TRACE

ALSO BY ARCHER MAYOR

TRACE

A Joe Gunther Novel

ARCHER MAYOR

Minotaur Books
New York

TRACE. Copyright © 2017 by Archer Mayor. All rights reserved. Printed in the United States of America. For information, address St. Martin's Press, 175 Fifth Avenue, New York, N.Y. 10010.

www.minotaurbooks.com

The Library of Congress Cataloging-in-Publication Data
is available upon request.

ISBN 978-1-250-11326-9 (hardcover)
ISBN 978-1-250-11327-6 (ebook)

Our books may be purchased in bulk for promotional, educational, or business use. Please contact your local bookseller or the Macmillan Corporate and Premium Sales Department at 1-800-221-7945, extension 5442, or by email at MacmillanSpecialMarkets@macmillan.com.

First Edition: September 2017

10 9 8 7 6 5 4 3 2 1

ACKNOWLEDGMENTS

As must be clear from the long list below, I do not create my stories without help. My deepest thanks to all these bright, informed, talented people for their time, interest, and support. Although I write fiction, I've always tried to at least reflect the reality of my world. If you find the stamp of truth resonating from within the following pages, thank them, not me. Theirs are the voices I heed. I can only hope they'll find that I made it worth their while.

Elizabeth Mayor

Julie Lavorgna

Mike Mayor

Chuck Rataj

Lyman Wood

Ray Walker

Windsor PD

Frankie Bailey

Paul Grondahl

Robert Wolfgang

Jack McEneny

John Currier

Castle Freeman, Jr.

Margot Zalkind Mayor

Joe Donahue

Stanilaus Skarzynski, Jr.

John Alexander

American Precision Museum

Laurie Fenlason

Gordon Norwood

Jay Fenlason

Barb Zonay

Tim Stevens

Mike Kokko

Albany PD

Jay Wilson

Ruth Constantine

Mark Franklin

Josiah Jones

Harrell Perkins

Tracy Shriver

Chris Morrell

Eric Buel

Douglas Van Citters

John Coleman

Vermont State Police

Zack Bennis

Walter Mangel

John Martin

Windham Co. SA's Office

Paul Perreault

and of course, Brio

TRACE

CHAPTER ONE

Jayla Robinson looked out across Albany's Lancaster Street at the three matching brownstones opposite. They were shorter than the one she was in, but more ornate, with arched first-floor entrances and windows, which made them appear classier, like squatty, potbellied rich men immaculately dressed in tailored suits.

She'd liked them at first, as she had the whole street and the lifestyle it reflected, back when. Now she needed to escape—this house, this neighborhood, this city. Above all, this man.

She switched focus to her reflection in the window's antique ripply glass, the midnight darkness of the street blending with the black room behind her and the chocolate cast of her own skin.

Somewhere between "coal black" and "high yellow," in the loaded vernacular of her culture. She recalled her darker-hued mother gazing at her sadly as a child, ruing that she hadn't "turned out lighter." The comment had baffled Jayla then, and angered her later. She was proud of being black, and of being a woman. Her mother's clear ambivalence about the first, and implied resignation concerning the second, had fueled Jayla's rebelliousness as she passed through high school and entered college.

They had also influenced some of her decisions—her hairstyle, her choice of clothing and jewelry, her music. Even her name. Jayla was her own creation. Charlotte Anne was what she'd been born with. In retrospect, her life since high school had been a succession of mile markers, all leading to the contradiction that had finally put her here, in this house, at this watershed moment.

Because, as with so many youthful journeys of self-discovery, especially for people with the means to choose their way, Jayla's progression had been stamped with awkward inconsistency. She had been blessed with her parents' work ethic, broad-mindedness, and, unacknowledged by her, occasional thick skin. And she had gained from their insistence on good schools, self-respect, and a regard for others. Educators both, and living embodiments of responsibility, they had been evenhanded, generous, forgiving, and encouraging.

Which at times had driven her crazy.

In part, if only that, it helped explain how she'd ended up as the college-dropout mistress of a scary white man with a short fuse and an inexplicably large income. Of course, even that had begun benignly enough: Jared Wylie had shown up as a guest-speaker expert on lobbying at a poli-sci class and had, over the first half year of their relationship, appeared urbane, educated, worldly, funny, and, most ironically now, kind.

She stepped back into the living room, still dressed in one of the short, sheer nightgowns he preferred—and which had gone from once making her feel sexy and appreciated to seeing herself as his latest and, given how she was feeling now, increasingly short-lived acquisition.

Things had not been going well over the past few months. For reasons unexplained to her, Wylie had shape-shifted from being the sophisticated, savvy monitor of Albany's politically charged government corridors to something less definable and much more ominous. A purported lobbyist, yes, and a lawyer from what she'd gotten off the framed documents lining his office. But Jared was clearly something more. Something malevolent.

Prompted by the thought, she raised her fingertips to her left breast, still sore after his latest assault. Not a blow this time. Nothing that overt. He clearly was a fast learner. Rather, just the latest in a series of escalating manipulations spread over a longer time than she was willing to admit. All delivered by hand or mouth or instrument and couched in the guise of erotica. But finally unmistakable to her as increasingly unbridled sadism.

Which fit other aspects of his persona, in her delayed perception. As she would have benefited from a blinding light swinging away from her eyes, in search of newer targets, she'd at last recognized the mannerisms she'd judged earlier to be eccentricities, or even intriguing in their novelty, as the harbingers of menace.

Brutal confirmation of this unease had come a couple of months ago. By convention or cliché, he should have been drunk at the time, in order to rationalize his excess. But he'd been sober and angry and very, very cold. Stimulated by what, she hadn't known, he'd come at her out of the blue, torn her clothes, thrown her about, hurting her in the process, and finally raped her on the kitchen floor. What had followed was almost boringly predictable—the apologies, the excuses, the promises of better behavior. Unimpressed, she'd called 911.

Only to then receive an unexpected education.

In response to her action, knowing he couldn't stop the police from appearing at their front door, Jared had made it crystal clear what would happen if she went beyond calling the cops and actually told them what had happened.

He'd been convincing enough that when two uniformed men did show up, she downplayed the assault, stating that she'd wanted to get back at her boyfriend for a perceived infidelity.

Beyond the humiliation of that moment, it had made her queasy to realize that Jared's feigned sensitivity and good manners had masked a man of Machiavellian and amoral propensities—a frightening mixture that had eventually imprisoned her.

At first, despite his displays of evil, she tried writing off her doubts as youthful paranoia. She challenged reality by ascribing his actions to a really bad day at the office and tried showing more independence. She went for a dinner with friends and looked up an old boyfriend for an after-dinner drink. The friends were quickly targeted with Facebook revelations of past indiscretions, with the implication that she'd been their source; the old boyfriend was mugged by a stranger and put into the hospital. The message was clear: Jayla was under surveillance, her privacy gone, and Jared's brutal tendencies no longer restricted to the odd sexual outburst.

Jared hadn't confessed to these two actions, but he hadn't denied them, either, making it clear that her efforts to distance herself carried a promise of future violence, to her and her friends and family, and that he was capable of worse, were she to challenge that conclusion.

She realized that her life had gone from uncomfortably claustrophobic to out of control. Only then had she focused—since by now she was barely allowed out of the house—on Jared's interactions with some of the people who entered his ground-floor office. Almost to a person, they looked trapped, as if visits to Jared Wylie were for root canal surgery, a sensation she now shared.

She'd considered calling the police again, before realizing she had nothing to report and no credibility in any case. She'd thought of her parents, and then remembered the old boyfriend's trip to the ER. And she'd already been made to imagine what might happen if she simply told Jared to screw himself, and returned to her life of old.

She was stuck. And, after tonight's near rape, assisted by so-called toys, she was struggling not to panic. Nothing in her short, happy, sheltered life so far had prepared her for anything like this. To her own embarrassment, she wasn't finding within herself any of the militant self-reliance she'd so admired in idols of her past. Now that such grit was being called for within herself, all she could think of was to run.

She sat on the bottom step of the staircase to the bedrooms overhead and ran her fingers through her long hair, pressing her palms against her temples.

"What're you doing?" she heard from above.

She whirled around, half collapsing onto the floor, her legs splayed out. Jared stood naked in the shadows at the top, more a menacing outline than a man.

"Get your ass to bed," he ordered.

Her earlier frustration and anger yielded to fear as she gathered herself together, saying, "I couldn't sleep."

He let out a short laugh. "I'll give you something that'll wear you out. Come on."

His shadowy arm gestured to her to join him, which she did meekly and without protest, feeling the dread rise, along with the soreness that he'd visited upon her hours earlier. As she drew up next to him, he slipped a hand beneath her nightgown and groped her painfully.

The effect was electric. Unlike ever before, without thought or hesitation, she countermanded all her paralyzing self-doubts, swung on her heel, and drove her raised elbow into his temple.

With a grunt, he fell from view and tumbled down the stairs, landing in a heap at the bottom.

Jayla stood stock-still in the sudden silence, her arm suspended in midair, staring at his motionless form. In the light from the street, she could just make out his chest moving slightly.

She reacted to that as to a starter's pistol, running to their bedroom. She dressed quickly in jeans, tennis shoes, and a top and raced downstairs to the front door as if wolves were on her heels, which, in her mind, they might as well have been as she jumped over Jared's still motionless body, expecting him to lash out and seize her ankle.

At the door, she grabbed a hoodie he'd left there upon coming home that night, swept up her small backpack containing phone and wallet, and without pause ran onto the brownstone's landing, slamming the door behind her.

It was spring, the night air cool but comfortable, making the hoodie all she needed to begin running east along Lancaster, toward Albany's downtown. By instinct, she was heading for the bus station. With no destination in mind, she was convinced of two things: She needed to get away from Jared fast and far, and she couldn't lead him toward anyone she knew or loved.

Because, as ignorant as she'd been of his true character upon meeting him, she knew in her bones that he was going to pursue her—the irony being that with her violent reaction of minutes ago, she'd just legally turned the tables on their mutual grievance. Jared Wylie, as she interpreted the law, had become the primary injured party—meaning that she'd officially cut off her own access to the police. Assuming she hadn't actually broken his neck, she'd given Jared free rein to hunt her down.

At the end of the block, she came up against a high, blank, shimmering marble wall, as subtle as anything once associated with Berlin, put there decades ago by New York governor Nelson Rockefeller as part of Albany's most startling and controversial landmark: the nearly one-hundred-acre-large Empire State Plaza.

Jayla ran to her left, along South Swan Street, before entering the plaza via a pedestrian path that cut across the marble expanse.

It was ghostly, eerie, and deeply disquieting, given what she'd just been through—abruptly being transported from a quaint collection of historic brownstones in Albany's trendy Center Square to what felt like the set of a cold and dystopian movie. The builders of this monument to ego and power had tried here and there to soften the place's sharp edges with some trees, but beyond such minor touches lay the plaza's primary feature, which no degree of subtle plantings could ameliorate—a vast, flat, featureless stone expanse, empty aside from a row of towering, monolithic office slabs and a huge half sphere that looked like a giant's abandoned golf tee but was referred to as the Egg, which it didn't come close to resembling.

Crossing this no-man's-land at full tilt, the thought of Jared fresh in her mind, Jayla had never felt so vulnerable or minute—a single speck populating a gigantic, white-painted architectural model. She stared down at her pounding feet as she went, half expecting them to start fading from view as she vanished into nothingness.

Relief came inside the blocks-long covered pedestrian corridor at the far end—which led to the parking garage adjacent to the Times Union Center. By the time she stepped free of the whole interconnected, labyrinthine mass, onto the relative normalcy of Beaver Street, Jayla felt she'd survived an imaginative rite of passage through fire. She paused for only a minute, her hands on her knees, blowing off some of the accumulated stress and collecting her thoughts, before proceeding more calmly down a couple of side streets to the bus depot on Liberty.

She'd come to a decision. Perhaps it wasn't well thought out, but it played to her need for something familiar while simultaneously—she hoped—supplying a solution at once unexpected and idiosyncratic.

If Jared was going to come after her, he'd start with her family and friends, her old haunts, and maybe places where he'd think she'd go to blend in—like New York or Boston. She racked her memory as she ran, trying to recall any trips or vacations she'd ever mentioned to him, knowing what an extraordinary memory he had for people's personal details.

She'd finally hit on an answer, if perhaps only short term: a spot she'd been to briefly years ago, while shopping for colleges, and rejected for some of the very reasons she was now finding it attractive.

She entered the flat, ugly, virtually abandoned Greyhound station, walked up to the counter, donning a pair of plastic sunglasses she found in the pocket of Jared's stolen hoodie, and bought a one-way ticket to Burlington, Vermont.

CHAPTER TWO

Joe Gunther opened his eyes at the phone's ring, distinguishing between it and the sound of his cell phone. No one called him on the landline anymore, not even Beverly.

He was lying on the couch, as usual, having dozed off rather than going to bed—one of the perks of living alone. His cat, Gilbert, was asleep on his chest. Or he had been; he was now eyeing Joe balefully at being disturbed.

"Hello?" Joe asked, expecting his mother's voice. An ancient woman with predictably aged habits, she avoided calling cell phones on principle.

But it wasn't her. "Joey?" his brother asked. "You okay? You sound weird."

"It's near midnight, Leo," he answered, checking his watch. "I was asleep."

"Oh, right. Well, I was at work till really late—couldn't get to a phone."

Leo ran a butcher shop in the town where they had been born—Thetford, Vermont—and lived with their mother, tending to her, supposedly, although she was famously and stubbornly low maintenance. Still, what could have been a pretentious comment from anyone else was probably true for Leo. The shop, their mother, and what time he had left for a social life did make for a very busy man.

"I hear you," Joe sympathized. "What's on your mind?"

"Mom. She's in a bad way."

Joe straightened, causing Gilbert to leap for safety. "What happened?"

Leo had expected the reaction. Joe was a cop, after all, had been for decades, trained to expect the worst. "I'm sorry, Joey. I didn't know how else to phrase it, but it's the same crap she's been denying for a couple of weeks. She couldn't hide it anymore. It was getting worse, so I forced her to go to the doc."

"The headaches?"

"Headaches, sleepiness, the tingling—all of it. But here's the pisser, Joey. It's Lyme disease. And that's not the worst of it."

By now, Joe had swung his feet onto the ground and was hunched forward. "What's that mean?"

"He called it Lyme encephalitis. It's gone to her head, and I know that's true, 'cause just today, she started acting really weird."

"Where is she?" Joe asked, hoping to cut through the escalating emotion in his brother's voice.

Leo paused. "I had to put her in the hospital. That's why I'm calling so late."

Joe stood up, still speaking. "Where are you?"

"I'm there, too—Mary Hitchcock."

That was the old name of what had become decades earlier the Dartmouth—Hitchcock Medical Center, in Lebanon, New Hampshire, which made it about a seventy-minute drive from Joe's home in Brattleboro, Vermont, near the Massachusetts border.

"Take a breath, Leo," he counseled, locating his shoes by the door. "Have you eaten yet?"

"No." Leo sounded calmer—and grateful.

"Grab a sandwich," Joe said. "I'll be there in forty-five minutes."

* * *

It was a late night as well for Dr. Tina Sackman, working at home in Moretown, Vermont, a tiny village bordering the Mad River, near her office at the crime lab in Waterbury.

Vermont had a disproportionately impressive forensic facility, given the state's small size. It was spacious, modern, well equipped, and very professionally staffed. From the old days when an ever-changing rotation of state troopers cycled through the lab, learning the ropes—more or less—before yielding to the next newcomer in line, this modern incarnation, made up entirely of civilian experts in their fields, was a remarkable improvement.

Given, of course, the realities of a largely rural state with little industry, a small budget, a hefty tax burden, and a population of just over a half million.

Which in turn meant that for all its impressive attributes, the lab had a few noticeable gaps. One of them being a freestanding latent prints department.

Nevertheless, some of the staff, like Dr. Sackman, despite being employed as a biologist primarily focusing on DNA analysis, took an interest in disciplines outside their fields, like photography, blood pattern analysis—and evidentiary prints. It was her belief that while you should trust your colleagues and rely upon their experience, it was helpful and flattering to acquaint yourself with their fields.

It also didn't hurt to admit—in Tina's case—that she was interested in becoming director of the lab someday, and thought her chances of success wouldn't be hurt by knowing as much about each section's discipline as possible.

Right now, she was putting together a graduate-level lecture on issues concerning what most laypeople called fingerprints. Her own field played a growing role here, of course, given how advances in forensic science had encouraged the melding of DNA and latent prints. Increasingly, criminals were being convicted as much on the genetic material mixed in with their prints as on the latent impressions themselves—especially when those prints were mostly smudges. The whole area of study was being called "touch DNA."

As with all lectures, however, virtually regardless of the audience, a show-and-tell approach made absorption that much easier. So Dr. Sackman had decided to use a recent headline-grabbing, successfully closed case as her starting place—the shooting of a Vermont state trooper three years ago by a man he'd killed with return fire just before dying.

It had thankfully been an open-and-shut case, with no margin for error, and investigators had been able to present a solid narrative of events in a timely fashion, even before the last of the forensics had wended its way back from the lab.

But therein lay part of Sackman's current problem, and the primary reason she was still up at this hour. In her effort to use the double-death case as an example of her lecture's thesis, she had hit a major obstacle. She'd found what she considered a gap in the ironclad narrative detailing what had transpired that night between Senior Trooper Ryan Paine and the motorist he'd pulled over, Kyle Kennedy.

She straightened from her labors and stared dejectedly at the paperwork on her desk, realizing that she now faced two obligations: to return to the archives and find another case, and to notify someone of her troubling suspicions.

The first was going to be a pain in the neck, and would certainly result in a less catchy crowd-pleaser for her audience. The second was less challenging. She pulled her laptop before her and began typing an email to Lester Spinney, an old state police acquaintance who she knew had joined the state's elite major crimes unit, the Vermont Bureau of Investigation.

Abigail Elizabeth Murray was ten years old—precocious, stubborn, and willfully independent. Fortunately for her, as far as she was concerned, she also lived in Windsor, Vermont. According to whatever adult was opining, this was a mixed blessing, because Windsor was either an old industrial New England throwback, out of luck and void of options, or it was the historic cradle of Vermont's constitution, quaint, pretty, ripe for improvement, and poised to make a comeback if only the right combination of money and entrepreneurship would recognize and finance its potential.

None of which interested Abigail. She lived in a tiny rental on Jarvis Street, high on the bank of the Connecticut River, with her mishmash of a family consisting of her mother, her mother's boyfriend, and three siblings, each with a different last name. The boyfriend called it a box of gerbils, but to Abigail—in the spring and summer, at least—it was the jumping-off spot for heaven on earth. She didn't care that its waterfront location—potentially prime in any other town—was on a potholed dead-end avenue trapped between the garbage-strewn riverbank and the remnants of a torn-down Goodyear factory—suspected of being an industrial waste site.

In her view, the virtual wasteland separating her street from the village farther inland was a playground at once vast and intricately confusing. In successive parallel swatches, from the river toward Main Street, high on the bluff, it had dark old conduits designed for industrial runoff, abandoned ancient buildings filled with mysterious offerings, acres of concrete slab littered with piled treasure, and a railroad track that marked its boundary like the dotted line on a printed form the lower half of which was designed to be removed and discarded.

Abigail loved Windsor.

This morning, with the night's chill just yielding to the sun rising over the New Hampshire hills on the far shore, she was rooting alongside the railroad tracks, looking for anything interesting.

Unlike her friends, she enjoyed this time of day, and in general happily rolled out of bed to greet it. The domestic noises she lived with hadn't begun, few people were up and traveling within the neighborhood, and the air outside was quiet and fresh—and starting to get warm, which was always a plus. Abigail liked winter, but spring and summer were like her mom's embrace—soft and warm and filled with good smells.

Railroads fascinated her, with their locomotives larger than her house, their carriages filled with people destined for mysterious places. In Windsor, the old station house had been converted into a fancy restaurant, leaving passengers to detrain on the concrete slab just shy of it—something she thought emblematic of the whole town, not that she could have put the thought into words.

Nevertheless, whenever she could, she made a point of witnessing Amtrak's two scheduled stops per day, one northbound, the other south, just to see who was getting on or off. She rarely recognized anyone. That wasn't the point. In fact, the enjoyment was only enhanced by ignorance. Who were they? What were they up to? And what had they seen beyond Abigail's horizons?

But if the train was nowhere near, as now, she still had the tracks to entertain her, if illegally, and there again, she was often mesmerized by what she found. Despite her having been told that the carriages were tightly sealed, incapable of leaving more in their wake than a passing thought, she found something new every time she explored. She'd slowly processed everything from discarded pens and lighters and crumpled scraps of paper to odd hunks of metal, a cell phone or two, and, weirdest of all, a toy soldier with a small parachute still attached, which now resided near her bed at home.

Weirdest that was, until today.

She crouched down—the picture of a child in a near desolate landscape, like a scrap of humanity scrounging for discarded bits of rice—and eagerly gathered up her discovery.

Colin Guyette was one of only two Windsor police officers with any notion of the "old days"—meaning before the closings of Goodyear, Cone-Blanchard, and the Mt. Ascutney ski resort. And he wasn't all that old. He'd been a kid in the '80s—or at least a young man. But the era remained fresh in his mind, as did the painful contrast between those headier days and now.

He had been on the police force a long time—steady, dependable, hardworking—a local boy with no ambitions to move someplace flashier. Which had helped him to survive the succession of selectmen and/or police chiefs who had ended the careers of so many of his colleagues. Guyette was like a boulder in midstream, all but immune from the passing ravages of politics and fashion.

He was a sergeant by now, which was as high as he aspired to go, and his one concession to the passing years and their toll on him was that he worked the day shift exclusively, leaving the more action-packed evening hours to those more eager to deal with them.

He was therefore on duty when dispatch announced the presence of someone in the lobby. Out of habit, he stepped into the front office first, his eyebrows raised in inquiry. The young woman at the radio console motioned to the bullet-resistant window overlooking the building's waiting room.

"She said she has something to show a policeman, and only a policeman."

Guyette opened his mouth to respond as the woman quickly held up a hand to stop him. "I have no clue. She was very specific."

He shut his mouth, glanced at the skinny girl sitting on the bench by the door, and nodded. "If that's what she wants, that's what she'll get."

He circled around to the electronically locked door leading into the lobby and approached the child, displaying a friendly smile. "I been told you have something to show me."

The girl took him in solemnly for a moment, as if appraising the validity of his uniform. She then pursed her lips, possibly in approval, reached into her jacket pocket, and silently extended her hand, her fingers opening to reveal her prize.

Nestled in her palm were three broken, bloodstained teeth.

CHAPTER THREE

Dartmouth–Hitchcock Medical Center jarred with its rural setting, in Joe's eyes. He'd been coming here since they imploded the old Mary Hitchcock Hospital in Hanover to great fanfare in the 1990s, but upon every visit, especially at night, like now, he empathized with its nickname among medevac chopper pilots: the Emerald City. It was vast, modern, towering, bright green, and white, and as urbane and architecturally ambitious as its wooded surroundings were not.

It was also the best such facility within a huge radius, rivaled only by a distant competitor in Burlington, Vermont, and of course the clusters of major hospitals in and around far-off cities like Boston or Springfield, Mass. If you had a big problem and you lived within a two-hour drive, chances were good you were going to end up here.

In the case of Joe and Leo's mom, who lived fifteen minutes up the river, checking into DHMC was virtually instinctive.

Finding it, however, versus finding anyone within it were two different prospects. Joe didn't even bother trying to seek out the room number Leo had given him on the phone, and asked reception for directions instead. Only then, following a near marathon course down corridors and up stairs, including through a so-called mall with sixty-foot ceilings, did he find his brother anxiously pacing around a nurse's station.

"Where is she?" Joe asked without preamble, putting his hand on Leo's shoulder, as much to slow him down as to make physical contact.

Leo looked at him a moment and threw both burly arms around him in an unexpected hug. "Joey. Jesus, man. You came."

Leo was the family extrovert. Joe favored their late father—a thoughtful watcher.

"Of course I did," he said, patting Leo on the back. "How's she doing?"

Leo broke off to wave down the hall. "Doc's with her now. She's hurtin', and you know her—tough old broad. Never says a thing. She is now, though."

"They sure about the Lyme disease thing?" Joe asked.

It was the wrong question. Leo's eyes welled up. "I try to watch her. You'd think it'd be like falling off a log—her in a wheelchair. But she gets out, down the ramp, and onto the lawn in the time it takes me to take a leak. Tick must've got her then. I never thought about it."

Joe laid his hand on his brother's cheek. "Leo, for Christ's sake. You couldn't've seen this coming. Let it go. Anyone tell you what to expect?"

"Shit. I don't know. She could die. She was acting crazy, Joey. None of it makes sense." Leo's attention was abruptly drawn to a distant figure in a lab coat. "That's her doc."

Joe turned to meet the woman as she drew near. "I'm Joe Gunther, Doctor. My brother phoned me. What's the news?"

"Dr. Lacombe," she responded a little stiffly, glancing at Leo as if expecting him to say that Joe was an impostor. Seeing no such reaction, she indicated a small alcove nearby. "Let's step over here for a minute."

The three of them moved beyond potential foot traffic, thin as it was this late at night.

Lacombe gestured to a small scattering of chairs. "Sit, sit. Are you all the family Mrs. Gunther has?"

"Yes," Joe answered. "Just the two of us. Our father died decades ago. What do you think's going on?"

"The common label is Lyme encephalitis. It's a variation on Lyme disease that attacks the brain."

"Can you fix it?"

Lacombe had apparently already reached a conclusion about Joe's likely preference for the unadorned truth. "No. I mean, we could waste time trying, and maybe get lucky, but while we can certainly stabilize her in the short term, she'd be better served at a more specialized facility."

Leo hunched over, his hands between his knees. Joe kept his eyes on the doctor. "This is no teenager, Doc," Joe said. "Are you talking about an end-of-life place?"

Lacombe's eyes widened in surprise. "What? No, no. Let me back up." She hesitated a moment and then asked, "What do you do, Mr. Gunther?"

"He's a cop," Leo answered.

The doctor straightened and smiled, clearly relieved. "Okay. You're used to bad news. What I'm saying is just the opposite—that your mother is in incredible shape, aside from this. Her vitals are strong, her history is unremarkable, despite the immobility. Everything in her record indicates she's facing many more years of good health. This situation could be lethal—it's true—but it could also be survived, virtually without a scratch. I just don't know. That's why I'm suggesting more specialized care. I'm not speaking in euphemisms here. Please don't misunderstand."

Joe nodded. "Okay. Got it. What's the timing on this? You said something about helping her in the short term."

Lacombe pulled a card from her lab coat pocket. "This is the place I'd recommend. The Francis Rehabilitation Institute, nicknamed the Frank or the FREE because of its impressive endowment. It's near St. Louis, Medicare covers the costs, and the endowment does the rest for those in need, which includes putting up family members." She gave

Joe a pointed look and added, "I'd recommend that, too, by the way, because of her age and the disease presentation in this case. Are you ready and willing to accompany your mom?"

Joe opened his mouth to answer, but Leo spoke first. "I'll do it."

He faced his younger brother directly, speaking kindly but forcefully. "You are the driving force behind your butcher shop, Leo. You're sure as hell the guy loyal customers travel miles to see at the meat counter. Without you—or knowing what stretch of time the doc's talking about—there's no telling how business might suffer."

"Joey . . . ," Leo began before Joe cut him off by asking Lacombe, "How long?"

Lacombe hesitated. "No way to know. It could be two weeks; it could be much longer."

"I'm your man," Joe said. "I probably have years of time off in the bank by now. I'll do it."

Again, Leo tried to speak.

"No," Joe said flatly. "You're the Rock of Gibraltar—always there, always available. Let me do this—brother to brother. It would do me good and make me feel a little less useless."

To his surprise, Leo considered that for a couple of seconds before saying, "You got it."

"No shit?" Willy asked.

Lester Spinney leaned back, linking his fingers behind his neck and stretching his legs into the narrow aisle between the four desks squeezed into the VBI squad room—an impressive sight, given his extraordinarily long and skinny frame. "Nope. Check your email. We got a new boss."

The office was located on the second floor of Brattleboro's municipal building, above the police department, and virtually unknown to anyone in town. The Vermont Bureau of Investigation was a major crime-only unit made up of elite detectives culled from agencies across the state—although mostly the state police, as in Lester's case. They were specialists, primarily called upon by departments or prosecutors in need of their expertise. They didn't have uniforms or marked cars or a prominent public image. Their charter made it clear: They were to assist and fade away, leaving the limelight to others.

"Joe's mom needs special care out West somewhere," Lester was saying as Willy settled in behind his desk. "He found out last night and he's already home packin'. Bada bing, bada boom."

Willy wasn't particularly interested in his boss's domestic troubles. "Who's God while he's gone?"

Lester was enjoying breaking the news. "You'll love it. The mother of your bouncing baby girl."

The reaction was typically Willy. He ducked his head so Les couldn't see his expression, opened his drawer, and said evenly, "She'll do a good job."

Les instantly regretted his approach. "Sure she will. Didn't mean to spring it on you."

Although not married, Willy Kunkle and Samantha Martens shared a child, Emma; a house, once Willy's own; and a propensity for exchanging mostly friendly, if often barbed, one-liners. They'd been fellow detectives downstairs, before VBI was created, and had forged a Mutt-and-Jeff image of contrasting styles that had therefore left most onlookers stunned by their romantic coupling.

"Nah. That's okay," Willy muttered, still pretending to forage around in his desk.

Lester stayed silent. Like so many others, he often took Willy's hard, abrasive outer shell for granted, forgetting the man's baggage of combat-born PTSD, past alcoholism, and instinctive paranoia—not to mention a crippled left arm, the result of a bullet he'd received on the job years earlier. An intuitive, natural-born cop, Willy could be judgmental, dismissive, and unmannered at one moment, while being thoughtful, sensitive, and generous at the next.

God only knew what Lester had poked with his playful announce-ment, if anything, but he wasn't about to worsen the situation by saying more.

Fortunately, he didn't have to. The door to the office opened to reveal Sammie Martens, fresh from having dropped Emma off at preschool.

"Hey," she said, taking them both in warily.

"Hey, yourself," Willy answered neutrally. "Long time, no see."

She didn't respond right away, instead registering Lester's embarrass-ment before saying, "You heard."

"I did."

She held up her iPhone. "Just got it when I was delivering Emma. Kind of a kick in the butt."

"Woulda been nice if he'd told us face-to-face," Lester said, moving to safer ground.

"Doesn't matter," Willy announced. "It was a family crisis. You do what you gotta do." He looked at Sammie directly. "You'll be great. It's not like you don't act like the boss half the time anyhow."

Lester laughed, he hoped supportively, but it only caused Willy to darken slightly and reach into his pocket, saying, "I gotta get this."

He pulled two stacked cell phones out of his pocket, one of which he deftly tucked away again before lifting the other to his ear and heading back out to the corridor for privacy.

Sammie gazed down at Spinney and shook her head. "That went well," she said.

"The Frank?" Beverly Hillstrom responded. "Absolutely. Best place for her. I wouldn't have thought of it. Will they take her? I imagine there's a waiting line."

Joe Gunther hadn't doubted Dr. Lacombe's recommendation of

where to send his mother, but it was nice to get a second opinion from the state's long-standing medical examiner and Joe's romantic partner for the last couple of years. His natural prejudice aside, he'd never met a more motivated, learned, and dogged MD in his life. Beverly was the first person he'd called after leaving his mother's side, following a very long night preparing for the transfer from Dartmouth-Hitchcock to the Frank—and informing his squad, via email, and his boss, VBI director Bill Allard.

As straightforward as it appeared, that seemingly mundane process, even with Leo in tow, had been tougher than Joe anticipated. Their mother was admittedly old, restricted to a wheelchair, and although quicker-witted than many twenty-year-olds, not slated biologically to be around for much longer. He knew that. Nevertheless, seeing her in that bed—guarded by monitors and IV drips, her face haggard, her eyes wandering like a cornered animal's, and babbling nonsensically—had thrown him badly.

Joe had been the one to leave the family farm after his father's death, enrolling in the military and fighting overseas. Even though he'd returned to Vermont, it hadn't been to his birthplace. Leo was the local—never married, no wanderlust, content to envision dying where he'd been born. His contentedness had allowed Joe to slip free without guilt, even after their mother was confined to the wheelchair. The three of them had developed an unusual emotional dance step through the years, with Leo traveling the inner orbit, Joe the outer, and their mother holding the center.

That was what had rattled Joe the most. His mother, self-reliant, alert, perpetually engaged, and always available, had served both her sons more as a force of nature than as a parental guide. She set the tone by example, and instructed by inference. To see her so at sea bypassed a defense mechanism on which he'd relied for his entire professional life, and left him at an emotional loss.

Joe addressed Beverly's inquiry. "I don't know the details, but her doc must've pulled some strings. It was like the waving of a wand."

"Does that mean you'll be leaving soon?"

It was asked pragmatically. Beverly had a reputation for keeping cool in a crisis. But he knew her better than most now. He heard the sadness in her voice like the far-off fluttering from a hummingbird's wings—so faint as to avoid notice—and he loved her for it.

"Tomorrow. Even Dr. Lacombe was impressed. I don't understand much about encephalitis, but I guess there're enough interesting things going on with her that she's being looked at as a prime candidate for treatment." He paused before adding, sincerely, "I do wish I could come up to see you before, though. There's just too much to do."

The Office of the Chief Medical Examiner, or the OCME, as everyone called it who knew to call it anything, was located in the depths of Vermont's largest hospital, in Burlington, a good two-and-a-half-hour drive from Joe's home in Brattleboro. His and Beverly's long-distance romance hadn't suffered much yet, as they were both workaholic loners by instinct, but this was a clear exception.

"I wish you could, too," she answered honestly.

The longing in her voice—this time clear and unfiltered—was sweet and surprising, and touched him deeply. He faltered before trying to respond. "I know—"

"So do I, Joe," she cut him off, sounding more her old self. "This needs to be done. You and I have all the time in the world."

"Willy, it's Colin Guyette, in Windsor."

Kunkle walked to the end of the municipal center's broad hallway to stand at the window overlooking the rear parking lot. "Okay," he said. Guyette was one of dozens of cops across the state whom he'd cultivated over the years. Not at any of the usual trainings, meetings, or especially shared family outings, however. Willy disliked his fellow humans broadly enough to consider such interactions with barely suppressed horror, as Sammie knew well. Nevertheless, he got around a lot, traveling far and wide, and always made himself known to the locals, however quietly. The arm helped, and the reputation. There weren't many crippled cops who'd been military snipers, complete with impressive kill lists, who not only were still employed—thanks to the Americans with Disabilities Act—but also maintained the "up yours" attitude that so many people in uniform aspired to.

Kunkle was the much-envied mascot of institutional dysfunction.

He also made sure he was a good man to know. He helped his colleagues, showing little prejudice or preference, often by doing things they didn't dare try themselves. As a result, along with spreading his bad boy aura, he'd subversively made himself useful, with never a claim for credit.

"I got handed something I can't do anything with," Guyette explained. "But it's offbeat enough, I thought you might be interested."

"Okay," Willy repeated.

"A little kid just gave me some broken teeth. Said she found them on the railroad tracks near the old Goodyear plant. I figured it was a couple of guys from the hood punching it out as usual, but I had some time on my hands and I wanted the kid to feel good about bringing it in, so I drove out to take a look, just for the hell of it, you know?"

"Yup."

Most people knew Willy for his terseness—indeed, preferred it to his often caustic one-liners—so Guyette spoke on. "Well, I found something else, right where the teeth were, according to the kid. Don't know what it is, but it was burned up pretty bad, and it looks electronic, and kind of important, if that doesn't sound stupid."

"That it?"

"Yeah. Sorry. It's not like anything I ever seen before. I coulda chucked it and not bothered you, but I figured, what the hell? If you ain't interested, I'll let it go. It's probably nothing—a piece of trash not even connected to the teeth, but—"

Willy cut him off, not wanting to hear more or—worse—hear it all over again. It's what geezers like Guyette did. "I'm coming up. You around?"

"Till seventeen hundred hours."

"Don't get killed in the meantime."

Jayla Robinson adjusted Jared's oversized sunglasses for the twelfth time and joined the row of people shuffling down the center aisle to leave the bus. It had been a long and sleepless trip. Instead of feeling the relief she'd hoped for, an angry string of texts on her smartphone had reminded her of her tormentor's ongoing proximity—"You'll pay, you bitch." "Watch your back, whore." "Where're my fucking glasses?" "You have no idea how bad you're about to feel."

And so on. The glasses reference was a little nuts, but the rest of it only confirmed what had made her run, and rewarded her wisdom in escaping to parts unknown. She'd fallen in with a very bad man. Everyone she'd left behind, it seemed, was about to find that out, too, but at least none of them could be found accountable for giving her shelter.

She looked at her phone as she progressed toward the door, deleting all his texts and wondering if she should nevertheless warn her parents. What would she say, though, that wouldn't expose them to possible harm? And they wouldn't have the sense to run. They'd go the conventional route, calling the police or something, which would really get Jared wound up. Best they know nothing; that he'd accept.

She reached the sidewalk, emerged into the early-morning sun, and looked around. The bus had let them off in the heart of the University of Vermont, near the Davis Center, at the top of the long bluff that marks the last small upheaval of the Green Mountain range, before it falls—

straight, flat, and steep—into the enormous, perpetually cold embrace of Lake Champlain below, with most of the city clinging to its slope.

The street was a busy east–west corridor, connecting downtown to the interstate and thus slicing between the dorms to the south and UVM's central campus opposite. The college was no SUNY Albany, with whose enormity Jayla was very familiar, but it did feature some twelve thousand students of all stripes, most of whom, it seemed, were swarming around the bus like army ants circling a boulder.

They were used to navigating this potentially lethal intersection of pedestrians and vehicles, of course, while Jayla was not. As urbane as she was, and as used to a big town's circulatory system, that didn't exclude a newcomer's learning curve. So it was that, in a moment's inattention, she stepped out into the street and was hit by a car.

It was actually more of a nudge. She didn't even fall. But she was jarred enough to drop her bag onto the car's hood, cause a few people to react, and make the driver slam on her brakes.

"*Oh, my God*," the young woman yelled, leaping out so fast that Jayla worried the car might keep rolling. "Are you okay? I'm so sorry. I didn't see you."

"Were you hit?" a man asked from beside her.

Jayla had already retrieved her bag and was shaking her head, looking for a gap in the renewed press of humanity around them. "I'm fine," she muttered, dreading what attention might come her way next.

The driver put both her hands on her shoulders, looking her straight in the eyes. "That's probably the adrenaline and the endorphins. They'll mask any initial pain. Do you feel anything going on with your neck? Whiplash, maybe? How 'bout your pelvis?"

Jayla stared at her, thrown by the questions and her general demeanor—sure and matter-of-fact—despite having just run into someone. Jayla envied her poise, since she just wanted to run.

"No, no. I'm fine," she stammered. "Really. Are you a doctor?"

The driver laughed, obviously relieved by Jayla's apparent good health. "God, no. My mom is. Not that you'd want to end up in her wait-ing room." She looked around quickly before suggesting, "Get in the car. I have to get out of traffic anyway. Then we can really find out how you're doing. I'm not letting you go till we do."

"Why wouldn't I want to meet your mother?" Jayla asked, letting herself be steered toward the car's passenger door.

"She's the state medical examiner."

CHAPTER FOUR

Joe stopped at the office door and watched unobserved for a moment as Lester and Sam sat at their desks, exchanging comments while poring over open file folders and computer screens. Popular fiction aside, most police work amounted to research and a hunt for continuity. How was the crime committed? Who was involved, directly or peripherally? What actions, items, and/or processes were needed for its completion? Times, people, movements, alibis—all of them called for scrutiny and linkage, and most of them were applied in the office, via phone, fax, computer, and interoffice dialogue.

As Joe was about to take leave of this comforting cocoon, he let a moment's nostalgia tug at him. A widower in his twenties, childless and a bachelor ever since, although involved in three serious romantic relationships along the way, Joe had spent the decades thereafter reading history books, practicing a little woodworking, and doing this job. Even he had to admit that he'd led a limited social life.

But he in no way begrudged his choices. His experiences had been rich, and life's evolutionary surprises, like discovering Beverly in a new context, had usually come at just the right time—the mishap involving his mother notwithstanding.

That was one reason why he had joined the VBI, and so appreciated his colleagues within it. Each of them, their eccentricities aside, had made the sacrifices and commitments this level of performance required. It was the apex that every career deserved after untold years of effort, and which he'd been fortunate enough to find.

Sam was the first to look up and end his contemplative moment. "Hey, boss," she said, rising to welcome him. "How're you holding up?"

Lester stood also and shook his hand. "I was really sorry to hear about Mrs. Gunther."

Joe placed the animal carrier he was holding on the the floor and thanked them both, answering, "I'm the one who's sorry to leave you holding the bag. There's just nobody—"

"Save it," Sam interrupted, dropping to the floor to peer through the wire door of the carrier. "Hey, Gilbert . . . Oh, that's right, you're leaving today." She looked up at her boss. "You want me to take care of the cat?"

"I think Gilbert's spoken for," Joe answered, indicating Lester. "And you're right. I'm about to head north to pick up our patient."

The tall detective grabbed the carrier and placed it by his desk. "Yup. The kids're psyched. He'll be in good hands. You got a place to stay once you get out West?" he then asked.

"Free housing for the first month," Joe told them both. "It's a dorm or something. Apparently, family members are a part of rehab, so I guess I'll be put to work. I hope so, to be honest. I might go crazy if I have to sit around too much."

"Not to worry," Sam reassured him. "I'm freaked out enough about running things that I'll be calling you five times a day."

Joe waved that away. "Walk in the park. You're a natural for this. You all are."

Lester laughed outright. "All of us?"

Joe joined him ruefully. "Okay. Some more diplomatically than others. Where is he, anyhow?"

"Oh, you know," Sam said. "He took a call and vanished, as usual. Not a word said. He'll resurface. I'll tell him you said hi."

"Did anything come in overnight?" Joe asked.

"It didn't, and you don't need to know anyhow," Sam told him sternly. "Go take care of your mom. I was kidding when I said I'd be bugging you, okay? We'll be fine."

"You'll be gone for three days, max," Les said supportively, "and we won't even get a jaywalking case."

The other two looked at him silently before Joe voiced the obvious rejoinder, "Now you done it. You're gonna get buried."

Ten minutes later, after Joe had departed, Lester Spinney asked Sammie, as he was scanning through his emails, "Are you really nervous?"

"I just don't want to fuck up," she answered truthfully. "What if we do get buried?"

Les was about to answer reassuringly when he stopped to reread a message that had come in overnight. He canceled the platitude he'd been about to utter. "Well, if I'm reading between the lines right, this may be the first shovelful. I just got an email about an evidentiary discrepancy with the Ryan Paine–Kyle Kennedy shoot-out, a few years ago."

"Great," Sammie said, joining him to peer over his shoulder. "Why start with a ground ball?"

"Technically, we're trespassing," Colin Guyette said.

"Technically, I don't give a rat's ass," Willy responded, crouching low between the train tracks.

"Couple of weeks ago, a local ball team posed in front of the Windsor Station Restaurant for Facebook, from the tracks side instead of the parking lot. The Amtrak police showed up and violated them."

"They can violate me all they want," Willy growled. "They won't like what happens. Where were these teeth found—exactly?"

Guyette chose his words carefully. "She brought 'em in, so I don't know *exactly*, but I asked her to show me, and she said right here."

"And the burned-up thing?"

Now the Windsor cop was more in his element. He got down beside Willy, opened the bag he'd brought with him containing a charred, book-shaped object with wires sticking out of one end, and held up his smartphone so that he could place his evidence on the track bed to match the photo on the phone.

"There," he said. "That's pretty close."

Willy nodded and stood up, looking north. Windsor presented itself to him in three parallel strips from this vantage point: the river to his right; the poor industrial section they were in, with the tracks defining its far edge; and the actual historic town—complete with church spires, old buildings, lofty mansions, and businesses—high on the rise to his left, clearly demarking the land of the haves from that of the have-nots.

Organizationally, it made good sense. A century ago, the river and the railroad—until both were replaced by the interstate highway system—had served the town's industries in turn, while the town's elite had sat above it all, enjoying the view and raking in the money. Riverfront property in most factory towns had amounted to what a delivery alleyway is now.

It helped explain why so many older communities had corrupted their most coveted modern real estate and left beautiful, peaceful rivers to be flanked by blighted, polluted shorelines.

"What do you think?" Colin asked his guest. "A waste of time?"

"Maybe," Willy conceded. He pointed at the steel rail on the right. "I like how the broken teeth, that thingamabob, and the tracks all fit into the same frame, like they're interconnected."

"How?"

Kunkle kicked at a small stone with his toe. "You find stuff like this, you try to build a story around it, right? When you first saw the teeth, you thought fistfight."

"Right," Colin agreed.

"Has that changed?"

"Because of this?" Colin waved his hand around to include their surroundings.

"Yeah." Willy watched him, enjoying seeing him reason his way toward clarity. If cops get a consistent kick out of anything, it's usually in locating what they call that "aha moment."

"You mean the owner of the teeth maybe had a hard encounter with the train?"

"Maybe," Willy said. "That's a little dramatic. Most encounters with trains don't end with a few broken teeth. We'd have more evidence than just this, and probably a medical examiner. Plus, that doesn't explain the burned metal box."

Guyette chuckled. "I see what you mean. A passenger, then?"

"Train comes through twice a day?" Willy asked.

"Yup. Noon heading south, and just shy of six heading north."

"And the kid found the teeth early?"

Colin was nodding, seeing where Willy was headed. "I asked her how often she checked the tracks, as part of her treasure hunt. She said she'd done a sweep the day before, after school, meaning the teeth must've come from the northbound train. But you think the guy fell off?" He gestured up the tracks. "It stops about an eighth of a mile farther up. It's still moving right here. Why would he jump or get pushed so close to the platform?"

Willy pointed to the charred hunk. "Could be where that thing comes in. Anything around here that connects with it? A plant or an electronics store?"

Guyette shook his head. "Don't even know what it is. What about getting DNA off the teeth?"

"Costs money," Willy said. "You even bother punching a case number for this?"

Guyette pushed his lips out resignedly. "I see what you're sayin'. It's barely littering at this point, since we don't have a suspect."

He hunkered down, retrieved their burned object of interest, and roughly shoved it into his paper bag. "Another item for the Dumpster. So much for not wanting to waste your time."

But Willy smiled and took the bag. "Not so fast. Let's find out what that is, first."

"Really?" Colin asked, raising his eyebrows.

"You don't know till you know, right?"

The other man hesitated. "I guess. You give everything this close a look?"

"You'd be all by your lonesome right now if I didn't. Not every case begins with a knife dripping blood. Plus, I'm fond of the offbeat."

Tina Sackman had offered to discuss her concern on the phone, or set up a video call to better explain what she'd discovered, but Lester told her that he preferred a face-to-face meeting.

It was a pretty day to take a drive, something cops do to an inordinate degree in rural areas, but his other motivation was that he'd wanted to get out of the office. Watching Sammie had been increasingly distracting. He admired her stamina, trusted her judgment, and was happy to have her backing in a fight. But watching her figure out her new command role was something he wanted to avoid.

In fairness, Joe was more than the head of their small squad, which was only one of five all told, geographically sprinkled across the state. Theirs was in the southeastern corner—where Joe had spent his entire career—but it was also from where he additionally served as the field force commander for the entire VBI, just under the director. Sam had therefore been made the number two person of the organization, not just their unit.

Lester wouldn't have touched it with the proverbial pole. Sammie, on the other hand, couldn't have said no if her hair had been on fire.

And therein lay one of Lester's primary concerns for her.

Not that he knew the details, but he was aware of Sam's having endured the childhood of a Dickens novel. It had influenced her choice of careers and played a big role in her attraction to men with poor social skills. Lester thought that she'd gotten lucky with Willy, but saying that revealed how badly she'd done in the past. He'd heard a colleague crack years ago that if your arrest stats were running thin, you could always bust whomever Martens was dating at the time.

That notwithstanding—or taking it into account—he found her organized, efficient, practical, and flexible. The hallmarks of a perfect boss. He'd also known her to be sentimental, insecure, a chronic worrier during good times, and—most concerning—occasionally inclined to override her own better judgment. That, even more rarely, had led to impulsive and careless actions—moments that Willy's influence had done little to curb.

It was seeing many of those traits in play, as she worked the phone to establish her abrupt primacy within the agency, that had driven Les from the office. He'd felt like he was seeing a comic strip's conflicting thought balloons floating above her head.

He knew she'd get it right, but for his own peace of mind, he needed her to do the basic spadework alone. Excess insight into a boss's makeup had never been a good thing, in his experience.

Vermont's forensic lab was part of the state police headquarters building, in Waterbury—one of a complex of old brick structures that had once been the sprawling campus of a heavily populated insane asylum, back in the unenlightened 1890s. Conveniently for modern, government-related needs, it was centrally located, not far from the capital, and equipped with a growing number of old brick buildings that had become increasingly available as mental health philosophies modernized and the patient population plummeted. With the corresponding expansion of state bureaucracy, the campus segued very elegantly over time into an office complex, including the state police.

Until the whole thing—flat, verdant, and surrounded by the Winooski River on three sides—went underwater during a tropical storm.

Local wags used to find it suitable that what had once housed nutcases now sheltered bureaucrats, but in fact the flood devastated the town and the facility, making everyone eager and happy to see any improvements come into view.

The forensic lab had been brand new when the flood hit, and had survived it in better shape than many of its neighbors, including the structure to which it was attached, where reams of state police records had suffered in the basement, along with some important computer hardware.

Tina Sackman gave Lester a hug in the lobby, along with a slightly reproving look. "You know we could have done this electronically. We have the means."

"I know, I know," he answered. "None of which would have given me the pleasure of seeing you in person."

She patted his chest before turning toward the lab's inner entrance, waving her key card at the lock. "Oh, you smoothie. I'm the one who called you. You don't have to sweet-talk me into anything."

He fell into line behind her, looking around at the building's surprising modernity—not something he got to enjoy much in the context of Vermont's chronically tight budgets. "I am cut to the bone, Tina."

She waved her hand at him without turning back. "Yeah, yeah, yeah. You'll recover. How's the family?"

"Sue's still at the hospital, happily cursing the system and everyone running it; Wendy's turned into a frighteningly attractive young woman with a growing interest in boys; and Dave's learning the ropes at the sheriff's office and loving it. You and Brad ought to travel across the mountains for a visit."

She led him down a long corridor, up a flight of stairs, and eventually to her office overlooking the parking lot. On a small conference table against the wall was a row of files, neatly arranged. Two chairs had been placed side by side, facing it.

Tina indicated his seat as she settled into the other. "How familiar are you with the Paine versus Kennedy case?"

He arranged his long legs comfortably under the table. "Trooper Ryan Paine pulled over Kyle Kennedy late one night about three years ago, more or less, somewhere between Guilford and Halifax, presumably for a routine car stop. They exchanged shots and both died of their wounds. The police academy's been stressing officer safety issues to recruits ever since. That about right? Not that I don't know you're about to reeducate me."

"No, no," she corrected him quickly. "I'm just here to show you what I found. You're the investigator. I don't even know if there's enough here for you to investigate."

She reached out for one of the folders and opened it. "You weren't wrong in your recollection, of course. It was front-page news. But obviously there were many more details supporting the story."

"I knew a prosecutor once," Lester responded, "who warned me that the word 'story' applied only to make-believe, and never to use it on the stand."

Tina reacted indirectly. "Well, let's find out, because even at the time, there were questions about the actual sequence of events."

"Oh? That doesn't sound good."

"Yeah. That's why I emailed you." She was spreading pages and photographs around in a semicircle before him as she spoke. "With no one left alive, there was a small contest between the 'what you see is what you got' people and others who thought the reality might be a little trickier. But the second group had no evidence to back them up."

She suddenly sat back and fixed Lester with a look. "Is it true what I heard about Beverly Hillstrom and your boss?"

He laughed at the non sequitur. "That they're a couple? Yeah."

She nodded approvingly. "Good for them. Then you won't be surprised to hear she was one of the . . . if not doubters, then at least questioners. If I remember, that was true of Gunther, too, but it wasn't his case."

"Huh," Lester grunted, not having retained many of the details. While technically, the investigation should have gone to the VBI, it didn't. Politics had intervened, and the state police kept control of it.

"What was the hang-up?" he asked.

"Hillstrom stuck to her specialty, of course, so for her, it was about the bullet wounds. She wasn't emphatic either way—we would've heard about that—but she wasn't happy with the foregone conclusion that Paine could have survived long enough to shoot Kennedy. Although that's what everybody went with, finally, mostly for political reasons."

"It wasn't legit?"

"It was as legit as any other scenario," she emphasized. "That's what I'm saying, or trying to. This whole thing may not've been as cut-and-dried as they made out in the press releases, but nobody compromised their integrity. In the end, everyone agreed to the playbook you just rattled off: boy stops boy; boys shoot each other; one boy's buried as a hero; the other's forever labeled a cop-killer."

"So where do the politics come in?"

"You know how these things get. Everybody leaning on everybody else to get results fast. The primary investigators on the case were pretty quick to stand before the media and say, 'case closed.' But in their defense, nobody's proved them wrong, either, so no miss, no foul."

"Until now," he prompted her.

She smiled. "You keep trying to corner me on that. I'm just bringing you . . . Call it an after-the-fact anomaly."

"All right, all right. Tell me about your anomaly."

She reached for another file. "Only part of what I'm about to tell you played a role in the initial case findings. It involves DNA and finger-prints, after all, which—then as now—can take a while to come back. And in this particular situation, since things were moving along at such a clip, everyone had moved on by then. Not only that, but the lab's find-ings didn't debunk anything, so all was considered safe and sound."

She opened the file and laid out a series of fingerprint images. "Fit-ting what was found at the scene, there were two weapons—one for each man, and each with one round fired. Ballistics did their thing and the facts lined up perfectly. As part of that same routine, each of the guns was tested for prints. Again, as you can see here, nothing but consistency—each man's prints were where they were supposed to be. No muss, no fuss. So far, so good."

"You do know how to build things up," Lester commented.

"Hey. Allow me a little fun. Okay, now, I'm assuming you've been in a situation like this before, right? Lifting prints for comparison?"

"Sure."

"And on those occasions, what did you do with the print or prints you lifted?"

He glanced at her, looking for the trap. "Sent them to the lab?"

"Right. Who then plugged them into AFIS to see what kicked out."

"That and the state's database," he reminded her.

"Correct," she agreed. "But in either case, the hope's always that the person's prints will be on file, and you'd all end up exchanging high fives."

"Okay," he said cautiously, wondering where this was heading.

She twisted in her chair to face him before asking, "But successful or not, did you ever—in a situation where you had several prints—compare the lifted prints with each other?"

He hesitated before asking, "Why would I?"

She didn't answer the question, asking instead, "And, if you got lucky and did get a hit, did you then push to have a DNA analysis done of the print, to double-check that the latent matched the person's genetic code—assuming they also were on record?"

He shook his head. "Why would I do that? A match is a match."

"That's what I would have thought," Tina said. "It's what we all would've thought. It's cumbersome, expensive, and redundant."

She opened a file to show two shots of the same enlarged image of a single fingerprint.

"What's that show you?"

Playing along, he studied them closely before stating, "Same picture, times two. One's got a bit less showing at the edge there." He tapped the image. "But you can tell they're the same print. Like a Xerox."

She covered them with an evidence report. "And yet one was collected from Kennedy's trigger, while the other came off the revolver's cylinder."

Lester shoved aside the report to look again at the prints. "Weird. They're almost exactly the same."

Tina sat back, beaming with pride. "They *are* exactly the same."

Lester was nonplussed. "What're you saying? Aren't they Kyle Kennedy's?"

"Yes, but they aren't separate prints. They're duplicates, and since every lifted print is compared to what's in the data bank, and not to the other prints in any given collection, no one tumbled to it."

"That they were manufactured?" he asked incredulously.

"In this situation, I think people in the latents field use the term 'forged.' But, yes."

She slid over a textbook and opened it to a marked page. "See here? This is a display of an individual's thumbprints, lifted from the same drinking glass, five different times. Each one shares the same characteristics, as you'd expect, and each resulted with a hit from AFIS, proving they were valid. But compared to each other, you can see that they're all a little different. This one's very slightly smudged, this one's lighter, this one had more pressure behind it, this one emphasizes the heel more than this other one. . . . It's the nature of the beast. It's essentially impossible to leave exactly the same impression behind, twice in a row.

If you really work at it hard, the differences can be subtle, but you can always tell."

She pulled out another picture of a print from the Paine–Kennedy case. "This one was lifted from a bullet casing—a round surface."

He stared at it. "It's not the same print, but it looks good."

"Too good," she said, "less consistent with touching and more with being planted there. It's the same with all of them, although only the two I showed you first were identical. The others belong to different fingers, all fitting the same man, like you'd expect." She added, "And here's the kicker. I did run DNA on all of them, on my own, since that's my thing, just to see what I'd find."

"And?"

"There was none. On any of them. Each one was pristine. They weren't the result of a real finger touching *anything*. They were placed there using some sort of transfer technique I can only imagine, given the ubiquity of computers and fancy printers."

"But transferred from what?" he asked.

"Beats me," she replied. "Something else he'd touched earlier? A computer file featuring his prints? An old fingerprint card? I can't tell you."

"All to make it look like Kennedy had handled a gun he'd never touched."

"*Maybe*," she stressed, laying a cautioning hand on his forearm. "That's where you have to be super careful. Scientifically speaking, there's nothing saying he never handled the gun—only that he didn't leave those impressions in the traditional manner."

Lester got up and began pacing the room, his chin tucked in. "You're tiptoeing toward saying this case is baloney," he said.

"I'm saying that there seems to be an—"

"I know, I know," he interrupted a little irritably, a rarity for him. "An anomaly. I get it. You can call it subtle. I call it a disaster—especially once I yank it out of the bag for everyone to see."

"Do you have to do that?"

He stopped to look at her. "Yeah, I do. Not at a press conference, but this is a can of worms I need to spill out." At last, he let show a half smile before finishing, "Which you knew when you called me. Nicely played, Dr. Sackman."

CHAPTER FIVE

"I'm Rachel, by the way, Rachel Reiling." Jayla's driver reached out awkwardly for a quick handshake as she drove downhill toward the lake into the embrace of Burlington's downtown.

Jayla opened her mouth to respond, hesitated a moment, and answered, "Charlotte Collins," stealing her last name from SUNY Albany's Collins Circle. She felt embarrassed for lying, and even wondered why she'd done so. The fact that Jared sounded ready to kill her in his texts didn't mean he actually would. His ego had taken a bigger hit than the side of his head. And he certainly wouldn't be interested in this girl, who seemed only concerned with being helpful.

"Where're you from?" Rachel asked.

"New York," Jayla said vaguely. "How do you feel about your mom being a medical examiner?"

"It's cool. It's what she's done my whole life, so it's not like it's awkward or anything. Not for me. I kind of like it. My dad's a lawyer, which is really boring. How're you feeling, now that the adrenaline's worn off?"

"I'm fine," Jayla reassured her. "It wasn't anything. Barely a tap. You can let me off anywhere here, if you want."

Rachel took her eyes off the road long enough to cast her a severe glance. "I'll do whatever you want, Charlotte, but let me offer you some tea at my place, just to make sure, unless you're already feeling kidnapped. It's the least I can do. But you call the shots."

When Rachel had first made that offer, Jayla almost refused and walked away. A moment's reflection, however, had reversed her thinking. She was a stranger in a strange land, on the run and unsure of her choices. Why not seize what fate had delivered and see what developed? She sure as hell had no Plan B.

"Maybe some tea would be nice."

"Great," Rachel said happily, turning left onto St. Paul Street.

She lived on the second floor of a ramshackle rental, clad with what looked to be old-time asbestos shingles but obviously weren't—not in this town of seriously leftist leanings. Being PC, green, culturally sensitive, and inclined toward veganism were just some of the traits commonly associated with what was called the Queen City, in part because of its dominant size.

The two women tramped up the narrow stairs just inside the rear entrance, Rachel chatting all the way. "I hope you like herb tea. I'm afraid I don't have anything else. I do have lots of maple syrup to sweeten it, though. I'm not that much of a purist."

"Maple syrup?" Jayla asked, partly to stay conversational as she studied her surroundings. There wasn't much startling about Rachel's apartment—from the bricks-and-boards bookcase to the foldout couch, it was pretty standard student or post-student fare—and as far a cry from Jared's digs as she could imagine.

"Yeah. I put it in my coffee, too. My mom's boyfriend taught me that. It was a total revelation. I didn't even like coffee before then."

"Is he a doctor, too?"

By this point, Rachel had stepped into the kitchenette off the living/dining room to put a kettle on, leaving Jayla to expand her studies to the pictures and books lining the walls.

"He's a cop."

Jayla stopped and looked up at the ceiling briefly. Great. Of course he is. "That must be interesting."

"It is," Rachel's voice floated over the top of the small counter between them as she scrounged around in a low cabinet. "I even helped him out a while ago, taking videos of one of his crime scenes. I was kind of hoping it would turn into a real job, but nobody had the funding for that."

"Exciting. So what do you do instead?"

"I'm in grad school. Art. Video mostly, but still photography, too. I'd like to be a documentarian, like Frederick Wiseman, although his stuff drives me a little nuts."

Rachel emerged finally, carrying a tray of mugs, milk, some Oreo cookies, and the syrup. "It's almost ready. Water's nearly boiling. How 'bout you? What do you do, Charlotte?"

Jayla smiled at the use of her actual name. She'd been calling herself Jayla for several years, and associated Charlotte with her parents only. It sounded odd to hear it being used again.

"I'm in between jobs," she answered.

"Is that why you came to Burlington? Lots of people do. Maybe I can help."

Once more, Jayla suppressed her impulse to reject the offer. Why fight finding herself under a roof, being entertained and fed by a generous, pleasant, safe-seeming extrovert within minutes of arriving in town?

"I probably need all the help I can get," she answered honestly.

Rachel stared at her as if something had sprouted from her forehead. "Holy cow. Does that mean you need a place to stay?"

Jayla looked back in surprise, unable to squelch her reaction. "You don't even know me."

Rachel laughed. "Right, and you do look like an ax murderer." She turned on her heel at the sound of the kettle whistling and continued speaking. "I have that couch 'cause I thought I'd be having friends over and stuff. But that never happens. All my friends live in the city. It would be a total waste for you not to use it. The sheets are even on it—right now."

She stepped around from behind the counter with the kettle and a trivet. "How 'bout you try it for a couple of days, at least? You get sick of me, or vice versa, we can call it off. I'd love the company."

The two sat down at the small dining table, Rachel filling the two mugs from the kettle.

Jayla pretended to give the offer some thought before raising her mug in a mock toast. "To roommates," she said. "At least for a few days."

By the time Joe Gunther arrived at the Francis Institute with his mother, he knew only that he was somewhere between St. Louis and Hannibal, Missouri. Where, precisely, he had no clue. For a man used to driving back roads and walking the woods, a day filled with planes, limos, taxis, airports, waiting lines, and doting or not-so-doting airport employees had made him completely self-absorbed, focused solely on the care and management of his addle-minded mother.

That had been the resounding worst aspect of the trip, of course, drumming home repeatedly his reason for being here. Her flights of fancy, her violent mood swings between tearful and madly cheerful, her sudden dead drops into profound slumber, regardless of circumstances, had filled him with sorrow, fear, and frustration. As he navigated her wheelchair through the facility's twin glass doors, into a cavernous, softly lit, and pleasantly appointed front lobby, he was ready to plead before any celestial entity for the return of his mother of old. Despite his past experience with abnormal human behavior, he had never seen such a complete change of character, shy of someone seized in the throes of a meth trip.

His expression must have told of his anguish and exhaustion, given the empathy of the woman who approached them as they entered. She crouched down before Joe's sleeping mother as he rolled her to a stop, took her withered hand into both of hers, and glanced up at Joe as she said in greeting, "Welcome. Everyone in this building will do their utmost to put you both back on track. You will get the best we've got. I promise you."

To his surprise and embarrassment, Joe was at a loss for words.

Sam dropped her belongings near the front door as her tiny daughter ran to greet her. She crouched down, gathered the child up in her arms, and allowed herself to fall backwards so that the two of them rolled across the rug in a laughing embrace—a standard evening routine. Willy, standing at the kitchen door, looked on, smiling.

"Oh, God," Sammie let out with relief. "Just what the doctor ordered. My two favorite people."

"The burdens of leadership?" Willy asked, settling onto the floor next to them.

"The burdens of bureaucratic nitpicking, more like it," she answered, tickling Emma and making her giggle. "I thought it would be like when I've had to run the squad for a day or two—do a little extra paperwork, handle a few moron phone calls. But what a bunch of kids some of our esteemed colleagues are. No disrespect to you," she addressed Emma, renewing her attack.

"Money, time sheets, and scheduling, right?" Willy suggested.

Sammie looked at him wide-eyed. "*Yes.* Summer's coming up. The whole VBI wants the same weeks off. I worked that stupid phone all day. So-and-so got that slot last year; someone else's been milking their sick days; and when're the cost-of-living increases kicking in; am I gonna get overtime for that detail that was clearly marked 'volunteer time only'? Endless. People are getting raped, killed, and robbed out there, and these bitchy clowns're all staring at their time sheets. I thought we were better than that. I now officially hate being texted—for the record. For any reason."

Willy stayed silent. He knew Sam's habits, and that she'd work through her rant in short order.

Sam brought her face up from having buried it in Emma's belly. "Okay," she resumed, as if he'd interrupted her. "I'm griping about two or three of 'em, I know. But it sticks in your craw. Infects the whole day. I don't know how the boss keeps such an even keel all the time. I was thinking of buying a punching bag for the office, just to keep you guys safe."

"Good day, in other words," he said, rolling over so Emma could use his body as a jungle gym.

Sam propped herself up on one elbow and watched them, now philosophical. "Yeah. It wasn't bad, now that it's over. I just had to blow off steam." She reached out and waggled Emma's bare foot. "And see you two. How was your day? You disappeared. Smart man."

"Pal up in Windsor wanted me to see something," Willy said.

"New case?" she asked, trying to sound casual. More than anyone except possibly Joe, she knew of Willy's chronic problems with authority, following the chain of command, and even exchanging information. Working with him—living with him, for that matter—was like trying to walk a lone wolf through a room full of noisy people. It was complicated, difficult, and sometimes dangerous.

Or it was nothing at all.

His present silence was characteristic of the man. "Probably not," he said as he got up and went into the kitchen to prepare dinner, leaving mother and daughter alone.

Sam continued playing with Emma, wondering—given his reaction just now and today's statewide squabbling—what being Willy's boss might lead to.

Lester was sitting on the couch when Sue came home, still dressed in a pair of pale blue scrubs. They lived in Springfield, forty minutes north of Brattleboro, along the Connecticut River, where Les had been born and Sue worked as a nurse at the local hospital. It was a cliché, a marriage of these two professions, but it made sense. The routinely weird hours, the influence of sometimes violent energy on the workday, and the always lingering expectation of an adrenaline explosion fueled both jobs and employees.

She put her bag and keys on the side table and plopped down onto the couch for a kiss, snuggling in beside him as he looped an arm around her shoulders. He'd been staring at the television, drinking a beer, when she entered.

"Kids around?" she asked, reaching for the bottle.

"Wendy's upstairs doing homework. Dave's covering a high school basketball game for the sheriff's office. You have a good day?"

"Short version? Two overdoses—one terminal, one not—one pregnancy gone nutso and sent to surgery, and the usual aches, coughs, cuts, and bruises lined up out the front door."

As if dropped from the ceiling, Joe's cat Gilbert landed on Sue's lap. "*Damn.*" She burst out laughing, ruffling his ears in surprise. "Where did this come from?"

Lester ran his hand along the purring animal's back. "He's Joe's. We're official custodians for a while. Meet Gilbert; Gilbert, this is Sue."

Gilbert almost instantly made himself comfortable against Sue's stomach.

Lester nodded approvingly, taking back his beer. "He's clearly fond of good-looking women. Smart cat."

"And we have him, why?" she asked.

Her husband looked at her closely. "He a problem? I thought it would be okay."

She rubbed Gilbert under the chin with her finger and put him into a trance. "No, no. It's fine. Is Joe on a trip?"

"Little weirder than that. His mom came down with something, so he's taken her out West to a treatment center in Missouri, I think. I guess his brother couldn't get away."

Sue poked him in the ribs, jostling Gilbert slightly. "Sounds a little worse than 'coming down with something.'"

"I don't know the details," her husband admitted. "Lyme disease was mentioned. Guess it's pretty bad."

She let out a laugh. "Ya think? How long's he gone for? He just dropping her off?"

"Nope. He's stickin' it out. The place they went to has free lodging for family, so who knows when we'll see him next."

"What's it called?"

"The M. Frank . . . no . . . I forget," he said vaguely, looking a little shamefaced. "I wasn't paying much attention."

"He's your boss, Les."

"I know, I know, but remembering the name of the hospital isn't gonna change anything. I was interested in getting out of the office so I didn't have to watch Sammie strip her gears getting into substitute boss mode."

"You're a terrible person." She reached for his beer again, which he happily gave up.

"It's true," he agreed. "Too bad you're stuck with me. You may be seeing me in the papers again, by the way. I caught a case that could turn into a real wasp's nest."

"Oh?"

"Yup. Famous double homicide, complete with hero cop. Remember the Ryan Paine shooting?"

"Sure. That was just a few years ago. Real O.K. Corral stuff."

"That's it. Well, I got a call from an old forensics pal of mine who said she's discovered something fishy about it."

"Uh-oh."

"Yeah. It may not mean anything, but it's right up there with somebody asking you to retrieve an old beer can, out in a field—except that the field's loaded with land mines."

She craned her neck to kiss him. "You come up with the nicest images. You watch your step, okay?"

CHAPTER SIX

Devin Lambert straightened, pushed away the combination magnifying lens–fluorescent light clamped to his worktable, and blinked a couple of times. Caught in a dazzling white halo before him were the charred remains of what Willy had handed him from the Windsor railroad tracks.

"It's a battery. Specifically, a lithium-ion polymer battery. All the rage right now. You've got at least a smaller version in your pocket as we speak."

Willy frowned.

"Your cell phone," Lambert elaborated. "They're the latest in what they call energy density, until they figure out cold fusion or miniaturize nuclear or a way to feed some other kind of gerbil so you can wear it on your wrist. Or brain implants, like in the movies."

Willy looked away from the battery to glance at him. "What the fuck're you talking about?"

It was early the next morning, and they were in the basement of a Vermont-based, nationally known purveyor of bed and bath products, where Lambert, once a government computer engineer with top secret clearance and a drug problem, now worked on the company's website and fixed employee doodads, as he called the flow of computers, cell phones, tablets, and the like—several of which lay stacked at the far end of his workbench like discarded props from a sci-fi movie.

"Nothing," Devin mumbled, prodding the body in question with a pair of tweezers. Willy had picked him up as a peripheral player in a drug raid years ago, tucked him surreptitiously into his car after realizing the man's potential, and had been using him as a private technical consultant ever since. Lambert may have been a self-acknowledged disaster as a human being, but he recognized a favor when he saw it. Both men knew that he'd eventually get himself into a jam Willy wouldn't be able to dislodge, but until then, he was happy to oblige the cranky one-armed cop whenever he asked for help.

"You'll find a lot of them looking like this," Lambert was saying.

"Burned?"

"Yup. Without getting into details you won't understand or remember—no offense—these guys are built like sandwiches of material that react violently to each other if they come into direct contact. The trick is to get the layers close enough so they can do their magic, but not so close that they burst into flames. I had a marriage like that."

Willy didn't find the last comment original or insightful. Even with a companion as accommodating as Sam, he still had days when he couldn't understand why anyone sane would choose to live with someone else. The catch in his case, of course, was that he saw her as the sane one, while he was the one she'd be better off without.

"They're fun to watch when they go off," Devin went on, presumably speaking of batteries again. "The internet is full of footage. People sticking them with knives and clawhammers—real Darwin Award candidates." He swung the magnifier back into place and showed Willy a minute scrap of some shiny, flimsy fabric. "See this? It's supposed to be flame retardant—wraps around the whole device like a sock. 'Cept it's not designed to keep fire out, like a fireman's coat; it's supposed to give you enough time to get the hell out of the way when the guts of these things malfunction. If you're lucky, that's when you'll see the wrapping puff up like one of those funky tropical fish just before it explodes, complete with hydrogen gas, and tries to kill you. Not a healthy environment. That's what caused that plane crash in the headlines recently. Hoverboards got into trouble, too, 'cause wear and tear on the batteries was making them burn up."

Unconsciously, Willy slipped his hand into his pocket and felt the contours of his cell phone.

Lambert caught sight of the gesture. "Made you nervous."

Willy extracted his hand quickly. "You're an asshole."

The other man wasn't laughing. "I wouldn't worry. Cell phones are burning up, too, but chances are you're okay—law of averages. Mostly, I'm talking about batteries that're subquality, or somehow get damaged, like the ones you'll see on the internet. It's when you breach their integrity in some way that they get nasty. Mostly," he added with a sly look, "but not always. There're a few far-out videos of guys with their pants on fire because of their Samsungs. We have less and less of a clue about what we're doing in this field these days."

He tapped on the carcass before them. "As for this one, there's not enough left of it to tell one way or the other. Where did you find it?"

Cops are cautious about sharing details of a case, but Willy figured a little insight might be of benefit. "On a railroad bed."

Lambert was surprised. "*Really?* Jesus. I wasn't expecting that. Was there a train crash?"

"No. It was just there." His own statement made Willy wonder—not for the first time—why he was pursuing this. Railroad beds were littered with garbage. Why not a ruined battery?

The scientist looked back at the item of interest. "Well, no wonder it burned up. If it got wing-dinged by a train wheel or smashed against a track, that would sure as hell set it off. Remember I mentioned knives and clawhammers? That's because they're metal. The chemicals in these things are very sensitive to metal."

The two of them stared at the battery for a moment, as if expecting it to speak. Willy, however, was now thinking back to those broken teeth—more evidence of a hard and sudden encounter. It was a coincidence he used to reduce his self-doubt.

"So, if there wasn't a train wreck," Devin said then, as if eavesdropping on Willy's thoughts. "What happened?"

Willy ignored the question, wanting to get on firmer ground. "You said this is the same thing I got in my phone. But this is the size of a paperback."

"Right. Your phone doesn't pull much energy. Batteries like this run things like drills, Weedwackers, remote-control toys—old-fashioned power-suckers."

Willy made a face. He imagined two bums fighting over a stolen Weedwacker in the middle of the night, one of them losing his teeth and the tool being destroyed. Maybe Colin Guyette's vision of a simple duke-out was right.

But Lambert wasn't finished. "This particular one, though," he was saying, "looks familiar from the old days. I won't take you down memory lane, but context is everything. Batteries are ordered up and manufactured to fit specific things, right? So your run-of-the-mill Tonka truck cell will be different from the drill I mentioned."

"This looks familiar?" Willy asked, interpreting what he was hearing.

"Yes and no. The size and shape, the way some of the connectors present—or used to. It reminds me of mil-spec stuff I used to futz with in my previous life, before the evil weed brought me down."

"Your stupidity brought you down, Devin," Willy reminded him, perhaps incautiously. "What're you not saying?"

Lambert didn't take issue. He smiled and slid his stool away from the table. "I am dancing around a little. I'm guessing you've got something interesting here—maybe something hot. I don't think it actually does fit a tool or a toy. But there's not enough of it left to tell for sure. It *reminds* me of the military-grade units I knew back in the day, but that was . . .

well, back in the day. And in this high-tech world, things change monthly. That's one problem: This could be something I know nothing about 'cause it's too new. A second problem is that, by law, anything that's built for the U.S. military has to be made here. That"—he pointed to the dead battery—"was made in China, so I'm probably wrong."

Willy pondered that a moment before grunting. "No shit."

"If I'm *not* wrong," Lambert continued. "It wouldn't be the first time I've seen a little corner-cutting going on where inspectors aren't likely to look. I only know it's Chinese 'cause the wrapper burned off. You wouldn't necessarily find out otherwise.

"Let's say you're a small-fry manufacturer and you get a contract for remote-controlled bomb sniffers for the army. As soon as things're up and running smoothly and everybody gets relaxed, you swap out the American-made batteries for something like this. Some Chinese-made components are top-notch, after all. So maybe you rationalize it. Either way, it makes a difference, 'cause a Chinese battery's a lot cheaper for you to buy. All you have to do is disguise it to look like the original. Who in his right mind's gonna open up a dangerous thing like this to read the fine print?"

"Where do you get them?" Willy wanted to know.

"Everywhere. The government might have a law about where they buy their junk, but the rest of us go to China. There are importers in every state in the country with batteries on their shelves."

He poked the item before them again. "Course, this is all hypothetical. I just said this *reminded* me of what I used to see in my old job. CBP or Homeland Security might be able to help you out. They're the import–export hawks who keep up to date. You're a cop. You must have federal friends."

CBP stood for Customs and Border Patrol, a blending that had emerged after the 9/11 security shakeup. Willy knew people in federal agencies, but his personality and methods usually dictated that he couldn't call them friends.

"Yeah," he said. "I'll look into that. You said every state had import-ers. Who's in Vermont?"

Lambert looked down at his hands a moment, clearly caught out. "Okay, maybe I exaggerated. Sort of. You'll have people in Burlington importing general-purpose batteries, or possibly using ones at this level of sophistication on their own assembly lines. But importing them for sale? Not likely."

Willy considered where the battery had been found—the town and actual location, both. The Amtrak line ran from just shy of the Cana-dian border to Massachusetts and beyond. If there was any logic con-necting the railroad and Windsor to the battery and the teeth, why not a reasonably situated place of origin?

"What about Springfield, Mass?" he asked.

"Sure," Lambert said without pause. "It's a major crossroads between Boston Harbor and the rest of the country, which is exactly what Ver-mont ain't. Absolutely."

Willy sat in his car after leaving Devin Lambert and stared sightlessly at the people entering and leaving the building before him. The alarm bell that had gone off in his head when Colin Guyette began his explanation had only gotten louder.

The major problem confronting Willy, however, remained stub-bornly the same: Willy had no proof of a crime.

Even given her mood, Beverly Hillstrom couldn't repress a smile as she spotted her daughter from across the cafeteria. The day at the morgue so far had been busy, complicated, and bureaucratically charged, and she'd been missing Joe terrifically, somewhat to her surprise. The opportunity of a lunch with her daughter had appeared like a gift.

Joe had been texting her regularly—a major accomplishment for him—since their arrival at the Frank, and he'd phoned last night. But somehow, the fact that he was out of state, beyond her ability to reach him by car on pure impulse, made him appear impossibly remote. It was a longing no texting or phone call could address.

"Hi, sweetie," she greeted Rachel as she reached the girl's table.

Rachel gave her a hug and indicated a cup of tea, a bowl of soup, a small salad, and a yogurt. "I know you don't have much time, so I got those to spare you waiting in line. I hope there's at least one thing in there you like."

In fact, Beverly had bolted down a salad she'd brought from home before crossing campus to get here, thinking of the same time constraint as her daughter had mentioned. But the gesture truly touched her, especially today, and so she positioned the bowl of soup before her as she sat down. "That was incredibly thoughtful. This'll hit the spot."

Rachel beamed, happy to please a mother whose intellect and abilities had overwhelmed her from childhood—not that Beverly had ever lorded over her. The love and admiration were mutual, in fact, as Beverly had always envied Rachel's artistic abilities, not to mention her engaging people skills. Hillstrom may have been the beneficiary of many talents, but sociability was not among them.

"Has Joe given you an update?" Rachel asked, having heard of his situation.

Beverly took a sip of her meal before responding. "Yes. They're both settled in. Today's been a familiarity crash course, with lots of meet and greet. Tomorrow will be tests and examinations. After that, it depends on what they find. I'll tell him you asked."

"How's he taking it?"

Beverly did not take the question offhandedly. It wasn't in her nature. Also, she knew that Rachel's regard for Joe Gunther went beyond his being her mother's boyfriend. Rachel had worked for him on a case, and the two had greatly enjoyed the experience—all the more so because it was safely over and everyone had survived. Things had gotten a little dicey at times.

"He's on edge," Beverly said honestly. "He didn't see this coming, and I think his mother's disorientation has come as a shock."

"It must be tough."

Beverly took another sip and moved on to what she imagined was the real reason behind her daughter's invitation. "And what's been going on with you? The apartment working out? It must feel better living off campus at last."

"I have a roommate," Rachel said brightly, her words a shade more rushed than normal.

Her mother's reaction was polite and carefully open-ended. "Really? That's interesting."

"Yeah. I sort of bumped into her, and we've become pretty good friends. She's from New York."

"A student?"

"She's taking a break, so she's looking for a job—just something to do while she thinks things over. Also, she'd like . . . No. That doesn't matter. Never mind."

"What?"

"I was going to say that since she's obviously new in town, she'd love to move in with me. For a little while, at least. She'd help with the rent, of course."

Beverly kept her expression neutral. "What's her name?"

"Charlotte Collins. She's really nice."

"How did you meet? This sounds kind of sudden."

Beverly was watching Rachel's face carefully, expecting the slight signs of tension around her daughter's eyes that she knew well from past experience. Rachel didn't disappoint.

"It's a little crazy, actually. I wasn't kidding when I said I bumped into her. I hit her with my car."

The normally imperturbable Hillstrom almost choked. "My God, Rachel. When—?"

But Rachel was already cutting her off. "No, no, no. It was a tap. Nothing happened. It was fine. That's why I didn't call you or anything. It was like spilling a drink on somebody's lap and then becoming friends."

"A drink doesn't weigh a few thousand pounds, honey."

"I know, I know. Okay, so maybe it's not like a drink, but it was just as minor. She might as well've walked into the side of my car. It was that light."

"All right, but I'm confused," Beverly said. "Where was she living before this bump? There seem to be a few pieces missing from all this."

Rachel didn't quite roll her eyes, but close. "Mom. No crime was committed. It's no different from meeting someone at somebody's house for dinner and hitting it off. People move, they switch jobs. It happens."

Beverly pretended to dive in for another taste of her soup while pondering her next comment. From Rachel's viewpoint, she was absolutely right: People do bump into each other, form a friendship, and sometimes even move in together. That's what had happened with Beverly and Rachel's father, after all, when they weren't any older.

But somehow, it had felt different, which was giving Beverly the most trouble. Was she reflecting the sensibilities of an aging mother still adjusting to empty-nest syndrome? That's what she'd seen in Rachel's expression. Or was she—as she believed—asking the right questions about a chance encounter perhaps too good to be true?

"Of course it does, sweetheart," she eventually picked up. "You have to admit that how you met is near the top of the charts. Give me that much."

"You'll really like her," Rachel said reassuringly. "She's really cool."

Great, Beverly thought—the ultimate praise. What could go wrong?

She wiped her mouth with her napkin and glanced at her watch.

"Well, I hope I do get to meet her. I'm sure I'll like her as much as you do."

"Okay," Sammie said, sitting on the edge of her desk, in part to gain a slight height advantage over her two seated colleagues. "We might as well get started. Our midday briefings have become a habit by now, so I thought we might keep them going while the boss is out of town. Les, I read in the dailies where you got handed a wrinkle on the old Ryan Paine case. What's that looking like?"

The dailies were the equivalent of a squad log, or diary, where members were supposed to enter what they were up to. It was less a legal document than a computerized version of an update around the water cooler.

Lester was noncommittal. "Too early to tell. The prints I wrote about barely featured in the initial investigation—they had enough to close the case without them. And nothing surfaced afterwards to debunk the theory that Kennedy shot Paine after being pulled over for an infraction, and that Paine returned fire and got lucky as he was going down. But the duplicate prints are pretty far out, as discoveries go."

"I say they stink to high heaven," Willy commented.

"To what point, though?" Sam asked them both. "If they don't change the end result?"

"Don't know yet," Lester emphasized. "I'll definitely be digging into it, including checking into any screwup on the lab's part, after the fact."

"Is it going to derail anything else you got going?" Sam asked.

"Shouldn't," he answered. "My other cases're humming along at a reasonable pace. The prosecutor hasn't been bitching, has he?"

She smiled at the familiarity of the complaint. "Not yet." But the comment did prompt her to look at Willy, about whom the local state's attorney and their own prosecutor, the attorney general, had voiced concerns in the past. Willy was in fact extraordinarily good with his paperwork, as befitted his compulsive personality. His methods, how-ever, and the coyness with which he alluded to them in his reports, often made lawyers either squeamish or bloodthirsty, depending on which party they represented.

"How's your caseload going?" she asked.

"Good. Yours?"

She ignored the belligerent undertone. "What about the Windsor thing you mentioned at home? You were AWOL for most of the day. Anything there? There's nothing in the dailies."

Willy laughed shortly. "Uh-oh. Pillow talk making it into the office. Dirty pool. You know how I work."

Sammie straightened in surprise. "Where did that come from? I was asking for the briefing."

"And I said it was fine. Anyone complaining?"

She felt her cheeks redden, which increased her irritation. "Don't be a jerk. If you got something new going on, we need to know about it in case something happens. It's standard protocol."

"Or a yank on the leash," he argued. "Joe was okay with me wander-ing off the rez now and then."

Sam bit off the rejoinder that she wasn't Joe and that he'd put her in charge—precisely the comeback she imagined Willy was angling for. She took a breath, struggling to understand why this was happening. "Nobody's prying, Willy. It's a security issue. We can't watch your back if we don't know what you're doing."

There was an awkward pause in the room—Sam staring at Willy; he looking stubbornly out the window; and Lester watching them both with his mouth half open.

As if he had a stiff neck, Willy brought his gaze to bear on her. "Sorry," he said. "My bad. Complicated day."

She looked at him a moment longer before letting it drop and return-ing to Lester with a face-saving follow-up question of no particular importance.

As the meeting continued, Willy applied all his self-discipline to keep from bolting from the office. He'd been a juvenile idiot, reacting to her running things in Joe's absence—which he knew she was doing well—and to the fact that she'd mentioned a case where even he felt he might be chasing next to nothing.

His response was a self-reminder that he was overdue for some bad news. He'd been happy, stable, rewarded by work and family. It wouldn't last, and he could smell it nearing an end—even if he was the cause.

The young New York state trooper stood nervously on the doorstep, his finger still hovering above the door buzzer. He hadn't been on the job long, and found the system and its workings at once scary and intoxicating. And that was just the standard rules, procedures, and protocols. In addition, he was baffled by the maze of alliances, friendships, and unstated understandings that seemed in play wherever he looked. A case in point being what he was doing here, dressed in plainclothes, ringing the bell of a man he'd never heard of, and told to do so by his immediate superior.

The door opened, promising to put an end to his discomfort.

"Yeah?" The man before him was slim, young, well dressed, and appropriate to the elegant brownstone to his back. His face, however, reminded the trooper of some of the neighborhood thugs he'd grown up with. There are those whose very features—although outwardly perfectly normal—bespeak menace. This was such a man, to the point where the trooper took a half step backwards.

"Sorry to disturb you, sir. I was told you'd be expecting me."

"You have an envelope?"

It was instantly pulled from an inner pocket and proffered. "Yes, sir."

The young man didn't immediately let go of it, however, his training and instincts coming to the fore. "I was told to get your name before I handed it over—just to be sure."

Jared Wylie smiled unpleasantly as he snatched the envelope away. "No you weren't. Get lost."

The door slammed shut in the trooper's face.

Inside, Nick Gargiulo watched his boss rip open the unaddressed envelope.

"Son of a bitch," Wylie said, pleased by its contents.

"Good news?"

"The stupid cow turned on her phone," he said. "They got a ping. According to this, she's in Burlington."

Gargiulo smiled in turn. "Guess that means I'm going to Vermont."

Wylie's expression was grim. "Don't come home empty-handed."

CHAPTER SEVEN

Lester stood before the bulletin board in the lobby of the Vermont State Police barracks in Rutland, absorbing not one iota of the information thumbtacked before him. He was here to meet with James "Sturdy" Foster, a member of the agency's Bureau of Criminal Investigations— the same branch that Lester had left to join VBI, and whose major crimes responsibilities had been curtailed as a result of the VBI's creation. A lot of time had gone by since, and Joe Gunther and Bill Allard, VBI's director, had worked extensively to maintain and nurture cordial relations, but feelings had run raw at the beginning, and Lester to this day encountered remnants of those times, from accusations of his being a deserter to the VBI's being the expedient product of a single, long-gone governor's pen, and therefore deserving of disposal.

This old baggage was relevant now, since Sturdy had not only chosen to stay with BCI, but had also been the lead investigator on the Paine versus Kennedy shoot-out. In addition to ancient rancor, therefore, there possibly lurked a claim that Lester was reopening the Paine case because he believed that the BCI had loused it up—or, worse, had cooked up evidence.

To say he was on edge only scratched the surface.

Sturdy Foster, however, wasn't so nicknamed without cause. When he threw open the inner door to the barracks and welcomed Spinney in, Lester sensed that his misgivings had been anticipated. Foster made his greeting friendly and welcoming, and directly addressed the major issue potentially standing between them.

"According to your phone call, you got poked by an unhappy scientist," he commented as they walked down the hallway to his office. "They saying I screwed something up?"

Lester matched his tone to his host's. "They bent over backwards not to say that. But by pure dumb luck, they did find something I'd never seen before. That's why I wanted to fly it by you first. You know the ins and outs of this thing better than anyone."

Foster credited his tactfulness with a supportive "Okay. Well, let's take a look at it, then, and see what you got."

Foster escorted him into an office cut from the how-to-drive-a-state-worker-mad handbook—starting with narrow slit windows placed too high on the wall to allow anyone a view of anything—and offered him a metal chair, commenting, "Sorry for all the frilly amenities."

Lester laid Tina Sackman's file folder on the desk and flipped it open to the first document. "You want to plow through it first or hear my takeaway? Your choice."

Sturdy made himself comfortable, leaning far back in his chair, which Les found to be interesting and perhaps telling body language. "Fire away."

"In brief," Lester began, "while the fingerprints the lab lifted from Kennedy's revolver all belonged to him, two of them were exactly the same print, carbon copies, while the rest were too perfect to belong to anyone shooting a gun. Also, none of them had any DNA attached."

"None at all?"

"Nope. They're like transpositions from some neutral, nonhuman source."

Sturdy didn't react for a long, slow count, fixing his guest with a steady, impenetrable gaze. "Nonhuman," he finally repeated.

"As if transferred from a source other than a finger, like an old finger-print card or a wax impression or a rubber mold or something. The person who brought this to me—Tina Sackman—said she couldn't tell."

"And the lab didn't catch this at the time because?"

Lester shuffled through the file to a document deeper inside the pile. "That's pretty interesting. Or I thought so. Since I started this job, I've always compared any lift I've collected to what's in AFIS. I think it's what we all do. But I've never once compared one lift to another. Why would you? That's what Sackman did, and when she found the duplicate set, she looked closer. That's when she called me."

Foster absentmindedly chewed the inside of his cheek before asking, "Got anything else?"

Lester played the only card he had: "Only that a case with no margin of error now has a murder weapon where all the latents appear to have been planted by a third party."

Foster slowly sat forward, reached out, repositioned his stapler, and returned to his previous position, all without uttering a word.

Lester stayed quiet.

"There is one very large elephant in the room you haven't mentioned," the older cop finally said.

Lester winced slightly, knowing he'd been overly optimistic. "I'm not saying you screwed up, or that you're the third party," he said quietly.

"Thank you for that. Why not?"

It wasn't the response he'd expected. "I read the reports," he replied. "And I mean all of them—yours and everybody else's who worked the case. I couldn't see where anyone had exclusive access to the gun. I thought of it. I won't deny. But I couldn't make it fit. I looked at how the lab might've cooked up the results, too, but that didn't work, either."

Foster nodded, as if to himself. "So, what's your theory?"

Les felt like he'd passed inspection, if perhaps only temporarily. He turned both palms toward the ceiling. "That's why I'm here. Damned if I know. I figured I'd start with you, for the insider's guide, and then maybe—I hope with your help—start looking at the case all over again, from the ground up."

Foster gave a final, single curt nod. "All right. Tell me what you need."

Lester smiled with relief. "Great. I can't thank you enough. How 'bout laying it out for me from the beginning."

"On the night in question," Foster began, "Ryan Paine was on patrol as usual, outside Halifax. He called in a stop per protocol, including his location and a 10-28 for a vehicle registered to Kyle Kennedy. He was never heard from again. Dispatch issued an 11-20 after the suitable time lapse, like they're supposed to, repeated it several times without success, and dispatched backup to find out what had happened. As luck would have it, two cruisers showed up at almost exactly the same time—one of ours and a sheriff's deputy—and found Kennedy dead of a gunshot wound inside his vehicle, and Paine on his back in the middle of the road, his weapon out and a hole in his throat. Both men were dead, there was blood everywhere, given that Paine's carotid had been severed, and we never found a witness to any of it. It was an empty stretch of road, with no homes nearby, and late enough that traffic was nonexistent."

"And ballistics matched perfectly," Lester recalled.

"Right. Paine's weapon was missing a single round, later found in Kennedy's chest at autopsy—right through the heart, if you can believe that. Kennedy had a Taurus .357 revolver. Assuming he went in with a full cylinder, only one bullet had been fired, consistent with the hole in Paine's throat."

"But it was never found?"

"No. Given the proximity and the fleshiness of the target, the bullet kept on going into the puckerbrush. The lab people busted their humps trying to find it, but with no luck. On the other hand, they did an angle analysis of both trajectories, which fit the narrative to a T."

Lester imagined how Sturdy came across on the stand at trial—another context in which his nickname made sense. "Where was Kennedy's gun found?"

"On his lap inside the vehicle, sprinkled with his own blood, and"—he gave a small smile—"covered with his prints."

"But was his hand on it or just near it?"

Foster hesitated. "Near it only. And before you ask, there was no GSR found, either."

Lester already knew that from the reports he'd read. However, gunshot residue was not a given in a shooting, although more likely with a revolver. Depending on a variety of factors, it might or might not be found on a shooter's hand—popular belief and too many forensic TV shows notwithstanding.

"Let's step back from the actual scene for a sec," he suggested. "What about the two guys in general? Did they know each other?"

"Kind of," Foster told him. "Ryan Paine was what I call a locked-in-the-job trooper. Not ambitious, not a self-starter, not a volunteer by nature—a punch in–punch out type. He got assigned his first barracks because of where he was already living—in this case, west of Guilford—and never made a move to change that. As a result, he got to know the same neighborhood players, basically because neither he nor they ever went anywhere, except maybe to jail now and then. That's the context where we later found out that he'd run into Kyle Kennedy in the past."

"Kennedy was a bad boy?" Lester asked, still playing ignorant.

Foster knew the routine, however. It was never a bad idea to rehash known information. You never knew what new might pop up.

"Kennedy was a woodchuck," he said. "Neither bad nor good. Just regular. He drank and drove, he slapped his girlfriends around sometimes, he did a little weed, didn't get his car inspected on time, bought cigarettes for minors, was loud and disorderly, and so on. A jerk by society's standards, but by ours? Pretty average."

"And Paine nailed him for a few of those?"

"A couple, at most. And we never found where they had a run-in, like with Kennedy threatening to sue or anything. If Paine had later told me he'd never heard of Kennedy, I wouldn't've been surprised. Guys like him're a dime a dozen. You stop paying attention."

"Any charges involving guns?"

"Nope."

"How 'bout Paine? What was his home life like?"

"Wife, now living with some new boyfriend in the house she'd shared with Paine. There was a stepchild, belonging to her, who's since grown and moved cross-country. Paine's long-divorced mom also lived nearby. Looked plain vanilla to us. That said, I don't know that he was looking at keeping his job with us for much longer."

"Oh?"

"Not to speak ill of the dead—a dead hero, for that matter—but his last performance evals were pretty bad. We have a strong and protective union, but even they were running out of excuses. It was Rule 32 stuff—training, weapons recertification. There's irony for you, given the last bull's-eye of his life. Still, he'd been putting off his obligations and burning up goodwill by not meeting anybody halfway. I didn't get anyone to tell me this afterwards, but I'm pretty sure it was about to get ugly."

"He was going to be fired for acting retired while still on the job," Spinney filled in. "If only there were such a category."

Foster nodded. "Just a gut feeling, based on what I was seein'."

"Had he had his come-to-Jesus talk with his supervisor?"

"More than once. He had thirteen years on the job. You know how it goes. People feel they're owed a few extra swings. He might not've ever qualified as trooper of the year, but he put in his time, and had never fucked up big-time."

"Or been caught at it," Lester said less charitably.

Sturdy didn't take offense. "Or that."

"Any rumors surface after the dust settled? About either one of them?"

Foster pushed out his lips contemplatively. "Not that I heard. His mom died recently—lung cancer, I think. She wasn't in great shape when I met her. At the funeral, she was a basket case. You were there, weren't you?"

"Yeah, lost in the crowd. I think everyone in law enforcement was there, from all around New England. It was a zoo in uniforms."

Foster laughed. "That it was. Anyway, the old lady went downhill after that, I guess."

"And the widow?"

"Dee Rollins," Sturdy reminisced. "She was a tough nut. Not someone I'd marry, but she passed all the tests at the time—properly distraught, nothing in her background to raise suspicions, not that there was much room for suspicion anyhow, given the circumstances. Still, we checked her out, just to be thorough. She'd been married once before—that's where the kid came from. Had been with Paine for fifteen years. Don't know what she's up to now aside from the new boyfriend—and I just heard about that incidentally."

"Did you or anyone else put an interview into her?" Lester asked.

"As in, did we turn up the heat a little?"

"I know there was no particular reason—," Lester began.

But Sturdy cut him off, still sounding unperturbed. "Ya gotta remember how hot this was. I mean, three years later, we can say, 'Oh, yeah, this was headline news,' but it was more than that. You referenced the funeral. There were thousands there, including from beyond New England. This wasn't our first law enforcement death, but by gunfire it was. This ain't New York—everybody from both U.S. senators on down were weighing in. There was no way I was gonna grill the mom and widow, or the adult stepkid—not with the scenario we'd worked out and which has stood the test of time—latent prints or no latent prints. I would've had my head handed to me. So, the answer is, yes, I met them both, and conducted interviews, but more than that? No."

The conversation stalled for a moment as each of them mulled over what they were facing. Lester spoke first, purposefully keeping things practical: "All right. So, a cop slowly melting into his boots, about to be fired; a crook of no distinction and with no history of violence; and a midnight encounter with bullets flying. Dispatch had no clue why Paine pulled him over in the first place, correct?"

"It's not generally said over the air. You know that. Comes at the end, when the stop's wrapping up and Dispatch's told whether it was a ticket or a warning—and for what. The only exception might be for a high-speed chase or when a trooper requests backup, neither of which happened here."

Lester nodded, not wishing to overstay his welcome. He wanted this man as an ally, after all. "Okay. I appreciate the guided tour. As I said at the top, I'll be poking through it all, trying to make sense of the fingerprint angle. I hear you loud and clear about the facts probably being solid, but it's a kinky detail, and I feel I ought to check it out."

But despite his diplomatic tone, Foster was already shaking his head sympathetically. "No, no, no. Don't tiptoe on my account. In fact, what I'm thinking may piss you off, but you might consider inviting IA to the party, so everyone's butt is covered."

"Internal Affairs?" Lester parroted, impressed.

Foster hitched a shoulder. "That's how this conversation started, wasn't it? With my thinking you were maybe accusing us of planting those prints? Ninety percent of the time, IA clears the cop being looked at. Those're good odds, and since I was the lead on this one—and know for a fact no malfeasance occurred—I got everything to gain asking them in. I can't explain what your scientist discovered, and maybe it'll lead to some new insight on the case—God knows, we don't know everything—but I seriously doubt anyone's pecker'll be going into the wringer. Asking IA to play'll make us look like saints in the meantime. There's no downside, as I see it."

Lester smiled, shook his head, and stood up to leave. "It's your call, Sturdy. You're a better man than I."

CHAPTER EIGHT

"Joe, how're things progressing?"

Joe settled back against the pillow in his small, sparsely furnished, but kindly provided room, the cell phone cradled against his cheek. The Residence, as the staff called the entire building, was built like a dorm for grown-ups, with decorative touches and architectural details the average college kid would overlook—or destroy without thought. The floors were polished hardwood, curtains covered the windows, each room had a bathroom, there were communal kitchens on each floor. It was a livable compromise between a soulless hotel and a furnished apartment building from which the permanent inhabitants had mysteriously vanished.

A relieved smile creased his face. "Hey, yourself. I'm okay. How's life at the morgue?"

"Very funny. Is this where I say, 'Still as the grave'? You know I hate that kind of humor."

"Yes, Doctor. I do. My deepest apologies."

"Humbug," Beverly said severely. "How's your mother?"

"I'm not the one to ask. They plug me in here and there, mostly to supply a familiar voice and presence, but they're the ones with the know-how. Supposedly, she's showing promise, but I can't tell much of a difference yet. She still seems pretty out of it to me."

"It hasn't been very long," Beverly tried soothing him.

"I know. I'm not bent out of shape. It's more that I just feel awkward. I've watched Leo deal with her over the years, as natural as you like, and even then—when she was a hundred percent—I wasn't sure how he did it. I guess I've been on my own for too long."

Beverly laughed quietly. "Why do you think I deal with dead people? My bedside manner? I know you cops have nicknamed me the Ice Queen. For what it's worth, I think you're very good with people, your mother being a case in point. I also know for a fact that she adores you, so your being there is probably the best thing for her—perhaps even better than your brother."

He let that sink in for a moment before grudgingly saying, "I guess, maybe. I do feel useless, though. What's been going on with you?"

"I've been having my own parent-child issues. Rachel told me that she's taken in a roommate."

"Don't tell me. A boy?"

"No. It's a girl, but someone she met by pure happenstance. Apparently, she almost ran her down with her car, and now the girl's moved in."

"You met her yet?" Joe asked, surprised.

"No. Rachel and I had lunch, which is the first I heard of it. I got a name—Charlotte Collins—and then I did something that will no doubt come back to haunt me. I got hold of Samantha and asked her to check her out. I hope that was all right."

"Of course it was," Joe reassured her, although in fact, it wasn't. Police are not supposed to use their databases for personal reasons, but it's a hard regulation to enforce. Who's to know, after all, when a small preemptive inquiry might head off a larger, possibly criminal situation in the making?

"I think you and Samantha are lying through your teeth," Beverly said, "but I love you for it."

"I take it Sam hasn't reported back yet."

"No. I only screwed up my courage to ask her a couple of hours ago. I had to wrestle with myself about Rachel's right to privacy first."

"How did you find Sam, when you had her on the phone?" Joe asked, spurred by Beverly's revelation. "Any comments about being the boss? Not that you would've asked."

"I didn't," she admitted, "but she gave me some insight anyhow. From what I gathered, if she ever aspired to your lofty heights of authority, this assignment is nipping it in the bud."

"Good Lord," he said. "So soon? What's been going on?"

"In a word? Her other half."

Joe groaned. "I should've known. What's he done now?"

"You'll have to ask her. And I must stress that she wasn't complaining, nor did she sound out of her depths. More frustrated than anything else. She also made a comment about having had no idea of the amount of bullshit—her word—that you must deal with every day. She paid you a high compliment by saying that she'd never heard you grumble once about that."

He was laughing by now. "Damn. She must've gotten seriously dumped on. It's not that bad."

"Not for you, perhaps, but I think Samantha would beg to differ."

"Did she mention any cases that might've popped up while I've been gone?"

"She's much more professional than that, Joe," Beverly chastised. "You'll have to ask her yourself."

"I know, I know. I haven't wanted to micromanage, so I've left them alone. I have been reading their daily log entries, but that's all."

"There is a difference between managing and being supportive, you know." It wasn't phrased as a question.

"Point taken, Doctor."

At that precise moment, the call-waiting function on his phone buzzed, informing him that Sam Martens was calling in.

"Speak of the devil," he told Beverly. "That's her ringing me now."

"Take it, Joe," Beverly quickly urged him. "She needs to hear your voice."

"I know the feeling," he said softly.

"I love you, too," she replied. "Now, hang up."

Smiling, he switched over to Sammie. "Is this the big boss?" he asked.

"I hate your job," Sammie told him.

"I was just chatting with Beverly. I asked her if you were less than thrilled. But you know her—very tactful."

"I sound like a whiner, though. Sorry. I'll suck it up. Write it off to the shock of the new."

"You're allowed," he counseled her. "There is an inordinate amount of nitpicking involved. Don't feel bad. I'm just used to it. You guys trained me well."

She laughed. "Oh, thanks a lot."

"Think nothing of it. Is Willy getting under your skin as well? That's what he tries on me."

She sounded resigned to fate. "He is who he is. He's always doing his own thing, which is God knows what. It's fine when I'm working with him; not so fine when I'm trying to manage him. That's all."

Joe had pulled his laptop over from the night table while they'd been speaking, and now opened it up to the secure site they used to file their dailies. "I've got the log open," he said to her, "in case you want to refer to anything. I don't see Willy mentioned at all."

"That's my point. I think he's working on something in Windsor, but he won't tell me what."

Joe was reading ahead. "Lester looks like he's got something interesting."

"Might be. He's just rolling up his sleeves. Sturdy Foster was a big help."

"I can't believe he urged us to invite IA to participate."

"Yeah, well. Say what you will about the state police, they do play by the book."

"Good for them. I'll be watching this one with interest. Speaking of playing by the book, Beverly was embarrassed to admit that she'd asked you to check out Rachel's new roommate."

Sammie paused before answering, "I gave it a stab."

Joe was surprised. "Meaning you didn't find her?"

"She only gave me a name, and I got no hits with that alone. A date of birth might help, especially if I'm to go outside the state system. I just sent her an email asking if she can get me that."

"Any warning bells go off in your head when she brought the subject up?" Joe asked her in a colleague-to-colleague tone. "Beverly's obviously concerned, but it does sound like the sort of thing a kid fresh out of dorm life would do."

"I don't know," Sam answered honestly. "It did sound spontaneous enough to be true, but I don't have much to work with."

"Okay. Well, do keep an eye on it, if you would. The rationalization can be that the state's medical examiner is peripherally involved, and we want to maintain her security. That ought to do it."

"Roger that," Sam said. "How're things going out there? Your mom any better?"

"Slow but steady," he said without going into details. "Thanks for asking."

She could tell by his phrasing that he wasn't keen on pursuing the subject. "All right, Joe. Tell her hi from all of us, and take care of yourself. You keeping busy?"

"They're doing that for me. I help out at PT and at the cognition labs. We're still settling into a routine."

"Not much fun, I bet," she said sympathetically.

"Not much."

Sam stared at the phone in her hand, reviewing her conversation with Joe. It wasn't its contents that were giving her pause. She was fine with that. She was pondering what he'd told her first—that he'd just been talking with Hillstrom.

There was someone to model, she thought. Imperturbable, organized, respected. Maybe she was called the Ice Queen, but usually from people who'd been told to their faces that they'd come up short. Hillstrom didn't mince words when it came to incompetence.

And she and Joe had been talking about Sam.

Which prompted Sam to make a move she'd usually instinctively avoid: She dialed Hillstrom's number.

"Samantha?" Beverly answered, reading the display on her phone.

"Call me Sam, please. I've always wanted to ask you that. My mom called me Samantha, and it mostly wasn't 'cause she had something happy to share. I know you like to use full names, though, so if you have to—"

"*Of course,*" Beverly interrupted her. "Sam is fine. I'm just old-fashioned that way. Were you already able to find out something about Charlotte Collins? That was incredibly fast. I'm not sure that's good news."

"I'm sorry, no," Sam replied, flustered by Hillstrom's reasonable assumption about why she'd called.

But Beverly's follow-up removed the awkwardness. Laughing, she said, "Of couse not. I should have known better. I got off the phone with Joe because you were calling in. There's been no time. Write that off to the vagaries of an aging brain."

As if, Sam thought, imagining that Hillstrom's brain at a hundred would still be one of the brightest things in a crowded room.

"Tell me how I can help," Beverly added.

"It's pretty stupid," Sam confessed, deciding to forge ahead. "I just gave in to impulse. I have a lot of respect for you, Dr. Hillstrom, and now that you're with Joe, you're sort of like family, if you get what I mean. So I was wondering if maybe I could ask you an off-the-wall question."

"Naturally."

Sam spoke quickly, wanting to get through this as quickly as possible. "How do you do what you do? Run an office, fight with your bosses, do your job? Even go to the statehouse to argue about funding, or whatever you do with them?"

Beverly laughed gently. "Feeling a little overwhelmed?"

"I guess," Sam admitted.

"May I ask you something, Sam?"

"Sure."

"Is there anything that you're doing now that you haven't done at one time or another, for example, when Joe's been out of the office even for a few hours?"

Sam gave that some thought before answering, "Not exactly. I've either done it or I've seen him do it."

"Because in a way," Beverly suggested, "you've been in training for this for some time, no?"

"I guess."

"I don't think you are overwhelmed, Sam. I think you're simply on the entry ramp and building up speed. In no time at all, you'll be traveling at the same rate as the rest of us. We're just bureaucrats—in the literal sense of the word. We know how to work within a structure of rules and procedures in order to get things done. It simply takes a little practice and self-confidence.

"And keep in mind," she threw in as a bonus that under normal circumstances she would never have volunteered, "virtually none of us has Mr. Kunkle to contend with."

Sammie burst out laughing. "No shit, Doc. Oh, Christ . . . I'm so sorry."

But Beverly had joined her. "You're right, Sam. No shit, indeed. Does any of that help?"

"You have no idea," Sam acknowledged. "I guess I just needed another woman's opinion."

"Call anytime, Sam. There is no reason for you to feel alone out there."

Willy Kunkle waited until he saw the man he was looking for appear from the tiny Amtrak office. It was cut like a mousehole into the bottom of the austere, multistory rock and cinder block wall that was the back side of the Brattleboro Museum and Art Center—which, incidentally, had once been the train station. Having just been to Windsor's dispossessed counterpart—now a restaurant—he had no further doubts that the railroad had left its glory days behind.

That was a shame, in his opinion. He'd always loved the train, be it New York's subway or the interstate version he was anticipating now. Despite his antagonism toward most people-filled environments, he found trains soothingly communal—sealed vessels filled with unrelated, generally quiet strangers, rocketing through space as if on a hopeful shared journey. It didn't make much sense to him—and he'd heard all the counterarguments—but his fondness for trains, and the unexpected optimism they brought him, had never abated.

He stepped free of the alcove he'd been standing in, out of the light mist that filled the air, and approached his man from the rear. Keely Hooper was an engineer for Amtrak. An affable, easygoing person, he seemed perfectly suited to his job, riding atop a roughly 135-ton giant as if he were on a Sunday drive. On the other hand, Willy imagined, Amtrak probably didn't have too many train drivers who were twitchy and excitable. At least he hoped not.

"Hey, Keely," he said from right behind the man's shoulder.

Hooper smiled lazily as he said, "Trying to get a rise out of me, Kunkle? After you've hit a truck or two with one of those things"—he pointed down the track—"it takes a lot more than a creepy, gimpy cop to make you jump."

Willy laughed as they both took in the northbound locomotive coming into the station, its large headlight burning like a Cyclops's eye on fire.

"They always make me think of a hippo riding a skateboard," Willy commented.

"I like that," Hooper said. "Massive and dainty at the same time. Very good."

Keely was about to take over the head of the train—as they called it—from another engineer, and continue to St. Albans. He did this on a regular basis, which is why Willy had contacted him to ask if he could hitch a ride to Windsor. The only thing Hooper had asked was whether the request was professional in nature. Willy had assured him it was.

They walked to where the street crossed the tracks, near the flashing lights and barriers, and waited for the fourteen-foot-tall engine to draw abreast of them, like a submarine gliding to a halt. They circled its broad nose, waited for the end-of-shift engineer to descend, and then—following an exchange of greetings—climbed the exterior ladder to the cab.

Hooper motioned his guest to a comfortable chair mounted before the broad front windows on the cab's left side.

"Ever been up here before?" he asked.

Willy settled in, not bothering to answer. They were almost ten feet apart, before a long counter faced with instruments, screens, levers, knobs, and controls, the majority of which were clustered before Hooper. In his left rearview mirror, Willy could see the distant passengers leaving and boarding the train, mostly oblivious, no doubt, to the complexity of the machine pulling them.

"Lousy weather," Keely muttered as he laid his hands on the controls.

"Could be raining," Willy countered.

"Be better if it was. Mist and fog turn the rails into grease. Rain gives you a better grip. That's called a paradox in your world."

"That's what I always say," Willy kidded him. "So, what do you do about it?"

Hooper touched a raised button to the left of the throttle. "Drop a little sand in front of the drive wheels. It's not like they haven't figured most of this out by now."

Slowly, smoothly, the train pulled out of the station. Willy stared ahead at the parallel strips of steel they were riding, ridiculously skinny, narrow, and far below them. "What were you saying about hitting a truck or two?" he asked.

"Deer, cows, people, trucks, trees, rock slides, you name it," Hooper said in a matter-of-fact voice. "Glad you asked, in fact. It's not likely—and I bear witness to that personally—but if something comes up, just do what I do."

"What'll you do?" Willy wanted to know.

"Generally, not much. But I might hit the deck." He motioned to the steel flooring directly behind their chairs. "You never know when something might come through the windshield. If it's really hairy, I'll be heading that way." He jerked his thumb over his shoulder, toward a narrow metal door mounted in the right-hand corner of the rear wall.

"What's that?"

"A set of steps and a corridor leading back toward the engine and the first car beyond. Not that you'd make it that far."

"Jesus, Keely. What're we talking about?"

"Worst-case scenario? A gas truck at sixty miles an hour." He waved his hand around his head. "This whole area could fill with flames. It's not gonna happen, and I'm not pulling your chain. But I thought you should know."

Willy nodded grimly. "Thanks."

"Sorry," Keely said, sounding genuinely contrite. "Didn't mean to be a buzzkill. You never told me why you wanted to come along."

"It's a case I'm working on," Willy explained, still transfixed by the view of buildings ever more rapidly flashing by, and the sight of a girder bridge looming up. "I'm working on a theory that somebody might've been using the train to transport something they shouldn't've been."

Keely laughed outright. "I'll guarantee you you're right. I used to be an assistant conductor back in the day, down south. You'd see these guys—always alone, always quiet, always carrying a rucksack they kept on their laps, and always looking a little iffy. They'd ride in the middle of the night, when there was almost nobody on board, and mind their manners. We actually got to know some of them, at least by sight. They were all mules or couriers. They might as well've worn signs."

"Why the train?" Willy asked.

"Cheap, anonymous, pretty reliable, and most of all, no security. Even post–9/11, anybody can bring anything on the train. I think in part word got out about the troopers watching the interstates, too, and pulling people over for pissant violations. No such problem with us. What's your guy carrying?"

"Maybe electronics," Willy said. "I'm just starting, so I'm not sure yet. That's another reason for the hitchhike."

"You want to talk to the Drum, then. I just drive this thing." Hooper patted the console affectionately.

"The Drum?"

"The conductor. I was showing off. That's super old-school. Nobody actually calls them that anymore, but I like it. We all have to march to the sound of the drum. That's where it comes from; at least I think it does. Anyhow, it's because the conductor's in charge of the train, at all times. People think he's just the schlunk who punches your ticket, but he's the boss man. The drum. And you're in luck, 'cause the regular guy's on today. Al Clay. You'll like him. A true veteran. He might even know who you're after."

"How do I talk to him?"

"He'll be up in a while," Keely reassured him. "He kind of treats the cab like his office. You're actually in his chair, at his desk, so to speak."

"Should I move?" Willy asked, not wanting to ruffle the very man he was seeking out.

"Nah. Better you stay put, just in case you fall down and sue the railroad. I don't need the hassle and Al won't care. He comes and goes anyhow, keeping an eye on the herd. Not that big a deal."

"What is he, security as well as ticket taker?"

"Train security, yeah. Your kind? As in a cop? Not him. He doesn't mess with people like you do. As long as they're minding their manners and not being visibly dangerous, we leave 'em alone. But he keeps track of who's on board, where they're going, and he lets them know when their station's coming up. It's all on his cell phone, transferred there as soon as the ticket's purchased—name, destination, where they boarded, the works."

Outstanding, Willy thought to himself—almost worth joking about the light at the end of the tunnel. But not quite.

Al Clay arrived shortly thereafter. A tall barrel of a man, his stomach stretching the front of his dark blue uniform coat, he looked as comfortable in his clothes as others do in their pajamas.

Hooper made the introductions as Clay rested his forearms on the back of the engineer's chair, looking like a sea captain of old, staring beyond the rail of the poop deck.

Willy let them discuss their trade at first and watched as Clay grabbed a phone from the console and spoke to some far-flung dispatcher, probably sitting in Philadelphia. Finally, Keely informed his colleague of the reason behind Willy's visit.

"These big parts or small ones—that your smuggler was carrying?" Clay asked Willy after the briefing.

"I don't know that he was a smuggler," Willy corrected him, "but what I found burned to a crisp in Windsor was about the size of a book."

"So, backpack-sized."

"If that's all he was carrying, yeah. This entire line of inquiry is based on little more than a hunch."

"You find a ticket stub or something?"

"Don't I wish. I actually found what I did between the rails, along with three broken teeth."

Hooper laughed, hearing that, but Clay merely became thoughtful, suggesting, "And that made you think he maybe came off the train—most likely out the rearmost door. It's a bigger drop than people think."

It was Willy's turn to now carefully study Al. "Why so specific? Did you notice something?"

Al nodded. "Yup. When did this happen? Just a few days ago?"

"Yeah." Willy gave him the precise date, one day before young Abigail Murray made her treasure hunt discovery.

Al reached into his pocket and removed his smartphone, commenting to Keely, "Remember when I held the train at Windsor that day? 'Cause I had a miscount?"

"I guess. Yeah."

"That's the same day another passenger complained later in the trip about the rear door banging. At the time, I didn't connect the two. Once in a blue moon, maintenance leaves it open by mistake. Plus, that was after we picked up a sniffer dog detail."

He turned toward Willy to explain, "Every two months or so, we pick up a patrol of our own people—Amtrak police—who run a dog through the train to smell for bombs or whatever. I thought the unlocked door might've been them, by mistake."

"Can I see it?" Willy asked.

"The door? Sure," Clay said simply, turning on his heel and gesturing with his hand to follow.

The two of them proceeded single file through the narrow door Hooper had mentioned, along an extremely tight, short corridor through a second door, into an eardrum-shattering chamber as wide as the locomotive and filled with its screaming, clattering, massive, 4,250-horsepower diesel-electric engine. At the end of this area, they reached a center-mounted door that led them to the first car.

Willy was blinking slightly as he emerged into the train's public section, but Clay, seemingly impervious to the noise they'd left and the gentle swaying beneath them, marched forward like an old tar.

In this fashion, marching by clumps of passengers as settled into their seats as crouching animals harboring from a storm—and surrounded by their belongings, laptops, and small bags of food—Al Clay took Willy to the end of the train.

Only there did he stand aside and indicate the door he'd mentioned with a sweep of one meaty hand. "All you need to do is swing the lever over. It activates like a cam—one hundred eighty degrees—and out you go. No signal, no warning light, nothing."

Willy checked that they were alone. The only passengers were a couple at the far end of the car. "And when did you notice it was open?"

"It sticks a little, so it stays closed even if it's unlocked. Like I said, I never saw it was unsecured till that passenger complained. That was long after Windsor."

"Keely said you keep everyone's name on your phone," Willy said leadingly.

Clay pulled it out, as readily as a cop producing his handcuffs—a long-practiced gesture. "Yeah, but we get the name they give us, you know? I don't have it anymore on this, but I remember it was Samuel Jones, 'cause I kept yelling it as I looked for him, after nobody got off at Windsor. We don't assign seats on this train, but the name'll list each passenger's destination. It happens sometimes, though—when there's a snag in the system."

He touched his temple. "Or I mess up somehow. Not often, but I ain't gettin' any younger. I finally wrote it off to that. I sure didn't check this like I should've." He looked at the door accusingly, concluding, "That's what makes me think you're probably right: Your guy came off this train, but he did it by jumping off the rear. The good news is that he fucked up and busted his teeth in the process. Revenge is sweet."

Willy looked baffled. "But why? You said he was ticketed for Windsor. Why jump off and risk breaking your neck when you're a few hundred feet from the landing?"

Clay shrugged. "You wanna avoid whoever's waiting for you?"

Willy considered that a moment. "I like it. I'm assuming you wrote a report?"

"Yup. Filed it by end of trip. Never heard anything back."

"But it'll tell me where he got on, won't it?"

"I can tell you that. It's still in my head. Springfield, Mass."

Nick Gargiulo was doing his own analysis of mass transportation, sitting in a parked car within the University of Vermont's Davis Center oval, facing busy Route 2. He was watching the Middlebury bus unloading its occupants—the one that catered to passengers originating from Albany.

This was the same bus that Jayla Robinson had taken to Burlington a few days earlier. He knew that from flashing her photo around two depots and several drivers, along with a little cash and a counterfeit law enforcement badge Wylie had secured him to help in loosening people's tongues. Nick knew better than to overexpose them, but the badge and the credentials supporting it bore up under most scrutiny—unless someone contacted the actual issuing agency. Wylie did have his ways of making things happen; Nick would grant him that much.

He worked his door handle and stepped out into the cool, somewhat misty weather. That had been easy enough. Now came the tougher part: either finding her or what she'd stolen in a spread-out, extended metroplex of over 200,000 people.

But how hard could that be, in actual fact? One of the reasons he'd been so successful with this assignment was that, as soon as he'd crossed into Vermont, asking people about sightings of an attractive young black woman had suddenly become a breeze.

He did love this job, and thought his boss was okay at least. And as for the perks? Hey—case in point: He'd been told that if he got ahold of what Jayla Robinson had grabbed, then the girl could be considered disposable.

It was entirely his choice.

CHAPTER NINE

Jayla stepped out of the hair salon and looked up and down Church Street, aptly named for the historic redbrick Unitarian church anchoring its northern end. Church was a pedestrian boulevard in downtown Burlington, closed to traffic, four blocks long, and often teeming with people in search of its cafés, shops, and restaurants, most notably on weekend evenings. It wasn't too busy now, however, at midday, which made seeing Rachel approaching all the easier.

"Ohmygod," the latter said, drawing near. "You look totally different. What a great look."

Jayla was pleased, as she'd been hoping for as big a change as she could reasonably expect. Jared had often commented on her long hair; she was hoping its near complete removal, in favor of something as short as a boy's, might at least be a step toward anonymity. She remained one of the few black faces in a near snow-white town, but not uniquely so. Her hopes remained strong that the preponderance of college-aged people, Burlington's well-known extrovert nature, and the unlikelihood that she would've chosen this place to hide in the first place were all in her favor.

"I got a job, too," she told her new friend as they wandered toward a small café nearby.

"You're kidding. Boy, you don't fool around, do you? What did you get?"

Jayla tilted her head, as if slightly embarrassed. "It's not much. That's why it was so easy. There's a clothes store a couple of blocks down. They needed a stock girl. It pays next to nothing, and I'll probably never know what the weather's doing outside, but it's a start."

"Of course it is," Rachel said supportively, hesitating before asking, "Are you also going to look at UVM for some courses, like you said?"

"I will, for sure. I think I want to settle down a little first."

They sat at a small round table outside, enjoying the afternoon sun filtering through the bordering trees, and ordered two coffees. Rachel's timetable as a grad student and teaching assistant allowed for a scattering of openings in an otherwise eccentric schedule.

It was a magic time of year in Vermont for her—just after the "unlocking" of winter's grip and the first tentative forays of warm weather and bright sunshine, and just before the same heat became uncomfortable and unleashed the summer's annual crop of blackflies and mosquitoes.

"Of course," Rachel said after their server had left, "there's more than UVM available. Champlain College is good, and St. Mike's, in Colchester. And there are others." She laughed. "A lot of people say it's a hard town to leave 'cause of everything it offers. Course, I'm prejudiced, having lived here my whole life. Where in New York do you come from?"

Jayla had anticipated the question earlier. "Buffalo," she answered quickly, hoping Rachel didn't know the place. Certainly Jayla didn't. She'd thought of it because of its distance from here, and—purely based on its reputation, mostly among comedians—she thought it an unlikely destination.

She got lucky.

"Gosh," Rachel said. "I've never been there. Seems so far from every-thing."

Jayla laughed. "Now you know why I'm here."

"Must've been rough, though," Rachel said, her voice still easygoing. "I mean, you got off the bus with just the clothes on your back."

Shit, Jayla thought. Here it comes—the inevitable third degree. Mom's boyfriend was a cop, after all.

She looked down at her hands, conjuring up an expression that was half embarrassed, and half coconspiratorial, before saying in a low voice, "I can trust you, right? I feel I can, seeing what you've done for me."

Rachel matched her tone, leaning in slightly. "Of course."

"I didn't really tell you everything. Well, I guess I haven't told you anything at all, to be honest."

"I figured you'd pick the right time. I knew something had to be up."

Jayla nodded, thinking fast to create a story her new friend could eas-ily grasp, but poignant enough to forestall much more prying. "You're good. Yeah, I had to get out of town. My mom got a new boyfriend, and . . ." She made sure her voice had a catch in it before finishing, "things started getting a little weird whenever we were alone."

"Oh, that's gross," Rachel said sympathetically.

"I tried telling Mom," Rachel continued, "but you can figure how that went. We're not that close—not since my dad died. . . ." She let the words trail off, aiming for her listener to fill in the blanks.

She wasn't disappointed.

Rachel reached out and grabbed her hand. "Did he do anything to you?"

Jayla thought again of the mysterious cop hovering over Rachel's shoulder. "No, that's why I ran. I could feel it coming. My mom works nights sometimes, whenever she pulls a double shift, and I knew that's when he was going to make his move. So I just left."

The waitress returned with their coffees. Rachel patted Jayla's hand and pulled away to make room. "You were right. But that's really hard, leaving everything behind."

Jayla was glad to drift into generalities. "It's more like a big relief. I've been champing at the bit for a while, wanting to travel. I wouldn't have planned it this way, but—you know—what am I missing? Clothes I can replace, a few friends I wasn't that close to anymore, a home life that was going downhill fast. And look what's happened—I step off the bus, and the nicest person I've met in years almost runs me down. How cool is that?"

They laughed together, began drinking their coffee, and drifted onto other subjects—Jayla still wrestling with her deception. She wasn't a liar by nature, and genuinely liked her companion—more and more with each day. Whatever else she may have been, Rachel Reiling appeared to be one of the most sincere and trusting people Jayla had ever met.

Perhaps, Jayla thought—once she'd figured out a plan beyond a haircut and a lousy job—she'd become more open and let Rachel in on her situation. Who knows? Maybe even Rachel's invisible cop could be brought in for advice.

But not yet. For the time being, Jayla was going to lie low, watch her back, and wait. She had no proof that Jared Wylie was after her—just a fear that such would be his instinctive course of action. He was a brutal, manipulative, fundamentally cruel man, if sociopathically smooth and easy in manner and speech. It was the latter, she realized now, that had reeled her in.

In her heart, she truly didn't think she was overstating her vulnerability—or his desire to pay her back with interest. The sexual assaults she'd suffered, the virtual imprisonment toward the end—those were her validations, along with his possessiveness.

Which thought gave rise to another as she watched Rachel's animated and friendly face: What was to become of this girl, if Jayla wasn't being delusional and Jared was on her trail?

He'd stopped the string of threatening and damning texts that had been cluttering Jayla's phone since Albany. But the sudden silence had not struck her as good news. It had instead made her feel stalked—as if the birds overhead had suddenly quieted, seeing the stealthy approach of a feared predator.

If that was true, what would happen to anyone close to her? Jayla wrestled with the possible consequences of what she'd done. What had at first appeared as an act of pure providence—Rachel's miraculously sweeping her up and supplying friendship and shelter—was beginning to feel like a huge mistake.

But was it, truly? What, in the midst of her present turmoil, was reality? And should she sacrifice what good fortune had handed her out of unfounded paranoia? Jared had treated her as a cat did a mouse—tossing her around, essentially for sport. It was possible her escape had broken that cycle, and allowed him to be drawn off by a different, newer distraction.

It wasn't as if she had left with anything of value to him, after all.

Nick Gargiulo was having a good day. While scouting out the area where the bus had dropped off Jayla Robinson, he'd spotted a closed-circuit camera on a pole, which he'd traced back to the UVM police services. It had taken some doing, and the use once more of his questionable law enforcement credentials, but he had finally smooth-talked his way past any requirements like a warrant, gotten access to the pole's video footage, and ended up actually seeing Jayla getting off the bus, to be immediately bumped into by a young woman driving a car.

A car whose registration he'd been able to jot down as the driver pulled over to give Jayla a lift.

Things in life sometimes worked out. Now it was simply a matter of using the phone and some of his old police contacts to get a name and address.

Sam worked the lock and stepped inside their home, closing the door behind her and standing in the darkened living room. It was late, and she was tired and—most taxing of all—depressed. The workday had contained its obstacles. On top of monitoring the agency-wide caseload, she'd had to deal with several lamebrained commotions: a bogus complaint of VBI high-handedness from a municipal department, a conflict between two agents in the same office over competing vacation requests— which the Special Agent in Charge should have handled but had kicked to her—and a very long conference call with two legislators who wanted to know why the hell the VBI even existed, much less why Vermonters had to pay for it, and who should've been bitching to the VBI's director in the first place.

Worse than any of that, however, was what was going on between her and Willy. Indeed, one of the reasons she was so late coming home was that she'd dreaded leaving the security and sanctity of the office— even with her cherished, if sleeping, Emma being available for a soul-cleansing kiss at the receiving end. Bureaucratic hassles could be a pain, but at least they had shape and a shelf life she could recognize and address. Relationship problems, at which she'd sucked her entire life, remained amorphous, elusive, and generally irrational—even before they'd involved Willy Kunkle.

People too numerous to count had warned her away from Willy, as she'd felt Hillstrom had hinted with her otherwise helpful pep talk. Even Sam had been one of them. She'd worked side by side with him for years, when they manned the Brattleboro PD's detective squad under Joe. She'd seen Willy at his worst. She'd been there when he lost the use of his arm on the job, when he worked at the town library while his Americans with Disabilities suit ran its course, and when his ex-wife was found murdered in New York City and he went AWOL to find her killer. She'd witnessed him pissing off, embarrassing, alienating, and lashing out against more people than she could possibly recall, mostly in the name of his sacred sense of honor, but sometimes just because he could be impulsive, insensitive, and careless.

When they moved in together, she'd heard references to everything from the proverbial train wreck to the *Titanic* to the end of the world as she knew it. But while no one had been utterly wrong, in general terms, all of them had missed the mark concerning the man she'd come to love.

Sammie had not chosen him to be her child's father because she was running out of time on the biological clock. She had done so because of her faith in his honesty, integrity, and devotion. Yes, he could be a screwed-up son of a bitch, brusque, intolerant, short-tempered, and dismissive. But rarely to her and never to Emma. And his trustworthiness was absolute.

She surveyed the room. This had once been his house, alone, and it reflected his taste and sense of order. That was another trait—the man was obsessively neat, and a monk in his rejection of material possessions. He was as organized and spare as his psychology was anarchic.

This was not a casual observation. In some ways, it ran to the core of why she'd finally chosen him as a partner. She was messy—in her lifestyle, her past lovers, her impulsive emotionalism. She'd often acted before thinking and been quick to let her heart rule her judgment. One of the huge benefits she'd absorbed from living with Willy—the combat sniper of old—was the value of that crucial reflective pause, when poised on the very edge of battle.

But there was a giant "if" in the midst of all this rational analysis, whose influence occasionally made the ground they stood upon as unstable as quicksand: Both of them—for different reasons and from different influences—were not who they were now by natural evolution. Their current status in the world—as responsible, if sometimes unusual, police officers and parents—had come about through hard work, conscious choice, and extreme sacrifice. From dysfunctional, violent roots soaked in betrayal and human carelessness, they'd each fought against fate to get here.

Which meant that they had all that baggage still on board, lashed down as securely as possible, but often teetering on the brink of collapse. To mix a metaphor, she'd once thought of them both as solid citizen snowmen, praying that the weather would never get too warm.

His voice, when it came, was quiet and unaccompanied by any warning, as usual. It didn't startle her. She'd grown used to it. The man could be like an illusion. The ghost she'd chosen to lean on.

Plus, she knew he had to be here. The babysitter's car hadn't been by the curb.

"I made a mess of things, didn't I?"

She let him remain in the darkness, knowing how he was struggling to make an opening in his armor. She understood his dilemma—she was inclined to tell him to fuck off and figure it out on his own.

"Your timing could've been better. I didn't think I was being *that* type A."

"You weren't."

"I never accused you of goofing off."

She felt that hesitation from him—the one that controls an initial reaction—which rewarded her for practicing the same restraint. "I didn't use those words," she added.

"No, you didn't," he acknowledged, stepping out of the shadows and removing her bag from her hand to place it on the table by the front door.

She bridged the barrier between them by touching his good arm. "We walk on such thin ice, you and I."

"I didn't think it was such a big deal," he said in his defense.

She understood what he meant. "I know you didn't. It was your timing. At the exact minute I needed support, you gave me crap—accusing me of pulling your leash—and then you took off. I know you didn't mean it, and that you have your own thing against authority, and maybe even that you were scared I was gonna start bossing you around. But it hurt, and I don't think I deserved it."

"You didn't."

He seemed contrite enough that she risked pushing her advantage a bit. "So why did you do it? As much as anything, it caught me by surprise—you usually keep that shit for other people."

His answer completely surprised her. "It was like I was afraid everything we had would fall apart. You know how I am—always trying to get off the first shot."

Impulsively, she cupped his cheek with her hand—a gesture she knew he usually shied from, like a not-quite-tamed animal. "Oh, Willy," she said softly, and kissed him tentatively. "Why would that happen? I'm just filling in till Joe gets back."

He touched her in return, softening a little. "It's not that. I just picked on that, maybe out of convenience. I can't get used to good things lasting, and things have been good for a long time, now."

She looped both arms around his neck and hugged him tight. "You are such a head case, you know?"

"That's why I think you'll get rid of me, finally."

She pulled back to look him in the eyes. "That's shit thinking, Mr. Kunkle. We're building something here—all three of us. Don't you dare make up some story that'll tear that apart. If we make a mess of this, it'll be because you and I fuck it up together. Deal?"

He gave her a small smile and kissed her back. "Deal."

"Come here." She grabbed his large hand and tugged him into the hallway and down to their daughter's room, where the night-light revealed Emma sleeping peacefully, her arms clutching a favorite stuffed bear.

"What did the Three Musketeers say?" she asked.

He chuckled softly. "Sure. I'm the literary scholar of the family. 'One for all and all for one'? Or something."

"Right," she said.

CHAPTER TEN

Ongoing criminal cases vary from one extreme, where the cops are left scratching their heads, to the other, where they know who did it—along with his location—and can peacefully build a case so tight, the prosecutor won't even have to go to trial.

To dedicated hunters like Lester Spinney, each had its appeal—the intellectual challenges of one might be offset by the legal gamesmanship of the other, and influenced in various ways by the forensic intricacies required by both. It was this reliable unpredictability that kept most investigators coming back for more, despite the mind-numbing paperwork and occasional verbal abuse from suspects, witnesses, and even testy colleagues that accompanied it.

A brainteaser like Paine versus Kennedy, however, was rare enough to warrant its own category. A headline-making major case of yore, a police-involved homicide that had dominated conversation for weeks, it was nevertheless considered ancient history. Except that Lester knew it no longer was. He felt like the guy in those movies who has to tiptoe past a bunch of sleeping ogres in order to reach his goal. In his case, the ogres were the media and the public, who would have a field day if they discovered what he was investigating.

Which fortunately didn't bother him. Lester was almost perfectly suited to his job. The son of a man who'd once worked in the machine tool industry, back in Springfield, during Vermont's heyday as a center of that world, Les appreciated order and precision and a cool approach to problem solving. Complementing this, as a man of intelligence, independence, and a wit poorly suffered by bureaucrats, he was designed by temperament to flourish working on his own. Being a detective gave him the best of both worlds.

After studying the details of the case and meeting with Sturdy Foster, Lester had pondered how best to approach his delicate—and, for the moment, clandestine—assignment. It was that latter feature that had encouraged him to initially avoid people like Paine's or Kennedy's families, who had been so bathed in the limelight of the moment, and instead approach some of the outlying players in the drama.

The irresistibly named Molly Blaze, for instance—a cousin of the late Kyle Kennedy. In his scrutiny of the investigation, Lester had found Blaze mentioned but once, in notes by one of Sturdy's colleagues. She'd shed no light on the events of that night, and hadn't seen her cousin in several days before he died.

But Lester had liked what he'd read, given his slightly different mission. His predecessors had been out to establish the facts—who'd done what to whom, in what way, and in what sequence. Les was after those same touchstones, but his focus was more on the why, in the hope it might give him everything else in sharper relief—or in a different light altogether. Molly Blaze, while not a front-row witness, had struck him as reflective and clear-sighted on the subject of her cousin. If Les was lucky, that insight would be available concerning the rest of her family as well.

The confrontation between Kyle Kennedy and Ryan Paine had occurred within a little-recognized, eight-by-forty-mile rectangle of land parallel to the Massachusetts–Vermont state line, running from New Hampshire to New York—east to west—and marked in the middle by the Harriman Reservoir. The western half of this patch is claimed by the

Green Mountain National Forest and remains very thinly populated; the other half is sprinkled by a few tiny communities like Guilford, Halifax, Jacksonville, and Whitingham—scattered along a flimsy web of twisting, hilly, narrow, largely dirt roads that can confuse even the most dependable GPS unit. It was the kind of country made famous in a string of Vermont one-liners concerning flatlanders seeking directions.

Other jokes, however, had a more mean-spirited edge. Unlike other rural pockets in an already unpopulated state—some much touted, like the Northeast Kingdom—this isolated and largely unnamed area was only rarely referred to within Vermont, and often dismissed as being either "single-string-banjo land" or simply an extension of Massachusetts.

Lester found that a great shame. A native of the old urbanized New England rust belt, he loved this quiet, pretty, overlooked mountainous retreat. The tourists could have their Stowes and Killingtons and Quechee Gorges. He'd been bringing his family here for years, in all seasons, for canoeing and ice fishing and hunting and just plain relaxing. He didn't wish it more popularity, as with those other places; but he didn't think it deserved disparagement.

Molly Blaze lived a mile or so below Jacksonville, up a short dirt lane in a trailer that had—like so many others—grown a peaked roof, an extensive deck, and a ramshackle garage to protect the family pickup. The only destination left for this once mobile home was to slowly sink into the ground beneath it.

But that appeared to be a fair way off. Though old and a little worn in spots, the place was presentably tidy, with a vegetable garden being prepared to the side and new flowers beginning to appear in boxes hung under the windows. With the recent damp weather, now followed by cool but welcomed sunshine, everything capable of growth was responding eagerly, enriching the multihued green surroundings with a welcome fresh embrace.

Lester parked at the end of the rough driveway and waited briefly behind the wheel—observing backcountry rules of etiquette—for any protective dogs to appear and function as surrogate doorbells.

Sure enough, something close to a black Lab came out from under the house, but with tail wagging and tongue out, its white muzzle speaking of too many years to put up much of a fuss anymore.

As Lester opened his door and stepped out, he heard a woman's voice call out, "Brutus. You stay. That man does not want his face licked."

Dog and man both stopped five feet apart, each questioning the woman's accuracy. Brutus was exactly Lester's kind of mutt.

Nevertheless, he passed the dog by, trailing his hand so Brutus could touch his fingers with his nose, and approached the front door, where a slim woman with long hair had opened the screen and was holding it ajar with one hand.

"I help you?"

He flipped his jacket open to reveal the badge clipped to his belt. "Lester Spinney, ma'am. I'm from the VBI."

She gave him a wry smile. "Ooh. You guys are a big deal, right?"

He laughed. "We like to think so, but it depends on who you ask."

"Does that mean I'm in trouble?" It didn't seem to bother her much.

"Not as far as I know," he said. "Are you Molly Blaze?"

The smile broadened. "The one and only."

"I know I'm coming from out of the blue with this, but I was wondering if I could ask you a few things about your cousin Kyle."

Her expression became questioning. "You know he's dead, right?"

"Yeah. Right. I'm sorry," he retreated slightly. "I shoulda put that better. It's how he died that I'm asking about."

"One of you guys shot him," she said simply but, interestingly, without bitterness or rancor.

"I guess that's right," he said. "I was assigned to other things back then, so I suppose I heard about it like everybody else did. It was a big shock."

"Surprised me, too," Blaze concurred. "It's not the way I saw Kyle goin' out."

Lester was taken by her response. "Really? Not a go-with-my-boots-on kind of guy?"

She laughed, yet another good sign. "You want a Coke or a coffee or something? It's a pretty day. Might as well use the deck—if nothing else, to justify the time and money we put into it."

She stepped back into the trailer, leaving the door open for him to follow. Without answering, he accepted her implied invitation and entered the home.

"Coke would be great," he said once he crossed the threshold. Looking around, he saw a beautifully kept kitchen and living room, with a hallway beyond—tastefully decorated, clean-smelling, with fresh flowers in a vase on the coffee table. Molly Blaze had crossed over to the fridge and was preparing their drinks.

"Really nice place you got," he commented. "You live here alone?"

"Thanks," she replied, keeping to her task. "Looks that way, doesn't it? I have a husband and two kids—not here right now, of course. They'd probably tell you I torture them to keep things tidy, but this is mostly my doing. I tend to pick up after people. Just a habit—compensates for the usual messy life."

Lester read behind her words. "Tough growing up?"

"Like everybody else," she allowed, "we all have our stories." She handed him a Coke and led him out through a double glass door onto the deck and into the sunshine.

She chose a chair and settled down, waving him into the seat across from her. "I should've asked," she said. "You want lemon in that? Or lime? I got both."

Lester got comfortable, crossed his legs, and reached for the drink, shaking his head. "I'm all set. Thanks."

"What do you want to know about Kyle?" she asked. "And why? Isn't this old news?"

"Well, you're right," he told her, keeping his voice casual. "It is. Every once in a while, though, people like me poke into a closed case, just to make sure everything's squared away."

"And the poor slob who's been in jail for twenty years isn't suddenly proved innocent?" she asked.

He looked slightly pained as he took a sip of his Coke. "That's a worst-case example, and obviously not the case here."

"You saying Kyle didn't shoot that cop?"

"No, no, no," he reassured her. "None of the facts have changed. What happened, happened." He paused to take another sip, playing for enough time to think through what he wanted to say, now that he'd sized up his audience.

"It's just that at the time, because of the headlines and publicity, there was a big push to get everything squared away, so that passions could settle down as soon as possible."

"And the lawsuits would go away," she suggested with a small smile, watching him carefully.

"Those, too, I guess," he conceded. "I don't doubt a few lawyers were hoping they had a cash cow on their hands. That's actually one thing I haven't researched." He then said, "Were there any suits filed in the end? I never knew."

She shook her head. "No. It's like you said. Once the Attorney General or whoever it was said they shot each other during a traffic stop, that was sort of it. The family went back to drinking and feeling sorry for itself."

"Ouch," he said, almost despite himself.

She shrugged it off. "It's not my branch, not really. My mom and Kyle's were sisters, and they never liked each other. Actually, Kyle was about the only one of them I thought had something on the ball. The rest of them're a waste of time. I shouldn't say that—his sister Lorraine's okay."

"You spend a lot of time with Kyle?" he asked.

"Enough," she said. "He had an attitude—don't get me wrong. The man could be an asshole, 'specially around women—course, what man isn't? But never with me. We were buddies, plus we were family, like I said, so that made it different. I was like the older sister he didn't have. Well, Lorraine's older, by a lot, but she had her own problems."

"You'd give him advice?"

"Yeah—which he'd never take. I'd give it a shot now and then, even if it was like trying to teach a preschooler rocket science."

Lester laughed. "Sounds like you had a lot of practice. Is that why the first investigators looked you up? To ask you about Kyle's personality?"

"Not really," she said. "They just wanted to know when I'd last seen him, what we'd talked about, and if he ever had a grudge against the cop."

"Ryan Paine."

"Right."

"What did you tell them?"

She lifted three fingers, one at a time. "A few days earlier, nothing much, and I never heard the name Ryan Paine before this whole thing blew up. We talked for twenty minutes, tops, and they didn't seem super interested in anything I had to say, outside of answering those three questions. It was kinda lame, if you ask me."

"Point taken," he said. "Tell me about Kyle. What was he like? You said he was different from the rest of his family."

She sounded wistful. "He could be sweet, for one thing. He thought he was a ladies' man, but it was more he was a sloppy jerk who couldn't take no for an answer. Women would like him at first, 'cause of his manners and the attention he'd give 'em, but then one side of the equation or the other would get tired of it, and that would be the end of it. I kept warning him to cool his jets and pick on a higher class of chick, but he kept rooting around in the beer section, hoping to find champagne—if you get my meaning."

Lester did. "Did he ever get violent because of these fallouts?"

Blaze shook her head. "He'd get drunk and lick his wounds—usually come crying to me. He might've got into a shoving match. I think I heard about one girl calling the cops, but I never saw him raise a hand to anybody—ever."

He heard the conviction in her voice. Still, "The gun they found on him was definitely his," he told her. "And it wasn't for hunting."

She looked at him pityingly. "It's Vermont, Detective. Everybody has guns."

"They don't necessarily drive around at night with them," Lester insisted.

She studied his face a moment in thoughtful silence, prompting him to ask further, "Did he usually carry a gun, to your knowledge?"

"Nope," she said.

"So why was he then?"

"I don't know."

Lester kept with that line of questioning. "And what about that night? Do you have any idea what he was up to?"

She reflected a moment before answering. "No. I always wondered, too. He was heading away from his apartment, and unless he was aiming for North Adams or someplace in Mass, there's no bar nearer by, and it was probably too late for that anyhow. I could never figure that part out."

"How'd he been behaving up to then? Any ongoing arguments or love affairs gone bad?"

"None that I knew about."

"I didn't find any reference to a girlfriend in the file. Had he been seeing anyone?"

"It seemed like he always had something going on. That's what I meant about his being a ladies' man." She paused before suggesting, "Maybe that's where he was heading that night."

Lester considered that before asking, "How 'bout married women? He go after them, too?"

She tucked in her chin slightly in response. "I don't think so. I never heard about it if he did. Why would you ask that?"

"It would be an extra reason for him to be cautious," he said. "Did he have other people he confided in, besides you? A best buddy, maybe?"

"He had a lot of friends," she said. "High school, the fire department, the road crew—where he worked—and just people around town. He was a local and well liked. But even if the cops didn't ask the kind of questions you are now, we talked about it among ourselves afterwards. I mean, we couldn't make sense of it, either. How did he seem? What was he doing? Who was he hanging with? What about this Paine guy? Stuff like that. There was a lot of buzz. Nothing came of it, though—that's what I'm saying. This was totally out of the blue."

Lester was nodding as she reached her conclusion. "What about his family, besides you, that is?"

"What *about* them? How would any of them have anything to do with his shooting a cop?" She frowned suddenly and looked frustrated, adding, "Or his friends or girlfriends or anything else, for that matter? Two people shot each other, for Christ's sake. Why all the questions?"

Les held up his hands in a placating gesture. "Whoa—hang on. I got no dog in the fight. How else'm I supposed to learn? You said the first guys with badges weren't interested. Well, I am."

She took a long pull on her drink before saying, "Sorry. You're right. I don't have a ton of people available to me. My husband's gone most of the time, my kids are being kids, my dad's who-knows-where, and my mom was useless before she died. Kyle was somebody I could depend on for company, if nothing else. I miss him."

Lester let a moment's-worth of birds chirping and breeze passing through the trees add to her recovery.

"You wanted to know about his family," Molly finally said. "Not much there, really. Hard to tell who was worse between his mom and dad; they were both lost causes. Dead now. Kyle had an older brother who's in the service somewhere, and hasn't been back to Vermont in years. There's the sister I mentioned—Lorraine. She's outside of Ludlow nowadays, on permanent disability 'cause of a back injury. And a younger sister who headed over the hill almost as soon as she could stick a thumb out for a ride. That's it, sad to say."

The latter reference caught Lester's attention. "When did the younger sister leave?"

But Molly brushed it off. "Way before when you're talking about. Plus, it was same-ol', same-ol' soap opera stuff. They know where she is—California, I think—it's just that she burned all bridges. She really hated her dad. Blamed him for everything. I didn't mean it was a mystery or anything. She just doesn't want anything to do with here."

"And Lorraine?"

"She's fine. Kind of a wise old bird, even if she's not that old. Just seems that way, maybe 'cause of her problems. You could talk to her. Actually, come to think of it, you should. Kyle used to see her regularly. You were asking if there was somebody he leaned on. I bet she'd have a different take on him than I would. We were more like buddies. Lorraine was maybe like the mom he never had."

Lester gazed off into the surrounding woods, reviewing his thoughts.

"What happened to his stuff?" she asked him.

He looked at her, surprised. "What stuff?"

"In his apartment. He was living in Wilmington—a rented room above a bar or restaurant or something. I always wondered what they did with his junk."

Lester was nonplussed. He had no idea, and was embarrassed that he hadn't thought of it.

"It's on my list of things to do," he answered vaguely.

CHAPTER ELEVEN

"How goes the battle?" Joe asked.

Sam smiled at the phone. "Better. You were right. It does get easier. I'm learning how to separate the people from the things they say."

His response was leading. "Oh?"

Sam knew better than to mention names, however. "Well, you know: the ones who go on and on about overtime, benefits, and vacation days, but who'd be stunned if you did anything about it. Or the guy who's hot to turn one of the local cop shops upside down for corruption, until I found out his ex-wife was sleeping with the chief. Or half the paperwork coming from the top that apparently isn't as urgent as it says on the cover sheet. I completed a form a couple of days ago—filled everything out— and sent it back to a clerk who had no idea why I'd gotten it in the first place."

Joe was laughing by now. "You do know you can pile about fifty percent of that on my desk for later, don't you?"

"I do now." Sam was feeling that she might have gone on for too long about herself—not a rare circumstance. "How're things out there?" she therefore asked.

"We're settling in," he said, in fact sounding happier than last time.

"Mom's improving. She's got a way to go, but everyone agrees progress is being made. She's definitely not so out of it as she was. Part of it is just sticking to a routine. She's learning to anticipate things happening at a certain time, in a certain place, which turns out to be pretty soothing in itself. And the people are extraordinary—it's like they're hooked on happy pills. No matter how grouchy she gets—or me, for that matter—they have an upbeat comeback and a solution to offer. It is an impressive place."

"Leo must be super relieved."

He laughed. "You have no idea. He's been driving me nuts, calling all the time. So, yes. He's doing better, too."

"You said they put you to work, too?"

"Yeah. I think the staff's just keeping me busy, but it works. They make me dress like them and help out with a lot of the physical and occupational therapy. It gives Mom a familiar face to look at through the day, and makes me feel more like part of the solution. It's odd to be away—made me realize how long it's been since I even had a full weekend without work. On the other hand, I'm starting to take notes about how to apply some of what they do here to our operation."

"Oh, great," she commented. "We all gonna have to wear matching outfits?"

"You'll love 'em," he countered. "Pale mauve. Go great with your hair. And Willy'll never look better."

"I don't know, boss," she said resignedly. "I may have to send him out there to extract you. You been checking the dailies in your spare time?" she asked.

"Oh, sure. Sounds like Willy's thing in Windsor is developing into something."

"Yeah—took him long enough to spill the beans, but I have to admit, it's got me curious, too. We also had a heart-to-heart—just the two of us—so things are better there, too."

Joe didn't pry, instead asking, "I take it that the mysterious and toothless Samuel Jones, who presumably jumped from the train, was a totally made-up name?"

"Let's say that nobody matches any Sam Jones we got in our database. Course, you know what that's worth."

"So, what's the plan?"

"Willy's inclined to sniff around in Springfield, Mass. That's supposedly where Mr. Jones got on board. I don't want to go all crazy, though. There's still no smoking gun, so I'm putting him on a short rope."

Joe made no comment, but he was tempted to wish her good luck in that department.

Instead, he moved on. "Tell me how Lester's doing on the Paine shooting—I want to hear your thoughts about what we're facing. Is this about to go haywire?"

"Honestly?" she asked. "I don't know. We're walking a tightrope, trying to dig into it without letting anyone find out. But it's gonna blow, sooner than later, probably. And then, you're right—all hell will probably break loose."

"As well it should," he mused.

"What?"

"Something's not right, Sam," he reasoned. "I'm not wishing us prime-time news coverage, but what're those prints doing in the middle of an easy case? That needs to be explained."

"I know, boss. I know," she said quickly.

"*You're* the boss," he reminded her. "How're you feeling about this?"

"I'm good," she said, not feeling good at all. "In a way, we can only improve from where we are. We've got two dead people, killed in a mutual shoot-out. That's not gonna change. Meaning that if we come up with another player we knew nothing about, it'll only be to our advantage— show how thorough we are."

"Okay," he said doubtfully after a moment. "But if you ever want to consider a change of careers, I'd recommend becoming a negotiator. You'd be terrific."

"Thanks—I think."

He laughed. "Hey, did you ever get that background information for Beverly? Rachel's new roommate?"

"No," Sam reported. "I needed a birth date, like I told you, but I guess Beverly found that was too awkward to get diplomatically, so it's been left hanging. Rachel really likes the girl—they've become best pals—and even Beverly told me her radar hasn't picked up anything creepy yet. I can get more aggressive, if you want."

"No, no," he said quickly. "I was just asking. Best leave it be."

By birth and upbringing, Willy was a city boy—New York, specifically. Vermont had won him over, at last, but never to where he'd renounced his roots. Cities had value to him—supplying a vibrancy that fueled the culture in ways the boondocks, as he still called his adopted home, could never touch.

That being said, Springfield, Massachusetts, impressed him not at all—not in its present incarnation, at least. He granted that it was in awkward transition. But the question remained: to what end? Would it take on a new identity, becoming New England's first primarily multi-ethnic metropolis, and supply a completely novel and modern urban template for the rest of the nation?

That was one hopeful line of thought.

But it was being chewed over by two opposing groups. One represented commerce, business, and tourism. It wanted to transform the city with hotels, museums, a casino, and a modern version of the industry that once had been a Springfield trademark. The other side argued for something less timeworn and more radical—a new model reflecting its current mixed-culture population and striving for an identity as yet unseen in the nation's aging metropolitan landscape.

To Willy, the uninspired wishful thinking of the first group was almost equally matched by the lack of cash, power, and political influence—or any agreed-upon grand plan—of the second.

Not to mention that the movers and shakers had all the money anyway, which explained why most of downtown was already a construction site involving the new casino and the revamped interstate causeway making room for it.

Nor the fact that neither side was tackling the black hole metaphor currently implied by places like Detroit, where the whole purpose of an erstwhile industrial powerhouse was under scrutiny. New York City might have been considered "too big to fail," in today's convoluted global vernacular, but Springfield? Who was to say?

Certainly not Willy, whose frequent up-or-down judgments spent little time processing such philosophical conundrums. To him, Springfield was a dump, as it had been for years. How it addressed its problems—much less solved them—was of no interest to him.

His focus at the moment was to meet with the man Keely Hooper and Al Clay had recommended: Aaron Hinkle, of the Amtrak police in Springfield. According to both sources, Hinkle was an old hand, a "good guy," and a friend of Vermont law enforcement—having coordinated, all too often, with various Vermont agencies in documenting so-called whacks, or the one-sided encounters between locomotives and trespassing pedestrians.

Willy found his man in a featureless, windowless, concrete office buried beneath the stark elevated platform that had serviced Springfield since the 1970s, when the grandiose old Union Station across the tracks had been closed as an expensive dinosaur. All of Amtrak's local workers had been toiling in the decades since in an increasingly decrepit hodgepodge of cell-like cubbyholes, waiting for Providence or retirement to help them escape. Miraculously, the former was about to happen. For enough money to make Croesus weep, the city had embraced mass transit once more, and was reinventing the mothballed antique Union Station as a rail, bus, and auto hub to envy.

As Willy and Aaron Hinkle exchanged handshakes, Kunkle imagined, looking around, that his host had to be counting the days—Willy had only rarely been surrounded by a more depressing set of four walls.

Hinkle, as advertised, was generous, affable, and helpful. It didn't hurt that Willy had called ahead about his interest in Windsor's minor "mishap" of the missing passenger, or that he'd asked Colin Guyette to throw in a good word—thereby enhancing Willy's bona fides. But Hinkle didn't hesitate to make available what he had, in any case. That amounted to video footage of the passengers boarding the Amtrak *Vermonter* on the day it was presumed that the mysterious Samuel Jones had lost his teeth later, falling or jumping off the back of the train.

As both men made themselves as comfortable as possible in front of Hinkle's computer screen, the Amtrak cop told Willy, "I think you may be in luck. It was a super slow day—a standard crowd getting off, but not too many boarding. I also thought it might help you to see everything we got, and not just the platform footage."

"What's that mean?" Willy asked, peering closely at the images before them.

"We got three cameras, mostly because of problems in the past. One's on the sidewalk outside, above the taxi stand on Lyman; the other's mounted behind the guys at the ticket counter; and the last one's what you asked for—the platform unit."

Hinkle began manipulating the mouse beside his keyboard. "The key was what you got off of Al—Mr. Jones's ticket info. From that, I could get the exact time of his purchase, and from *that*, I got this."

He froze the image where it framed a skinny young man standing before the bullet-resistant glass, receiving his ticket in exchange for a crumpled wad of cash. A date and time stamp hovered in the lower right-hand corner of the screen.

"Meet Mr. Jones," Hinkle said. "Or at least I think so. He fit what you're looking for?"

Willy leaned forward and tapped the monitor with his finger. "That sure as hell does." He was indicating a large rucksack, slung over the young man's shoulder. "Did you check the people before and after him, just to make sure the clocks are all lined up?"

In response, Hinkle quickly flashed ahead and back on the footage, speaking as he did. "Yup. There was a girl with a pack, who got off in Northampton, and another guy traveling alone, but he's accounted for, too—rode all the way to Essex Junction. That was it for people even close to your profile. There are a few old folks, families, people with companions—I have a list for you of everybody's names, et cetera. But that's Jones, all right."

He did his magic with the mouse again. "And here he is getting on board. That's where you can see some of the others, too." He pointed at another man and laughed. "I wondered about him for a second, 'cause I didn't see him buy a ticket, but then I found him. He's a relative of the engineer who was on that day. Happens sometimes."

Willy nodded and pulled back from his scrutiny. "Will you be able to print out a face shot from the ticket counter shot?"

Hinkle proudly handed him an envelope. "Thought you might want one. I included a thumb drive with the footage, too."

Willy gave him an admiring smile. "Nice. You got his home address?"

Hinkle couldn't resist a broad grin. "Open the envelope."

"You're kidding." Willy placed it flat on the desk and worked it open expertly with his one hand. He extracted two photos, one of the shot he'd requested, and a second of a high-angle view of the taxi stand by the station's entrance, revealing the same young man getting out of a readily identifiable cab—its driver clearly visible.

"Not quite that good," Hinkle conceded, "but I thought it might give you a leg up on finding where he came from."

Willy reached over and patted the man's shoulder—a rare show of appreciation from him. "You like Vermont maple syrup?" he asked. "Give me your mailing address."

Two hours later, Willy sat in his car, in the McKnight section of Springfield, Massachusetts, smiling to himself as he observed a modest, low-slung warehouse on Albany Street.

Aaron Hinkle had been right to be hopeful. After leaving the Amtrak cop's company, complete with photos, Willy had contacted Doug Murphy of the Springfield PD—an acquaintance from when the two had exchanged business cards at a training years earlier—and asked him for a little help in chatting with the taxi company's dispatcher.

With the resulting uniformed officer in tow, Willy had then appeared at the cab company and asked the woman at the counter to see her logbook for the same time and date stamped on Hinkle's photograph. Without complaint or hesitation, she'd done so, supplying Willy with the address he was now observing.

Sometimes, he thought now, the fates rewarded even the likes of him. The signage above the small warehouse's entrance read: PURE COMPUTERS—*THE* IMPORTED ELECTRONICS EMPORIUM. And on a smaller, vertical plaque to the right of the door was written:

CHIPS
BOARDS
BATTERIES
You name it.
If you need it, we've got it.

"Let's hope so," Willy said to himself, reaching into his pocket and producing his cell phone.

"Murphy," came the answer after a single ring on the receiving end.

"Hey, Murph. It's Kunkle again. I wanted to thank you for smoothing the skids with the cab company."

Doug Murphy was sounding slightly more harassed than earlier. "Sure. You get what you wanted?"

Willy forged ahead anyhow. "I did. I'm parked in front of the place right now, wondering if you'd like a piece of the action."

Murphy let out a humorless cross between a grunt and a laugh. "Great. Just what I need. What *are* you working on, anyhow? I didn't ask before."

There was some shouting in Murphy's background, which Willy let quiet down before he answered, "A bunch of suspicions right now, but I think I've stumbled over an electronics smuggling operation of some kind."

"Based on what?"

Even as the words left his mouth, Willy was aware of their apparent inanity. "I found a maybe bogus lithium-ion battery in Vermont, in Windsor. The guy I had analyze it said it reminded him of some mil-spec work he'd handled back in the day."

"Military?" Murphy echoed.

"Yeah."

"And . . . ?"

"I think I've traced it back to an electronics importer on Albany Street. That's where I am now."

There was a repeat of the noise on Murphy's end, just before he asked, "Where're you going with this? Sounds like you found a lost battery. I don't get it."

"If it was built to U.S. military specifications," Willy argued, "it's not supposed to be imported."

"You know anyone at HSI?" Murphy asked brusquely.

"Homeland Security? Not really. Rumor has it I don't play well with them."

Murphy was running low on patience. "Look, I don't wanna play with you, either. Maybe you got somethin', maybe you don't, but if you're right about the mil-spec thing, you should call Alex Dorman at HSI. He's a good guy and he might want to help. To me, this sounds more like a Customs and Border Patrol case, but Alex is better to work with. Plus, I don't know anybody at CBP."

Willy dived into his pocket for a pen to write down Dorman's contact information that Murphy quickly rattled off before saying, "Good luck, man," and abruptly hanging up.

Willy didn't mind. Unlike many who shared his abrasive personality, he didn't mind being on the receiving end now and then, even more when he could empathize with the messenger. He didn't know Murphy well, but he'd heard that his department had been under fire politically for years. That could not have made it a fun place to work.

Plus, not only was Willy still on track, following a case that had begun as a mere hunch, but throughout its escalating stages he'd been learning how to improve his pitch. When it came time to win over Alex Dorman, Willy was already calculating how best to appeal to federal law enforcement's refined appetite.

Nick Gargiulo's phone vibrated on his belt.

"What?" he asked without preamble.

Jared Wylie took no notice. "You find her yet?"

Nick was amused. Wylie had been calling him every few hours. "Like I wouldn't tell you to get you off my back?"

"Don't give me attitude. You're not irreplaceable."

"Maybe not, but I got your girl."

"The fuck you do. Really?"

"I'm looking at her right now," Gargiulo replied. "Like the song says: Just walkin' down the street."

"God, you're irritating, you know that? Where are you?"

"You know where I am. You want me to do this right, I gotta get off the phone."

"She have it with her—?" Wylie was asking as Gargiulo cut him off. He absentmindedly slid the phone back into its holster, dropped a five-dollar bill next to his coffee cup on the counter, and walked to the café's front door. He waited a few moments for Jayla to get partway down the block from the clothing store where she worked, before stepping out and following her from a distance.

Shouldn't be much longer now.

CHAPTER TWELVE

Jayla stopped chewing in midbite, taking in Rachel's surprised expression as she said, "Oh—I thought when you said you'd come from Buffalo, that's where you were born. What a dummy."

Rachel gently slapped her own forehead as Jayla silently cursed her slip of the tongue. Enjoying dinner at the apartment—consisting of soup and sandwiches—they'd been chatting, when Jayla had let slip that she'd attended high school in Guilderland.

Okay, she then thought, what was the damage? They'd been roommates for almost a week, they got along, Jayla knew in her bones that Rachel represented no threat, and she hadn't heard a word or seen a sign of Jared lurking anywhere in all that time. Maybe her legitimate but fading paranoia was losing its grip.

"I wasn't exactly honest when I told you about Buffalo," she said tentatively, testing her new theory. "I've never even been there."

Almost as a reward, Rachel smiled encouragingly. "That a cover story?"

Jayla looked down. "I'm sorry. I was trying to be careful."

"Smart," Rachel said. "So you're a Guilderland girl. Where is that? I never heard of it."

"It's right outside Albany. That's not all, by the way. My dad's not dead, and my mother would be the last person on earth to have a boyfriend. I just thought it would put you off asking more questions. I'm really sorry."

Rachel took it in stride. "Don't be. I get it. I've done that before. I mean, I never killed off my dad, but I've tossed out smoke bombs at guys getting too nosy. It's handy sometimes. Does that mean you were taking classes in Albany, at SUNY?"

Relieved, Jayla nodded.

"Oh, God," Rachel said enthusiastically, "I was soooo tempted when I was applying. My mom would've been cool about it, but my dad had a fit—said it was too far away. Total joke, of course, since I barely see him since he remarried. Not that I'm complaining. UVM's been good, but I always wondered if SUNY wouldn't have had much more to choose from."

Jayla rolled her eyes. "Parents, right?"

Rachel laughed. "So now that you have parents again, what do they do?"

"They're both in the Albany school system. My dad's an administrator; my mom's a librarian. Super nice, super straight . . ."

"Super controlling?" Rachel suggested.

"Kind of. My mom's worse. That's what I meant about her never having a boyfriend. I know my dad was her one and only, period. Maybe it's the mother-daughter thing, but we kind of get on each other's nerves. She says I don't respect what they've achieved—that's her favorite phrase—and I say she's sold out her heritage."

She quickly held up one hand, as though Rachel were about to interrupt, which she wasn't. "I know, I know. Harsh. Makes her sound like an Uncle Tom or whatever. I don't mean that. They did well for us and she's not really a sellout. They were part of the Civil Rights movement and everything, and they still belong to all the right groups. It's just they're so protective, you know what I mean?"

In that way, Rachel actually didn't. Her parents had been remarkably trusting and freehanded as she and her older sister were growing up, even if that had been in Burlington, Vermont.

"You know Albany at all?" Jayla asked, not just warming to her topic, but also enjoying speaking freely after so many days of self-guardedness.

"Not really," Rachel admitted.

"It's a fun town. I mean, it's got all the political junk going on that everyone talks about, but underneath, it's a huge melting pot of cultures and ethnicities and different traditions—all the things that Burlington could have if it were bigger, and not so white.

"Anyway," she went on, "there are two sections that are mostly black—South Side and Arbor Hill—and when I started getting older, I used to go to Arbor Hill to do volunteer work and find out more about it. Drove my mom crazy. That's where she and my dad came from originally, before they headed for the burbs."

"So she saw you as trying to set back the clock?" Rachel asked.

"I guess. But it wasn't my clock. It was hers. I get it, you know? I totally understand why they left. It was a different time and they had their reasons, and it's true that parts of those neighborhoods are pretty bad. But there's a ton of good going on, too, and if all you do is leave a place, how're you gonna make it better?"

Jayla suddenly laughed and sat back. "Jeez. Where did all that come from?" She looked at her watch. "Did you want to catch the early show? We could get some ice cream before."

Nick Gargiulo watched the two young women leave the apartment house on foot from across the street, and quickly pondered his next move. Wylie had given him an open contract—grab the package, kill the girl if she got in the way. He didn't care. As for Nick, he didn't mind killing the girl. That part of his job had its appeal, which is partly why he so missed the military, after they'd been stupid enough to throw him out, ruining a good career and wasting a useful asset.

Of course, killing civilians over here was trickier—he admitted that. And he wouldn't miss watching his back if he did let her get away.

He shifted his gaze from the girls to the apartment they'd just left. It was unlikely the target had the package with her. So, just this once, discretion being the better part of valor, maybe he would keep it simple. It's not like he couldn't find her again. He crossed the street.

Rachel Reiling's building was a cardboard box against Nick's particular talents—and that was before he discovered that the common entryway servicing both second- and first-floor apartments had been left unlocked.

He therefore slipped up the narrow interior staircase, careful of squeaking floorboards—in case the downstairs neighbors were around—and expertly bypassed the simple door lock he found at the top.

The girls had thoughtfully left a couple of lights on, allowing him to use his pocket torch sparingly. And, befitting her age, lifestyle, and income level, Rachel hadn't yet caught the habit of acquisition. The apartment—given some of the ratholes he'd burgled—was so uncluttered, it was almost spare.

That in no way reduced the pleasant shiver he experienced every time he entered someone's place uninvited—especially if it belonged to a young woman. Regardless of whatever he was after, Gargiulo never passed up the chance of searching through an underwear drawer, for example. In his own self-defense, such recreations weren't entirely illegitimate—people did often bury their valuables in precisely that spot, for reasons he never understood. But truthfully? He would have pawed in there anyhow.

It was fair to say that the whole enterprise was of dubious merit, of course. It was Rachel's apartment, not Jayla's. Jayla had arrived literally with the clothes on her back, which had only minimally been added to in the interim. Gargiulo's careful ransacking of the place, while entertaining, should have taken all of five minutes, instead of the hour he gave it, and the end result was that he learned much more about Rachel than he did Jayla Robinson, including her family members, her mother's interesting occupation, and the name of the latter's policeman boyfriend.

It was proof to Nick Gargiulo that no search—regardless how fruitless in appearance—was ever a complete waste. In his profession, information was currency, and always worth having tucked away.

But it wasn't what he'd come for. The target must've taken the package with her, after all. His earlier optimism for a quick and bloodless resolution had foundered. He was still lacking what would bring his employer satisfaction.

It was time to step things up. Fortunately, he was now perfectly situated to do just that.

"You know, it's weird," Jayla said as they entered the apartment and Rachel locked the door behind them. "It's like every movie's better in a real theater. I watch everything on my phone, almost—maybe a laptop, sometimes. But that was *fun*. And the whole place was so . . . I don't know. *Old*."

Rachel was laughing. "Leave it to Burlington to keep the traditions alive. That movie house is older than my mom. I don't go anywhere else, though. It's pretty dumpy, but it's like the movie's *got* to be showing there. *Then* I'll start worrying about if it's any good."

Jayla rolled her eyes, having been less than impressed by the venue. "You got it bad, girl."

"I know, I know. Country girl, trapped in the sticks."

They had moved into the living room/dining room/kitchenette portion of the flat and were dumping their purses, Rachel's sweater, and—in Jayla's case—her hoodie onto the furniture.

"What do you have lined up for tomorrow?" Rachel asked.

Jayla checked her watch. "I've been thinking about what you said a couple of days ago, so I'm going over to UVM before work tomorrow morning to check out their courses. See if there's something I like."

Rachel was delighted. "Really? That is so neat. I can't believe all this is happening. If you find something, you could move in for sure. Get your stuff from Albany. We could find a bigger place."

Jayla gave her a hug. "You are too much. One step at a time."

Rachel patted her back. "Okay, okay. I know. I won't get my hopes up. Well, I will get my hopes up, but . . . You know what I mean."

It was late. Jayla lay on the foldout bed, gazing at the ceiling and the occasional lights of passing traffic. Who in their right mind would have come up with this outcome, considering how it had begun, with her running down the street, convinced that Jared would come flying after her like a condor-sized vampire bat? From that degree of fear and paranoia—just a few days before—she'd reached here.

It was like a miracle. She closed her eyes and drifted off to sleep.

Gargiulo had taken his time, concealing himself in the back of the hall closet. It was, naturally enough, where Rachel had piled her little-used junk. The trick had been how to rearrange it so he could later emerge without making any noise. That meant shifting hangers so they wouldn't slide, piling luggage so it wouldn't fall, and heaping clothes so they could be moved without a sound. Just as important, he'd had to settle into a comfortable-enough position to stay immobilized for several hours.

He began moving at around one in the morning, slowly working his way to where, after fifteen minutes of painstaking effort, he finally stepped out into the hallway. Once there, he indulged briefly in stretching his arms above his head, straightening his spine, and fully articulating his stiff neck.

He stayed stock-still for an additional, drawn-out moment, acquiring and cataloging the apartment's symphony of tiny sights and sounds—the outside lights, regularly altered by a light breeze through the trees, the ticking of a clock, the fridge's steady hum, Jayla's deep and regular breathing.

He then adjusted his ski mask and glided soundlessly toward the center room, having memorized which boards creaked and which could silently bear his weight. Having reached a spot about four feet from Jayla's head, which was helpfully turned away, he looked around carefully. There was still no reason to make a fuss if his goal was lying in plain sight.

He saw the two purses, a small paper bag, the sweater and the hoodie, all newcomers to the scene he'd inventoried before hiding out. Which purse was Jayla's, he didn't know. Hers had to be new, or at least newly purchased at a used clothing store, but that didn't help. They both looked old. The paper bag he ruled out as being too noisy to deal with first. The hoodie, he knew for a fact belonged to the target—he'd seen her wearing it. And it was lying in a heap in the chair by his leg.

He bent over, running his fingers across the soft fabric, searching for the center pocket. He felt something hard in its folds, shifted the hoodie slightly to pursue it, and tried reaching in. His otherwise delicate gesture proved just enough to nudge the object he'd felt—a pair of sunglasses— onto the floor.

Shit, he thought as the plastic frames clattered onto the wooden floorboards.

There was a rustling from the bed, followed by a sleepy, "Rachel? What's up?"

Gargiulo swiveled on his heel, took one step over to the bed, and clamped his gloved hand across the startled girl's mouth.

"One move, one sound, and you die. Do you understand?" he hissed into her ear.

For a moment, she seemed to comply, staying utterly still. But apparently she was merely gathering her wits, because one second later, her hand flew out from under the sheet, improbably armed with her cell phone, with which she struck him on the temple with her full might.

He was stunned by the blow, and staggered backwards slightly. It was enough for her to roll free of his grip and make for the far side of the bed, screaming Rachel's name.

He threw himself at her, caution abandoned, hoping to neutralize her before her roommate could respond. He caught her around the waist as she fought to free herself of the entangling sheet, and they both crashed to the floor, knocking over the nearby table lamp.

Jayla was on her back, Gargiulo partially on top of her, kicking, punching, and scratching like a woman possessed, screaming all the while, when Rachel appeared at her bedroom door, confused and alarmed.

"Hey!" she yelled, looking around desperately. Hanging from a hook over the kitchenette's counter was a frying pan that she now wrestled free.

Nick Gargiulo, seeing her grab the skillet, wasted no time. He grabbed the broken table lamp, smacked Jayla across the head with it, and scrambled to his feet to deal with Rachel.

She didn't wait for him. As he jumped onto the bed to vault toward her, she ducked low and lashed out with the pan, striking him hard on the left knee. He uttered a scream and fell forward; she let him tumble over the arch of her back and then pivoted around to hit him again on the shoulder.

He'd had enough. Throwing the chair at Rachel to pitch her off balance, he found Jayla's phone by chance under his hand on the floor, took it, and ran, limping, toward the entryway. He tore open the door and vanished, his feet thundering on the steps as he went.

Rachel fought off the chair and got to her feet, yelling at the top of her voice, already hearing concerned voices from the downstairs neighbors.

"Charlotte!" she shouted to her friend, still lying beyond the bed. "Are you okay?"

The frying pan in hand, she saw her own phone on the breakfast table. Keeping her eyes on the gaping front door, she dialed 911 with her free hand.

"Charlotte," she repeated loudly, working her way through the destruction to where Jayla lay, at once watching the door and trying to listen to the operator.

She rapidly explained what had happened and announced her name and address before tossing the phone onto the bed, trusting 911 to do the rest.

She reached Jayla's outstretched legs between the open bed and the wall, and crawled up alongside her, repeating her name again and again, never getting a response.

There was no blood, as she'd feared. The lamp—a heavy metal remnant of a piece of farm equipment, once considered quaintly ornamental—rested like the ponderous hulk it was beside Jayla's head.

Rachel carefully slid her hand under her friend's neck and cradled it. "Charlotte," she said softly. "Say something. Can you hear me?"

But there was no response. Nor would there be.

CHAPTER THIRTEEN

"I keep telling myself I shouldn't do it," Don Heustis said, maneuvering his electric wheelchair to where he could fit his key into the storage locker's padlock. "My wife says I need my head examined. These four units're a decent size—worth some money. I own this whole storage business, as well as a bunch of apartments, but still—she's right. I could rent these out if I made 'em available."

"Why don't you?" Lester asked, mostly to be friendly, but also mildly curious. Heustis had been the late Kyle Kennedy's landlord, and was the owner of several businesses around Wilmington, including the storage park—his entrepreneurial energy at odds with his appearance.

Heustis paused to cast Spinney a glance. "You know? The folks I rent to tend to be down-and-out. People call me a slumlord, and I know my places aren't the Ritz. A lot of other scumbags make a ton ripping off the poor and cutting corners. But I used to be down-and-out. Me and my wife, both. We haven't forgotten. Do I make money? Sure, but not like people think." He waved his hand at the row of locked cabinets facing them. "And I do things like this—keep people's property for years after they're gone—just in case someone might care enough to want them back. It's like a community service I don't advertise. But it helps some-times, like with you, right now."

Lester couldn't argue the point. Once he'd been reminded of Kyle's belongings by Molly Blaze, he'd contacted Sturdy Foster to ask after them, and was told that, while they'd been processed, virtually nothing had been kept as evidence. Only a hunch and pure curiosity had en-couraged Les to then locate Don Heustis, so he was grateful for the older man's benevolent packrat instincts.

"I really appreciate it," he told his guide. "Has anyone else asked to see any of this?"

"Not since I inherited it," Don said, getting the lock open. "They better hurry up, though. I have my limits. I keep this junk for maybe three years, more or less. Just the small stuff, of course. I sell the furniture, or reuse it or trash it, depending. But whatever'll fit into these four units, I'll keep." He patted a nearby partition. "This one's due to become available again, so I'm glad you came."

His chair whirred backwards a couple of feet and he nodded once definitively. "Don't bother calling me when you're done." He laughed. "*You*, I think I can trust. Just lock everything up."

"What if I want to keep something?"

"Send me an email describing it. I'll print it out and put it in the bin to represent the original. That way, everything's complete—in theory, at least." He tilted his head. "Till I throw it out later."

"Right," Les acknowledged. "Well, thanks again."

"You bet," Heustis said, and trundled away down the aisle, toward the warehouse's distant open door.

The phone went off in Lester's pocket. It was Sam.

"Hey," he answered.

"Hey, yourself. What're you doing? I didn't see you at the office this morning."

"I'm in Wilmington, about to paw through Kyle Kennedy's old

belongings, from his apartment. Just wondering if there's anything in them that might tell me what he was up to, the night he got killed. I figured I'd drive straight here, instead of bothering with Brattleboro traffic. Anything going on?"

"Yeah," she told him. "I'm heading up to Burlington, on a homicide."

Lester was surprised. "Doesn't the BPD usually handle their own? I thought that was a matter of pride for them—the whole twenty-four/ seven, full-service thing. We almost never get invited to play in Burlington."

Her voice remained grim. "We weren't this time, either. Beverly Hillstrom weighed in, and I guess they didn't want to piss her off. I think the governor and the commissioner were lurking in the background, too. Hillstrom's daughter's roommate was bludgeoned to death last night— an unidentified intruder."

"Holy shit," Lester burst out. "Is she okay? Rachel, right? She worked with us."

"Same one, and she's fine. She actually beat the bastard off, but it was too late for the roomie. Anyhow, Beverly called me and I called McReady at the PD up there. You know how it goes. I informed Joe, to keep him in the loop. Course, Hillstrom had already called him."

"McReady good with it?" Les asked, knowing the politics she was re- ferring to all too well. In a state this small, everyone in fact did know everyone else.

"He didn't have much of a choice," she said. "But he's a good guy—and a realist. He said he totally understood, had no problems with my tagging along. But he also made it clear he wasn't handing anything over."

"That okay with the bigwigs?"

"They're all on their best behavior—so far. It's early yet."

"The boss gonna come home?"

"He can't," Sam said. "His mom's not out of the woods and his brother still can't relieve him. It wouldn't make any difference. Rachel's fine, like I said, and her mom can definitely handle a crisis."

Lester laughed. "No kidding. Okay. Well, happy trails, then. What's Willy up to?"

He could visualize her rolling her eyes. "Very funny. He's south of the border somewhere. Have a good time in Wilmington."

The phone went dead.

Lester opened the cabinet's battered metal door and peered inside. Every time he was called upon to paw through someone's possessions—like now, or during a search warrant, or even glancing at the personal detritus attending a car crash, strewn across the road—he was confronted with the same pathetic reminder of how little of true value most humans leave behind. The keepsakes and mementos, the once-cherished scraps that stimulated a memory, so often resembled flotsam from a sunken vessel—objects without resonance, open to misinterpretation, criticism, and/or mockery.

With this in mind, he paused before the relics of the life of Kyle Kennedy, almost forgotten in this dim, anonymous repository, looking like trash left by the curb and labeled FREE.

These were the tailings Lester hoped to mine, and maybe use to explain Kyle's death.

Lester assembled a couple of cardboard boxes and a piece of plywood into an uneven table, across which he began spreading the contents of the storage locker. He made four piles—clothes, CDs, papers, and everything else, including keys, some cheap pens, a telephone answering machine, a couple of pocketknives, a comb, and a watch. Then he took inventory.

He started with the paperwork—bills, notices, Post-its, a parking ticket, bank records, pay stubs, a checkbook, and other predictable odds and ends. Sorting through them, methodically taking notes as he went, he built a timeline and a portrait of an average Vermont blue-collar citizen, neither surprising nor particularly revealing. Kyle Kennedy drank, smoked, cavorted, worked, loved, and lived like most of the people Lester had known since birth. By the time he moved the last shred of paper from one edge of the table to the other, Lester felt he'd merely glimpsed a variation of his own reflection in the mirror. He'd made different life choices than Kyle, and thus chosen a different road, but fundamentally, there were more similarities than differences between them.

He moved to the next pile—the clothing—and made fast work of that, going through pockets, checking labels and general appearances for anything outstanding, again without success. After that, he hunted down an electrical outlet, plugged in the answering machine, and played what few messages there were—from his employer, an unidentified female asking if he wanted to have dinner, and a final one, presumably from a friend, that caught his full attention.

"*Hey.* It's Chad. When the fuck're we gonna throw some lead again? You ever find the sixty-five? Come on, man. I'm boooooored."

Lester played the recording twice. The time stamp on the machine had been lost when it was unplugged, but Chad's call was second to the last in line. It had to have been fairly close to the time of Kyle's death.

Lester briefly abandoned his labors to walk out into the welcome sunshine to his car, unlock the back door, and open the old case file that he'd brought for easy reference.

He flipped to the section containing the crime scene photos and went to the ones showing Kyle's bloodstained body, sprawled in the driver's seat of his pickup. Nestled in his lap was the revolver he'd used to shoot Ryan Paine. It was a .357 Taurus Model 65.

Beverly shifted her daughter's head slightly against her chest, causing Rachel to look up and ask, "You okay?"

Beverly stroked her hair and kissed her forehead. They were stretched out together on Beverly's large bed at home, facing the windows over-looking Lake Champlain, the blush of the rising sun just starting to paint the peaks of the Adirondacks, far to the west.

"No, I'm not," Beverly told her. "You just witnessed a friend's murder. I'm not the least bit okay."

They'd been up all night, ever since the attack, first at the scene, then the hospital, so Rachel could be checked out, and finally the police department, where she detailed what had happened. It was there that Beverly had made her request that the VBI—and specifically Sammie Martens—be invited. That went over like the proverbial fart in church, not that Beverly had cared.

Lastly, and speaking well of each of them, both Dan Reiling and Joe had made immediate contact—Dan by coming to the ER to see his daughter, and Joe, regretfully by phone only from the Midwest, asking to speak to the girl so he could offer his sympathy directly.

Beverly had taken comfort in all this—the mechanisms of the very system she represented working quickly and well. It helped her keep at bay the true horror of what Rachel had been through. Of the usual list of things no parent wants their child to experience, this one was so exotic as to rarely be mentioned.

"I really liked her, Mom," Rachel said quietly.

Beverly tightened her hug slightly. "I know, sweetheart."

"She was a nice person."

"I realize that you told everything to the police, but do you think Charlotte knew the man who attacked you? Now that a little time's passed by?"

Rachel shook her head. "There's like a disconnect. If you do have a normal mom and dad and you went to school like everybody else some-where in an Albany suburb, you don't just step off a bus without even a toothbrush. When we first met, I knew there was something off. She covered it first by saying she'd run away from Buffalo and a bad home situation, but I didn't care when she later said that wasn't true. She did it 'cause she was being careful, like we do sometimes when we're not sure of a situation."

She twisted around again to look her mother in the eyes. "It didn't matter. It *never* mattered—she was so . . . alive. I mean, I got it when you asked me about her at lunch. I knew you were worried I'd taken in someone I knew nothing about. But I felt in my bones it was okay. That was just the way she was." She sagged again in Beverly's arms, staring back out at the dawning day. "Or that was how I saw her."

"Perhaps the man had nothing to do with her," Beverly suggested. "Is there anything to say that they were definitely connected?"

"Maybe not," Rachel replied. "It *could've* been random, I suppose." But her heart wasn't in it.

Nor was Beverly's. Being of an analytical nature, and never having met the mysterious Charlotte Collins, she'd been far more concerned than her daughter by the girl's sudden and unexplained appearance. There was little doubt in Beverly's mind that Rachel's new roommate and the attack were related. It was one of the primary reasons she'd pulled rank and manipulated the VBI, and specifically Sammie, with whom she now felt she had a real connection, into being invited by the Burlington PD.

But Beverly's insistence wasn't purely sentimental. Her inner alarm system was ringing loudly—whoever was behind Charlotte's murder was most likely also involved in causing her to get on a bus to Burlington. The question therefore had broadened, as Beverly saw it, beyond who had killed Charlotte Collins to why.

This young woman's murder was not a freestanding event. It was the second act in a drama that predated her encounter with Rachel. Of that, Beverly was convinced.

CHAPTER FOURTEEN

To Sammie, the common denominator around the conference room was that everybody looked exhausted, from Captain Mike McReady and his entire detective squad to the attending forensic types and the uniformed brass, including Mike's boss, the police chief. All told, there might have been twenty people either sitting at the table or lining the walls.

The Burlington Police Department was housed in an enormous, remodeled, pre–World War II car dealership. It was sprawling, soared overhead, and generally had an open-ceiling design to most of its offices, allowing for better air circulation and—for a few cynics—the feeling that its occupants were rats in a maze. Therefore, depending on your outlook, the exceptional presence of a ceiling in this special soundproofed room was either a relief or a claustrophobic disappointment.

For Sam, who was already feeling the effects of everyone's body heat before the briefing had even begun, the rats had it good.

Psychologically, her isolation was all the greater since—for now, at least—she was a guest. The VBI generally took on cases only upon invitation. That had been understood since its creation. Thus, McReady's opening the door only halfway: VBI could sit in, but no more.

Sam, however, did have two more personal incentives for being here:

First, Hillstrom had requested her by name—without Joe acting as intermediary; second, this was to be the first of two meetings in Burlington. The second was slated for later at the VBI office down the street, to involve only the squad. She'd used this high-profile, lethal home invasion to call for a special meeting—including Joe via video—to simultaneously assert her leadership and guarantee that everyone was on the same page.

There was, in addition, an unspoken third reason for her being here: She was laying the ground for what she was convinced would be the VBI's eventual inheriting of this case—or at least for its taking the leading role. Notwithstanding the commissioner's and the governor's influence—and Rachel's mother's high profile, politically—Sam felt that there was much more going on here than just a thief who got surprised sneaking around an apartment.

McReady ran the briefing. Experienced, professional, and level-headed, Mike had ended up where he was through merit and years on the job. Most knowledgeable people assumed that the same factors would make him the next chief of the department.

He began with a computerized slide show, displayed on a wall-mounted screen. Using a progression of neighborhood establishing shots and crime scene photos, maps, and sketches, he outlined Jayla's and Rachel's evening—the outing for ice cream and a movie, the routine retiring to the apartment and separate bedrooms, the unexpected and unforewarned nature of the attack.

He then split the screen and itemized what they knew so far about each victim, beginning with Rachel, in part because of the small role they suspected she'd played in this drama. With Jayla, however, he slowed down and spoke to greater effect.

"Charlotte Collins," he began, showing various images of her dead body. "Which—surprise, surprise—is an alias, as is her alternate first name, Jayla, which we found on a couple of documents in her purse. Real name, according to her license, is Charlotte Anne Robinson. I should mention that Rachel Reiling was unaware of this. She had no clue Robinson was using a pseudonym. She did say that she wasn't too surprised, since she'd wondered about the victim's backstory from the get-go. We expect to find out more about Robinson soon. She told Reiling she was from Albany, attended SUNY, had parents who lived in Guilderland, just outside town, and that they both worked for the Albany school system. We've sent inquiries to both PDs out there. It shouldn't be long before one or both kick something back."

The screen returned to Rachel's semi-destroyed living room.

"Reiling was positive that she locked the door before they left," McReady resumed. He glanced across the room to inquire, "Bob?"

One of the men with his back to the wall filled in, "The lock was crap. You could breach it with a paper clip or credit card. The guy wore gloves, so the only prints we've found belong to the vics. We also think he came in while they were out. We found things arranged in the hall closet that're not how the owner remembers them, and which allow someone to hide behind them. That's what we think he did."

"So," McReady picked up. "He sneaks out after everyone's asleep, tiptoes into the central room where Robinson is sleeping, and then . . . What?"

Bob—who appeared to Sam to be their primary evidence processor—spoke again. "Creaky floor, light sleeper, he bumps his knee. We don't know."

"Could be he was there just to snuff her," a voice suggested.

"I would argue against that," Bob retorted. "The use of the lamp, the mess after all that careful planning, the noise waking up the neighbors and Reiling, the way he ran downstairs after she clocked him with the frying pan—it speaks of things going sour in a hurry. I see Robinson waking up for some reason and catching him."

"So, he was after something that's missing," another voice threw in.

"Yes," Bob agreed. "Her phone, I think. And he got it."

McReady added, "We asked Rachel specifically about Robinson having one. There's no doubt about the phone being gone."

"Rachel gave us the number," Bob explained further. "We've pinged it, or tried to, but it's not responding, meaning it's been turned off or the killer removed the battery."

"So we're nowhere on him?"

"Correct—for the time being. We've put out a BOL to area clinics, hospitals, and pharmacies, in case the frying pan did some serious damage, and we're checking any reasonably located CCTVs for footage. Nothing yet."

"Reiling can't give us anything?"

"Nope. Just a big guy in a mask. No more description. She does confirm the gloves. If we're lucky, he now has a permanent limp or an arm in a sling, given that she whacked him twice."

"He killed her for her phone?" the first voice asked. "Why not just grab her purse at the movies, or whatever? If we're saying this guy's a good planner, what the hell's he doing making such a dog's breakfast?"

Nobody answered him.

"Are we sure the phone was the goal?" someone asked.

"It's the only thing of hers that's missing," Bob said. "She didn't have much else. She came off the bus—which is another avenue we're checking—with just a small backpack-style purse with her wallet and the phone. Reiling said she purchased a few basics since then—underwear, extra clothes, an actual purse—but that was it."

"If she came off the bus," came a question, "how did her killer find her? Through the phone? And if that's true, then why so many days between her arriving here and his trying to whack her?"

"Fair questions," McReady finally said. "Along with a bunch of others. We've got a lot of work to do."

"How'd it go?" Lester asked two hours later. He'd made the trip to attend Sammie's second meeting, but he was the only one. Joe was there only as an image on a computer screen, while Willy had chosen to appear on speakerphone, which gave the meeting a distinctly disjointed, sci-fi flavoring.

They were gathered at the VBI's Burlington address, on Cherry Street, which was the largest facility in the agency's five-office network, including the director's in Waterbury—a reflection of the so-called Queen City's disproportionate workload. Chittenden, Burlington's host county, laid claim to over a quarter of the entire state's population, making this branch deserve its size.

"They're doing a good job," Sam reported. "And McReady didn't have a problem with me in the room, although all he did was introduce me. So far, they don't have much—the victim's real name was Charlotte Anne Robinson, from Albany. Her assailant is a complete unknown. Rachel just saw a big guy in a mask, wearing gloves. She hit him with a pan, so the hope is he'll seek treatment somewhere for a knee or shoulder injury."

"Yeah—right," Willy predictably commented over the speaker at the same time Lester said, "Good for her. How's she doing?"

Joe answered that, his face oddly pixelated, and his lips and words out of sync. "Remarkably well, considering. Beverly's got her at home. The deputy ME's doing the autopsy. So mother and daughter are working through it together. Thanks for asking."

"*Good* boy, Les," Willy said, sounding like he was praising a pet.

Lester eyed the phone with an exasperated expression.

Sam spoke up, hoping to maintain control and stick to her agenda. "The reason I asked for us all to be in the same room at the same time— sort of—is that I suspect this case is going to wind up in our lap, and therefore stress our resources. So I wanted to identify priorities. For one thing, I could tell at the meeting earlier that the BPD is on the edge of having to send people outside their turf, what with Albany being mentioned. That's probably where we'll be asked to come in and play—as a diplomatic way of ceding at least partial jurisdiction."

"Actually," Joe said, "if I can briefly interrupt . . ." He let his request hang a moment.

"Sure," Sam blurted out.

"This should've gone directly to you, Sam, so I apologize for our current slightly fuzzy chain of command. But I just received marching orders to that effect. I didn't want you going on without knowing about them."

"Uh-oh," Willy said. "Here it comes."

Joe smiled. "I'd tell you to get stuffed, Willy, but this time you're right. Burlington's chief, the commissioner of public safety with the governor's backing, and our own director have apparently had a pow-wow, virtually as we speak." He held his cell phone up to the camera. "I got the call three minutes before coming online."

Sam controlled her disappointment at being bypassed. "What did they say?" she asked neutrally.

"You called it, including diplomacy being a factor. They're calling for a Burlington–VBI–Albany task force, where we'll be the liaison between the two city departments. Our AG will be the prosecutor, meaning, for all intents and purposes, that it'll now be our case. Of course, that means the usual, where we do all the work and let them take the credit. But we're used to that. We won't be stepping on toes, anyhow. Burlington and Albany are to run things in their backyards, like always. We're like the air traffic controllers, handling everything they aren't interested in."

In the silence that greeted this, Joe continued, "Good news, Sam, is that you'll get to dump some of the bureaucratic load you've been shoveling. You were specifically mentioned as the point person on this—at Beverly's urging, I might add, along with mine—so it's yours to organize and run with. The other good news is that, because of the task force design, VBI actually shouldn't be overly stretched in terms of manpower."

Sam felt her cheeks redden, flushed with a complicated mixture of pride, frustration, and embarrassment—the last two emanating from an irrepressibly childish response to feeling marginalized by the grown-ups, who'd essentially met in another room to decide her fate.

Joe predictably tried to address this by saying, "This didn't happen as it should have. Time was tight, Sam, you were in transit between the last meeting and this one, and the other players contacted me on instinct. You are the agency's field force commander. I made that clear to them once again, just now. I hope it was okay, and you should feel free to let me know otherwise."

Swell, she thought. What the hell can I say? "Not a problem, boss."

"Great. Thanks," he said, sounding relieved. "And again, my apologies."

"Nice, Sam," Lester said. "You nailed it."

"Yeah, good luck," Willy chimed in. "Albany's an armpit."

Sam shook her head slightly, muttering, "Jesus." Was that the best he could do? She knew he was capable of real support. He proved it all the time to her and Emma in private—and to complete strangers when he wanted to win them over. Why was it such a goddamn burden this time?

She squared her shoulders and resumed leading the meeting.

"Okay, now that we know where we stand, how're you two faring with your cases? 'Cause I'll guarantee that some of what I was doing'll probably fall to you." She looked at the screen. "Unless the gods on Mount Olympus have come up with a way to manage that, too."

"No, no," Joe quickly reassured her. "Like I said, nobody's expecting you to do everything at once, so delegating your workload sounds good to me, including, like I said before, just dumping it on my desk for later."

"All right," she said, somewhat mollified. Her earlier pique aside, not to mention the effect of Willy's one-liner, the vote of confidence was clear and rewarding, even if brought about clumsily. "Lester, what've you got with the Paine case?"

Les looked slightly embarrassed. "Well, given what we just heard, I'm almost sorry to say that it's starting to take off. Nobody made any mistakes that I can tell so far, and nothing's surfaced to say that Kennedy shooting Paine and vice versa didn't happen like people think, but there are some serious questions bubbling up."

"Like what?"

"According to the source that got this rolling," he answered carefully, "the fingerprints on the gun are possibly looking forged."

"Damn," Willy said. "How the hell do you do that?"

"I'm not sure. Simply speaking, you lift a print from one source, make a copy somehow—maybe using a digital transference process—and then deposit it where you want it to be found. In this case, on the murder weapon."

"All while the owner of said weapon holds the light for you?" Willy asked sourly.

"That's another problem," Lester acknowledged. "What I meant by things bubbling up is that I'm also not positive Kyle Kennedy had uninterrupted possession of the gun used in the shooting."

"You're sounding like a lawyer, Les," Willy criticized. "Spit it out."

But Les wouldn't play. He was uncomfortable enough poking into a case that former friends and colleagues had closed. He wasn't about to discuss any suspicions with the likes of Willy Kunkle before they became facts. His loyalty ran deeper than that.

"Not till I'm done investigating," he said simply.

"What about you, Willy?" Sam asked quickly, hoping to pull him off Lester's back. "Last we heard, nothing you had was even that solid."

"True enough," he said cheerfully, she thought in part to irritate her. "I've been spending some quality time in Springfield, Mass, which makes Albany look like Capri. I'm in the same boat as Les—pokin' around in the dark with my eyes closed—but it's startin' to look like the battery they found in Windsor might be military grade and not home-made, which would make having it a federal violation, from what I hear. Anyhow, I've got a date with Homeland Security today, which is why I'm not up there, to see if I can get their help in connecting a few dots I lined up."

It was textbook Kunkle-speak—at once vague and attention-grabbing. It told everyone listening precisely nothing, while holding out the hope of something bigger to come.

They all knew the routine well enough to let it be. Their shared experience with this man, while often punctuated by annoyance and impatience, was more than offset by his proven record of reliability—and a compulsion to find the truth.

None of which meant that Sammie wouldn't rib him a little, feeling the way she was right now. "The way you have with bullshit, if Les sounds like a lawyer, you should run for governor. Be careful with the feds, Willy. If I end up a single mother 'cause you've been tossed into Leavenworth, I will teach your daughter to kick your ass every time we come visit."

"That's sweet, dear," he replied. "I look forward to seeing you both every fourth Sunday."

"What dots?" Joe pointedly asked him, gently challenging the unspoken protocol not to put Kunkle under a microscope.

Willy took a strategically well-timed step toward sincerity and full disclosure. "You know me, boss. I'm flying mostly on intuition. The battery, the broken teeth, the use of the train, and now a Springfield importer. It stinks, and I don't want to walk away from it without a little more digging. Just so you know, I'm not alone. To get their interest, I forwarded a couple of photographs to HSI—of what's left of the battery and the man on the train—so my meeting ain't just a meet and greet. An agent named Alex Dorman wants to know more. I think I've struck a nerve, and I'm betting it's the battery. So—yeah—I'm throwing a little horse manure around, but I think I'm onto something."

Joe, feeling fidgety and out of the action, knew he should keep quiet and let Sam maintain control, but couldn't resist commenting, "It's all you needed to say."

Sammie took the hint and moved along. "Okay. I guess we're squared away. Thanks, everybody, for making an appearance. Keep your dailies up to date, and for Christ's sake—especially you, Willy—call for help *before* you feel your head going underwater. All right?"

"You got it, boss lady," he said as Joe thanked them all and severed his connection—in large part to avoid further crowding Sam's action.

To that point, Sammie made sure Willy was still on the line after Joe hung up. "Where are you right now, Willy?" she asked tersely and without preamble. "Physically?"

"Massachusetts—my meeting's in an hour. You want me to pick up Emma after daycare?"

She paused, brought up short by the very traits she'd been so missing in him minutes ago. Despite her irritation, she smiled at his having read the meaning behind her question, and assuming responsibility.

"Play it by ear," she said. "If you can, great, but I'll call Louise and tell her she's first in line unless you tell her otherwise. I have a feeling I'll be stuck in Burlington for a while."

"You got it, babe," he said. "And I'll call Louise. Knock 'em dead."

Sammie looked at Lester after Willy had hung up. "You all set?"

He smiled as he collected his things and prepared to leave. "Me? Sure. I'm just going back to what I was doing. You're the one on top of the slippery slope. Good luck, by the way. I'm sure you'll wow 'em. But if you need help, call, okay? Day or night." He waved a hand to indicate the offices lining the hallway outside. "And don't forget you have all these dudes available, too."

She nodded her acknowledgment. "Got it, Les. Thanks. And thanks for making the drive. It was nice to have at least one other human being in the room."

He laughed and left, closing the door behind him.

Sammie sat down before the blank computer. Her irritation with Willy aside, he had won points, mentioning Emma as he had. In pre-Emma days, it had been a virtual contest between them to see who could work the hardest, or put in the most hours. Now Emma continually tugged at her conscience. In no way did Sam want her daughter to suffer the kind of childhood she'd endured. But it was that childhood in part that had produced Sam's drive, dedication, and sensitivity, along with her insecurity, fear of rejection, and need to show control.

How was she to supply the kind of upbringing she knew so little about, while avoiding the pitfalls to which she knew she was prone—on top of being teamed with someone as complex as Willy? She didn't question his devotion to their child—he demonstrated it as regularly as he changed moods. But given his baggage, wasn't he almost fated to screw up?

Sam rubbed her forehead in frustration, trying to will herself to stop and return to work.

Or, she kept thinking, perhaps given *her* past, wasn't she fated to sell him short anyhow? Isn't that precisely what had just happened during the meeting, where her focus on his shortcomings had been abruptly upset by his spontaneous and genuine helpfulness? The irony was that despite Willy's reliability, she was fearful of his failing as a parent unless he proved his worth daily. Thus any demonstrated self-doubts from him—as legitimate as her own—rang louder than his constancy. How unfair was that?

It was enough to warrant a lobotomy, she finally concluded—or a distraction like the task ahead. Any port in a storm—wasn't that the saying?

Joe Gunther unhooked his earphones, disconnected his smartphone from Skype, and put it away with a sigh. He looked up from the borrowed PT supervisor's desk and gazed through the observation window into the therapy room beyond, where he could see his mother being put through her scheduled regimen of exercises.

He'd been up half the night, talking with Beverly and Rachel alternately, and then the management types necessary to have Sammie officially invited by the Burlington police to head up the subsequent task force—or however they were going to put it in the eventual press release. Of course, this had to have happened when he was stuck far from home. There'd been jokes that his leaving Vermont would guarantee some crisis occurring.

But to this degree?

He rose and crossed to the window. His mother was doing better, improving by the day. The symptoms mimicking dementia had eased, and her coordination skills were increasing. But it remained a long haul, as she quickly tired and relapsed. He'd had a couple of near lucid conversations with her, but depression had dictated most of their content, with her suggesting that all this fuss and bother wasn't worth the effort—"No one lives forever," and so forth.

Normally, such talk didn't pull at him unduly, even from someone so stoic by nature, nor was he much given to brooding. People were allowed to feel down-and-out, after all. But the near miss involving Rachel had been a bad piece of timing, catching him away from the steadying distractions of running an entire agency. He was free to worry now about Beverly, her daughter, Sammie, and the others, even Leo, whose twice-daily need for updates bespoke his rising anxiety.

Joe had rarely felt so powerless—or so assailed by such emotions.

CHAPTER FIFTEEN

The office of Homeland Security Investigations in Springfield had once belonged to the Marshals Service, and was equipped with all the appropriate law enforcement bells and whistles—multiple locked doors, a processing center, holding cells, a weapons room, and the like. Otherwise, by contrast, it was a typical cube farm, as mundane in appearance as an insurance company call center.

A further jarring note was that had it been the latter, times were clearly tough, because most of the cubicles were empty or had been put to other uses—from housing a printer station to becoming an oversized parking place for the office coffee machine.

HSI Special Agent Alex Dorman swept his arm across the whole expanse as he led Willy to his office overlooking Main Street, and said, "Welcome to the hub. First time in my entire career I've ever found myself surrounded by too much space."

"Don't say that, Alex," came a disembodied voice from one of the cubicles. "I keep telling you. The gods will be angry."

Dorman laughed, opened his glass door, and ushered Willy across the threshold, indicating a guest chair for his use.

He wasted no time thereafter. Dragging over another chair so as not to put a desk between them, Dorman sat down himself, crossed his legs, and said, "Nice information you sent along—enough to catch our interest, while being too vague for us to grab it and run without you. Clever."

"Thanks." Willy nodded. "High praise, considering the source."

Dorman half rose to retrieve a couple of documents from his desk and settled back down. "Okay. Two photographs. One of what looks like a cremated battery, the other of a train traveler buying a ticket. Your implication is that the battery's military, the dude is a terrorist, and you've just saved us from another 9/11. Is that about it?"

Willy was impressed. He was clearly in a room with his own kind. "In shorthand?" he said. "That's a definite maybe. But I won't know till I dig deeper, and it seemed like I had enough to qualify for a little federal assistance."

"Very little," Dorman told him, pointing toward the interior of the office. "The real meaning of all that available space out there is that we're understaffed, overworked, and committed not only to our standard casework, but also to farming out the people who normally work here to the FBI, ATF, DEA, and even the Berkshire County Task Force. We could fill every desk we got and still have enough cases to keep us more than happily occupied."

The agent smiled encouragingly. "None of which is to say bye-bye. I just wanted you to know that you'll have to lobby hard to gain our interest. I'm not being snotty—I promise. It's just our reality. I came out of local law enforcement. I'm no Ivy Leaguer. I used to piss all over the feds. I get it. But now that the shoe's on the other foot, I'm forced to spout what I hated to hear in the old days."

He held up the photos. "So, convince me. What more do you have?"

"How 'bout Pure Computers, on Albany Street, here in Springfield?" Willy offered. "I traced our rail rider to there, where the sign clearly says 'imports,' which, from what I hear, would not be kosher for any U.S. military ware."

Dorman rose and got behind his desk, bringing his computer to life.

Willy kept speaking: "I was also told that Customs and Border Patrol keeps an eye on outfits like that, to make sure they're playing according to our rules."

"CBP," Dorman said half to himself as he worked the keyboard, his eyes on the screen. "I showed them your crispy-critter battery. They were interested, in a vague kind of way."

"I know the feeling," Willy cracked.

"Hey," Dorman argued without emphasis, "you're here, right? I'm fluffing your ego. Stop bitching."

Willy liked this man.

"Got it," Dorman said after a few more minutes. "Pure Computers, owned by a man named Sunny Malik, from Pakistan. There's a note here that says that Pakistan means 'land of the pure,' ergo the name of the store. Cute."

"They got anything on him?" Willy asked.

Dorman was shaking his head. "Nope. He's married to Amra, has a daughter, Sarah. They live on South Branch Parkway, in the Sixteen Acres section of town. Not too bad." He sat back. "No red flags."

"So?" Willy asked.

"I'll have Customs run his import and shipping records, receipts, incorporation filings, the rest. Just because nothing pops out immediately doesn't necessarily mean much—mostly that he's not on the FBI's top ten list. You were smart to send me that high-res shot of the battery ahead of time, by the way. It is mil-spec. People who know that kind of thing confirmed it for me—that's why I called you back."

Willy's eyes widened. "So we're good? I get an attaboy and you take this off my hands?"

His host laughed. "Don't you wish. You got a long way to go. Our involvement may stop here and now, depending on what CBP kicks back. If, and only if, they show some interest, we *might* move up to a document search, surveillance, possibly wiretaps. That could take a long time, and even then, if we still don't find a bunch of covert money, or discover that Malik's got known terrorist connections, I can't promise that we'll do anything more."

He held up a finger for emphasis. "And finally—to rub salt in the wound—since you told me in your email that the local PD's already passed on the case, without us, you're pretty much up shit creek. The state police CPAC won't touch it, and none of the other federal alphabets'll be interested. You'll be considered old news.

"Course that doesn't mean anything if you come back later with something sexy. The door's never closed. Find another battery that's intact, for example. A pristine, Chinese-made, U.S. mil-spec version, complete with serial numbers and manufacturer stamps? Then it would be off to the races—at least more than you are now."

This was a clear turning point for Willy: He could either hand over an incompletely defined case, poorly supported by hard evidence, and watch it vanish as surely as a stone thrown into a tar pit, or he could fight the odds as usual. If the latter, he might right a wrong, achieve the impossible, put some bad guys in jail, and make the feds look like morons—all while playing the maverick.

It wasn't even a choice.

"What's that address on South Branch Parkway?" he asked.

Alex Dorman didn't answer at first, probably recognizing the cowboy he'd been himself before being tamed by federal employment. Almost mournfully, he recited the address and added, "I'm giving you that because it's already public record, but there are a couple of things you should know if you really do want our help."

"Sure."

"Working with us doesn't give you authority to do anything in the state. When you're here, we have to know what you're up to at all times. That means you have to ask permission to do *anything*. Any surveillance, taking of photographs, seizing evidence, entering properties on your own—any stunts like that will create a firestorm and cause you to be immediately sidelined. Plus, none of what you collect will be deemed usable legally, so it really would be a waste. By law, I couldn't hear or look at anything you brought in—not without sabotaging the entire case and probably bringing the AG's office down on my neck."

"Seems a little shortsighted," Willy commented blandly. "I'm an asset. You said you were shorthanded."

For Dorman, that was a virtual confirmation of his misgivings moments earlier. He placed his elbows on his desk to better make his point, eye to eye. "I get that you think we're crap artists and won't do squat, but try to look at this from our perspective. You've given us Sunny Malik and his business. We don't see anything there yet, but I'll be putting a note on his information, for future reference. For us, that matters. It amounts to something. Next time his name comes up, that note'll be there, and our interest will be heightened. If nothing else develops right now with you, we've still got that."

He got up and stood with his back to the window, still looking at Willy closely. "That makes this meeting worth our while, and—like I said—I will start the ball rolling by running a short check on Pure Computers. But if you go gonzo on us, acting on your own, we'll waste all that, throw the book at you instead, and drop the case like a hot rock." He leaned forward slightly to add, "Am I misreading your character, Agent Kunkle?"

Willy smiled where others might have taken offense. "It's like you've read my file," he confessed.

Dorman smiled back, but genuinely and with empathy. "Thought so. Takes one to know one. I can't tell you how tough it was for me to conform to this outfit's rules and regs. Damn near got fired at least three times."

He walked to the door and opened it as Willy rose to his feet. "I gotta get back to work." He gestured as he had earlier, for Willy to precede him. "So I'll walk you out." At the door, however, he laid his hand on Willy's shoulder, which the other man rarely appreciated.

"Don't fuck me over. I like you and I think you may have something here, but it's gonna take time. Deal?"

Willy smiled at him again, their faces inches apart. "You got it."

Ten minutes after escorting Kunkle to the lobby, Alex Dorman settled back behind his desk and picked up the phone. He dialed the number of a local drug task force member—a cop who had been so deep undercover for so long that his uniform no longer fit him, and who had helped Alex with the odd favor now and then because of his absolute and utter discretion.

"Yeah?" the man said, knowing from Alex's disguised caller ID who was on the line.

"I just had a Vermont cop in here, pitching me a case. It may have merit; it may not. But my nose tells me he's gonna go rogue. I could tell he didn't like listening to my trust-me lecture."

"The one where we're all one happy family but we can't piss without your say-so?"

"That's the one. I'm sending you his specifics. He'll most likely be hanging around either Albany Road or South Branch Parkway." Dorman gave him the addresses. "If you see him, let me know, okay? I'm not gonna jam him up; I just need to know. That fit with your schedule?"

"Sure. I'll keep an eye open. Won't be twenty-four/seven or anything."

"I know. Anything's helpful. Keep making people unhappy out there."

The answering chuckle sounded ominous.

Later that night, having returned home to pick up Emma and coordinate with Sam—still in Burlington—to have Louise spend the night at their home, Willy was back in Springfield, tucked out of sight along

South Branch Parkway. He'd understood from Dorman's lecture—both what he'd said and what he'd meant—that he wouldn't be the only one here acting invisible. Dorman had to have called for an extra pair of eyes, just as Willy would've done in his place. And for Willy Kunkle— the old sniper—there were few greater pleasures than playing the urban version of who's-the-stalker. With a psyche as convoluted and pessimistic as his, Willy found absolute peace nowadays in two environments only: within his family and on the hunt. The former was a late-blooming and unexpected haven; the latter had been a refuge since maturity. If one of your problems is the human race and all that it can throw at you, being armed with a rifle and hiding in wait can be a true, if complex, salvation.

Willy had driven here earlier in a rental. His own car was rounding the distant corner at the moment, with a cohort at the wheel. If Dorman had issued orders, the only visual he had to pass along was Willy's license plate and vehicle description. So why disappoint him? It had been a simple matter for Willy to call on one of his many contacts—yet another person with a checkered past and a debt to pay—and request a small favor.

Willy brought up his night vision scope and focused on an older parked sedan he'd been watching for half an hour. He saw the long-haired driver level his own binoculars to study the rear plate of Willy's car as it crawled down the street before sliding into an open spot.

Smiling, Willy moved at last. South Branch Parkway is a curving, residential street in a Springfield neighborhood named Sixteen Acres. For most of its length, it is bordered by suburban-style family houses on one side, and woodlands and a couple of golf courses that follow a meandering waterway on the other, suggesting that the street is more in the countryside than it is. Sunny Malik's home was among the houses across from this artificial wilderness, and Willy had requested his surrogate to park prominently near that address, stay put, and enjoy listening to the radio or drinking a cup of coffee.

For his part, Willy drifted like a shadow across several backyards until he was positioned at the rear of Malik's property, again within view of the surveillance car. Willy could now better see the man at the wheel, who looked more like a biker than a cop, complete with beard, tats, and pierced ears. Willy was impressed—Alex Dorman had called upon friends in low places.

Friends that Willy assumed had by now made a quiet phone call to Dorman.

He put away his scope and paid closer attention to Malik's house. It was a standard two-story residence with attached garage. Willy took his time to inventory the layout as much as possible through the back windows, and establish the security system, which turned out to be nonexistent—always helpful.

From Dorman earlier, he'd heard that Malik lived with a wife and daughter, neither of whom appeared inside tonight. Judging from the neat, almost abandoned look of the daughter's bedroom, Willy thought that she might be away at school. The wife? Who knew? But there was an empty slot in the garage. He would risk the possibility that she'd be returning home later.

As for Sunny, he was visibly accounted for, with his stockinged feet straight out, a drink in his hand, his butt in a La-Z-Boy, and watching a ball game on TV.

Willy decided to seize his opportunity, as imperfect as it was. Malik's being alone for the moment, mollified and surrounded by distracting noise, was too good to pass up. Checking one last time on Dorman's long-haired guardian angel—who had by now decamped, no doubt to allow the local police an open field to disturb Willy's decoy—Willy easily entered Malik's home.

Trusting Malik to stay put, Willy quickly toured the house from the inside, confirming his earlier conclusions, before entering the den, directly behind the Lay-Z-Boy.

He paused on the threshold a moment, absorbing the scene—the large TV, the back of Sonny's head outlined against it, both of them swathed in cheers, music, and that endless commentator twaddle.

Willy knew he was about to cross a line—had already, in fact, simply by entering without cause or a warrant. Additionally, his conversation with Dorman had highlighted how isolated he was this time. His fellow VBI agents were used to his ways, and even tolerant of his methods, so long as they were spared the details. But the federal government? And outside his own jurisdiction? Dorman's rules of engagement had been made very clear.

And were—from Willy's viewpoint—all the encouragement he needed for a little clandestine independent action.

He approached Sunny Malik, positioned himself comfortably right behind his head, and—with a gloved hand—smoothly reached around and took hold of the man's chin, pressing him against the headrest of his chair and making it impossible for him to see Willy's face.

Malik's whole body spasmed with surprise as Willy whispered into his ear. "Do not move, or you will die, as will Amra when she returns home. Do you understand?"

His victim struggled some more, but without conviction. The chair, so perfectly designed for all-encompassing comfort, was Willy's perfect confederate, keeping Malik immobilized.

"I have a knife in my hand, aimed at your other ear, Sunny," Willy lied. "Do I need to prove that to you? I will, but it'll piss me off."

"What do you want?" Sunny managed to say through his clamped jaw.

"First, hit the mute button on your remote."

Malik did so, plunging them into silence.

"Very good," Willy continued. "I do want something. And keep in mind that I know all about you and your family and what your habits are. We've been watching you for a long time, around the clock. Do you believe me, Sunny?"

Malik nodded.

"Outstanding. Here's the good news: All I want is some information."

"What?" Malik's voice sounded incredulous.

"We both know what you've been up to, Sunny—involving imported lithium-ion batteries. Don't we?"

Malik's body language gave him away. Willy chuckled malevolently. "Right. Now—either I can prove how I know what I do, which'll again piss me off, waste time, and end up with you suffering. Or you can just cut to the chase and give me a few missing names. 'Cause that's why we're meeting like this, Sunny."

"What names?" his voice had climbed a few octaves.

"There's a man who came by in a cab, a few days ago. He picked up several batteries made in China but to American military specifications. That ring a bell?"

Malik stiffened. "Who are you?" The fear in his voice was clear and sharp.

"You really need to ask?" Willy tightened his grip slightly.

"No. No. I am sorry. But that's not absolutely true."

"What isn't?" Willy asked, picking up on the man's careful wording.

"The batteries. They can be converted to what you're saying, but they are not one hundred percent complete."

"You think that leaves you off the hook?"

"I am not breaking the law."

"Then why're you so scared, Sunny? I'm the other shoe dropping you've been so worried about. You think I believe this is the only magic act you're pulling? If my people drop by your business and tear it apart, how many years do you think you'll spend in federal prison? Do you know what we do to terrorists in this country, Sunny?"

"I am not a terrorist," he squealed, wriggling again.

"The names, Sunny," Willy ordered.

Malik was almost crying by now. "I don't have names. It's not like I wrote an invoice."

"Cute. Sure sounds like a completely legitimate transaction. Details. How did it work?"

"It's true, I import partial batteries. They still have to be wired and finished so that they'll work as designed."

"Mil-spec batteries?"

"Not technically. That's what I was saying." He tensed as Willy shifted his hold. "All right, all right. I admit, they are illegal, but that is the business. People are cutting corners—even people making things for the U.S. military. That is how they increase their profit. They quote one figure to the government, then they undercut that figure every way they can to make more money. It is true everywhere. It has been true forever. It is the way of business."

"Cut the crap," Willy growled, conscious of his narrowing time window. "I don't care about history. How did this one deal work?"

"A man in Vermont heard about what I import. His money was good, his system with that courier worked well, and he was happy with the batteries being only halfway finished."

"That's bullshit," Willy swore at him. "All that hush-hush and he tells you he's from Vermont? How dumb do you think I am, Sunny?"

"He didn't," Malik protested, trying to turn his head. "It was the courier. A very stupid man. He talked and talked. He even said he lived in Windsor, specifically. I did not *want* to hear. I told him once to be quiet—that his boss would be angry. That is why I cannot give you their identities."

Willy found that completely believable, given so many of the crooks he'd met. "When's this very stupid man scheduled to pick up another load?"

"He's not. The last purchase was when you're talking about."

Jesus, Willy thought. Almost missed it. I'm not usually the lucky one in something like this.

"How did you keep in touch?"

"I didn't. He would call me. That is how it works with many of these people."

"That's how it *used* to work," Willy cautioned him, seeing the flicker of emergency LEDs flashing against the street-side curtains.

"What is that?" Malik asked.

"Colleagues, more or less," Willy said truthfully, not eager to meet them. "But nobody you want to talk to about me. Remember what I said about your family, Sunny? Their safety depends on your silence and flying straight from now on. Clear?"

Malik nodded. "Yes, sir."

"One last question," Willy proposed. "What're these batteries for?"

"I do not know. But I suspect drones. I have seen such cells used that way before."

Damn, Willy thought, his rebellious independence rewarded yet again. This thing won't quit. He gave Malik an extra painful tweak with his hand. "You find some other way to pad your wallet. Don't move."

Willy let go of his head, reached for his gun, and tapped it against Malik's cheekbone. "Know what this is?"

"Yes."

"I will shoot you if you move a muscle for the next five minutes."

Willy didn't wait. He was gone in an instant, and out in the backyard by the time he heard the doorbell ring. He circled around unobtrusively and saw two cops by the door, and two more interviewing his hapless friend across the street.

Not to worry, he thought. And not a bad night's work. With this, he had enough to return to firmer ground in Vermont.

CHAPTER SIXTEEN

The Guilderland, New York, residential street Sammie Martens observed as she parked her car reminded her of photographs of old Hollywood back lots, featuring perfect suburban neighborhoods stripped clean of people or trash. Checking in both directions as she crossed over, she half expected someone to yell *"Action"* and for a sitcom kid to come barreling out of the house ahead of her.

He didn't, of course. Nor was it that kind of show. To no surprise, when it came to notifying Charlotte Anne Robinson's parents of their daughter's death, Sam had found no takers from her Burlington colleagues or the Albany cops she was scheduled to meet with afterwards. Death notices were anathema to cops, who, despite their fictionalized portrayals, tended to dislike dead bodies or any of the emotional drama attached to them.

The door opened before she reached it, revealing a woman with perfectly brushed, shoulder-length hair and immaculately applied makeup—all in jarring contrast to her expression of unbridled anguish.

"Who are you?" she demanded in a strangled voice.

Sam displayed her badge. "Special Agent Samantha Martens, of the Vermont Bureau of Investigation. Are you Mrs. Robinson?"

The woman's hand left the doorframe and crept to her neck. "Where is she?"

"I'm sorry," Sam responded. "I'm afraid I have to know: Are you Harriet Robinson?"

A clean-shaven man wearing a white shirt and a tie appeared by the woman's side. His voice was deep and powerful, and his words carefully chosen. "We are Thomas and Harriet Robinson. Are you here about our daughter?"

"Yes, sir. I am. May I come in?"

Harriet Robinson was about to say something—to somehow upset the formalities—until her husband placed his hand on her shoulder and squeezed it gently, before stepping back. "Please."

Sammie slid by them into a surgically clean front hallway. Thomas Robinson gestured with his hand. "Right ahead, to the living room. Would you like something to drink? Iced tea, perhaps?"

Sam looked back at them. "No, thanks. I'm really sorry to be meeting under these circumstances."

Robinson continued with his hand directions, pointing out one of two opposing sofas, separated by a long, low coffee table. The room looked lifted from a two-decades-old magazine article on interior decorating. Over the mantelpiece were framed oversized graduation photos of two girls, one of whom Sam immediately recognized as a longer-haired Charlotte.

The Robinsons sat across from Sam, holding hands. "You haven't explained the circumstances," he said calmly, almost professorially, as if easing her through a tough moment, which—in a way—he was.

"I'm afraid I have bad news," Sam began, feeling pedantic. "I know you realize that. I'm really sorry."

"Our daughter is dead," Robinson stated gently as his wife's shoulders slumped and her head bowed to her chest.

"Yes," Sam replied. "She was killed in Burlington, Vermont, during a break-in."

After a long pause, "Tell us," Thomas managed to get out.

"We don't have much," Sam told them. "That's another reason I'm here. It seems a man broke into the apartment where Charlotte was staying and attacked her. We don't know why, and we don't know who. We have put every available resource onto the case, though."

By now, Harriet was weeping and Thomas rubbing her back.

"When was the last time you communicated with your daughter?" Sam asked him.

That caused Harriet to cry harder as her husband explained, "It's been a long time. We had a falling out."

Great, Sam thought. "What would you say? Weeks, months?"

"Well over a year. She found us too controlling, to use her words."

Harriet suddenly looked up. "I'm the one. I was the controlling one. She ran because of me."

Thomas tried consoling her, whispering into her ear for a while. In the end, the woman couldn't take it any longer, rose to her feet, and left the room without a word.

"Where is she?" he asked Sam.

Sammie processed the question for a second before she understood. "Burlington. By law, they had to do a postmortem. But she's ready to be released whenever you want."

"I'll give you the name of a funeral home," he said evenly. "They've handled other family members. Where should I tell them to go?"

"The chief medical examiner's office at the UVM Medical Center," she replied. She pulled out one of her business cards and wrote the information on its back before handing it over. "Just give them that. They may be familiar with it."

"Thank you."

"Mr. Robinson, I don't want to be a pest, but I hope you understand that in order to move forward with our investigation, we're going to need whatever information you can give us."

"Of course."

"For example, while I realize you weren't in touch with Charlotte, you might've known what she was up to. Where she was living, for example, or going to school, or work, or who her friends were. Things like that."

He sat with his hands now slack between his knees, staring into space. "I don't know much," he said, sounding lost.

"Where was she living?" Sam tried again. "In Albany? Maybe at a dorm?"

"Not a dorm," he said, looking at her.

"Okay. There we go. An apartment?"

"She was at an apartment, with a couple of other girls, but that ended. I called once to talk to her, and was told she'd moved."

"That's all right," Sam encouraged him. "It's a start. Where was it?"

He gave her the address in a monotone.

"We heard she was attending SUNY," Sam went on. "Is that right?"

But here, he shook his head. "That was partly what caused the rift. I guess you know that both Mrs. Robinson and I are employed by the school system?"

Sam nodded.

"Education is very important to us. It was the gateway we both used to get out of the neighborhood we lived in as children. Are you familiar with Albany, Special Agent Martens?"

"Not really," Sam said to keep him going.

"There's a large black neighborhood named Arbor Hill, near the river, north of downtown. Harriet and I started out there. Our educations got us out."

His voice grew as he gathered momentum. "We are proud people, Agent Martens—proud of being black, of being successful, of making something of ourselves, and of passing along the benefits of hard work to our daughters."

Sam nodded. "Yes, sir."

"It has not been easy, as you can imagine, and perhaps we didn't do as good a job as we might have in sharing those lessons properly with Charlotte Anne."

His eyes were glistening as he spoke, and Sam understood that she was perhaps less his audience than were his own guilt and loss.

"In any case," he continued, "she rebelled, as children do, and we dug in our heels, as parents will. We lost touch with our daughter as she dropped out of college, associated with people we didn't approve of, and returned to Arbor Hill in search of her roots, as she put it."

"Was she living there?"

"Not that we knew of. I know she was working at a halfway house there, which was commendable in itself, but it led to other, less savory and admirable things."

Sam could only imagine what some of the arguments must have sounded like in this pristine, almost sterile home.

"What about her sister?" she asked. "Was Charlotte close with her?"

"As children. But Angela moved away and got married. I don't think they've been in touch for several years."

Sam paused to reflect before asking, "Charlotte's roommate in Burlington said she was calling herself Charlotte Collins. Do you know what that might've been about?"

Robinson looked baffled. "Collins? I don't know anyone named that. Another argument we had with her did concern her name, but it was her first name. She preferred to go by Jayla. Her mother had a real problem with that."

Sam recalled Mike McReady mentioning the alternate first name in Burlington. "So that's probably how I should be referring to her, when I look into her past?" she surmised.

"Most likely, yes," Thomas said sadly, as if hearing of the loss of his daughter all over again. "Charlotte Anne ceased to exist long ago."

The large, short-cropped blond man rose upon Sammie's entrance and circled his desk with his hand extended in greeting. "Special Agent Martens? I'm Chief of Detectives Ted McTaggart, welcome to Albany."

He motioned to another man on a couch against the wall, also rising, "And this is Scott Gagne, who'll be your counterpart while you're here. Scott's a detective with our Child/Family Services unit, one of our specialty branches."

Sam performed the welcoming ritual, wondering why Child/Family Services had been chosen to babysit her.

"How did it go with the Robinsons?" McTaggart asked as they all took chairs and got comfortable. "I hope that wasn't too rough. If it's any comfort, we've been busy on our end while you got stuck with the notification. Did they give you anything, or would you like us to go first?"

"No, that's fine," Sam said. "Not much. They and Charlotte went their separate ways well over a year ago, which of course is tearing them up now. According to the father, Charlotte wanted more involvement with the same black roots that the elder Robinsons had spent their lives escaping. As a result, Thomas Robinson didn't have much on where his daughter was living, who her friends were, or even what she'd been doing after dropping out of SUNY."

She produced a pad from her pocket and waved it in the air. "He did give me the address of where she once lived with two roommates, along with a list of the few friends he could recall. He also said she'd started calling herself Jayla, instead of Charlotte, in case that name comes up."

"It has," McTaggart said, pointing to Gagne. "That's actually why I tapped Scott to be your liaison. Charlotte 'Jayla' Robinson popped up on our computer in relation to a domestic dispute a couple of months ago, which made it his bailiwick."

The chief of detectives shifted in his chair. "I should give you the crash course on how we do most things over here first, though, just so there're no misunderstandings later. I've heard good things about VBI—"

"As we have about you folks," she quickly threw in diplomatically, but truthfully, as well.

He smiled. "Thank you. I understand you're kind of the top dogs in Vermont—brought in for big cases whenever other agencies ask for help. We're more like one of those other agencies. We're a full-service operation, and like to think we're good at our job, but we still have municipal restrictions. A case like this—an adult female killed in Vermont, who left here under her own steam—that would normally fall to the state police."

He held up one finger theatrically. "*But*—since Scott got a hit on that domestic, and since you told us this girl died in a home invasion—which could be an extension of the domestic, till proven otherwise—we'd like to see more of it before kicking it loose. That sound reasonable to you?"

"Totally," she said. "Whatever works best for you. Can you tell me about the domestic?"

Gagne took over the narrative. "That's actually why we're interested. The call was to the home of a lobbyist-lawyer named Jared Wylie, who's a rich white guy living in a fancy neighborhood downtown. Robinson was the complainant—calling herself Jayla—but there wasn't enough traction to the case to interest the DA in pursuing it."

His face grew animated. "But if this homicide ends up being connected, like the captain was saying, we could try ramping up the old domestic to a felony assault, death resulting, which would be a nice way to stick it to a prick who's gotten used to walking away from the misery he causes. It would take a bunch of lawyers from both our states putting their heads together, but it's an idea."

Sam was struck by the man's passion. "A wild guess: You've had runins with Mr. Wylie before?"

Gagne nodded. "And he's walked every time. Nailing his hide would be a real pleasure."

"Okay," she responded, slipping off her jacket and hanging it on the back of her chair. "Sounds good to me—assuming we can connect the two cases. Let's lay everything we got side by side right now and see what matches up. And not to sound pushy, but is there any coffee to be had nearby?"

* * *

Lester stood on the dirt road beside his car and watched the house for a few moments, like a hunter studying for movement in the woods. Driving up to people's residences uninvited was always to be done cautiously. Being a cop only increased his wariness. Even while off duty, visiting friends, he found himself checking perimeters, windows, parked cars, the general surroundings, and listening for things that fit—like TVs, yelling kids, and dogs—and things that did not—like utter silence.

What he heard as he began approaching was a TV and a dog barking.

"*McKenzie*. Shut the fuck up."

Even better.

In Lester's experience, there were four basic styles of home in the state: trailers—including upscale, permanently rooted ones like Molly Blaze's; nineteenth-century Greek Revival piles in various states of repair; modern houses in search of a suburb, rich or poor; and shacks. This was one of the last, situated in the woods, possibly having started as a hunting camp, and now a disintegrating, much-patched, Frankenstein's monster of plywood, tar, metal roofing, torn screens, and a few moldy antlers hanging under the eaves. The yard was a pinup for backwoods accessorizing, complete with two rotting car carcasses, a rusty washing machine, and the standard assortment of auto parts, broken farming implements, and scattered tools.

Lester felt on familiar ground. He had spent much of his professional life visiting such properties, and had several friends whose places looked indistinguishable from this.

A big man in a full ginger beard and a greasy baseball cap appeared at the door, a mastiff by his side.

"You a cop?"

"Murder police," Lester told him, keeping things simple. "Not here to hassle."

"I haven't murdered anybody."

The dog growled as Lester got nearer.

Its owner glared down. "*McKenzie.* I told you to shut the fuck up."

"You Chad Raney?" Lester opened his jacket to show his badge.

"What d'you want?"

"Talk about Kyle Kennedy."

Chad's face showed surprise. "Kyle's dead, man. One of you shot him."

Lester shrugged, getting used to the response. "Looks like he gave as good as he got."

The other man barked out a laugh. "Jesus. That's cold."

"Maybe. But that's why I'm here."

Raney narrowed his eyes. "You saying it didn't happen that way?"

"Just making sure it did or it didn't. I don't have a vested interest, either way. You were tight with Kyle, weren't you?"

Chad stepped outside, leaving his companion behind the flimsy screen door. "Sure. Best friends."

"Shooting buddies," Les stated.

"That, too." Raney moved over to one of the wrecks, sat on what was left of its fender, and fished around in his breast pocket, preparing to roll a cigarette.

"Police ever talk to you after Kyle died?"

"Nope. You're the first."

Lester hid his disappointment. "When did you last see him?"

Chad was intent on his task, pouring tobacco evenly along a rolling paper. "That week, drinking beer, watching TV. The usual."

"He seem different in any way?"

"Nope. Same ol', same ol'."

"How 'bout what he was doing?" Lester kept going. "At work, with his folks. He have a girlfriend at the time?"

"Not right then. He'd just broken up with somebody."

"That a big deal for him?"

Chad glanced up. "The girlfriend? Nah. He did that all the time."

"What was her name?"

He licked the edge of the paper and twirled it expertly. "Who knows? I never kept track. He might not've even known. Fuck 'em and forget 'em. That was his motto. Seemed to work for them, too."

"You know every one of them?"

"Nah—a few, by chance. It's not like he brought 'em around. Kyle was a dog, you know? You should talk to his sister, Lorraine. They were super tight. She was always the woman he went back to. I always thought it was a little creepy, but it's Vermont, right?"

He accompanied that with a laugh Lester didn't share. "Kidding. Sorry. They were just close."

Lester thought back to a comment that Molly Blaze had made, and asked, "You know the stretch of road where the shooting took place?"

"Sure."

"Where do you think Kyle was headed, late at night? You know anybody who lives out that way?"

Raney actually seemed to give it some thought before answering, "Nope. That's like no-man's-land out there."

"Did he know the cop that shot him?" Lester asked as the other man then lit up.

Raney tilted his head back and blew out a stream of smoke. "Paine? Good name for a cop. What's yours?"

"Spinney."

Chad seemed to consider that, as if sampling a sip of wine. "Never heard of you."

"Just as well, given what I work on."

He laughed. "Good point. Nah. Not that I know of."

"Kyle didn't know Paine?"

"That's what I said."

"Right," Lester mused. "When did you two last go shooting?"

"Me and Kyle? Shit, I dunno. A while. He lost his piece."

"The Taurus?"

"Yeah."

"Tell me about that."

Chad took another drag. "Nothing to tell. He either lost it or it was stolen. That dump he lived in, coulda been either."

"He had it with him when he died," Lester told him. "You know that?"

Chad looked mildly interested. "Guess he found it again."

"He ever drive around with it?"

"When he came here to shoot."

"How 'bout in general?"

Chad shook his head. "Couldn't lock his car. He didn't want it stolen."

"Where did he keep it at home?"

"Under the bed, like most people."

Maybe, Lester thought. Maybe not. What was becoming clear was that a once neat and tidy case was increasingly showing signs of questions left dangling and lines of inquiry ignored.

Rachel looked down at her iPhone.

"U up?" she read, startled to see Joe Gunther's name under the trendily typed question.

She made sure to respond with complete words, just in case. "Yes. You TEXT?!?!"

She was comforted by the reply, and smiled to read, "Not even close. Fingers not nimble nuff. U up for a call? Can't do this much longer."

"Sure," she typed, her own fingers a blur.

The phone buzzed moments later.

"Thanks for that," Joe said. "I can only show off so much. And you have no idea how many times I backtyped just to write that."

She laughed. "Even with the time difference, it's late for you, isn't it?"

"Hey," he said, mocking offense. "I've had my Geritol. I'm good for hours. You busy right now? Am I interrupting anything?"

"It's two in the morning, Joe. Most of my drinking buddies are gone and the circus animals just left. What's Geritol?" she asked after a hesitation.

"Never mind. In other words, you're staring at the ceiling and either can't get to sleep or don't want to."

She was in fact sitting on a built-in upholstered window seat in her old bedroom at home, overlooking the moonlit water. She'd said good night to her mother hours ago.

"You figured that out, huh?"

"Yeah. The wizard detective," he said. "That's me. How're you holding up?"

"Not great," she admitted. "I can't get it out of my head."

"No reason you should. It was a horrible thing to have happen."

"You sound like Mom."

"You flatter me. You seeing a counselor or someone?"

"Yeah. I'm not too impressed."

"That's because you're thinking they'll make it go away. They're only there to make you say it out loud—to sort through it yourself."

"Damn. I should do *that* after I graduate."

"Given some of the ones I've seen," he told her, "you'd be slumming. I like what you're studying. You having second thoughts?"

"No," she gave in. "I still love being behind a camera. I'm just having a hard time being enthusiastic about anything right now."

"It's gonna take time to replace the images you have in your head," he guessed.

"Yeah."

"They will fade," he suggested. "No matter how real they are now."

"You must have hundreds," she said.

"Not like yours." He paused. "Well, maybe a few, but I usually get there after the fact. Plus, I chose to do this. She was your friend. It's totally different."

"Yeah," she repeated.

"What was she like?" he asked.

"Funny, smart, lively," she said slowly, thoughtfully. "And a little sad. She never went into details, but I sort of got that she'd had some trouble in the past."

"What kind?"

She sighed wearily. "Guys, of course. I think her parents may've been really strict, too, her mom in particular. I told her about mine, and she was clearly envious. But it didn't pull her down. It wasn't like she was here in zombie mode, all beaten up by bad memories. What I got was that this was someplace for her to start over."

Rachel paused before adding, "She was so full of life."

"She never mentioned who might've done this?" Joe asked. "I realize I'm not the first to bring it up."

"Hardly," she replied tiredly. "But I understand. What I don't get is the why. Why would anyone have to kill somebody else just 'cause they fell out?"

Joe was stumped, as he had been countless times in the past by such a basic question.

Shy of a platitude, which he couldn't conjure up in any case, he mentioned, "We're not sure that was the reason."

"What else could it've been?" she asked.

But Joe had no idea.

CHAPTER SEVENTEEN

Sgt. Colin Guyette looked up as Willy Kunkle appeared at the door of his office. "Again?" he said, surprised. "You up to somethin' else, or are you still on those missing teeth?"

"45 CFR 164.512(f)(2)," Willy recited. "Ever hear of it?"

"She as attractive as she sounds?"

"Better, if we're lucky. It's from the *Code of Federal Regulations*. Allows us to get around HIPAA and find out if any local doc or nurse or PA, or whatever they call themselves now, treated anyone recently for three busted teeth, a split lip, and maybe more."

Guyette pushed his chair back and put his feet up on his desk. "You're serious. You telling me I did more than send you on a wild goose chase with this thing?"

Willy smiled. "Yeah. You fucked up if you were tryin' to waste my time."

Colin gestured to a chair. "Sit. Tell me."

Willy complied. "I'm working on the details, but the key is that burned-up battery. My money's riding on it being hot, and maybe tied into some kind of fraud to screw the feds on a government contract— or maybe worse. If we're right about the proximity of the teeth to the battery being relevant—considering that they both suffered from blunt impact and were deposited on the tracks at roughly the same time—then it stands to reason that the owner of the teeth might take us to the source of that battery."

Colin whistled. "Give me details. This going on in our fair city?"

"Don't know. That's why we need to find the toothless train rider. From what I got so far, he's sounding like the delivery boy between an importer of these batteries and whoever's putting them to use."

Guyette let that sink in before saying, "What else you got?"

"A bunch of pissed-off federal, local, and probably state cops from here to Springfield, Mass."

The Windsor cop nodded slowly. "Right. Is this where I wish you luck and later tell everybody that we didn't see each other today?"

"If you do, I'll know you're getting fat and soft."

Guyette laughed quietly, shook his head, and dropped his feet back onto the ground, preparing to head out on whatever screwy mission his old friend was about to suggest.

"Fat, maybe," he said, rising. "Let's find out how soft."

Willy's cited regulation allowed for a law enforcement officer to request of any relevant health-care supplier a person of interest's PHI. That stood for personal health information, which of course had been shortened to an initialization in the law, just to confuse matters. "For purposes of identifying or locating a suspect, fugitive, material witness, or missing person," it stated, the provider must deliver not the intimate medical details concerning their patient—those remained out of bounds—but the basic demographics, plus a few details like blood type. It was a tool cops like Guyette rarely needed, and therefore didn't know about. Willy, on the other hand, collected such tidbits like some enthusiasts went after butterflies. His only regret was that he hadn't thought of putting it to use until the train-riding courier's role had become so critical.

As he put it to Colin when they climbed into the latter's squad car and headed out to make the rounds of clinics, ERs, and doctors' offices, "I just hope to hell I didn't leave this too long. I'm guessing rodents like our toothless wonder have a dozen ratholes to call home."

But Guyette was more hopeful. "They may couch-surf, but they don't wander far. You know that. If this fella's local, we'll find him."

They didn't precisely find him, but they soon discovered who'd treated him. At the local hospital's ER, located on the western edge of town—and, tellingly, after Willy had invoked his open-sesame federal regulation to a slowly persuaded administrator—both men were introduced to a nurse sitting before a computer screen.

"When was this?" she asked.

Willy gave her the date, hoping he was right.

"And the injury?"

"Busted teeth," Colin supplied.

"And probably more," Willy added.

She kept her eyes on the data passing before her. "But you're saying you don't have a name?"

The two cops exchanged glances. "What the hell," Willy ventured. "Try Samuel Jones."

"That'll make it easier." She typed it in and instantly sat back. "Home run."

"You're putting me on," Colin muttered, leaning over to read the fine print.

"That doesn't necessarily mean it's his real name, though, right?" Willy asked. "It's not like you run background checks."

"That's true," she said. "And according to this, we don't have any additional records on him. This was a first-time visit."

"And what were his injuries?"

"He took a beating, all right," she announced. "Five lower teeth—numbers forty-three through thirty-two—badly lacerated lower lip, hairline fracture of the mandible, damage to the vestibular gingiva—which is doctor talk for 'the gum'—and a lacerated tongue." She stopped to read further and said, "Huh. That's weird."

"What?"

"He had a burned right hand, too. Pretty bad, from what I'm reading. Musta touched something really hot, or been too dumb to let go."

She turned to look at them. "All in all, looks like he was hit by a freight train."

Willy laughed. "You don't know the half of it. How'd they patch him up?"

"Reading between the lines, I'd say they did the best they could. He was not super cooperative, and of course he had no insurance." She read a little more. "Something here about an injection to dull the pain, ointment and bandage for the hand, and a recommendation to see a dentist about the teeth, only two of which he actually had with him. He was told not to eat hard foods—liquids only—because of the fracture. That was pretty much it."

"Okay," Willy said. "Here's where we cross our fingers and toes. To be honest, we don't really care about his health—or I don't. I just want to find out where he lives, who's his next of kin, his employer—anything like that."

She shifted to another window and scrolled through its contents, speaking almost to herself, "Don't hold your breath, given what we usually end up with, but . . . Hold it. I do have a couple of things. Not next of kin, but something, at least. Employer is listed as Robb Haag, with no particulars, and a residence—not home; it actually says, 'staying at'—this number on Central Street. That's all I got." She tapped the plastic surface of her monitor with an artistically decorated fingernail.

Colin squinted a moment at the information and said, "Got it."

Back in the privacy of the car, Willy asked, "You know Robb Haag?"

"Never heard of him," Colin replied, already calling Dispatch on his phone. While he was waiting for the computer there to be put through its paces, he told Willy, "But I sure as hell know Central Street, which sounds about right for where your Mr. Jones is hanging his hat. Which way do you want to move, assuming we get a fix on Haag?"

"Given our current suspicions-to-facts ratio," Willy said, "which I'd rate about piss-poor, I think Jones is the better target. He can't be in great shape, I doubt he was ever class genius, and he's the one we can lean on the hardest, given the little we got. I say we find him first—even if we do get a hit on Haag—and squeeze him as hard as we can. Haag may have nothing to do with all this, after all."

Guyette held up a hand as Dispatch spoke to him over the phone again. After a few moments, he hung up and announced, "Well, your wish has been granted, more or less. There is a Robb Haag. He's got a current driver's license and last-known address of South Burlington. But his most recent violation on record was for an out-of-date inspection sticker four years ago. Whoever he is and whatever he's doing now, we got zip."

He turned the ignition key and began backing out of the hospital parking lot. "Time for you to get up close and personal with Windsor's own poverty hollow."

"Swell."

Colin took them away from the hospital, downhill along State Street toward the business district—past the old nineteenth-century prison, now converted to public housing—and briefly onto Main. There, he doglegged onto River Street to resume aiming for the Connecticut River. Main Street was the dividing line, where genteel Windsor ceded to Abigail Murray's world of hardscrabble adventure and wonder. Just shy of the railroad tracks, however, Colin pulled on the wheel again, and entered Central. He came to a halt near the town's municipal garage—awkwardly straddling both sides of the street and occupying several beaten-down shop and storage buildings that exemplified how little money was available for the road crew's care and feeding.

He nodded toward a small, narrow, one-and-a-half-story ramshackle home—in appearance, like most of its neighbors—and said, "That's it."

Without comment, Willy swung out of the car, glanced up and down the remarkably quiet street, and walked up to the building's front door, Colin close behind him.

The person answering the door was a heavyset woman of indeterminate middle age wearing sweatpants, a tank top under extreme pressure, and a scowl. She looked straight past Willy at Colin, who was dressed in uniform, as usual.

"What do *you* want?"

"Hey, Brenda," he said. "I didn't know you lived here."

"Whatever. What do you want?" This time, the emphasis was on the last word.

Willy didn't bother introducing himself, nor did he use Samuel Jones's name, just in case Jones was flying under different colors here. If cops can avoid it, they don't reveal any doubts they may be harboring. Instead, he held out the picture taken from the Amtrak CCTV in Springfield.

"This guy," he said simply.

That brought Brenda's attention to him for the first time, and to his inert left arm.

"What's wrong with you?" she asked.

He moved the photo before her. "You didn't tell me where he is."

She avoided looking at the picture. "Don't know."

"Brenda," Colin warned her, drawing out her name.

"What?" she demanded angrily.

"Come on," he pleaded. "Why go through the whole rigamarole?"

"What'd you want with him?"

Willy cut off Colin's canned response. "Kill him."

Her eyes grew round. "What did you say?"

Colin let out an almost inaudible sigh as Willy said, "So, get him now or tell us where he is, so we can get it over with."

For no logical reason, it worked. Brenda leaned back as much as her physique would allow, and bellowed, "*Chris*. Get your ass down here. *Now.*"

Willy smiled, she thought at her response; in fact, it was because Sam Jones had apparently taken on a different identity, as he'd thought he might.

"You happy?" she demanded.

"Always," he said.

There was a clattering of booted feet as the two men dimly saw a pair of legs appearing from what looked like a ladder connecting the ground floor to a loft tucked in under the eaves.

An accompanying male voice querulously inquired, "What?"

Her explanation consisted of a single word, before she backed away from the doorway and vanished into the small house's inner gloom: "Cops."

The man now called Chris obviously would have appreciated a heads-up. He stepped into view, took Willy and Colin in with a glance, and moaned, "Fuck."

But he had nowhere to run, and didn't look in good-enough shape to do so anyhow.

Willy hooked a finger, gesturing to him to step outside. In the early summer sun, he was a sad sight to behold, his face bloated, bruised, and scarred with recent cuts.

"What's your name?" Willy demanded.

"Chris." The facial damage clearly had a painful effect on his ability to speak.

Willy said nothing, merely staring at him.

"Walker," he added, wincing again.

"That your real name?" Colin asked.

"Yeah."

"Prove it."

Favoring his bandaged right hand, Walker dug into the back pocket of his baggy cargo shorts with his left and pulled out a much-duct-taped canvas wallet, from which he awkwardly extracted a non–driver's license identity card. This he passed to the Windsor cop, who looked it over before handing it to Willy, who returned it without a glance.

Willy tilted his head toward their vehicle. "You wanna get in the car?"

Walker balked. "Why?"

"'Cause you've done bad things and it's time to get out from under them."

"What've I done?"

Willy barely leaned forward. "Are you refusing?"

"I didn't say that."

"Then get in the fucking car."

It had been Willy's quick test of Walker's complicity and grit, which the latter had passed and failed in turn, to Willy's satisfaction.

They drove back to the police department on Union Street, as modern and well appointed as the town garage was not, and resumed their conversation inside the confines of an interview room, where—although the door was left partially open—the implications of incarceration were thick in the air, as intended.

"For the record," Willy intoned as they all sat down. "This is a recorded conversation between Christopher Walker, William Kunkle of the VBI, and Sergeant Colin Guyette of the Windsor police. State your name and date of birth for the recording, Mr. Walker."

Walker did so, after which Willy added the time, date, and location of the conversation to follow. The practical reasons for all this were clear, but its true motivation was to continue the erosion of Walker's self-confidence.

This was working. Walker licked his lips as he looked from one of them to the other. "What do you *want*?"

"You prefer Chris or Christopher?" Willy asked.

"I don't know . . . Chris."

"That's good to know, 'cause we may be here for a while."

"Why?" Walker asked plaintively, his voice high-pitched. The contortion apparently strained his lip, as he winced and reached up to touch it tenderly.

"Like I said," Willy explained. "You been a bad boy, and it's time to confess your sins. How's the mouth doing?"

"It hurts."

"I bet. Why the hell'd you do that, anyway? When the train was a few yards away from stopping? Seems dumb."

Walker's mouth grew slack in astonishment at Kunkle's knowledge. "*What?*"

"You coulda just gotten off," Willy suggested. "Why'd you jump?"

It was an early shot in the dark—a calculated gamble. But not a wholly uneducated one, and certainly, if successful, a big step toward Walker's further destabilization.

He blinked and shook his head slightly. "Jeez. I don't know."

"Went with the whole covert thing?" Willy proposed. "The back-pack, the alias, the sneaking around Springfield? Something James Bond would do? 'Cept it was harder than it looked."

Walker bowed his head. "I guess," he muttered. "Sounds dumb. I wanted to show I was more than just a delivery guy. But it was higher than I thought."

"Did the battery burn right then?" Willy pointed to his bandaged hand. "Or did it take a few seconds? Bet you weren't told *that* could happen."

"Shit no, I wasn't."

"That's what you get for playing man in the middle, Chris," Willy commiserated. "You're kind of the disposable gofer, you know? Malik makes his money in Springfield, and as for . . ." He looked over to Guy-ette. "What's his name again?"

"Robb Haag," Colin supplied, building up the notion that there were no secrets in the room.

"Right." Willy repeated casually, "Haag. Well, as for him, the sky's the limit. I mean, who knows what he might make?"

Walker's eyes narrowed. "What's that mean?"

Willy looked surprised and cast another glance at his colleague.

"What's it *mean*? Are you kidding? With the high-tech widgets you're delivering to him?"

"I don't get it," Walker stammered. "They're batteries. What's the big deal?"

Willy laughed. "Wow. You are being screwed. You must owe Haag big-time, to stick your neck out this far. He must be laughin' at you now."

Walker's face flushed. "What the fuck're you talking about?"

"That guy you saw in Springfield," Willy tried explaining. "What was his name?"

"Malik. Sunny Malik."

"No, right, right. I meant his company. Where was it, again?"

"On Albany Street," Walker said. "Pure Computers."

"That's it. Foreign guy. I forget where he's from."

"Pakistan."

This was too easy, Willy thought. "Yeah, yeah. Well, anyhow, here's the thing, Chris. The way you got your hands on those batteries? The way they came into the country, and how they're gonna be used down the line? That puts you smack in the middle of a federal, Homeland Security black hole. That means terrorist charges, a vacation in Guanta-namo, no rights to a lawyer. Hello, waterboarding; good-bye, US of A. Get what I'm sayin'?"

Walker had raised his damaged hand to his cheek and was holding his face as if he'd been struck. "I'm no terrorist. I just carried that stuff for a couple of bucks."

"You know what they say about a bird in hand," Colin said quietly.

Walker looked dumbstruck.

"Of course," Willy threw in helpfully. "You're not without options."

He got a blank stare.

"Help us help you out, Chris," Willy tried again. "The more details you give us, the more we can tell the feds how cooperative you were."

"About Haag?"

Willy looked as if the idea hadn't occurred to him. "Sure. That's a good place to start. Why not? Where's he operating out of, for instance?"

Walker stared at him as if Willy were the one guy in the room not to know that water was wet. "You coulda damn near seen it from where you picked me up. In that old factory building, on the other side of the Goodyear slab, at the end of National Street."

"The same one where they got a woodworking shop at the southern end?" Colin asked.

"That's it. Robb's got the middle section, upstairs."

"He still there?" Willy wanted to know.

Walker was nonplussed. "How would I know? I'm with you guys."

"He still working there regularly?" Willy expanded patiently.

"Oh. Yeah. Sure."

"How did he deal with your little accident?"

"Deal with it? He was pissed, like I did it on purpose."

Willy made an effort to look sympathetic. "Right. You do all the humping and he gives you crap. Sounds like my boss. Did he pick up the medical bills, at least?"

"Fuck no. Lucky for me, they won't get any money out of me, either, but I'm still screwed with these." He tapped his lower lip, or what was left of it, destroyed by the missing teeth behind it. In all honesty, as Willy saw it, the poor bastard hadn't had much to work with before his swan dive onto the tracks, so his altered looks weren't a great loss. But that was just Willy's opinion.

"That's all you do for him?" he asked. "The runs back and forth? There must be other jobs."

"Hey," Walker said emphatically, "I'm his whole staff. He'd be nowhere without me. I do all sorts of things. That's what ticks me off about the medical bill."

Colin took that as his cue to play supportive second fiddle. "I was brought into this kind of late," he said. "What exactly *are* you doing in there? Something about batteries?"

Walker was caught out on his boast of moments earlier. "It's kinda technical. Electronics, you know? Pretty complicated."

"Right, but with batteries?"

"Yeah. I do soldering, screw around with wires, and packaging. It's like finishing up a car on the assembly line, or something."

"So the end product's still a battery," Willy surmised, "but it looks different?"

"Way different," Walker stressed.

"And what're they for?" Colin wanted to know.

"He supplies them to some dude down the line."

"What dude?"

"How do I know?" Walker grinned, as best he could, which looked both painful and unattractive. "Haag's management; I'm labor."

"Okay," Willy interjected. "This is good stuff, Chris. It's helping you out big-time. Tell us more about Haag. What's his story? Where'd he learn to do all the fancy electronics?"

"Burlington," Walker replied instantly, catching them both off guard. "He worked at a plant there, making these things."

"Batteries?"

"That's what we're talkin' about, ain't it?"

"It is. What was the name of this place?"

"Fuck if I know. I just asked him once, 'Where'd you learn how to do this shit?' and he told me."

"What else did he say?"

"Not much. Not a chatty guy. Plus, he's pretty stuck on himself, so we don't hang out. He did say he was fired, though, which I thought was pretty funny. I kept that to myself, course, 'cause I knew he was ticked off about it. I got the feeling what he's doing now is payback for that."

"Really?" Colin reacted, leaning forward and putting his elbows on his knees. "He's becoming a competitor?"

"Nah. He's out to fuck 'em up," Walker said. "That's what I got, at least."

"How?" Willy asked.

Walker's expression bordered on pity. "The batteries are crap. They don't last. That's the whole point."

Colin and Willy exchanged looks.

"And what're the batteries for, Chris? You know that?"

The answer was as eloquent as it was simple. "Sure. Drones."

Damn, Willy thought—drones now inadvertently designed to drop out of the sky, who knows where, on whom, or in what numbers.

CHAPTER EIGHTEEN

Sam twisted in the passenger seat of Scott Gagne's unmarked car and looked at her guide as he pulled onto Lancaster Street in Albany's Center Square district and parked. He'd taken the scenic route to get here, he explained, to show her the city in which he'd been born and brought up.

"You a native Vermonter?" he asked her. "I feel like I been talking nonstop."

"Born and bred," she said, determined not to be too specific—or even accurate, for that matter. In the reflection off her side window, she'd already noticed him taking her in when he thought she wasn't looking—scanning her from thighs to face whenever he could and with obvious appreciation. It didn't bother her. She was used to it, and even enjoyed it on occasion. When it stopped there and went no further.

There was a slight pause in the conversation before he nodded toward a stately brownstone ahead. "That's where Wylie lives."

She took it in appreciatively. "He's doing all right."

"He should be, for a walking, talking cliché. A lawyer-lobbyist with a bad reputation? Please. Not that we actually care much about his dirty dealings with government types. Like Ted was saying at the office, his corrupting officials isn't our business, strictly speaking. I want his ass for what he does to women; to hell with the politics. There're so many Albany assemblymen and -women in jail as it is that they'd probably reject him anyhow—for lack of available space."

"What's his background?"

"*Aha*." Gagne held up a finger. "There are roughly three categories of operators like him in town: the homegrown types, who have to watch where they piss, 'cause they might hit somebody related to them; the New York City high-class sleazos, who've got a wife and family in Westchester and at least one mistress up here, but whose big-city firm'll keep an eye on 'em, maybe; and the last bunch, which is where Wylie fits in. They're harder to define. He's from a D.C. firm that farms out lawyers all over the map, to capital cities of states where they have big-money clients. Most of these guys work solo, don't have leashes on them, but do have a mother ship they can call on in a pinch. Wylie's got contacts, money, influence, and none of the tie-downs that keep a lot of the less independent lawyers more or less under control. Plus, he's not too flashy, is kind to kids and old ladies, does pro bono work for the right high-visibility projects . . . You get the idea."

He paused a moment before adding, "Bottom line, with all those categories involved, it makes for quite a jungle. And, like I said, that's the part we don't mess with—unless we can finagle it with a locally rooted case like this." He smiled. "After all, if we didn't poach on state police turf every once in a while, we'd never get to work in the nicer neighborhoods."

"Looks like Greenwich Village," Sam commented. "Or what I know about it. I've been to New York only a couple of times."

"Not far off," he said. "Center Square, we call it. It's very narrowly defined, like a gated community without the gates. You couldn't find a Republican with a search party around here. You got your Yuppies, your Metros, your whatever the trendy set is now. They're not the filthy rich. That would be too tacky. But they're way up the politically correct tree, which is what makes Jared Wylie such a joke. They got the biggest offender to their value system living right in their midst, with no clue." He gave a theatrical sigh. "Such is life, I guess."

He checked over his shoulder to pull back into traffic.

"And nobody's ever jammed him up? Blackmail? Influence peddling? Corruption of public officials? Nothing?"

"Not yet. Here's hoping we can this time. It'll take some doing, though. I'll guarantee you that. All the stuff we and the state police have on him? It's circumstantial, guesswork, innuendo—nothing we can bring to the DA. This is a cagey dude."

They were almost at the end of the block, facing a high, white marble wall that forced them to turn right or left.

"What's that?" Sammie asked.

"Rockefeller Plaza," Gagne intoned. "It's got a longer, fancier name, but that's the acceptable short form. There are a bunch of ruder monikers for it—'Rocky's Last Erection' is my favorite."

He cut her a quick glance, to gauge her reaction to this vulgar reference.

Sam merely responded by craning forward—in full tourist mode—to take in the monumental, semi–sci-fi movie skyscrapers shooting up like futuristic dominoes. "I saw these driving in, but from a distance. I didn't realize they were sitting on a platform."

"Yup," he said, appreciating her self-restraint at his comment. "Between the plaza and the interstate, city planners pretty much destroyed downtown. No different from what they did all over the country after World War Two. The car was king, gas was cheap, everybody was driving, and the whole notion of ethnic neighborhoods was seen as backward and a reminder of the same corrupted Europe that had just killed so many GIs."

This time, she stared at him, her eyebrows raised. "Damn. Listen to you."

He chuckled. "History nut." He turned the wheel and began driving parallel to the bland marble wall. "And on top of all that, this eyesore ended up being a perfect souvenir of the tasteless '70s. Gotta love it. Rocky Rockefeller was governor. Story is he got embarrassed driving some head of state around town, so he gutted the old neighborhood— mostly Italian—and put down the best example of fascist architecture outside of Hitler's Germany. There's irony for you—given the European reference."

Sam shook her head. "Architecture buff, too?"

"Okay, okay," he admitted. "I read that somewhere. But it's great, ain't it? And it fits." He turned another corner and pulled over once more. "See? Ya gotta admit—that is one ugly mutha."

She laughed.

"Tourists love it, of course," he continued, pointing out the opposite window. "I saw a busload of Japanese stop here. Everybody piled out and began taking pictures. Not one of them turned around to take that in." He indicated the state capitol—gold-domed, intricate, as lushly adorned as a wedding cake. "I love that old heap, but it sure ain't stream-lined, and I guess that's what hot now, even though the damned plaza's like a half century old.

"Anyhow"—he spun them into the road again, made a U-turn, and headed west—"love it or hate it, three thousand state office workers call it home and we're stuck with it, and survivors like Center Square and its neighbors have thrived. So it goes, yet again."

With the discordant weirdness of the capitol area behind them, the view ahead settled down to a more predictable, beaten-down urban landscape. "Arbor Hill's to our right," Gagne said, "where Robinson ran away from the burbs now and then to get in touch with her roots, but I thought we should start with her old roommates. Maybe one of them kept in touch after she hooked up with Wylie."

They ended up traveling along Madison, into what he called the "student ghetto." Sam took in block after block of brownstones and row houses, some well kept, others less so, the scenery occasionally inter-rupted by a park or a stand of trees. As ghettos went, it looked pretty good. But Gagne had earlier demonstrated that Albany was a change-able town, often block by block. He'd also pointed out that along the Montreal–New York trail so popular among drug runners and illegal immigrants, Albany was a rare oasis for bad guys to pause and blend in. North of town was the long, affluent Lake George–Saratoga recreational stretch—not a great place to hide—while along the eighty miles to the south, until reaching comfortably down-at-the-heels Poughkeepsie, were the Berkshires, the Hudson Valley, and places like Rhinebeck and Kinderhook—all lousy hangouts for the average street gangster.

Albany may have been the state capital, the home of five major hospitals, and the anchor of the state's university system, but it remained a town with some serious, chronic, and malignant problems.

Which, as Gagne had said, made it a great place to work.

On a block of houses that reminded Sam of the old Archie Bunker TV show, Gagne pulled over one last time and finally killed the engine. "Let's see if we get lucky."

"You call ahead?"

He opened his door and got out. "Yeah, well. Students . . ."

At the building's entrance, tellingly flanked by multiple mailboxes, Scott stood aside to let Sam enter first, telling her, "Just so you know, I'm riding shotgun here. This is your case."

Sam stepped into a lobby blocked by a locked glass door flanked by a row of intercom buttons.

"There." Scott pressed the one with three names opposite it, written in tiny, childish writing.

"What?" a peeved young woman's voice answered.

"Police," Sammie said, instantly irritated by the tone. Having never attended college, she acknowledged the chip on her shoulder about what she saw as a campus's built-in aura of privilege.

The buzzer let them in, and they trudged up the stairs beyond. The house was dirty, didn't smell clean, and looked tired, heightening Sam's distaste.

On the second floor, they found a barefoot young woman in a loose tank top, high-cut gym shorts, and no bra. She watched them reach the top of the staircase with undisguised contempt.

"Did I forget to pay a parking ticket?" she asked.

Scott didn't respond, no doubt distracted by the view. Sammie walked up close to the woman, forcing her to adjust her affected slouch, and said, "Funny. Never heard that one. We're homicide detectives. Who're you?"

"Jamie Winslow," the girl said, caught off guard.

Still inches away, Sam asked, "You want to do this out here or inside?"

Winslow stepped back, confused, and waved her hand vaguely. "Sure. Come in. What's this about? What homicide? Who died?"

Sam waited until Scott had shut the door behind them. The central room fit the setting—messy, cluttered, clothes scattered across worn, mismatched furniture, walls decorated with posters, flags, pictures cut from magazines, thumbtacked souvenirs.

"Do you know Jayla Robinson?" Sam asked without preamble.

Winslow's voice became a whisper. "Sure."

"How?"

"She was my roommate. Is she the one who died?" Winslow reached behind her and groped for the edge of an armchair for support.

Sam kept her eyes locked on to the girl's. "Yes."

Winslow's legs weakened and she sat on the chair's arm. "Oh, my God."

"*That's* why we're here. Not a parking ticket. Do you understand that this will be a serious conversation?"

"Yes." Again, the small voice. Behind Sam, Scott was very still, taking it in.

"Are we alone here?" Sam asked, quickly glancing around.

"Yes."

"But you have two roommates?"

"They're at class. Well, Lizzie's away for the semester, studying abroad. Greece. She's a classics . . . I don't guess that matters. Sorry."

"And the other?"

"She is at class."

Sam pointed at the armchair. "Sit down." She lightly took the girl's elbow and steered her around to the front of the chair and eased her onto the cushion. She then sat on the coffee table directly before her.

"When did you last see Jayla?"

Her eyes down, Winslow touched her face lightly, as if exploring it. "We saw her a few weeks ago, for dinner. That sucked."

"Why? What happened?"

"Nothing then. It was afterwards, when we all got flamed on Facebook. She totally trash-talked us, for no reason. Bitchy shit—really upsetting."

"Back up. Who was at dinner?"

"The three of us, minus Lizzie—the old roommates and her. It was like a reunion. We had a good time. At least till later."

Sam cut her off to avoid a repeat. "How was she at dinner?"

"Fine. Funny, happy. Having a good time."

"Did she talk about what she'd been doing?"

Winslow looked like she'd bitten into something sour. "She'd moved in with Mister Smooth. To hear her, it was pure Cinderella. Not sure if I believed it, though."

"Mr. Smooth?"

"Jared Wylie. She met him when he gave a talk at SUNY. One of those guest-speaker things. I saw him, too—looked good, talked good, smelled good. Too good to be true—that's what I told Lizzie. But he swept Jayla off her feet, for sure. She was a goner."

"But you said you didn't believe it," Sam reminded her.

Winslow appeared thoughtful, and for the first time since they'd met, Sam saw a glimmer of intelligence flicker across the young woman's face. "Something was wrong. She'd cut us off after she split from here to be with him. Then, out of the blue, this dinner? And she acted weird—to me, at least—like she was trying too hard to be having a good time. You know how people get sometimes? Laughing too hard, almost hamming it up? Seemed . . . out of whack."

"She'd been living with Wylie for a year by then, more or less?"

"I don't know the exact timing, but that's where she was when we all met."

"She talk about him at dinner?"

"Oh, sure. Jared this and Jared that. Like I gave a damn. She dropped out, for Christ's sake. What kind of woman does that anymore? Prince Charming? I don't think so."

"You said something happened after? Something about Facebook?"

Winslow's manner had evolved by now, from attitudinal sulker to engaged conversationalist. She frowned at the memory. "Yeah. Maybe a day later we all got slimed. She posted stuff on our Walls making us look bad. And we knew it was her, 'cause it was stuff only she could've known about, dating back to when we were roommates. It was so random—and really mean."

"You ask her about it?"

"I tried to. Got nowhere. Left messages, texts, you name it. Nothin'. Might as well have saved my breath."

"Why did she reach out in the first place?" Sam asked. "I'm guessing she was the one behind getting together."

"She said it was 'cause she missed us. That was the only dark part of her walking advertisement about life with Jared—the implication that he was kind of a control freak. I even asked her if there was something going on she wasn't telling us. That just got a big denial. Maybe I was right, huh?"

"How so?"

"You said she was dead. Did he kill her?"

"I didn't say that, and we're still conducting our investigation. She ever mention going to Vermont to you?"

Winslow shook her head. "I don't think so. I mean, it might've come up, for skiing or something—in conversation—but nothing sticks out."

"Apart from you three," Sam asked, "do you know if she was keeping in touch with anyone else from the old days? It might help to get a better angle on her most recent activities." Sam thought back to her conversation with Mr. and Mrs. Robinson, and added, "Her parents, maybe?"

But Winslow reacted immediately to that suggestion. "Not them. That was pretty much a clean break for Jayla. They were too old-school for her. That's why she changed her name. You know Jayla isn't her real name, don't you?"

"Yeah. Charlotte Anne."

"Oh. You got that. Well, anyways, she told us they weren't in touch anymore. I always felt bad for them about that. I got the feeling the break was her thing, not theirs. Must be tough for your own kid to cut you off."

"So," Sam redirected her, knowing her fair share about alienated families, "anyone else?"

"Right. Sorry. Yeah. She had an old boyfriend. Aaron Goldman. They were a hot item before Jared. I heard later that she reached out to him, too, about the same time he got mugged. That's how I learned about it—somebody told me they'd seen him in the hospital."

"How do we get hold of Mr. Goldman?"

"You don't. He was way too radical and save-the-whales for me. You could call the Albany Alliance. He was tight with them. But I heard he took off. Probably charging at Japanese fishing boats in a rubber dinghy by now."

For the first time, Scott Gagne made his presence known, sighing gently from his spot by the door.

"We know them?" Sam asked him.

"Oh, yeah. They won't talk to us."

She returned her attention to Winslow. "Is there anything else you can think of to add, Jamie? You mentioned Lizzie a couple of times, for example. You think she might know something?"

"I doubt it. I'm the one who knew Jayla best. This place has only two bedrooms, and she and I bunked together, so we got to know each other pretty well." She stopped to shake her head sadly. "I still can't believe she's gone. She had her problems—fighting where she came from. She hated feeling like she was an Oreo, to use her word—black outside, white on the inside? But she was really good people, and I think she was wrong. Maybe her parents overdid the whole living-in-the-burbs bit, but Jayla was her own woman. I think the only screwup she ever made was that Jared Wylie creep."

"You said they met when he was guest teaching, that right?"

"Just for a day. A guest speaker at a class on local government for a poli-sci course. From what I could see, he took one look at her and figured he wanted her. She was like a fish in a barrel. I told her so, even though it pissed her off. But he was good. I'll give him that."

"You saw them a fair amount at the start?" Sam asked.

"Not really. It was super fast. After that, they were on their own and I have no clue what they were doing. She moved out pretty soon afterwards."

She lapsed briefly into silence before adding, "Men. Such assholes."

Sammie glanced at Scott, who merely smiled and shrugged.

The plan following the Jamie Winslow interview had been for Sam to stay overnight in Albany, and then return to Burlington to further debrief Rachel Reiling, now that she'd had a day or two to decompress.

But given her meeting with the Robinsons, and the references to parenting with Winslow, Sam wanted to get back to her daughter. Willy was already at home, according to his recent texts, so a familial fix was calling out as a priority.

Sam's feelings about motherhood were deepening as time elapsed. Given her childhood, she'd been surprised at her pleasure with becoming pregnant—she'd once thought that never having children would be her gift to the world. And now that Emma was undergoing such radical changes from week to week, being her mother had mutated from novelty with benefits to almost heart-wrenching love affair. It had been a transformation of soul-shifting proportions, and shaken some fundamental if simpleminded core beliefs.

No longer able to see herself solely as a wannabe Ninja overachiever—military- and SWAT-trained, athletic, rugged, aggressive, and resistant to pain and discomfort—Sam had been forced to deal with a new reality as a sensitive, caring mother and mate. That these traits had been long apparent to most who'd worked with her—most tellingly Joe Gunther—never penetrated her outer defensive shell.

Until Emma did so with no effort whatsoever.

The dilemma was: What to do now? Sam was feeling torn between dual personalities—one the driven detective, careless of appetite, lack of sleep, or degree of challenge; the other the doting mother, concerned with doing the best possible job, encouraged by childhood memories soaked with failure. Whenever she was in the midst of one, she was forever sensitive to the pull of the other.

The only useful aspect of all this was that it gave her some insight into some of Willy Kunkle's demons. Most people had never fathomed the rationale behind their union; but to her—with time, Emma, some therapy, and a lot of work—it had become a good match.

She couldn't wait to get back to her family.

CHAPTER NINETEEN

"Hey, hotshot. I thought I was supposed to be reading about you in the headlines."

Sue was dressed in almost fluorescent purple scrubs this time, but entering instead of leaving the house as Lester was pouring milk over his cereal. She dropped the newspaper onto the breakfast table and gave him a kiss before crossing to the coffee machine. Night shifts had started two days ago.

"Any kids underfoot?"

"Watch it, Mom," her daughter said, entering the kitchen. "Don't say or do anything you'll have to pay the shrink for later."

Her parents laughed as Sue hugged Wendy and kissed her on the cheek. "You're a brat."

Wendy returned the kiss. "But you love me."

Sue smiled. "I do. You get that history paper finished?"

"Handing it in this morning," Wendy said, pointing to her backpack in the corner. "Pretty good, if I say so myself."

A horn blast from outside made her head for the door, scooping up the pack and waving with the back of her hand. "Gotta go. Love you."

Sue sat across from Lester, the steaming coffee between her hands.

"Good night?" he asked.

"Not bad. Not too busy, not too boring. Goldilocks would've been pleased. So—did your shit-hits-the-fan case go down the drain?"

"Just the opposite. I'm just taking my time stepping up to the fan."

"The people who ran the case first screwed up, huh?"

He took a spoonful of cereal before responding. "Could be. That's one reason I'm taking my time—I think they were under more pressure than they should've been. Too many quarterbacks, maybe."

"You finding anything out of order?"

"I am," he said. "I just don't know what it amounts to yet."

He took another bite. "This whole thing is gonna shift one way or the other. I can guarantee that. But as to where the final pieces are gonna fall?" He smiled and shrugged. "Stay tuned."

Vermont is famous for its picturesque towns and villages, often outfitted with a common, a bandstand, even a Civil War monument, aging grace-fully. The surrounding buildings look transported from a century ear-lier, as can the overall pace of life. Barring the occasional tourist bus or fall harvest festival, the more remote among these places appear quiet enough to defy survival.

Which frequently runs to the heart of the matter. Many of them are barely hanging on, having become highly taxed virtual suburbs, depen-dent on larger neighbors for new identities as bedroom communities.

To Lester's practiced, jaundiced eye, each locale's architecture often told of its general vitality. He had, over time, identified most municipalities—rich and poor—as having four basic ingredients in tell-ingly variable quantities.

Most crucial were the businesses, spanning from plentiful to nonex-istent. They were the most obvious and easily visible indicators of a town's financial health.

There were usually a few mansions, owned by urban transplants in

L.L. Bean clothing, slumming in the countryside and either enjoying some time off or milking a windfall.

Third came the largest and most economically flexible quadrant—into which he fit himself: the single-family homes. They covered everything from tidy split-levels and modest Greek Revivals to patched and sagging structures sporting plastic sheeting over their windows and hay bales around their foundations. These housed a sliding scale of residents, from community movers and shakers to electricians, plumbers, teachers, carpenters, bus drivers, store clerks, loggers, farmhands, day workers, machine operators, and blue-collar wage earners who drove the pickups and rusty Subarus so common to Vermont's roads.

And last, and usually located downtown, were the ancient, sometimes remodeled buildings whose former function as hotels, rooming houses, or turn-of-the-century worker housing had been converted to partially state-supported apartment buildings for those less fortunately endowed, financially and otherwise.

The residents of the final category were not commuters, the self-employed, trust-funders, or retirees. They were the socially marginal, burdened by mischance, misbehavior, infirmity, or simple bad luck. Often goodhearted, well intentioned, and hardworking, they were nevertheless restricted in options, and lived their lives within limited spheres.

Lorraine Kennedy was one of them. At least, that's what Lester had been led to believe through his research. He'd confirmed, for example, that Lorraine was on full and permanent disability for a back injury sustained while working several years ago at a hardware box store outside Burlington.

The building she lived in was located in a village outside Ludlow, facing a green with an inoperative fountain in need of some paint. It was quiet and peaceful and looked faintly abandoned during the day, when he imagined most of its residents were working in the ski town and tourist attraction that was nearby Ludlow.

But not Lorraine. Lester hadn't called ahead, preferring the advantage of an unannounced visit. However, he knew enough to presume that he'd find somebody at home, regardless of the hour.

She was in. After knocking on the door of her third-floor apartment, he heard a shuffling gait approach, before the door was pulled open by a tired-looking woman with long, blond, dirty hair pulled back into a ponytail. She had a cigarette dangling from her lips, which stayed put as she asked, "Who're you?"

Her voice was husky and pleasant, her eyes bloodshot but alert, and her body language relaxed—all good signs to a man well used to the opposite. Early in the morning was no time for a screaming match or a brawl.

In his most self-effacing manner, Lester showed her his credentials and introduced himself.

"VBI?" she said. "You trying to say VSP?"

Lester laughed. "No, ma'am. I used to work for the state police, but I moved over to this outfit. Stands for Vermont Bureau of Investigation. We do things like bank robberies, murders—major cases."

"You don't say? I never run into you before."

"That's a good thing, right?" he said.

She tilted her head slightly, watching him. "That mean it's bad we're meeting now?"

He loved it. Insightful, smart, a little funny. He sensed he could work with this woman. "I hope not. I think I'm just here for a little information."

"About what?"

"Your brother, Kyle."

Her face didn't move at all, but in some extraordinarily subtle way, it transformed. From watchful and guarded, it became reflective and soft.

"Poor baby," she said, and stepped back, asking, "You want to come in? I got coffee on."

"Thank you," he said, and accepted her invitation.

The apartment contrasted with her untidy appearance. It was spare, open, and sun-filled with the morning light—at once startling, given his expectations, and instructive, considering the odds against her. He imagined that since her life had been all but reduced to this one small apartment, she was going to do the best she could to make it exemplary.

"It's a beautiful place," he complimented her. "You've done a great job."

"Thank you," she replied. "Have a seat by the window."

He did so, and watched her move painfully, stiff-legged, across to a kitchen counter, where she filled two cups. "Milk or sugar?"

"No. Straight is fine."

"Me, too," she commented, and slowly crossed over to join him, choosing a ladder-back chair she apparently found more comfortable than anything softer.

"How're you doing?" he asked, his meaning clear by his glancing at how carefully she moved.

"Some days are better than others," she answered indirectly, not addressing which kind this was.

"I can imagine," he said, taking a sip of coffee.

"Why're you here about Kyle?" she asked.

"I'm looking at his death," Les answered honestly. "Not because I think there's anything wrong with the conclusions reached, but mostly to satisfy my curiosity."

Her eyes widened slightly, as if amused by something very minor. "That the company line?"

He smiled politely. "For the moment. I guess so. I don't have anything else to go on."

She nodded in sympathy with his predicament. "I didn't either, at the time," she said. "I still don't. Two men are dead, each with the other's bullet in him. Hard to argue with that. But it still feels wrong to me."

"That kind of explains my visit," Lester told her. "I'd like to hear why."

She removed her cigarette and sipped from her cup before saying, somewhat doubtfully, "You're a strange sort of cop."

He chuckled. "So I've been told."

"Okay," she then said, cradling the cup and sitting back to get more comfortable, the cigarette forgotten in an ashtray. "For one thing, I can't figure out a situation where Kyle would ever use a gun."

"He owned one."

"Oh, I know," she agreed. "Like everybody else around here. He even used to shoot it with that knucklebrain friend of his, Chad. But there's a big difference between shooting at a target and another human being. One thing about Kyle you probably don't know: He never shot anything living. Never went hunting, never took potshots at squirrels or birds like most boys. When we were growing up, he'd cry whenever he saw a dead animal by the side of the road. It was a thing with him. I never knew why."

"People can be pushed over that line," Les suggested gently. "Pacifists driven to violence by the right circumstances."

"But isn't that because they got pushed there by what was happening?" she argued. "They say that cop and Kyle didn't know each other. What could happen in the two minutes it takes for a traffic stop to lead to people shooting each other?"

It was an excellent point, and one that lay at the heart of Lester's ongoing discomfort. "He could've been having the ultimate bad day," he suggested. "The kind of thing where one last push is all that's needed."

"I know what you mean," she said, surprising him again with her open-mindedness. If sister and brother had been blessed with similar temperaments, it was hard to imagine either one of them blowing up to the point of using violence.

"We've all had days like that," she was saying. "But that's when you yell or punch a pillow. You don't fire a gun at somebody. Sure as hell not a cop."

"It sounds like you two were pretty close," he said, changing approaches slightly.

"We were all we had left," she said, her tone wistful. "There's no other family to speak of—not in-state or nearby. There's a cousin, Molly

Blaze. She's a good egg. Lives down near Jacksonville, where we all came from. But that's it."

"Had you and Kyle been in touch that last week?"

"Oh, yes. Like usual. He was unhappy, but not mad—not like you're thinking."

"What was he unhappy about?"

Lorraine tossed her head slightly. "Oh, another woman, naturally. That was Kyle, through and through. If you wanted to pin a particular problem on him, it wasn't a short temper, it was his heart. That poor sap fell in love at the drop of a hat."

"Really?" Lester feigned surprise. "I had no idea he had it that bad."

"Oh, yes. That's what I meant before. All the crying at dead animals? He was a real softy. Women loved it. He could dance, cook, he had good manners. Compared with most of the lunkheads out there, he was a woman's dream come true."

"Okay," Les followed up. "So tell me about this latest love interest."

She looked a little surprised. "Oh, I don't know her name. I often didn't. He had a good turnover, like I said."

"You know anything about her at all?" he persisted. "Where he met her, maybe? Or where she worked?"

She was shaking her head. "No. Just that it was over, like all the others."

Lester placed his coffee mug on the floor beside his seat. "I'm not here to harass you, Lorraine, believe me. But this might be important for what happened that night. Anything might be. What exactly did he say about the breakup?"

She didn't roll her eyes or act impatient. It was as if from the start she'd accepted his reason for being here at face value, and thus saw him as an ally. She liked his manner, and trusted that he was in earnest. "Well, for all his successes, Kyle loved his independence. I only caught the tail end of these affairs, and only from him, but a lot of the time, they fell apart because the women wanted more of a commitment than he did." She laughed softly before admitting, "There's the irony, right? It was all about falling in love for him; after that, he couldn't wait to get out. He was always the most surprised when they beat him to it, and bailed first. Wounded his ego. He always claimed those would've been the true keepers, of course."

"Did you ever meet any of them?"

"Sometimes. For dinner, maybe. He'd bring one by. I never really knew why. He wasn't looking for my approval, and he never stayed with any of them long enough for it to matter. It was one of those things people do, I suppose."

"Any of them married?"

"Sometimes. It didn't seem to matter."

"You say he was the sentimental type, but these breakups can be hard to control. I heard he might've gotten a little physical sometimes."

She didn't take umbrage, smiling instead. "Love and liquor, right? The fateful combination. You get that from checking his record? It's true. He got arrested for domestic violence a couple of times, I think—maybe it was just once. They were shoving matches. I'm not saying it wasn't the right thing to do. Best way to break up a fight is to lock somebody up. But nothing came of it—couple of sloppy drunks throwing beer cans at each other. Look at those more carefully. I bet that's what you'll find."

In fact, he had, and she was right. He returned to his original inquiry. "All right. So, this last breakup."

She nodded. "Right, right. That's what you asked. Thinking back, I'm pretty sure she was married, now that you mention it. And I think that's what caused the rift—she wanted things to be more serious."

"Leave her husband?" Lester asked.

"That's what Kyle was worried about. I don't know if they'd actually started talking it, but he thought he saw the writing on the wall."

"Had he broken it off?"

"Oh, yes. That was why he was upset. She didn't take it well at all. Very worked up. And of course, there was no better way to drive him away faster."

"He didn't call her by name? Even a nickname?"

"Nope. Well . . . The dragon lady. But he'd used that one before."

Lester retrieved his coffee and took another sip, thinking back. Lorraine waited patiently.

"Did you ever see Kyle's gun?" he asked eventually.

"He showed it to me once," she said. "It was a revolver. That's about all I know. I've fired a gun a couple of times, but it's not my thing."

"What was the occasion?"

"He'd just gotten it. It was a few years ago. He got it secondhand."

"Did he carry it around often?"

She frowned. "Not that I know. I doubt it. I thought he'd lost it. That was another thing that surprised me when he died—I didn't know he'd found it again."

"He told you when it went missing?"

"Yes. He was pretty upset, I think mostly because he couldn't figure out what had happened to it."

"Did he think someone'd stolen it?"

"He didn't tell me if he did. At the time, I thought he blamed himself."

"When was this?"

She hesitated. "I don't really know."

"Near the time he died?"

"Oh, sure," she said without hesitation. "I just can't remember exactly."

"But within a week or something?"

"Maybe a little more."

Lester eyed her closely. "Lorraine, since we're on this topic, did the timing of the gun disappearing coincide with him and the mystery woman breaking up?"

She didn't answer immediately, returning his scrutiny. "You think they're related? How?"

"I'm not saying they are," he stated. "It just struck me as an interesting coincidence."

She nodded slightly, just once. "I thought you cops didn't like coincidences. That's what they always say on TV."

Lester smiled, but he was less amused than suddenly caught by the notion. "Yeah. Well, for once, they're right. We don't."

Some twenty minutes later, back outside in his car, Spinney pulled out his cell phone and dialed Sturdy Foster.

"You getting anywhere?" Foster wanted to know, in lieu of the standard greeting.

Lester laughed. "Hi to you, too. I'm pokin' along, trying not to make waves. I learned a couple of things which may or may not have anything to do with the price of eggs."

"Like?"

"Kennedy had just broken up with a married girlfriend, and he'd lost track of the .357 you later found in his lap."

"What'ya mean, lost track?"

"Lost it. Both his sister and his shooting buddy said he'd reported it missing."

"Stolen?"

"Not necessarily. Just missing."

"So he might've found it again, like under the couch?"

"Yup, but he never said so if he did."

Foster was impressively nondefensive. "Huh," he grunted. "Interesting. Who was the girlfriend?"

"Don't know. He didn't tell anyone I've met so far."

There was a momentary silence between both men as each mulled over what had just been said.

Lester took advantage of it to ask, "Was there anyone you met during your investigation who'd qualify as a best buddy to Ryan Paine?"

"Dylan Collier," Sturdy said quickly. "He's with A Troop—A4, specifically—St. J. He and Paine were joined at the hip. He made a total pest of himself during the investigation. Worse than the press, the SA, my boss, and the commissioner, combined."

"Why?"

"At first, I thought it was the whole 'thin blue line' thing—or green and gold, in our case—ramped up to the max. All he did was rant about how Paine had been killed in cold blood because of a lack of support for the troops from the top. It got so bad, I told his sergeant to yank his leash, which probably made it into his permanent file and put my name on his hate list. You talk to him, you better not mention me. I don't know what wound him up, but you should've heard him on Kyle Kennedy. It was like the man had raped his mother."

"He had killed his best friend, sounds like," Lester sympathized.

"I get it," Sturdy said irritably. "Trust me. I'm playing ball with you 'cause we go back and I know you. But don't read me wrong. I don't like that my case is being picked over and a cop-killer is being given the benefit of the doubt. But my saying that to you? That's nothin' compared to what I got from Collier. He was unhinged. It was like Kennedy had been acting on behalf of the VSP brass to get rid of people like Paine. Absurd. Totally went off track. It went beyond what you'd expect from a grieving man. Made me think the guy might be overdue for a psych eval."

Lester gazed across the empty town green, watching how a slight breeze was fluttering the uppermost foliage in the trees bordering the common. The leaves were new and translucently bright in the morning sun, looking freshly unpacked and ready for the summer ahead. He'd been struck into silence by Sturdy's honesty, which in turn reinforced the man's reputed integrity.

"Sorry," Sturdy said curtly.

"No need," Les told him. "You've been a stand-up guy, and I appreciate it. Don't apologize for being straight with me."

"Right. So why did you want the name of Paine's best bud?"

Lester proceeded gingerly. "I've been digging into Kennedy so far. Seemed like I shouldn't play favorites." Hearing the words out loud,

Lester wondered if he wasn't being disingenuous. It was accurate on its face, but he was being propelled by something less purely objective—an uncomfortable feeling, as though he was getting close to something that so far, and for unknown reasons, had been left undisturbed.

"Watch yourself with Collier," Sturdy recommended, his voice still sounding rigidly neutral. "I'll talk with you later."

The line went dead.

Lester started his car and left town, his earlier enthusiasm for the hunt replaced by a heavy heart. It was common, sometimes—perhaps self-protectively so—to exchange the wider picture for a more narrow focus. On the firing range, it was precisely what police instructors routinely warned you against doing. Be aware of the peripheral threat, they would say. "*Scan!*" was the constant reminder to look around and take heed.

Sturdy's words had reminded Lester of that, bringing alive the bigger story behind what had at first been merely an intriguing puzzle. As clichéd as it sounded, real people had died, one of them doing the kind of work that Lester had done more times than he could recall.

It was a sobering thought, and an encouragement to get everything right.

CHAPTER TWENTY

"I still say you're nuts," Sammie said, moving into the passing lane. "You should be in your own car."

Willy looked over at her. "We're both going to Burlington. We're carpooling, for Christ's sake. How much more crunchy-granola can you get? The governor or the commissioner gets wind of this, we'll be good for some environmental plaque. Crossed unicycles on a field rampant or something."

"You are so full of it," she said. "You're gonna rent a car to get back home. How crunchy is that? And how're you going to legitimize the expense?"

"Joe'll love it," he countered. "His troops carving out quality time while we're on the job? It's a win–win."

"You forget: I'm Joe," she reminded him. "And I say you pay for the rental out of your own pocket."

He laughed. "*Sold.* You think I care?" He reached far over with his right hand and gave her a poke in the ribs. "I get to spend a few daylight hours with my sweetie pie. When was the last time *that* happened?"

She squirmed away from his probing finger, laughing. "What the hell's gotten into you? You drinking again?"

He took it in stride. "No way. I was *never* a happy drunk. Much as that's hard to believe."

"Yeah, right." She took her eyes off the road long enough to look at him. "Seriously. This is almost creepy behavior."

He settled back in his seat and gazed out at the passing countryside. They were traveling north on I-91, in preparation for catching the state's only other interstate—I-89—that cut diagonally through the Green Mountains to reach Burlington on the western border. It was a beautiful, scenic, thinly traveled road, showing off some of the best views that northern New England had to offer. And at this time of year—the soothing, seductive, emerald green stretch of time between the end of mud season and early fall, when this patch of earth holds out the brief glimpse of perfection—it was difficult for even a hard-bitten soul not to be influenced.

"Not to worry," he said evenly. "It won't last."

Now she felt bad, and reached out to squeeze his leg. "What's going on?" she asked supportively.

The flash of effervescence had passed. "Not sure," he said briefly.

She stayed silent.

"How're we doin'?" he asked.

"I think we're okay," she said, struggling to keep her voice even against the surge of emotion his inquiry had caused. "You having doubts?"

"Not about us," he said, to her relief.

"Then what?"

"Me, as usual."

"Is it what Joe did? Putting me in charge? I know that caused some tension. I was hoping we'd talked that through."

"Yeah, we did. That was stupid."

"The other thing, then?" she ventured. "How everything you touch falls apart?"

He didn't answer for a while, before saying, "It always does."

"It doesn't, you know? Look at us—at Emma."

He didn't respond, keeping his eyes on the road.

She was at a loss. "You seemed happy to see me last night," she said almost wistfully.

He turned toward her. "I'm always happy to see you."

She felt her cheeks grow warm. Whatever was the relationship they'd forged over the years, this certainly wasn't it, with sentimental statements like that. Willy was not a man to tell her he loved her, or missed her, or couldn't wait to see her again. There were no notes delivered on birthdays or spontaneous gifts. He'd purchased her a box of bullets once, for self-protection. That had been it.

"That's one reason I came home," she said. "Instead of staying in Albany or Burlington. I'm always happy to see you, too."

"I thought that was Emma."

"Not only her," she told him honestly. "I knew you were with her, and not Louise. You're both my people, but I began this with you."

He rubbed an eye and sighed. "Maybe that's part of it. It's different for me—having people."

"That's true for both of us," she said. "You ever wonder about how folks said we wouldn't make it?"

"Nobody ever told me that to my face."

She couldn't help but laugh. "Gosh. I wonder why. You know they were saying it."

"Yeah."

"I used to think that's because you were such a nutjob, and they were being protective of me—not knowing you the way I did."

"But . . . ?"

"Well, you just said it. I'm thinking now it wasn't so one-sided—that they were saying that because neither one of us had a good history of hanging on to people, so how would we be able to hang on to each other? We'd be like double-damned."

He mulled that over.

"If that's true," she continued, on a roll, "then why's it so surprising if a little of that's gotten into you, too? You got good reason to have your doubts—about me and you, both. But I'm stuck on you. Just so you know. Come hell or high water."

She was tempted to say more, but stopped. This kind of conversation was foreign ground. She'd had soulful exchanges with Joe, who was a mentor and a trusted friend. But Willy and she had evolved to where they were virtually without dialogue. They each acted on their beliefs, with no commentary needed. In that way, she supposed, they resembled an older couple from a generation that valued endurance and taciturnity over sentiment and free expression.

"I got that last night, when you came home unexpected," he said after a long, silent pause.

"What?"

"That you and Emma are everything I've got."

"That's good, isn't it?"

"Maybe," he allowed. "But what happens now?"

She understood perfectly, and didn't downplay it. They were shipwreck survivors—two who'd managed to surface and swim to comparative safety. Who was she to tell him that everything was now safe? On that level, what better metaphor could there be than the useless left arm he carried between them—the result of a bullet being two inches off target?

"We do the best we can," she answered. "Like we're doing right now."

Willy's destination was in fact South Burlington, the hometown of Al-Tech Industries, Robb Haag's old employer.

As he turned from watching Sammie drive off, however, and took in his surroundings, Willy was struck by the value of a good business name. Al-Tech Industries had sounded impressive when he first connected it to Haag's background. Now, looking at the one-story, midsized, slightly decrepit building before him, he was left with a significantly less prosperous impression.

He crossed the cracked, weed-sprouting concrete lot to the narrow front door, and opened it to discover a small office containing one young woman at a desk, equipped with a phone, a computer, a copier, and a coffee machine.

"May I help you?" she asked brightly, as if seeing her first human of the day.

"I'm here to see Alan Summers," he said, not identifying himself.

"Mr. Kunkle? VBI?"

"Right," he replied, confirmed in his opinion about the amount of foot traffic the place enjoyed.

He gestured to their surroundings. "Slow day?"

She smiled. "Oh, no. But I get what you mean. We get trucks in here, not people. We're not retailers."

She reached for the phone and announced, "Mr. Kunkle's here," before motioning Willy to a side door and advising, "Go right on in. Mr. Summers is expecting you."

The next office was slightly more impressive, if only because its occupant had put down a rug, hung some pictures, and moved in something fancier than secondhand, industrial gray furniture.

The man behind the wooden desk rose to shake hands, but pointedly didn't abandon his station, indicating a guest chair instead. "Mr. Kunkle? Alan Summers. Glad to meet you. Have a seat." Willy imagined the body language was based on his host's diminutive size and slight build, which drove him to seek out props like the oversized desk. In that way, he made Willy think of a small wet dog trying to climb up onto a dock.

They sat at the same time, with Summers crossing his legs and tenting his hands before his chin as he resumed, "So you're a policeman."

"Right."

"How may I help you? You were a little mysterious on the phone."

"True," Willy said without apology. "What do you make here?"

"Energy cells," Summers said. "Among other things. 'Batteries' to the lay public, although that technically sells the product short."

"I bet. Who do you sell 'em to?"

Summers hesitated. "A variety of customers. We live in a world that's become increasingly independent of those," he indicated the electrical outlet in the wall near Willy's chair. "So it's a booming business. Of course, you don't buy AI-Tech power cells at the store, so it's understandable if you've never heard of us."

He chuckled as if this had been tremendously amusing.

Willy skipped smiling. "You sell to the military?"

Summers donned his serious face. "Ah. Well, without knowing why you're here, even though you represent the police, I'm sure you can understand my reluctance to have that sort of information spread around."

Willy was not liking this guy. "It says you do on your website."

The other man's cheeks flushed slightly. "Of course. Well—there you have it. Hard to duck the power of the marketing department."

"Like you wished you'd ducked this conversation?"

"No, no—not hardly," Summers protested. "You're here, aren't you? Because I agreed to it. Maybe we should get to the reason why. That may clear things up."

"Fair enough," Willy agreed. "You know a man named Robb Haag?"

"Is Robb in some sort of trouble?"

Willy just stared at him.

"Yes," Summers said after hesitating. "He used to work here."

"Doing what?"

"He was employed on the assembly line."

"Doing what?" Willy repeated.

Summers frowned. "Mr. Kunkle. I'm not sure I'm entirely comfortable with this."

Willy considered that, for all of a split second, before standing up. "Yeah. Me neither. I'll leave you in peace and come back at a more convenient time with a couple of friends from Homeland Security. They actually have an office nearby, as luck would have it. So we should be able to get down to nuts and bolts in no time, and make you much more comfortable."

Summers held up his hands as if in surrender and belted out a theatrical laugh. "Holy cow. My God, you're prickly. Sit down, sit down. We've clearly gotten off on the wrong foot."

Willy leaned on the man's desk with his right hand splayed out, his eyes boring into Summers's—purposefully emphasizing the man's small stature. "That happens when you dance around. I told you on the phone that I work for the VBI, and your response told me you know what that means. I'm not a labor board inspector, sir. Either be straight with your answers or I'll come back with reinforcements who have rules and regs that make Vermont's look like a summer camp handbook." He gestured to the chair he'd been using. "If I sit back down, it better be to have a conversation, and not some version of show-me-yours-and-I'll-show-you-mine. Are we clear?"

Summers licked his lips, nodded once curtly, and said, "Please, do sit back down. My apologies."

Willy did as requested. "Robb Haag," he repeated.

"He did work here, for about two and a half years. I had to fire him. He wasn't fitting in."

Willy turned his palm up and smiled. "There you go. Now give me the details. What does 'not fitting in' mean?"

Summers's irritation at the memory seemed to overtake his reluctance. "You name it. I put up with him much longer than I should have. The irony was that he was a good technician. He had the skills. But he was such a prima donna. He wanted better equipment, better lighting, better seating, more pay, shorter hours. Jesus, the list never stopped. And people didn't like him. It wasn't like I was pissing off the most popular guy on the floor. He treated everybody like dirt, from what I heard."

"And you put up with him for two and a half years?" Willy asked pointedly, his real question implied.

"I know. I'm an idiot. Look, what we do here encompasses a lot of skill sets, from people taping up cardboard boxes to chemists and engineers working to invent a better mousetrap. We're small, we're outnumbered by the big boys who dominate the market, and we're working in a business where a couple of cents here or there can cost a contract. I do the best I can with what I've got. But I'll be very honest, what I got to pick from ain't always the best and the brightest. I can woo some university types who don't want to leave Vermont, I can sell the charms of the region to people who can and do earn bigger bucks elsewhere, and I can bend over backwards to supply fringe benefits that'll buy people's loyalty. But in the end? I'm as far from Silicon Valley as I can be, shy of Bosnia."

He seemed almost exhausted by this outburst, and slumped back in his chair, looking at Willy as if he'd just been subjected to a vigorous interrogation.

Willy quietly said, "So?"

Summers understood. "So, Robb Haag, despite being a total jerk, had a talent I wanted badly enough to put up with a raft of poor attitude."

"Until you couldn't," Willy suggested.

"Until I couldn't," Summers confirmed.

"Was it anything in particular?"

"It was. I won't get into technical details, 'cause not even I understand all the ins and outs of it, but he got into a spitting match with one of the engineers about how to comply with the specs concerning one of our military products."

"A lithium-ion battery?" Willy quickly asked.

The CEO stared at him, making Willy regret his own impulse. He was usually better at keeping his mouth shut, and letting his interviewees supply all their own rope. Hubris or impatience had gotten the better of him.

"What exactly do you know?" Summers asked.

It is not to a cop's advantage to disclose details of a case. It's rarely helpful and usually backfires.

Willy shook his head, as much at himself as in response to the question. "Mr. Summers, I know I was rude earlier, and I appreciate your letting that go. Especially since what you implied about trade secrets or company discretion applies to me, too. I can tell you that Haag is a person of interest, and that the case is important enough that it involves our agency. I can also tell you that I've already been in communication with Homeland Security Investigations. After that, I have to protect the integrity of my case."

Summers was already waving the explanation away. "I understand, trust me. I deal with such issues every day. Yes—in answer to your question—it was a Li-poly design he was assigned to, and it was being assembled to military specifications. That was precisely the problem. He came forward with what he claimed was an improvement, but it didn't matter. You can't just arbitrarily change the terms of a military contract. It's a nonstarter."

"But he wouldn't accept that?"

Summers rubbed his face, finishing by squeezing the bridge of his nose between his index finger and thumb. "I don't know. Frankly, it might've been my fault by then. Generally, I'd been able to beat him back into line after one of these flare-ups. This time? I probably snapped."

He leaned toward Willy as if the latter had been about to argue the point. "He would never concede anything; never accept the other guy's viewpoint; never apologize for stopping everything in its tracks during one of his hissy fits. It was unrelenting. I would look at other people's faces during these things and see how they couldn't believe what was going on. I have a company to run. Mouths to feed. I just couldn't deal with him anymore."

Willy suggested, "So you fired him."

"On the spot," Summers admitted. "It wasn't pretty. He threatened to sue and stomped around till I had security throw him out. He actually chucked a coffee mug at me. People cheered when he hit the parking lot. Unbelievable. The real joke was that I'd done the guy a favor by taking him on. He didn't have the necessary degree when he applied. You could even call him a dropout. But I made an exception because of his natural abilities. I thought I had a whiz kid on my hands. Instead, I just had a spoiled brat. It became crystal clear to all of us why he hadn't finished his degree, or didn't have friends. I guess it was a mental problem, finally. That's all I could think of."

"Okay," Willy said. "Thanks for that. It fits and it's helpful, so I appreciate it. But I need to know a little about that battery."

"I can't—," Summers began before Willy interrupted him.

"I know, I know. I heard you. I was in the military. I don't need a blueprint. But if I were to tell you that he was maybe making these things now on his own, why would that be? What exactly might he be up to? I already know they're supposed to go into drones."

Summers was stunned into silence.

Willy waited him out, not having anything to add, and this time not ruing having told him too much.

"I . . . ," Summers began, searching for a response. "I . . . Look, it takes forever to land a DOD contract. . . . Okay. Maybe not always. I mean, they can come to you, too, if they know you've invented something extraordinary. But that doesn't fit what Haag . . ."

He rose and crossed to the window overlooking the parking lot, speaking as he did so. "No. He was wrong. That was the bottom line. He thought he had a shortcut, but it didn't work." He turned to face his guest. "After he was gone, I told my guys to look into it—to overcome their prejudice about the source and see if he'd had a point. There was nothing there."

He began pacing the office, his head tucked, virtually talking to himself. "We're all looking for the next breakout technology—bring in a power cell that delivers more in a smaller, safer package, lasts forever, is reliable, lightweight, and doesn't cost much." He stopped to address Willy directly. "Are you looking into him because he's set something up? Is he onto something?"

Willy told him with more honesty than Summers could know, "I can't tell you that."

But it raised the question: What the hell *was* Haag doing? Right now, all Willy had to go on was the opinion of a man who didn't know how to properly step off a train.

"Let's back up a bit," he suggested. "Just so I get it right. When we started this conversation, I got the feeling Haag worked on the assembly line, like someone turning the same screw four hundred times a day."

Summers dismissed that. "I'm sorry. I mean, yes, he was involved in the assembly process, but not like those Charlie Chaplin movies or an *I Love Lucy* episode. I was being coy, since I wasn't sure why you were here. We try to work as much as possible along open-ended lines. There's much more latitude among the workers that way—a freer exchange of ideas. Like I said, Robb didn't have a degree. I couldn't hire him as an engineer, but with the system we've established here, he could still have input—at all levels—if he knew how to pitch it. That was the sticking point—all he did was drive everybody crazy. He was so full of himself."

"He must've had some buddies," Willy argued. "Even jackasses have friends. I've been accused of having a couple myself."

Summers gave him a startled look, unsure of how to react. "Right. Well, you're right, of course. At least I guess so. I don't really know."

"Can I go out back and ask?"

The reply, despite its content, was delivered amiably: "Not without a court order and my lawyer tagging along. My contract makes that an obligation. It's a government security thing. I can't let anyone back there without the right paperwork. I doubt you'd find much joy, anyhow. If and when you meet the man, if you haven't already, you'll see what I mean. Your joke a minute ago notwithstanding, Robb Haag would have to pay to have friends."

Sammie found Beverly Hillstrom and Rachel Reiling sitting in Beverly's car on St. Paul Street, opposite Rachel's worse-for-wear apartment house. She walked up to the young woman's open window and crouched down so she could see both occupants.

"Hi, guys. I hope you just got here."

"Barely drove up two minutes ago," Beverly reassured her.

Sam laid her hand on Rachel's forearm, which was resting on the window's edge. "You okay? Still willing to do this?"

"Yes," she said firmly.

"We've been talking it through," Beverly volunteered. "That's why I tagged along. I hope that's all right."

Sam stood and opened Rachel's door. "I'm glad you did. I won't say 'the more, the merrier,' but maybe 'misery loves company'?"

Rachel smiled, if a little reluctantly as Sam added, "I know. Bad joke. I'll try to make this as quick and painless as possible."

They walked to the back of the building, and the common entrance to both floors, where they found a Burlington police officer. He logged them in and allowed them access to the stairway.

"Okay," Sam was explaining throughout, "it's like I said on the phone: What I'm looking for is basically a guided tour. I want you to tell me what looks moved, what doesn't, what's yours and what's not, and to tell me in detail what happened that night—now that a little time's gone by. Still sound doable?"

Rachel paused at the foot of the stairs and looked up. "Let's go."

There was a museum-like quality to the apartment for Rachel. The last visitors here had been the evidence collection team, after EMS, the initial police responders, and the subsequent investigators. A lot of people, all of them careful to not leave fingerprints or hair samples or other evidence of themselves behind, but none too neat and tidy. It made for a visual commingling of the foreign and the familiar, overlaid by an odd odor of other people, dusting powder, and luminol.

"Guess I won't be moving back in," she barely said out loud, pausing at the door.

The other two women let her take her time, following her at first without comment, so she could habituate to the surroundings.

Fortunately, Rachel had inherited some of her mother's clinical detachment, and thus maintained more composure than Sam could have hoped for.

Indeed, once the girl had reached the disrupted center of the living room, she turned to face the detective and asked, "Where do we start?"

"Let's get the hard part done first," Sam recommended. "Act out what happened."

It didn't take Rachel long. Quietly, without emotion, she slowly explained her actions, describing the screaming, the sight of two people wrestling, her seizing the frying pan just as the man hit Charlotte with the lamp, resulting in a horrible, dull-sounding thud.

She pointed out the chair he'd launched at her after she'd hit him, and finally, she circled the still-open sofa bed to point out where she'd cradled her new friend's head and called for help.

Throughout, Sam recorded the narrative on her cell phone camera. At the end, without comment, Rachel walked over to her mother and wrapped her arms around her neck.

Sammie gave them a few moments, after which Rachel broke free, wiped her eyes, and asked, "What now?"

"Let's go through the whole place, section by section, and identify everything. What I'm looking for is what's yours, what may be Charlotte's that we missed, and what you can't account for."

"That might belong to him?"

"Possibly. Or was left behind by someone else. It doesn't matter. And don't expect to find much of Charlotte's. If we've done our job right, that's all at the lab being analyzed."

They worked their way from the back of the tiny kitchenette, around the counter, along the wall, and into Rachel's bedroom, looking through cabinets and drawers, under furniture, along shelves, shaking out clothing, checking the backs of closets. Accounting for everything along the way, they reached the living room some forty-five minutes later, and started anew from the corner farthest from the sofa bed.

Fortunately, it was a small apartment, not overly stuffed with belongings, and—obviously—they didn't need to be careful about returning everything to its proper place.

Finally, at the doorway connecting the entrance hall to the living room, the three of them stood observing where they'd just been. They were about to turn their attention to the hall behind them, when Sam pointed to a pair of plastic dark glasses, half-wedged under the back pillow of the chair right beside them.

"Yours?" she asked, almost in passing.

But Rachel stopped. "No," she said. "Those were Charlotte's."

"You're kidding," Sam said softly, pulling a single latex glove from her pocket and slipping it on to retrieve the glasses. As she wiggled them from under the pillow, the right temple came loose.

"Oh, hell," she muttered, stopping to don a second glove for better control. She crouched to take more careful hold of the glasses and brought them into view of the other two women. The temple was still attached, but almost dangling from the actual frame.

"That looks odd," Beverly commented, leaning in for a better view. "It's not broken at the hinge."

Sam lifted her find to eye level. "You're right. It's not broken at all. It's designed to come apart."

She took hold of the frame in one hand and the loose temple in the other and gently tugged. They separated to reveal a shiny metal rectangle at the end of the temple, designed to snugly fit into a corresponding slot in the frame.

"I'll be damned," Beverly said, in a rare use of profanity.

"What is it?" Rachel asked.

Sammie was smiling, turning it in the light. "A handy solution for backing up your computer when you're on the go. It's a secret USB thumb drive."

CHAPTER TWENTY-ONE

Joe was struck by how emotional he felt, seeing his brother, Leo, enter the hospital lobby and look around to get his bearings. After so many days of dealing with their mother's recovery, experiencing Rachel's and Beverly's trauma from afar, and seeing his team get deeper into cases he could truly only glimpse, Joe was suddenly reminded of the cost of his isolation. He was beyond eager to get back home.

The feeling was all the sharper because of his mother's recent improvement. From very little change, day to day, in the beginning, she had hit her stride, and by now was virtually her old reliable self, making wry comments and suggestions, and increasingly asking when she might be allowed to return to the farm.

This had been the stimulus for Leo's appearance—the near guarantee of an official discharge within the next day, pending a couple of final, almost pro forma tests. He had overruled Joe's halfhearted objection, readied his staff to take the shop's reins for a couple of days, and flown out here to help Joe pack up the Old Lady, as he called her, and bring her back to where she belonged.

Joe crossed the lobby and greeted Leo with an unaccustomed bear hug. Leo, who was far more given to such gestures, burst out laughing and pounded his older brother on the back. "My God, Joey, you must be feeling like Robinson Crusoe."

"Close," Joe conceded. "Damn close. You had a good flight?"

"Yeah. I couldn't believe it. No delays, no screaming babies, no computer glitches. People were walking around in shock. How's Mom doin'? She really on the mend?"

"See for yourself." Joe grabbed his elbow and steered him toward the all-too-familiar inner workings of the FREE.

Two thousand miles to the east, Lester was pulling into the parking lot of the state police barracks near St. Johnsbury, in Vermont's Northeast Kingdom—a large, minimally populated, heavily forested section of the state, famous among law enforcement agencies for its isolation, occasionally peculiar residents, and slow backup response times. When a cop pulled over a car up here in the middle of the night, he or she was best advised to be prepared and fully focused.

It also had the reputation—deserved or not—of being a good place to put the odd, errant trooper out to pasture, either permanently or for a cooling off. Personally, Lester had enjoyed working there, back in his VSP days, even though he'd done so only as a plainclothes investigator, and not a road guy.

He was not looking forward to this interview. While he'd never met Dylan Collier and was hoping to be pleasantly surprised, he was familiar with the phenomenon of the on-the-job retiree, which is in part what he'd gathered about the man. In all walks of life, you got the same few folks—making police work no different—people who put in the bare minimum, never volunteered, always just squeaked by, and, for paradoxical reasons, bitched the most about the very work they were shirking.

Lester was also uncomfortable because, before his last tense conversation with Sturdy, he'd been hoping the veteran detective would be along for the trip. It was no stretch to imagine that having one of Collier's own in the room might make for an easier time. On the other hand, Les now rationalized, better to have no one along than a man harboring bruised feelings about what was being investigated.

One possible advantage to today's arrangement was that Lester had timed the interview for when Collier was off duty. He was hoping it would make the conversation more informal, less interrupted, and—most important—less encumbered by the trappings of duty. Police officers in uniform were more than just imposing in appearance; they could absorb the implied authority of their office into their personalities, becoming harder, less flexible, and more prone to combat—none of which was remotely appealing to the easygoing Spinney.

He was deep in such thoughts and approaching the building's front door, when he sensed a movement off to one side and turned to see a large man getting out of his pickup truck. He was dressed in jeans and a T-shirt, like a hundred thousand other men across the state at that same moment, but there was no mistaking this one's profession—he had the haircut, the eyes, and the cautious but powerful carriage of a cop.

Spinney smiled and stuck his hand out. "Dylan? Les. Thanks for agreeing to this."

Collier shook hands, his watchfulness unchanged. "Sure."

Lester looked around. "You want to go in, or drive someplace to talk? What's your pleasure? I'm happy to front you a cup of coffee."

But Collier was having none of such pleasantries. He pointed to a wooden picnic table on the grass bordering the parking lot, presumably there for lunch breaks. "That's good."

Lester led the way. "Sure. Okay by me."

Collier took the bench facing the lot and the feeder road beyond, forcing Les to expose his back by sitting opposite. This was also typical of the profession—not only did it allow Collier to see any and all potential oncoming threats, but it also placed Spinney at a disadvantage for the same reasons.

Except that Lester played along for exactly that reason. He wanted his subject to feel in control, especially as he recalled Sturdy's comments about Collier's irrationality.

"What's this about?" Collier began without preamble, seemingly used to being called to account by superiors.

"Ryan Paine," Lester said.

The effect was satisfying. Collier scowled, his remote detachment shaken. "What the fuck you want with him?"

"I'm taking another look at the case," Spinney told him, putting aside his earlier delicacy on the subject.

"The hell you are. Why?"

"It's a good idea. High-level case. Lots of distractions at the time. Everybody sticking their nose in, including the press and the politicians. The brass pushing to get it closed. It pays to let a little time go by and go over it again, just to make sure all the t's were crossed."

"You guys aren't busy enough?" Collier asked scornfully. "That's a total crock. You're up to something, and you're not gonna tell me what." He spread his large hands on the tabletop, as if preparing to leave.

"I do have some questions," Lester said. "But I'm looking for your help, not to screw you over. Why would I think you had anything to do with Paine's death?"

Collier's mouth opened. "*What?* Is that what's goin' on? You think I was involved?"

"I think you were never properly interviewed at the time. I think you were blown off as Paine's best buddy and that whatever opinions you might've had got derailed by other priorities. I also think you've had enough time to do some serious thinking about it and that you may be none too comfortable about what's rattling around inside your head."

In fact, Lester was sure of none of those things. The worn adage has it that you shouldn't ask suspects questions to which you don't already know the answers. But that's crap. There are no hard rules, and every once in while, it pays to take a flier into the unknown.

In this case, if nothing else, it got Dylan Collier to settle back into his seat. "What do you want, then?"

"I want to know what happened."

"It was a traffic stop, like we all been warned about from the first day at the academy. It went bad."

"'Cept you never believed it."

Collier hesitated a long time before saying, "No."

"Why not?"

The big man sighed. "It's not that I disagree about how things ended up. It's how they got that way that everybody missed."

Lester filled in the only option he could imagine. "The two men knew each other?"

Collier shook his head. "Don't know 'bout that. They each knew Dee."

Lester kept his voice calm despite a sudden leap in heart rate. In a single short sentence, Collier had revealed the secret cause behind the fulminating outrage that had caught Sturdy so off guard—there was a link between the two dead men. "Ryan Paine's wife?"

"Yeah."

"She was Kennedy's lover?"

"Yup."

"How do you know this?"

Collier straightened, hitched one shoulder, and stared out into the distance momentarily, apparently working his way toward a decision.

"I knew her, too."

Damn, Lester thought. Wait till Sturdy hears about this. "Okay," he said conversationally. "That had to've been a lot to sit on these last few years."

Collier dropped his gaze to his hands, still curled on the tabletop. "Yeah—hasn't been fun."

"You and Dee still an item?" Lester asked, knowing Collier was unmarried.

"Nah. That sorta messed everything up. She's with somebody else now—a cop, of course. Pat Hartnett, out of Wilmington. Plus, I got transferred up here, which put another strain on getting together."

"So," Lester said, his tone carefully offhand. "Tell me what happened."

"It was a setup," Collier said simply. "Kennedy knew Ryan's schedule, got himself pulled over for some bogus infraction, and then popped him—'cept it didn't work as planned."

Lester frowned. "That seems awfully easy. How'd he know Paine wouldn't be on another call? Or grabbing a coffee somewhere?"

"He kept doin' it till it worked."

"How do you know this?"

"Dee told me. Kennedy was pissed she wasn't gonna dump Ryan for him, so he said he'd help make up her mind."

"And nobody said anything after?"

Collier looked at him directly. "Why would we? It was over and done with. Dee didn't know exactly what that peckerhead had planned. She thought it was mostly hot air till the news came Ryan was dead. She called me that night. You wanna blame somebody, be my guest, but I didn't see how any of it would change anything. Ryan and Kennedy were still dead, Dee was still a widow. What was the point? Make a good man look like a fool and maybe fuck up Dee's survivor benefits somehow? That's one reason I went a little nuts at the time, accusing the bosses of throwing troopers under the bus. Ryan had died in the line of duty. More important, he still managed to take out the son of a bitch who killed him. Why tarnish all that by airing his dirty laundry? Who cares if some of the players knew each other?"

Lester challenged him, "So why tell me now?"

Collier paused again, once more scanning the distance for inspiration or solace. "Hell," he eventually said, "here you are. It's like you said, you're lookin' into it. It's clearly never goin' away, like I was hoping. How long would it be before you figured it out?"

He jerked a thumb over his shoulder. "These dumb bastards are achin' to find a way to kick my ass outta here before I reach full retirement. That's one of the reasons they moved me up here. They're not real subtle. I tell you this now, maybe it does go away. I'm cooperating, aren't I? But if I sit on it and make you work for it, whaddya think they'll say? Obstruction." He snapped his thick fingers. "Boom, I'd be history."

His shoulders slumped as he added, "Either way, I'm screwed. I'm just hopin' I'm less screwed this way."

Lester stared at him, once more recalling Sturdy's warning about Collier's mental health. Right now, he was looking like the most clear-sighted among them.

"For what it's worth," he told him, "I think you're doing the right thing. I'll make sure people know that when the time comes."

"Thanks, man," Collier muttered.

"I'll be talking to Dee soon," Lester continued. "But since I have you right here, you mind if I ask you a few questions of a personal nature?"

"Not gonna hold back now."

"I appreciate it. How sure're you that Ryan didn't know what was going on with Dee? Not to be judgmental, but she was cheating on him with two different guys." He stopped and added, "Or was it more? What about her current guy? When did he appear?"

Collier looked at him with a sour expression. "Later, and she wasn't a whore, if that's where you're goin'."

"I'm not," Lester said quickly, not wanting to lose his hard-won goodwill. "It's a reasonable question. I don't know any of you."

The trooper took that in thoughtfully. "Okay. Far as I know, it was just Kennedy and me—and Ryan."

"And how far back did you and she go?"

He smiled slightly. "Years. If it doesn't sound too sick, we were like brother and sister. I guess they call it 'friends with benefits'—somethin' like that. Sounds better, anyhow. Ryan and I were best pals—went through the academy together, worked to get assigned to the same barracks. I guess in that way, it was no surprise we ended up sharing the same woman."

"But he didn't know about it," Lester stated.

"No. He wasn't *that* bighearted. Me and Dee were real sensitive about that—making sure he'd never find out. The way I looked at it, I figured Ryan gave her everything her heart needed, and I gave her . . . Well, the other stuff."

"Ryan wasn't a sexual athlete?"

Collier laughed. "You're a funny guy. You know that? Yeah—that sort of sums it up. He was the greatest friend I'll ever have, but . . . Yeah, I guess he wasn't all that great in the sack. Feels kinda weird sayin' that."

"And where does Kyle Kennedy fit in?" Lester asked.

The other man smiled sheepishly. "Maybe Ryan wasn't the only one who came up a little short?"

Lester couldn't resist laughing. "Really? Did you know she was seeing him before the shooting? I didn't ask you that."

"Nah. But I didn't care. Friends with benefits—remember? That means no attachments."

"Meaning the same didn't hold for her and Kennedy."

Collier looked a little pityingly at him. "I guess not. I sure as hell wasn't running around with a gun to shoot Ryan."

"About that," Lester asked, "did she ever mention Kennedy having a gun, or target shooting? Anything like that?"

"Nope," Collier stated flatly. "Never came up."

"Let's back up," Les requested. "I know it sounds like I'm beating a dead horse, but I want to get this right. How did Dee tell you she'd been seeing Kennedy?"

"That night, when she called. They had a notification team come by, like they do, and offer a chaplain's services or whatever she needed. She turned it all down and then called me. I went over once I was sure she was alone, and that's when she told me."

"Details, Dylan. You know how this works."

"There's not a hell of a lot more to it. She was upset. She opened the door crying and I held her. She'd already told me on the phone Ryan had been killed, and I got more details through the grapevine as I drove over there, you know—workin' the phone. But right at the door, she said, 'Kyle was gunning for him. I didn't know he'd do it,' or something like that. That's when it came out that she'd been sleeping with Kennedy."

"You must've asked why."

"I did, sure. I mean, I didn't even know who the fuck Kyle was at first, much less that they'd been screwin'. It was seriously crazy shit for a few minutes. The way she told it, Kennedy had been growing more and more possessive, and pushing her to dump Ryan."

"How did she feel about that?" Spinney asked, struck by how others had described Kyle's habits with women differently.

"Not good. She loved Ryan. I know none of this sounds like it, but she's a special lady. She's not like other girls. Ryan was the center of her life. People get all hung up on the sex thing, but that wasn't it with her. It was like craving ice cream or some other quick fix. She had a real appetite. But at the center of it, Ryan and she were like that." He held up two fingers, intertwined.

Except, thought Lester, that for Ryan, the "sex thing" probably wasn't so easily equated with a craving for ice cream—nor was his wife's fondness for multiple flavors.

Especially if he'd found out about it.

"Indulge me with something," Lester requested.

"Sure."

"This is just a wild-ass, shot-in-the-dark, what-the-hell hypothesis, okay? It's not a theory, and it's not anything I'm pursuing. But since I got you here, I wanted to fly it by you, given that you know most of the players."

"Okay."

"What if Ryan did know about his wife and Kennedy? He could've pulled him over, killed him, and shot himself before dropping the gun in Kennedy's lap."

Collier stared at him as if he'd suddenly sprouted donkey's ears. His mouth silently formed, "What?" but when he actually did speak, he said, "No aliens from outer space? Damn. I thought I saw a movie deal comin'."

Lester was laughing. "I know, I know. I get it. But here's where I'm going: This whole story rests on Dee telling you that Kennedy was gunning for Ryan. What if she got it wrong? He might've said something threatening, but not actually acted on it. I mean, you have to admit, you wouldn't have come up with a fool stunt like that, would you? Get pulled over in your own vehicle, in a setting that'll guarantee your plate being run before the cop even leaves his car? That is lame, ain't it?"

Collier mulled it over. "I hadn't thought about that. But Ryan offing himself?"

Lester continued fleshing it out. "Let's say he'd discovered not just about Kennedy, but you, too. That would make it his best friend sleeping with his wife, as well as some other guy. If you're right about what Dee meant to him, then he's suddenly looking at his *two* best friends lying to him—you and her, both. Combine that with the way his career was going . . ." Lester let the line peter out.

Collier didn't protest. He looked tired and defeated as he said, "Maybe. Dee sounded so positive, and it *worked*—you know what I'm sayin'? Kennedy goin' after him so he could have her? We see that kind of dumb thinking all the time on the job."

"In retrospect," Lester asked, "and with this in mind, how was Ryan doing during the last month of his life? He must've known he was on the edge of being canned. Did you two talk about that?"

"Some. Not much. He seemed more resigned than depressed—like he was sick of the whole thing anyhow, so who cares? He wasn't having fun anymore."

"Are you?" Lester asked, seemingly out of nowhere.

"Not really," Collier conceded. "But it's a job. I know how to do it. I log in, I log out. When you get the hang of it and keep your head low, it's not too bad."

Neither one of them spoke for a few seconds before Collier commented, "It sounds so far out. I'm havin' a hard time swallowing it."

"You don't have to. It's just an alternate theory. I only wanted to hear your take on it. No big deal."

Collier smiled. "You gotta admit, it would be one hell of a way to go out with a bang. Were you at the funeral?"

"Yeah. Quite the deal."

"No kidding. And talk about a gift to the widow." Collier raised his eyebrows. "Dee made out like a bandit there—double life insurance, workman's comp for a monthly percentage of his salary, and a hunk of his retirement. Just that's close to a hundred grand a year, plus, she got over three hundred grand from the government through the Public Safety Officers' Benefits Program."

He abruptly straightened and fixed Lester with pure fury in his eyes, once more half rising from his seat. "You cocksucker." He leaned forward as Lester leaned back and started wondering how he could disentangle himself from the picnic table's bench before Collier took a swing at him.

"What?" Les half yelled.

"None of that happens if you pin a suicide on him."

"I'm not pinning anything on anybody," Lester complained. "I was spitballing, is all."

"Spitballing, my ass. This is the perfect frame, and you tried to tie me into it."

He brought his huge fist crashing down onto the table's surface. "You bastards. The guy's *dead*!" he shouted. "He died in the line of duty. So what if he wasn't Captain America? He still did his job and paid the ultimate price."

Lester had swung his legs out by now and stood back from the table. "Nobody's saying he didn't, Dylan. Take a breath."

"Fuck you, I'll take a breath. I got Dee telling me what Kennedy told her—that he set up Ryan and got killed in the process 'cause he was a screwup. That's straight from the horse's mouth, as I see it. What d'you got? Some fantasy about a heartbroken cop. Please. That's a crock and you know it." He pounded the table again. "I cannot believe you strung me along like that. What a flamer. Ryan Paine was a hero, you asshole. And all of you're just gonna have to keep shelling out survivor benefits, just like you're supposed to."

With that, he stormed off toward his truck, almost tore off its door, and left leaving twin rooster tails of gravel in his wake.

Lester stood quietly in the following stillness, caught between that explosive display of violence and his own much cooler view of things. Because while what Collier had said was fine and dandy on the surface, it still didn't explain Kennedy's prints being forged on the murder weapon.

CHAPTER TWENTY-TWO

"Have you even been home, boss?" Sam asked, giving Joe a hug at the office's doorway.

He smiled, patting her back while taking in the others in the room. "And miss this? I took a different flight from Mom and Leo, straight to Burlington. They were fine with it once I explained what you all were up to. You know what this mysterious USB is yet?"

"Just about to be briefed," she replied, eyeing him carefully. She was amused that her otherwise dependably avuncular, steady, and methodical boss had given her a teenager's rationalization about why he'd flown to Burlington rather than straight home. He may well have been interested in the contents of the USB. Who in the room wasn't? But he could have just as easily learned of them in an email, or face-to-face with Sammie in Brattleboro three hours from now. The missing link, of course, was Hillstrom, whom he hadn't seen in far too long. Sam could empathize.

Out of courtesy and the spirit of cooperation, they were at the Burlington PD, rather than at the VBI office, so Joe's next move was to extend his hand to Mike McReady. "Sam's been keeping me informed. You've been a rock, as always, Mike. Much appreciated."

"You're welcome, Joe," McReady replied. "How's your mom doin'?"

"For all intents and purposes? A hundred percent. In retrospect, it was the craziest thing, but—to use her words and not mine—for an old bat, she's as good as new."

Formalities followed, with the newly arrived Gunther being introduced to everyone in the room, including a thin, high-strung young man sitting before a computer console, who was transparently waiting for all these good ol' boys to settle down.

McReady finally granted the man's wish by stating, "Ned, here, was about to give us a show-and-tell concerning the thumb drive. He's already given me his recommendation, but if we all agree with it, there's not much time to pull it off. Ned? Take it away."

Ned hit a key and lit up the screen. "Not much to tell," he said in a fast staccato. "The drive contains data, and that data is encrypted." He pointed to the image displaying what appeared to be a chaotic blizzard of letters and numbers.

"No way to decode it?" someone asked.

"Not fast. The easiest solution would be to have the password."

McReady nudged Joe in the arm, saying in a stage whisper, "This is where it gets really interesting."

Ned pulled the drive from the computer and held it up. "And this Trojan horse," he explained, "is the way to get it. It's also," he added as an aside, "why I never use these things."

"Everybody uses thumb drives," a voice complained.

"Everybody puts their credit card information on the internet, too," Ned countered. "And uses their smartphones like the entire world wasn't looking over their shoulder."

As the drive was in fact wedded to the sunglasses temple, he twirled it before them between his thumb and index like a bent swizzle stick. "There are stick drives that have at least some element of protection," he began. "And there are high-security drives that're pretty reliable. This is neither of those. In exchange for the way-groovy design feature that makes it a pair of shades, and in order to keep it affordable, they used a cheap-ass USB stick."

He held up a finger to further focus his attentive audience. "On top of that, whoever owns this also made a personal error, because it's not the whole stick that's encrypted here, but just the file I showed you. That means that the rest of the device is available to us, just like the empty belly of the real Trojan horse."

Joe smiled, less at the language and style of the speaker, and more at his own pleasure to be at last among such company again. Much as he loved his mother and was pleased by her recovery, he was delighted to be back where he belonged.

"In layman's terms, what that allows us to do," Ned was saying, "is to infect the drive with a virus that will allow us to read everything on it after the owner types in his password. That means the encrypted file."

"Hold on, hold on," one of the cops protested. "What? How?"

Ned had been well trained to the sliding scale of his audience's computer savviness. Without breaking stride, he said, "We emplace a virus, which gives us two options. When the bad guy gets his drive back, he'll shove it into his computer to make sure everything's copacetic. Option one is that even if he runs a virus detector, we'll get to watch everything he does on that computer, from then on, because our virus will be privately sending it to us, undetected.

"Option two is that, since I just made a copy of the encrypted data, if all we get back is the password for some reason, that'll be enough, since we'll be able to use it to access the data. Needless to say, it'll be a lot more convenient and entertaining if Door Number One opens wide."

"Is any of that legal?"

Sam answered, "I ran it by the AG an hour ago. They called their Albany counterpart, since we're working on the premise that that's where this gizmo's from. Everybody's good to go."

"And we watch everything?"

"Just like in the movies," Ned replied, "assuming the internet's up and running. It's not instantaneous. The stick's got to stay in the computer for a couple of minutes to shake hands, but it'll take that long for the user to double-check its contents. After that, it doesn't matter. He can remove the stick and we'll still be able to monitor his every keystroke."

"I'm the new boy on the block," Joe said, "so I apologize if you already covered this. But what's the plan for getting the drive back into the bad guy's hands without his knowing we've fooled with it?"

McReady answered him obliquely: "We just removed the BOL on the man who killed Charlotte Robinson."

He showed Joe a slightly blurry but telling surveillance still of a man standing before a building entrance. "We think that's him. He used a badge to con his way into watching the college's campus security footage of Rachel bumping into Charlotte. To give the campus cops credit, the guy's credentials checked out via computer; it was only a phone call to the issuing agency that told us they'd never heard of him. Based on UVM's description and our going through their footage of the facility's front door—we got this image. The campus cops confirmed he's the man."

Joe nodded. "So you're going to put the dark glasses back where you found them, and open the apartment back up."

"Right," Sam said. "Until we found the thumb drive, we thought this dude was after Charlotte's phone, 'cause it was the one item that was missing. Now, with this"—she pointed at the computer—"we're thinking it's a good bet he missed what he came for."

"Meaning he'll finish the job if he sees an opportunity."

McReady gave him a lopsided smile. "Fingers crossed."

He then turned to the rest of the team in the room. "Everybody on board? Any more questions for Ned?"

"We gonna watch the place?" one of them asked.

"Yes, but we're not going crazy. It'll be low-key. The point of this is that the thumb drive itself will be our messenger. If we catch sight of the intruder and can slap a tail on him, great. That'll be our bonus. But I don't want to mess up the whole point of the operation."

"He's a murder suspect," the same man reminded him. "And now we're giving away a prime piece of evidence."

"Yes, he is and we are. But if we're right about this, and he was put in place by a higher-up, wouldn't it be nice to nail 'em both?"

A general silence greeted this, prompting McReady to collect the glasses temple from Ned and hand it to Sam. "It's all yours. I'll give our patrol officer at the apartment the heads-up. To fade away after you put that back."

"Then we wait," Joe commented.

"Then we wait," Mike agreed.

The meeting broke up, with most participants filing out of the room.

"You heading straight home?" Sam asked Joe nonchalantly.

"Oh . . . Well. I'm already here," he replied. "Might as well drop by and see Beverly."

Sammie laughed, confirmed in her earlier suspicion. "Right—might as well. Say hi for me."

Nick Gargiulo slowed down and did a double take before resuming his speed and continuing down St. Paul Street. There had been no yellow tape visible toward the back of the target's apartment building. Nor had there been the usual police car parked in the narrow driveway, as there had been for the past couple of days. Could it be the cops had released their crime scene?

He continued to Kilburn and turned right, parking in the large lot at the end of the block. It was dark, and late, and raining slightly, which suited his purposes, reducing visibility and the likelihood of people wandering around.

Dressed in black, including a hat, Nick soon became almost invisible as he stealthily and painfully worked his way north—limping still from the blow Rachel had delivered to his knee—to a mosaic of backyards approaching the rear of Rachel's apartment building.

It took some doing, cutting through hedges, squeezing between rotting cars, and watching for rubbish piled behind buildings like trash caught in a river eddy, but eventually he tucked into the shade of a neighboring house and began studying the building as the rain dripped off the edge of his hat.

What he'd seen from the street was confirmed—the cops had walked away and the place looked unoccupied.

The question was: What had they left behind?

Nick took his time, slowed by his handicap. He lived in a world where people watched each other, anticipating weaknesses, looking for openings. It was not beyond possibility that these hayseed cops were up to something, despite their inability to locate him during the previous forty-eight hours.

As a result, he moved smoothly, soundlessly, his eyes on every window and car, careful to note anything even slightly untoward—an unexplained movement, one curtain drawn aside, an exhaust plume from a seemingly empty vehicle.

But everything checked out, and he eventually reached the building's back entrance, his leg throbbing, but otherwise relatively comfortable about not having been seen.

Reinforcing the notion, as he removed his muddy shoes in the shared entryway, he heard the downstairs neighbors chatting softly against the background of a TV program, lending an air of returned normalcy to the scene.

Not unlike the first time he'd come here.

He moved slowly up the darkened staircase, still suspicious of a trap, using his good leg to pull the rest of him up, one step at a time. At the landing, however, after bypassing the front door lock as easily as before, he grew more confident. Ahead of him, the apartment loomed dark and silent, its very atmosphere bespeaking the loss it had suffered.

He was impressed by the mess the cops had created. He looked around, using the ambient glow of the surrounding city as an aid, and identified some of the damage he'd caused, directly or not.

Finally, he pulled out a small flashlight, cupped it in his hand, and turned it on, letting its beam leak into the room only gradually, between his fingers, so as not to attract attention from outside the nearby windows.

It took a while, which he found reassuring, but eventually, by progressing quadrant by quadrant, as if mapping an archeological site, he came to the armchair by the hallway and found the dark glasses almost completely wedged between the pillows.

Smiling, he pocketed the light, crossed the room, and took the glasses apart by the window, admiring the slight glimmer of the thumb drive's silver tip.

"Gotcha, you son of a bitch," he congratulated himself.

He added the glasses to the light in his pocket and, moving awkwardly but still silently, retreated the way he'd come. By the time he was back outside, shoes on and hat pulled low, it had been no more than twenty minutes.

After all the hassle, expense, time, misery, and pain, he could hardly believe this soap opera was finally about to end.

He was looking forward to a small vacation after this job.

"You get it all?" the one cop asked his partner.

The latter waited a moment for the man's shadow across the street to fully disappear back into the nearby bushes, before he operated a few controls on his tripod-mounted video camera in order to check his night vision footage. "Yeah. Let 'em know he's headed back to his car."

The first observer dialed his phone to make the call.

* * *

On the other side of the state, Willy Kunkle, similarly dressed in black, was crouched beside a pile of ancient building debris, on the edge of what used to be the Goodyear plant in Windsor—now an enormous, rubble-strewn slab.

A slab with a view, however, which did not include the peaceful Connecticut River or the New Hampshire forestland beyond it—now cloaked in darkness, a slight fog, and the same light rain that had shrouded Nick Gargiulo. What Willy was intent on was an old factory building in the middle distance, at the dead end of National Street, where Chris Walker, still being babysat, had said Rob Haag kept his workshop.

Willy had put himself in an awkward position—hardly a novelty, given his methods. He had assembled, against the odds and in violation of several rules of engagement, what he thought of as evidence of a federal crime.

But because of the way he'd gone about it, he was now stuck on how to carry it home legally.

Always resourceful, however, he was hoping that one last bit of unconventional investigating would supply him the missing piece to convince the likes of Special Agent Dorman—if not him personally—and present a credible narrative of cause and effect.

Willy had discovered early in his career that because cops often collected clues on their own, it fell to them to choose how best to present them. Police officers are trained to walk the straight and narrow—to reflect the truth at all times, regardless of consequences. They also learn almost as quickly the value of "officer discretion," with which they are supposed to act on that truth, depending on its context. Thus a little old lady with no prior speeding violations might be given a pass, despite having been caught driving too fast.

Willy had taken this practical, reasonable, occasionally used leeway and virtually made it his life's work. He was the master of officer discretion, and an expert at pitching the essence of a case, regardless of how he'd acquired its facts.

Inside the dark, still, forbidding embrace of the decrepit building before him, therefore, he was hoping to find the missing connective tissue between one Pakistani importer, three teeth and a charcoaled battery, and the supplier of power cells to military drones.

Either that, or he was going to have to explain having recently wasted so much time, bent so many rules, and irritated so many people, especially Sam—not to mention broken a few laws.

He stepped away from his cover at last and walked stealthily toward his goal, which was built in the classic hundred-year-old, flat-roofed, New England industrial style of stained brick and multiple tall windows. Ubiquitous when the entire region was a manufacturing powerhouse— and Yankee ingenuity the envy of emerging nations globally—such structures were now commonly deemed as monumental perhaps, but also drafty, inefficient, and probably built on chemical waste.

This one had found a way to survive both the wrecker's ball and being turned into condos by renting itself out piecemeal to entrepreneurs and small operators needing a little elbow room in which to function— sometimes discreetly.

The beauty of the architecture for Willy, however, lay not in its history but in its array of potential entry points—loading docks, equipment bays, garage doors, office entrances, and windows, to name a few. It didn't take long for him to find an overlooked opening only half covered by a flimsy piece of plywood.

Once inside, dry and free of incidental scrutiny, he took his time to decode the building's floor plan and pick his way toward what Walker had described as Haag's second-floor shop.

He'd entered at the back of a wood furniture manufacturer, its atmosphere rich with sawdust, glue, and varnish. Around him, silhouetted against the town's foggy lights through the windows, were spindly drill presses, vacuum hoses, overhead power cords, and robotic-looking band

saws and lathes—a crowd of silent, powerful, seemingly watchful senti-
nels through which he slipped without a sound.

The neighboring business dealt with automotive body work. Here
the odor was harsh and toxic, as industrial as the wood shop's had been
seductively artisanal. Willy made sure to stay clear of any counters, concerned that he might sideswipe a paint container or a precariously placed
grinder. Where the first place had been meticulously clean and neat,
this one was a mess, a potential obstacle course, all coated with a fine
gray dust.

It did have access to a central hallway, however, which in turn contained a broad wooden staircase heading up. At its base, Willy could just
make out the faint sound of distant music drifting down.

Curious, he stole his way up, pausing at each step and testing it for
creaks and groans. But they were all as old as the rest of the building,
and as settled in place as boulders. The only sound he ended up making
came from his own breathing.

On the second floor, the music louder, he found himself facing a
matching hallway, this one featuring a single glass door, about halfway
down its length. Light spilled out onto the worn wooden floor, remind-
ing him that when he'd been studying the factory's dark exterior, he
noticed two boarded-over upper-floor windows. Now he knew why.

He moved to the door and peered inside. The room beyond was vast
and high-ceilinged, but unlike its brethren below, it had few towering
tools or draping air-filtration equipment. It was more of a waist-level assembly plant—a row of end-on tables snaking through the room's center,
each loaded with serious-looking boxy apparatuses, their applications
arcane and oddly threatening in appearance. Articulated desk lamps accompanied most of them, creating a succession of lighted islands that
marched off in a line into the distance, leaving the rest of the vaulting
room in gloomy shadow.

Willy stayed put long enough to pinpoint the one human who was
supposedly accountable for the light and music—a thin, distant figure

wearing a lab coat and a circular fixture around his head equipped with magnifier lenses and a pair of powerful LED lights. He was intent on his labors, bent at the waist, his face inches from his work.

As confident as he could be that he and the mysterious lab tech were alone—Robb Haag, according to the employee photograph Al Summers had supplied earlier—Willy gingerly turned the doorknob and quietly stepped into the room, crouching low so that he was shielded by the first row of tables.

What he was seeking was simplicity itself—a single glimpse at Haag's end product. But despite carefully looking around, he could see no pile of rectangular, battery-like objects anywhere nearby. There were some next to Haag, mostly near the far wall, since that was the terminus of this peculiar assembly line. But at Willy's end, there were scant pickings. Significantly, also within Haag's reach, hanging on the same wall, were several large-caliber weapons, both pistols and long guns, semi- and fully automatic.

Willy began to work his way forward, maintaining his cover by crawling beneath the line of tables. This was no easy feat. Not only did the tables' underpinnings get in the way, but Willy's useless arm threw him badly off balance besides, forcing him to proceed slowly, awkwardly, and at considerable risk of making a noisy mistake. As before, the music proved as useful to him as to the lonely battery maker.

About a quarter of the way along, yielding to his contorted approach, he paused for a breather and to ease his aching body, sitting on the floor to stretch out for a moment.

That is when a loud, persistent buzzer went off directly above his head, sounding like a neighborhood fire alarm.

Almost immediately, he heard Haag say something to himself, followed by his footsteps approaching. Willy ducked down farther to see the man's legs headed his way, bathed in the halo of each successive pool of light.

Haag stopped two feet away, his toes pointed directly at Willy.

Overhead, Willy heard him open what sounded like a microwave oven and extract something hard that rattled on the tabletop. There was some more noise, of a practiced and rhythmic nature, like a repetitive task, before Haag stepped back, placed something on the adjacent table—presumably whatever it was he'd removed from the microwave—and returned to his point of origin.

Willy took advantage of Haag's retreat to roll soundlessly out into the aisle and move quickly, crouched over, along a parallel track, keeping well out of the other man's sight line.

It worked. Haag never broke stride, and returned to his labors almost instantly, happily on task. From his new vantage point, Willy could not only see the production line better, but also was close enough now to the stacked finished products to crawl along the floor for a few more yards, reach up, and remove a sample to carefully examine it.

What he saw supplied the missing piece he'd been seeking. The object in his hand was indeed a lithium-ion battery, shrink-wrapped, pristine, and equipped with wires to be plugged into its receiving unit. Most tellingly, it was colored army green and stamped with the logo of Al-Tech Industries.

Willy took a photo of it with his phone, returned it to its place, and quietly left Robb Haag to enjoy his music.

Beverly's expression blossomed as she looked up from her paperwork. "Joe," she said. "You made it in one piece."

She rose as he entered her office and they met beside her desk, folding around each other and kissing.

"You had doubts?" he teased, pulling back slightly.

"I only doubt the airlines," she replied, kissing him again. "My God, it's good to see you."

"Me, too," he told her. Holding her as close as he dared without cutting off her breathing. He could hardly believe how good she felt.

"You got a lot left to do?" he asked.

She looked up into his eyes. "And delay taking you to bed?" she asked with mock horror. "Not on your life. And I hope you ate earlier, 'cause you're not getting dinner for a couple of hours yet. I am going to see to that."

"I think I can cope," he said, running his hands down her back.

CHAPTER TWENTY-THREE

Joe sat on the edge of his desk and cast a fond look over his three investigators. "As hard as you may find this to believe, I have missed you guys something wicked."

"Your trip west must've been tougher than we thought," Willy cracked.

Sammie shook her head, as expected. "What he's trying not to say, boss, is that we're glad you're back and we hope your mom's in good shape."

"She is," Joe told them. He nodded toward Willy before adding, "Thank you for your touching concern."

Willy smiled. "Don't mention it. You gonna snap our leashes now that you've made nice?"

"So smooth," Lester said softly, as if to himself.

"Actually, no," Joe said good-naturedly. "I have been reading the dailies and talking with Sam throughout, so I know as much as you've been willing to admit." He gazed at Willy pointedly before continuing. "That makes me knowledgeable about some things, less so about others. What I'd like to propose is a more measured reentry. You three keep going with your separate investigations, and I'll play backup, catch any new cases, and take back the administrative duties Sam's been juggling." He looked directly at her. "Unless you've taken a liking to them, of course."

She looked slightly horrified. "No, no. Thanks for the vote of confidence, but if I never have to do that again, I'll be a happy woman."

"Maybe so," he said, "although from the Director's report card, you did very well under tough circumstances."

She looked slightly embarrassed, so he kept going. "Speaking of which, what's the current status of the Robinson homicide?"

"Last night," she responded, "the man we suspect killed Charlotte took the bait. He returned to the apartment and grabbed the USB-rigged glasses. The surveillance team Mike McReady put on it caught him on tape. They also recorded his vehicle registration and placed a GPS on the car. As we hoped, he made a beeline for Albany."

"He contact your lawyer guy?" Lester asked. "What's his name?"

"Wylie. Jared Wylie. No, that would've been too easy. He returned the car to a rental agency in Troy, and that's where the tag team lost him. So right now, we're waiting for some computer—Wylie's, if there's a God—to deliver the password after the drive's been plugged in."

"Which is presumably when we find out what cost Robinson her life," Joe suggested.

"Right."

"Is everyone sure the guy who took the glasses is the same one who killed the girl?" Willy asked.

Sam picked up a mug shot from her desk. "Yup. Name's Dominic 'Nick' Gargiulo. Military background, impressive rap sheet, definite ties to Wylie. He lives and works in Albany. This photograph has gotten us three confirmations: from the tag team last night, the car rental clerk when he turned in the vehicle he used in Burlington, and from UVM security, who ran his fake credentials before they helped him identify Charlotte as she was getting off the bus. Not to mention," she added, "that he's now walking with a serious limp, thanks to Rachel swatting him with that frying pan."

Joe turned to Willy. "And the mystery of the missing teeth? That's been a little underreported in the dailies."

Willy actually laughed, his mood—unknown to the rest of them—lifted by the results of the previous night's field trip. "This has turned out like a Sherlock Holmes story," he reported. "As far as I can tell, I've got one last egg to crack before I can deliver the full omelet, but I finally got a good idea what's goin' on."

"You want to share?" Sam asked sarcastically but with a smile, "or is this gonna be another rabbit out of the hat?"

Even Willy was a little sensitive about the toes he'd stepped on in Springfield, although he hadn't heard a word from Alex Dorman about having bushwhacked Sunny Malik. As a result, he was less coy with his response than he might have been.

"If I'm interpreting everything right," he said, "I think we stumbled over a plot to screw up a supply line of parts to the military."

"The battery you wrote about?" Joe asked. "Sabotage? Really?"

"Yeah. I'm hanging it all on one source telling me that the bogus energy cells are being made faulty in order to discredit the manufacturer, but the story fits everything else I've found out, so I want to chase down one last missing piece to make sure. And before you ask, yes, I will then generously lay it out before the appropriate federal law enforcement agency so that they can carve another notch on their bedpost and totally ignore our contribution. I've already made a courtesy call to Homeland Security."

"Okay," Joe said slowly, used to Willy's highly interpretive style. "But if you're uncomfortable laying it out here and now, might you want some backup anyhow?"

Willy astonished the entire room by saying, "Actually, yeah, I would. You volunteering?"

Joe didn't hide his surprise. "Sure. You got it."

He then gazed at Lester. "And how're you doing with both feet in a political quagmire? You wish your forensics friend had never called you about those fingerprints?"

Lester didn't need to go into as much background, since he'd been filing his case notes regularly, like Sam. Nevertheless, he hadn't updated his narrative since speaking with Dylan Collier.

"It is getting murkier, I'll give you that," he said. "Turns out Dee Rollins—Ryan Paine's grieving widow—has no middle gear when it comes to men. So far, I've found out she was sleeping with Paine; Kyle Kennedy; Paine's best friend, Dylan Collier—who gave me all this—and is now with a fourth one, who works for Wilmington PD. The first three were all at the same time, and the last one might've been, too, for all I know now.

"I'm already sure we're no longer dealing with just a trooper pulling some dude over and exchanging gunshots. The problem's become figuring out the choreography. Did Kennedy lure Paine by driving up and down that stretch like a maniac, waiting to be stopped? That's what Collier says Dee Rollins told him. Or did Paine lie in wait and ambush Kennedy because he was sleeping with his wife, and then get surprised 'cause Kennedy was packing heat? And in either case, what's the story behind the phony fingerprints on Kennedy's gun, which mysteriously went missing just prior to the shooting anyhow?

"I even took a flier and suggested to Collier that maybe Paine, distraught over his wife's cheating and knowing he was about to be fired, committed suicide somehow, at once killing his rival and coming out like a dead hero. Collier went ballistic, of course, since it sounded like I was trying to deprive Dee of her survivor benefits, but he didn't argue that Paine was bummed out about his career nose-diving."

Willy was chuckling and shaking his head. "Jesus, and I thought I had it bad with counterfeit mil-spec drone batteries. You should write for the movies. That's some crazy shit."

Lester laughed in agreement. "You think I don't know it? This thing's driving me nuts, mostly because I know when I put it on paper, the *Titanic*'s gonna look like a fender bender. Collier reminded me how many cops showed up for Paine's memorial. It's gonna be just swell telling 'em all that our hero's something else."

"But you know where you're headed with it?" Joe asked.

Spinney nodded. "I obviously got to have a sit-down with Dee. But staring at the ceiling last night in bed, I've also thought of another angle I want to look at first—just for what-the-hell."

Joe didn't press him. "Okay. Sounds good." He stood up. "Let's all get to it."

Lester stopped him, however, by reaching under his desk. "Almost, boss. Since you're heading home right now to find out who's been eating your porridge while you been away, I figured you might like company."

He pulled out Joe's cat carrier and placed it on his desk, to where Gilbert could see through the door and spy his roommate. He let out a meow and stuck a paw through the bars, to everyone's laughter.

Joe crossed over, opened the door, and took the cat into his arms, where the two of them touched noses.

"You gotta be kidding," Willy commented. "Really?"

Joe raised an eyebrow at him. "Hey, you can't be the only one to have a small creature love you."

The angle that Lester hadn't detailed at the meeting came to him during one of his routine rituals. In the dark, in bed, with Sue's rhythmic breathing for company—on the nights she wasn't at work—he liked to review the past day's events. Or, as this time, a case's inner workings. With no one to disturb him or ask distracting questions, he would let his mind wander among the details, as if window-shopping along a narrow, twisting, highly commercial street.

It was in that context, in the moonlit bedroom, that he recalled Sturdy Foster's offhand comment about the lack of gunshot residue either on Kyle Kennedy's hand or clothing.

At the time, he'd thought of how revolvers are more prone to leave such a deposit—the nature of a revolver's cylinder is such that there's a gap between where the cartridge resides and the opening to the barrel through which the fired bullet passes. It is that "cylinder gap"—not present in a semiautomatic gun—that typically allows a microscopic side-spray of burned gunpowder to escape.

In the commonly accepted scenario of the Kennedy–Paine confrontation, investigators like Sturdy had pictured Kyle Kennedy shooting one bullet into Ryan Paine through his open left window—meaning, since he was a righty, that he would most likely have held the revolver across the front of his chest.

This was not an absolute. Lester realized that. Kennedy might've twisted his body around or held his hand out the window. There were several explanations possible for why no cylinder gap powder stain had been found running lengthwise down the front of his T-shirt—or, for that matter, any blowback found on his shooting hand.

But Lester wasn't happy with some vaguely acceptable hypothesis. Even with all the political brouhaha at the time, the pressure to move fast, and feeling the loss of a colleague, his instinct would have been to take a very close look at Kennedy's car. The gunshot residue may have reasonably ended up somewhere other than Kennedy's chest, after all.

But that was the definition of Monday-morning quarterbacking. Nevertheless, before dropping off to sleep, Les had told himself to at least try to locate that car—even three years later.

It was not an absurd notion, not in Vermont. Old cars didn't vanish with the alacrity they did in major urban areas to the south. There, sheer numbers promoted efficiency—there were too many out-of-commission vehicles, too little space to absorb them, and too much money to be made recycling old metal.

In the rural north woods, however, the exact opposite was true. Locals even referred to an abandoned car—usually still sitting in a front yard—as a Vermont planter. Cars and trucks were driven for much longer than they were elsewhere, and when finally retired, they often ended up in an ex-pasture. Roaming along Vermont's back roads, one frequently came across a cluster of such retirees, sitting weed-choked by the dozen, side by side or stacked, often behind a sagging barn, awaiting a poorly defined future.

It tended to be a leisurely holding pattern, with vehicles resting sometimes for years between active service and demise in a smelter's cauldron—if ever.

The next morning, Lester got on the phone and, step by step, traced the route that Kyle Kennedy's bloodstained car had taken from its release as evidence by the crime lab. An hour later, he had the address of a substantially sized auto graveyard not far from the lab's location in Waterbury, near the center of the state.

When he arrived there two hours later, it turned out to be fairly typical of its kind—less a car and truck repository and more an old-fashioned junkyard, including everything from vehicles to large appliances to, in this case, a small herd of goats and some chickens.

A short gray-haired woman exited the farmhouse beside the dirt driveway when he pulled up.

"You the one who called?" she yelled at him before he'd fully rolled to a stop.

"Yes, ma'am," he said out the window.

She marched over and stood by the door as he unfolded himself from behind the wheel.

"Goodness," she said, checking him out. "You're a tall one."

"So I've been told," he replied, not commenting on the fact that she had to be under five feet, easily.

"Well," she told him, "I hate to be the bearer of bad news, but you'll probably be wanting to get right back into that car, 'cause the one you talked about is a good half mile down the way." She gestured toward the back of the house, where the driveway continued parallel to the piled junk he'd noticed coming in, over a small knoll, and around an outcropping of trees.

"Fine with me," he said, holding out a photograph. "It still look like this?"

She glanced at Kyle Kennedy's worn, dented, partially rusty sedan, documented at the lab on the day it had been brought in on a flatbed.

"Yup," she confirmed. "It's a whole lot dustier, but that's her. I wouldn't be likely to forget that one."

He slid back into his seat. "I bet. I'll check it out, then."

"Not without these, you won't." She dangled a set of keys before him, smiling.

He took them. "You're right. It's been locked all this time?"

She laughed. "Yup, despite the hundreds of people I get every day, asking to take a bloodstained beater out for a spin."

He joined her. "Okay. Dumb question. Thank you."

She stepped back to let him leave. "They say there're no dumb questions." The look on her face told him what she thought of that.

She was right about the dust, but once he'd found the car, parked perpendicular to the road, Lester was impressed by how unchanged it looked—as if someone had abandoned it at a drive-in theater long ago. He even glanced over his shoulder as he swung out of his car a second time, to check for a weather-beaten outdoor screen. What he saw instead were a few more of the wandering goats.

Nodding to them politely, he opened his back door and pulled out an evidence-gathering kit he'd brought along, which he deposited next to Kennedy's front passenger side door.

It was a sylvan scene, next to the field, complete with the goats, chirping birds, and a scattering of cumulus clouds against a bright blue sky—quite a contrast with what he encountered upon unlocking the door and swinging it wide against protesting rusty hinges.

Lester waited a moment for the faint breeze to whisk away the stale and rancid odor that hit him like a fog. Immediately before him, a few sharply angled drops of blood spatter led across the passenger seat's fabric like the tail of a meteor toward an age-blackened lump of gore, concentrated where Kennedy had sat, bleeding out from his heart wound.

Lester stood studying all this for a while, interpreting what he saw, section by section, some no larger than a playing card. He'd analyzed the crime photos earlier—the ones featuring Kennedy's body still in place—and now mentally superimposed the two sets of images.

They checked out. Everything confirmed what investigators had found—a man, dead of a gunshot to the chest delivered from an angle consistent with the open driver's window, had died in that seat. What projected blood there was had been deposited logically, thinning and spreading outward as it had traveled toward the vehicle's right side. The droplets that he could decipher—mostly the ones still adhering to hard surfaces—all pointed toward the point of origin.

It was textbook, and spoke without question of Ryan Paine's discharging his weapon at Kennedy, and catching him with devastating, close-range force.

Lester let his gaze return to where it had begun, on the passenger side. As befit the pacing of the initial investigation, the car's interior did not reflect a crime lab's full-fledged efforts. This had not been a who-dunit; no suspect was going to be facing charges in court later, where evidence would be presented. As a result, no swatches had been cut out for preservation, and no chemical stains left behind where tests had been conducted to support the sequence of events.

This had been a slam dunk. Sad, perhaps; "tragic," in the vernacular of the media. But easy. No muss, no fuss.

For Lester—now—that was good news. Although it had been three years, the car had gone straight from the lab to here and sat, pristine, locked up, and undisturbed. The family hadn't wanted it, for obvious reasons, and similarly, no one had expressed a desire to buy it. For his purposes—even though the technical chain of custody had long been broken—the car was an intact crime scene.

He looked directly before him. The fabric covering the right seat's vertical back section—as is commonly the case in cars—had suffered little wear or tear over time. Most Americans drive alone, and when they do have company, those companions usually drop their food and soda—or leave their paw prints—on the seat. Not against the back.

Lester leaned in so that his eyes were inches from the pale gray cloth, like a naturalist reading a butterfly's pattern. What he found is what had caught his imagination in the middle of the night and made his mind race at the possibilities.

He straightened, satisfied, and unsnapped the evidence case at his feet, extracting a cardboard box from a side compartment. From this in turn, he removed a small sheet covered with a slightly sticky substance, and an equally compact, flexible vial with a small quantity of fluid within it.

He methodically dabbed the sheet against the back of the car seat, working from top to bottom, dropped it into a plastic bag with a zipper-like seal—alongside the small vial—and crushed the vial to expose the sheet to the fumes of the vial's contents. Holding the bag up to his eye a couple of minutes later, he smiled as the sheet became speckled with a small galaxy of distinct blue dots.

"Son of a gun," he murmured happily.

CHAPTER TWENTY-FOUR

"Where're we going?" Willy asked, having just followed his boss's instruction to bypass the exit leading to Burlington, in order to stay on I-91, heading due north.

Despite Willy's general contempt for his fellow human beings, he liked Joe Gunther and enjoyed his company, and not only for the latitude that the older man routinely afforded him. There was a steadiness to Joe, a reliability that transcended their occasional disagreements, which had created a trust that Willy otherwise reserved solely for Sam.

Not that he would ever express any of that, of course.

"Little detour," Joe said. "If it's okay with you."

"Hey," Willy replied. "It's your dime."

Joe left it at that as they passed Hartford and Hanover and continued toward Thetford, some twelve miles on.

"You're kidding," Willy commented, suddenly recognizing the significance of following Joe's directions.

"Nope," Joe said. "I wanted to drop by anyhow, and it occurred to me you two had never met."

Willy let out a cautious grunt. "Okay."

The Gunther farm, where Joe had been born and raised, was almost

within sight of the exit. It wasn't large, even by Vermont standards—
tracts of it had been sold off over the years to set up a fund for Joe's
mother and lessen the burden on Leo. Nevertheless, the house still had
a couple of fields in proximity, and its appearance hadn't changed since
Joe and Leo minimally helped their father as kids.

Given the spontaneous nature of this impulse, Joe was pleased to see
the family car—usually at work with Leo—parked outside the attached
barn containing several less-than-perfect "classics" from the '60s, as Leo
put it, in which he was known to cruise the neighborhood, generally
with one of his fair-weather girlfriends.

Indeed, as they rolled to a stop, Leo appeared at the front door of
the house, his arms spread wide and a broad smile on his face—his
pleasure enhanced when he saw that Willy, whom he'd met only once
before, was at the wheel.

He marched over to Kunkle and gave him a bone-crushing hug,
which Joe could see Willy just barely resisted responding to with gunfire. Touchy-feely he was not—something Leo routinely ignored with
everyone.

"Willy," he now said with genuine pleasure. "A sight for sore eyes.
How long's it been?"

"Not long," Kunkle replied in a monotone.

"Well, it feels like it." Leo threw an arm across his shoulder. "How's
the bouncing baby girl? She's got to be roaring around like the Energizer
Bunny nowadays."

"She's fine," Willy said, as uncomfortable as if he'd been dressed in a
tutu at a funeral.

They all three began walking toward the house, with Leo still talking. "And Sam? Still happy balancing motherhood, crooks, and trying to
figure you out?"

"Yeah."

"Good luck on the last one, right?" Leo gave him a final squeeze before releasing him in order to throw open the door. Willy gratefully

entered the house in a near rush, leaving the two brothers behind to exchange conspiratorial smiles.

"You're a bad person," Joe whispered as he followed suit.

"You just say that 'cause Mom likes me more," Leo said.

"I heard that," came a woman's voice from beyond the mudroom. "You boys cut that out. We have a guest."

On cue, Joe motioned to Willy, who was more uneasy by the second, to pass through the far door.

They entered a living room, the true core of the house, where the boys' mother had long ago established her command center—a semicircular gathering of tables surrounding her wheelchair and loaded with books, newspapers, magazines, and remotes for radio, television, and various lights around the room, in case she wanted to take a nap. To Joe, the setup had always seemed like a Disney fantasy of an old lady who ran the world from her quaint, rural farmhouse.

Willy stood stock-still before her, at a loss, like a boy facing the principal.

Joe's mother stuck out her hand. "Mr. Kunkle, I presume? I hope you'll forgive my son's bad manners. Both of them, for that matter."

Willy quickly obliged by shaking hands. "Mrs. Gunther. Nice to meet you."

"By the looks of things, I doubt I was on your list of things to do today."

Willy half smiled. "No, ma'am."

She pointed to a seat by her chair. "Make yourself comfortable for a while. I'll let you go in under fifteen minutes, I promise. It shouldn't be too painful."

Willy obliged her as she fixed her sons with a glance. "And you two can retire to the kitchen, make us some tea, and talk about me in my absence. Sound good?"

Joe nodded. "Outstanding. Will do."

"Glad to hear you're doing better," Willy said after the other two had noisily retreated.

"Thank you," she said. "It was the oddest thing I've ever experienced, but it apparently left no ill effects, or so they tell me."

"Do you remember anything?"

She turned to better look at him. "Do you know? You're the first person to ask me that. Possibly a reflection of some of your own trials, from what Joe has told me. It can give you a less self-absorbed slant on life, regardless of what many people might say behind your back. I hope you don't mind my saying that."

Willy couldn't help being impressed. "No, ma'am."

"I do recall some things," she continued, "to answer your question. It was like being at the end of a long hallway, where I could see and hear people, but they couldn't do likewise. Or perhaps it was similar to being surrounded by a different culture and language. Neither image addresses the feeling of being awake and anesthetized at the same time. Hard to pin down, as you can see. But thank you for asking."

"Sure."

"How about yourself, if you don't mind the question? How are you holding up, having to care for a wife and small child when you once weren't sure you could care for yourself?"

If Willy had been given to such gestures, his jaw might've dropped open. Typical that it would take such an unlikely source to ask the very question that had been so plaguing him recently.

Instinctively, he tried sidestepping an answer—always one fond of smoke screens. "We're not married."

She laughed. "Well, of course you are. I wasn't talking about some scrap of paper. You don't know for a fact that I was married to the father of those two, do you?"

He smiled at the thought. "I guess I don't."

She kept studying him, awaiting a response. Despite her manners, she was one of the most direct people he'd met. And yet, he instinctively understood that she would either respect his confidences or accept his refusal to answer.

"It's hard sometimes," he admitted, surprised to be opening up to her. "I'm not sure I deserve them. I keep thinking they'd probably be better off without me."

"You consider yourself a handful?" she asked.

He was touched by her persistent concern. "Your son must've told you."

She tilted her head thoughtfully. "Actually, he counts himself lucky to have you around. In my experience—which would never come close to what you've gone through—things are usually much worse inside our heads than they are in fact. We are our own poorest counselors."

They could both hear Joe and Leo approaching from the kitchen, laden with a tray and talking. She took advantage of their remaining few seconds of isolation to reach out and place her hand on Willy's forearm and conclude, "For what it's worth, I think you're in the safest place you've ever been—right now—with all of them."

He turned his hand around to squeeze hers, genuinely moved. "Thank you—more than you know."

"You have a good chat with the old lady?" Joe asked him a half hour later, as they'd resumed their journey toward Burlington.

"Yeah. You lucked out with her."

Joe cast him a sideways glance. "Yeah," he acknowledged. "We all did."

As the two of them approached South Burlington, Willy told Joe of the conversation he'd had with Alan Summers, which ended when Summers had prohibited Willy's access to the factory floor—and thus to Robb Haag's coworkers—because of the company's restrictive contract with the military.

He also explained that Joe was here today less for backup than for the authority implied by his rank. Willy could readily admit that while he was perfectly happy intimidating people, playing toe-to-toe as a bureaucrat could be a challenge.

Joe listened, asked a few questions, and then nodded as they rolled into the parking lot, confirming, "I'll give it my best bluster."

He certainly began well enough once inside, striding up to the same receptionist Willy had seen on his last visit, presenting his credentials, and announcing, "My name is Joe Gunther. I'm the field force commander of the Vermont Bureau of Investigation. You've already met Special Agent Kunkle. We're working on a national security case and need to see Mr. Summers. Could you make that happen?"

The young woman stared in amazement before reaching for the phone. "Sure," she said simply. "I'll let him know you're here."

Joe sensed he probably could've achieved the same result by saying he and Willy were insurance salesmen, but he'd taken his assignment to heart—and with some amusement.

Almost as confirmation, Al Summers looked slightly befuddled when he stepped into the room to greet them, instantly recognizing Willy. "Did something happen?" he asked.

"We'll tell you in your office," Joe answered, reintroducing himself.

Summers ushered them inside, his curiosity plain, and addressed Willy directly. "I should've known you'd be back. It's like everything Robb touches—an immediate problem. What's he done now?"

Joe stayed in character. Without bothering to sit down, he told Summers, "We obviously have to be as circumspect as you about some of this, since it could easily segue into a federal investigation. As you know, Special Agent Kunkle has been in touch with HSI. The good news is, these things can be like isolated spot fires—if you contain them early and limit the damage, everyone gets to walk away happy. That's where we're hoping we are right now, but we still have a few missing pieces."

Summers was unstinting. "What do you need?"

Joe indicated Willy. "You gave us an employee photo of Robb Haag. I understand that unless we get some form of military waiver, you're not allowed to let us onto the factory floor. So here's a compromise: Give us ID photos of everyone who was ever friendly with Haag—even slightly— and we'll only watch the parking lot till those people come out. That should preserve your agreement with DOD and keep you up and running with minimum interference, while giving us what we want. You see any problems with that?"

Summers considered it before asking, "You wouldn't do anything in the parking lot itself? You'd wait until you were off the property?"

"If that's the way you want it."

Summers studied the floor for a moment before crossing to his desk and sitting before his computer, as he had at the end of his earlier meeting with Willy, when he'd printed out Haag's photograph. "There is one guy I thought about later," he said as he typed in commands. "Keith Cory. Works in fulfillment." He glanced up at Willy. "Basically, one of the box-tapers I mentioned when we met, although it's a little fancier than that. He and Robb seemed to be friends, or at least friendly. I saw them eating together out back only a couple of times, but for a loner like Haag, it stuck in my memory. I'm not saying they were actually friends. But I asked around after I thought of him, and Cory's the only one any of us can come up with."

"You didn't ask Cory as well, did you?" Willy asked.

"No." Summers rolled over to where his printer was coming alive. "If the two of them were pals, that's enough in my book to have as little to do with Cory as possible. He's not a fireworks show like Haag, but he doesn't need encouragement. I keep him because he does good work and keeps good records. He's also been around from the start, so we've all gotten used to him."

He swung around toward them, holding the printout of a sullen, fat-faced man with dull eyes. "Here he is. I'm still assuming you won't tell me what's going on?"

"Correct," Willy said quickly, hoping to cut off any further conversation.

But Joe—his figurehead role completed—honored his prior position as backup and stayed silent.

"We'll tell you after we've locked it in," Willy told Summers to soothe him.

The CEO had to live with that, and gave them both a wave of the hand. "Have at him, then. I'll prepare myself for the worst and hope for the best."

"Good plan," Willy said, leading the way out and smiling to himself.

Since his last visit to Al-Tech, Willy had considered how best to approach any potential ally of Robb Haag's. This was another reason why he'd asked for Joe's help.

Initially—had Summers been agreeable—Willy would have followed his instincts and sailed onto the assembly floor, revealing his identity in the process. Now, with the benefit of having Joe along, he was in fact grateful for Summers's request that they move on Keith Cory off campus. Not only would it distance them from any association with the plant, but it would also make their contact with Cory more private.

Willy's thinking here was that if Haag's plans did involve disrupting Al-Tech's operation via those Windsor-produced counterfeit batteries, then a quietly enlisted inside operator might prove useful. Also if more than one insider was involved, then initial contact with Cory was better kept quiet, so as not to spook any such coconspirator.

In any case, with Cory's photograph in hand, they waited within sight of the employee's exit at end of shift, watching for their overweight person of interest.

He turned out to be hard to miss.

"Look at the man," Willy commented, looking through his binoculars. "What a porker."

They saw him slowly trudge over to a tired Ford pickup, fire it up after a couple of tries and a resulting plume of oily smoke, and head out. They followed him through downtown Burlington, heading toward the Old North End, where he pulled over opposite a neighborhood market, eased himself out of the truck, adjusted his sagging pants with an unconscious jerk, and headed inside.

Willy glanced at Joe as he also parked by the curb. "Wanna grab him here?"

Joe looked around. "Why not?"

They opted for the sidewalk, rather than approaching Cory inside. The advantage of the latter would have been that any aisle could have served as a corral, making the job of two cops that much easier. The downside was that it was a commercial space, with other people to complicate such a maneuver. It also didn't account for the sheer size of their quarry, which guaranteed a massive amount of damage in case he resisted.

Resistance, however, turned out not to be a concern. As Cory stepped outside with a twelve-pack of beer under one massive arm, he saw the two cops approach from the flanks and stopped dead in his tracks.

"This about Robb?" he asked in a surprisingly high voice.

Willy took his advantage. "Yeah, big man. He fucked you over somethin' royal."

CHAPTER TWENTY-FIVE

"We meet again, as promised," Sam's host greeted her pleasantly. "And I hear you're bearing gifts."

She was back in Ted McTaggart's office in Albany—dark and wood-paneled, but like the storage room at a library, with no pretensions and lots of shelves. Before sitting down alongside Scott Gagne, who'd met her downstairs, she handed both men a thick file each. "Copies of what we've been up to. I sent Scott an email about Dominic Gargiulo and the thumb drive. Did he tell you about that?"

McTaggart nodded. "He mentioned it." He tapped the file with his finger. "This is the first hard copy stuff I've received, which is fine by me, by the way. I usually don't need to see much unless or until it really becomes a case for us, which I guess it has."

"I hope so," Sam said, pleased by his ready acceptance. "We put a tail on Gargiulo after he thought he'd successfully stolen the drive, and he brought us straight here. We lost him at the rental agency in Troy, but it's a safe bet all the dots connect back to Jared Wylie."

"In that email, you were waiting for Wylie to plug in the drive and enter his password," McTaggart suggested.

"We were, and he did. The techie at the Burlington PD is right now watching every keystroke being made. That puts the drive into Wylie's hands by default, and it ties Gargiulo to him as a result."

"Unless somebody else has the password and is doing that typing," Gagne suggested.

McTaggart looked at Sam questioningly as she laughed in agreement. "Great minds thinking alike," she said. "As this was coming together, I even started wondering—is all this Wylie getting his USB back, regardless of risk, or one of his victims wanting to blackmail him at any cost?"

"And your answer?"

"My *qualified* answer," she emphasized, "is Nick Gargiulo. He killed the girl, retrieved the drive, brought it back here, and works for Wylie. If we can muckle onto him and make him give us his boss—which is who I'm betting on—or, like Scott's suggesting, somebody who's gone to an amazing amount of effort to screw Wylie, we'll be set either way."

"I wasn't really suggesting it," Gagne clarified. "I just didn't want the possibility ignored."

"Well," she continued, "whatever it is, I do remember you saying that Wylie's been too slippery to catch until now. Maybe Gargiulo's the guy to make that happen. In any case, he's wanted for murder, so sooner or later, we're gonna want to bring him in."

"Agreed," McTaggart said, finally opening up the file. "So, let's talk about Wylie. What did your techie see when whoever it was opened up the drive?"

"We're still analyzing it," she said, her confidence growing with McTaggart's acceptance of her. There had been previous alliances in Vermont, where the VBI was purportedly the top dog, but in which she'd been made to feel like a second-class intruder. The Albany cops had been generous and accommodating from the start. "So far? It looks like a straight blackmail operation. He's got records, recordings, video footage, the works. You're the locals, so the names'll make sense to you, but the intel people in Burlington were saying that while several of them are Albany politicos—from top-ranking state senators to staffers and freshman assemblymen—there are a few D.C. representatives and some pure business types in there, too. It's quite a crowd. From what I was told, it's a prosecution task force's dream come true."

She turned to Gagne. "You said that once politicians start bubbling to the surface, this kind of thing usually goes to the state police, but I said task force just now 'cause it's sounding like there could be enough for everybody. Our AG and yours are already in bed over the thumb drive. You guys could have Wylie charged with ordering Jayla's homicide—depending on what Gargiulo has to say—and the troopers could have the rest. It would make lawyers on both sides happy for years."

Sammie was feeling a bit like a sales rep, but the indicators were telling. The already eager Gagne and his more circumspect boss were looking enthusiastic enough to give her heart.

It remained McTaggart's call, however, which he almost made now: "Okay. I want to read this through and phone a few people, but start setting things up. It's a qualified go unless I need to put on the brakes later." He held up the file. "Course, in this goddamn town, depending who's got their balls in a vise, anything might happen—or not—so keep part of yourself prepared for disappointment. It's been known to happen. I'll also issue an observe-and-report-only BOLO for Nick Gargiulo."

Sammie was heading back to Vermont when her cell phone came alive. She stuck it into the cradle on her dashboard so she could keep both hands on the wheel. "Hello?"

"Hi, Sam. It's Beverly Hillstrom."

Given the circumstances, Sam hadn't checked her caller ID, as she usually did, and now pulled over to get off the speakerphone, which she knew could be irritating on the receiving end. Hillstrom would forever be someone whom she held in awe, and she didn't want to commit any avoidable errors.

"Dr. Hillstrom," she said, moving the phone to her ear. "I mean, Beverly. Hi. Is everything okay?"

"It is on my end. Joe's back home and his mother's fully restored. I was calling in part to find out how you were doing."

Sammie felt her face flush. "Really? I'm good. I'm just driving back from Albany, where I had a super meeting with the PD. Things on Rachel's case are really coming together. How's she doing?"

"Much better, thanks. It's nice to hear you sounding so surefooted."

Sam laughed nervously. "Yeah. I guess so. I'm sorry I bugged you back when. I was feeling a little out of my depths."

"We all go there sometimes," Hillstrom reassured her. "Even now, I have days where I'm quite sure I'll be exposed as a child in disguise. I think that's true of every honest adult. Joe would tell you the same thing, I'm sure. I am delighted you found your pace, though. Joe tells me that he's been hearing from all sorts of people how impressive you were in his absence. I thought you should know that."

"Thank you," Sam said with feeling, truly touched by Hillstrom's telling her this. "He's actually mentioned it."

"I also wanted to thank you personally for what you did for my daughter," the older woman added. "You were far beyond professional with her. You hit all the right marks, and I wanted you to hear that clearly and directly. You are a terrific officer and a thoughtful, caring human being. I only rarely get to meet either, lately. You're entitled to your self-doubts, but don't think for a moment that they direct who you are."

Sam was almost overcome with emotion. "I'm not sure what to say."

Hillstrom laughed. "Don't say anything. Hang up and go back to driving home—with my best wishes and deepest thanks. That was an assumption, of course. I hope you're heading toward your family."

That said, Hillstrom hung up, leaving Sammie staring into the fading daylight ahead, her head swimming with happy confusion. She wasn't so naïve that she didn't suspect a bit of supportive manipulation at work behind Hillstrom's call. Not only was the medical examiner a good judge of character, but she'd also discussed Sammie's recent activities with Joe.

But that didn't mean Beverly had been obliged to make the call. That, Sam believed, went beyond old-fashioned good management.

"Neat," she said to herself, and pulled back onto the road.

Lester rose eagerly as Tina Stackman entered the room, dressed in her lab coat and carrying a manila folder. He'd come to Waterbury at her summons and had been waiting for only five minutes, anxiously anticipating what she might tell him about his findings.

She motioned to him to sit back down and joined him in an opposing seat, saying, "Who knew when I contacted you that we'd be dealing with all this?"

"Pat yourself on the back, Doc," he told her. "It was a good call."

She made a face. "I wouldn't go crazy there," she said. "If we'd done our homework properly the first time, we could've headed off what may turn out to be a huge black eye. It's not what any crime lab needs, especially in tight financial times."

"There's more than the fake fingerprints?" he asked.

She laid the folder on a table and opened it for reference as she spoke. "Sadly, yes, and I've already informed the director. That's one reason we were able to so quickly examine the samples you brought in from Kennedy's abandoned car. This whole case has become a high priority for us."

"What did you find?" he asked, caught by her almost grim demeanor.

"Another reason to hang on to old evidence, for one thing, regardless of how convinced everyone is that a case is a done deal. I will spare you the scientific mumbo jumbo that will feature at the review hearing later—to the possible cost of a couple of jobs around here—and simply tell you that the GSR you collected from the back of the passenger seat is a perfect match to the ammunition remaining in Kennedy's Taurus 65.

"What that implies, as you probably guessed when you went looking for its residue, is that the Taurus was fired too far right of Kennedy's position for him to have pulled the trigger—assuming he was always seated, as found, behind the wheel.

"Not only that, but a new, rigorous, highly detailed analysis of the stippling from around the wound in Paine's neck—which didn't go beyond a visual appreciation at the time of the shooting—has determined that the distance between muzzle and target was around four feet, or lined up with the center of the car's passenger seat."

She paused to catch her breath and added, "That introduces a different option to the scenario that Kennedy shot Paine point-blank, as he drew abreast of the front door."

Lester played devil's advocate. "Maybe Paine stepped back just before impact."

"Doubtful," she countered. "That doesn't fit with how the bodies were found upon discovery, with Paine's feet almost underneath Kennedy's car. It also doesn't match the stippling on Kennedy from Paine's gun, which had to have been fired almost point-blank, *and* it ignores what I just said, which is that the Taurus was shot from a position aligned with the front passenger seat."

Les couldn't deny his own adrenaline rush at hearing his theory confirmed scientifically. Still, he worked to keep his voice unemotional as he asked, "So what's the theory now?"

"The one that fits all the evidence, and makes rational and logical sense?" she asked. "I'm almost sorry to say it. It's looking as if Paine first shot Kennedy in the heart from close range, after which someone, wearing gloves to maintain the integrity of the counterfeit latents placed on the Taurus, aimed it through the passenger-side window from the outside, killed Paine in turn, and then dropped the gun onto Kennedy's dead lap, making sure some of his blood was deposited on it."

She handed a typed sheet from the folder. "That's my synopsis. It suggests that there had to have been three people at the scene that night, and that while Paine shot Kennedy, as suspected all along, a third person then shot Paine."

For a man his size, Keith Cory was disconcertingly meek. He sat like an enormous sack of damp laundry in the VBI's interrogation room in Burlington—pasty pale, glistening with sweat, his comb-over looking painted onto his head—and staring gloomily at the floor. Joe and Willy sat across from him.

"Okay, Keith," Willy began, "like I said from the top, this is a recorded conversation, but you're not under arrest. Do you understand that?"

The big man nodded.

"Gotta say it out loud, Keith," Willy informed him, his tone of voice supportive and helpful.

"Yeah."

"Yeah, what?"

"Yeah, I understand."

"Along the same lines, do you swear under penalty of law that everything you're about to say will be the truth to the best of your knowledge?"

"Yeah."

"Okay. Last but not least, do you understand that since you're not under arrest, you may leave whenever you choose?"

He nodded again.

"Speak, Keith."

"Yeah," Cory said wearily.

"All right," Willy continued, sounding almost chipper—an unusual thing for Joe to witness. "I've already recorded today's date, your full name, date of birth, and who else is in the room. You good with getting started, Keith?"

"Yeah."

"We're on a roll, then. Let's get right to it. Do you know a man named Robb Haag?"

"Yeah."

"From where?"

"Work."

"That would be Al-Tech Industries, of South Burlington, Vermont?"

"Yeah."

"And how long ago did you and Mr. Haag first meet?"

"Coupla years."

"Give us the circumstances."

Cory slowly lifted his head and gazed at his interlocutor. "Huh?"

Willy smiled encouragingly, enjoying the upbeat playacting for a change. "How did you meet? At lunch? On the assembly line? Walking to your cars after work? What?"

Cory blinked and looked around, as if he'd just been woken up and was establishing his surroundings. It occurred to Joe that the image might have value. Cory had appeared so deflated by their grabbing him outside the market that he'd seemingly entered a dreamlike state.

"I dunno," he reflected. "I guess it was all that stuff. Ya know, ya work together, ya get to know the other guy. Like that."

"But you became closer over time, is that correct?"

"Yeah."

"Tell me about that. Why did it happen?"

Cory shifted his attention to the ceiling. "I dunno. We were kinda on the outs from everybody else. There were a lot of ex-military types there, and eggheads. Real snotty. Robb was smart—super smart, I mean. But he was a good guy. Didn't treat me like crap."

"You became friends," Willy suggested.

"Yeah. You know how it goes. . . ."

"And you're still friends."

At last Cory made eye contact, slowly lowering his gaze to meet

Willy's. His response was familiar by now, but spoken tentatively this time—warily and drawn out. "Yeah."

Willy uncrossed his legs, leaned forward, and shifted his chair forward to where his and Cory's knees were almost touching. Their faces were only two feet apart when Willy asked, "What's he got you doing, Keith?"

Cory slowly tucked his chin in, but that was as far back as he could go. "Don't know what you're talkin' about."

Willy smiled again. "Everybody in this room knows what I'm talkin' about, Keith."

Cory swallowed.

"So does the Attorney General," Willy added.

The other man's voice was strained. "What does that mean?"

"It means that if you're straight with us here and now, we'll take it into consideration when we arrest you and Robb for terrorist acts against the United States and ship you to a prison cell somewhere in the Gulf of Mexico where *nobody* will hear from you ever again."

Cory's eyes widened to where the whites were visible all around his pupils. "*What?*" he asked, genuinely aghast.

"Robb didn't tell you that part?"

"He said it would fuck up that prick Al Summers, and all the jerk-offs who work for him."

"Is it becoming clear to you who's really gonna be fucked up, Keith?"

Cory worked his mouth a couple of times before actually saying, "That's not fair. I'm not *doing* anything."

"You sure as hell are, Keith. Don't lie to the Attorney General, or he might ship you south all by yourself."

"Tell us what you are doing," Joe said softly, speaking for the first time.

Cory stared at him as if he'd just materialized like a projection from the Starship *Enterprise*. "I just add them to some of the orders."

" 'Them' meaning what?"

Cory's voice dropped to a near whisper. "The batteries."

"The batteries that Haag supplied?"

"Yeah."

"And you blend them in?" Willy asked. "A few at a time?"

Cory nodded.

"Speak, Keith."

"Yeah."

"What's the plan?"

"They look the same as the others. No one'll know they'll fail and make the drones crash."

"And Al-Tech'll be blamed."

"Yeah."

"What about the people those drones kill when they crash?"

Cory looked from one of them to the other. "What?"

"That another thing Robb didn't discuss, and you chose not to think about?"

There was no response.

Willy got even closer, rising slightly from his seat. "This is important, Keith. How many have you added to the shipment stream so far?"

"Eighteen."

"Is there any way you can tell the counterfeits from the real ones?" Joe asked.

Cory stared at him as if he were all-knowing. "How did you—? Yeah. I put a dot on the upper right-hand corner of each one's label with a Magic Marker."

"You have any at the plant right now that you haven't fed in?"

"Only five."

"Where do you keep them?"

"In my locker."

"How's the process work? How do you do it?" Willy wanted to know.

"One at a time. I slip it under my shirt—maybe during a break or lunch or somethin'—and I add it to a shipment. Take a good one out, put a bad one in."

"What do you do with the good one?"

"Throw it in the lake later."

Joe was struck enough by the image that he blurted out, "Any in your car right now?"

Keith Cory nodded. "Six."

Fifteen minutes later, outside of the interrogation room, Joe was dialing the Al-Tech number in order to tell Alan Summers to immediately instruct his customers to pull any battery marked with the telling black dot.

As he was doing so, Willy asked, "What the hell made you think of asking him that?"

Joe was waiting for the call to be picked up. "Ego," he said. "Somehow or another, Haag had to have a way of delivering his message."

"Kilroy was here?" Willy suggested.

"Exactly."

CHAPTER TWENTY-SIX

Lester killed the engine and let his hands drop to his lap. He was staring at the staff entrance to the Bellows Falls Police Department, one of the odder buildings in town—purportedly an architecture student's project years ago—clumsily built of mismatched materials, poorly designed, incompetently insulated and heated, and capped with any number of graceless roof angles and pitches.

John Patrick Hartnett—universally called Pat—was the reason Les was here, and it sat on his heart like a stone. When Lester had started chasing this case, it presented as a scientific puzzle—prints that didn't make sense appearing as they did. Now it felt to him like all he was doing was chasing fellow cops. Ryan Paine, once the decorated hero, had become threadbare, desperate, and pathetic—saved by a bullet from being tossed onto the unemployment line. His best friend, Dylan Collier, was a self-professed, on-the-job-retirement candidate who'd been sleeping with Paine's wife, Dee Rollins—rationalizing it by saying they were just friends. And now Pat Hartnett, the same woman's current boyfriend, who Collier claimed had appeared onstage after the dust settled, but—according to Lester's most recent homework—appeared to have been standing in the wings, if not in the prompter's box, at the time of Paine's killing.

He let out a long sigh. He didn't have the prejudice against internal affairs so common among cops. He knew it was a job that needed doing, that most IA cases resulted in the subjects being cleared, and—in a suit-happy democracy—that IA ironically most often represented a cop's best chance.

But it didn't mean that he liked doing their job. He'd always prided himself on his integrity, his generosity toward others. Even people he was glad were going to jail received his courtesy and kindness. It was an aspect of his personality that he nurtured and protected.

Finding himself in this unusual role was proving difficult.

What he'd uncovered about Hartnett was possibly innocuous, but as part of his delving into the recent past, he'd included several hours reviewing the news footage of Ryan Paine's funeral—still and video, both. He'd studied the rows upon rows of uniformed officers—himself among them—marching, saluting, presenting arms over the coffin, and mingling afterwards. His primary focus throughout, however, had remained the grieving widow, Dee Rollins.

One by one, he'd separated and identified the people most closely connected to her. Family members—hers and Ryan's—friends of both of them, colleagues, even people assigned by the state police to deal with her needs.

Until he'd been left with a single man wearing the uniform of the Wilmington police.

Les had been slow to pin the man down. So many others were hovering around, holding Dee's arm as she sat or rose, opening doors or making room for her as she walked through the crowd. Prominent among them, unsurprisingly, was Dylan Collier. But too frequently for mere happenstance, Les saw this Wilmington cop—always in the background, just out of sight from those in the front, consciously watchful of the cameras, and thus frequently photographed in profile only, or with his face averted.

And twice, Lester had seen where—for a split second at best—this man and Dee Rollins had locked eyes.

It didn't prove anything, but to Les, it spoke of a connection. No other officer had hung close by so consistently, and no other person had attracted the gaze of the widow, who otherwise had devoted herself to studying the ground at her feet.

It hadn't been difficult thereafter for Lester to label the image with Pat Hartnett's name.

So why Bellows Falls right now? Because while Hartnett had been with Wilmington at the time of Paine's death, he was fresh from the BFPD, and Lester—who by now was questioning everyone's motives— wanted to find out more about him before a direct confrontation.

The sad fact at the bottom of all this was that as Les had worked his way, like a hunter circling his prey, through the tangles of this case, drawing ever closer to its primary actors, he'd become acutely aware of its no longer being a purely intellectual exercise. He was now looking for a killer—still alive, still unaccounted for, and quite possibly within law enforcement.

And although he was widely known for his sense of humor and easygoing ways—he'd been welcomed into the VBI for good reason—Lester Spinney was a good tracker of men, even more so for his self-effacing style.

As a result of this prowess, he'd become watchful of patterns, like what he'd discovered in that footage, where two people presumed to be strangers in fact shared a little-known history. Collier and Dee, for example—by the former's own admission—and, perhaps earlier than suspected, Dee and Pat Hartnett. Along similar lines, in yet another curious overlay, Les had recently found out that Kyle Kennedy had once been arrested in Bellows Falls—by none other than Officer Hartnett.

Les got out of the car, faced the closed-circuit camera by the building's employee entrance, pushed the doorbell nearby, and was buzzed in by Dispatch, along with a friendly, "*Lester*. Long time, no see."

He entered the lobby, circled around to the radio room, and gave the dispatcher a kiss on the cheek, leaning over her counter to do so.

"You're right, Jenn. Too long."

The woman laughed. "You're forgiven. It's not like you've been loafing around. How do you like VBI?"

"I'm a happy man," he said. "It's custom-made for oddballs like me. Is Nicole around today?"

"Right upstairs. I know she'd love to see you."

He waved good-bye as he retreated toward the door. "Thanks, Jenn. I'll try to drop by more often."

"We all do what we can, Les. Don't beat yourself up."

Nicole LaBrie was the department's lieutenant, a detective, and the chief's executive officer. A years-long veteran of the state's anti-drug task force, where she'd participated in undercover operations beyond counting, she was steady, dependable, unflappable, and a good friend.

Only a few inches shorter than he, dressed in a uniform shirt and blue jeans, she stood and gave him a bear hug as he entered the squad room on the second floor.

He looked around to make sure they were alone, which was all she needed in order to cut straight to business. "Uh-oh," she said, crossing to the coffee machine and pouring him a cup. "Looks like you're on the hunt."

"I'm on something, all right. Not sure what it is," he said coyly. "Did you know Pat Hartnett when he was here?"

"Sure. He in your sights for something?"

"Hardly. His name came up, and I just wanted to learn more about him. He worked here for a few years, didn't he?"

"Over ten," she said. "Longer, now that I think about it. He went to Wilmington, which you probably already know."

"Right," Lester replied vaguely. "It was actually one of his old cases I was interested in—involving a guy named Kyle Kennedy."

She gave him a knowing smile, along with the mug of coffee. "That's not just some guy. Don't kid a kidder. What're you up to?"

"I wish I knew," he admitted. "I am looking into Kennedy—and what made him famous—but it's too out of focus right now for me to tell you much. I'm still studying the puzzle pieces."

"And two of the pieces are Kennedy and Pat?"

"Pat arrested him for DUI, back in the stone ages. Here in BF."

"Okay," she said encouragingly.

"Well, it was long ago enough that you guys hadn't gone to electronic filing yet with your fingerprints. You still used ink. I was wondering if you kept those old cards somewhere."

"Far out," she said. "That is a shot in the dark. Paper files may be becoming ancient history, but fingerprint cards are prehistoric. On the other hand," she added, "we are New Englanders. We rarely throw anything away."

She retrieved the coffee mug she'd given him and placed it on her desk. "That being said, where we're going, you don't want that. Trust me."

She crooked a finger at him as she headed for the door. "Come with me, pilgrim. We're headed for the bowels of Middle Earth."

It did feel that way. The basement of this odd building was windowless, dank, concrete-lined, and only marginally illuminated, which explained why Nicole had brought along a flashlight.

She led him to a small mountain of decaying cardboard boxes occupying the far corner of a room otherwise filled with abandoned bikes, destroyed exercise equipment, and several home-built rusty racks designed to hold targets at the shooting range.

"What was the date?"

He rattled it off, and she scanned the labels on the boxes, although several had lost their tags over the years. "You do realize this is going to take you a while."

"Yup," he said, trying to open up some space in which to work.

She rapped her knuckle against a single box and added, "Unless you get lucky, of course."

He grabbed hold of her prize and put it where he could process its contents, as she handed him the light and headed back upstairs, saying, "See me when you're done."

His luck, as it turned out, was not what either one of them might have expected. In truth, he hadn't been sure what to expect—except for another hazily defined next step.

Or nothing at all, which is what turned out to be his reward in the end.

The contradictory eureka moment didn't come, however, until after he'd checked the file's chronologically arranged contents twice. DUI cases are complex structures, largely because—most cops believe—the laws enforcing them were written by drink-prone politicians who want to get out of trouble if they're ever caught under the influence. There are forms and test results and questionnaires and affidavits and video files and roadside dexterity demonstrations and much, much more.

Including booking records, complete with fingerprint cards.

Or not.

Lester sat back on his heels and wedged the borrowed flashlight under his chin before dealing the file's contents out like a cardsharp onto the concrete floor.

Fingerprinting had definitely taken place—the supporting documentation attested to it. But the actual card featuring the blackened blossoms of Kyle Kennedy's whorls, swirls, and loops was missing. Someone had removed it.

Someone, Lester had become educated by Tina Sackman, who'd created an alternate use for them.

Sam got the call a half hour after putting Emma to bed, dressed, as was her daughter, in a pair of pink pajamas—although minus the sewn-on feet.

"It's Gagne," said the familiar voice. "Some local yokel fucked up and went after Gargiulo—saw him in traffic and lit him up, instead of calling it in, like we asked."

"Where is he?" she asked, walking down the hall toward where Willy was watching TV, her adrenaline removing all weariness.

"That's the problem. They lost him in Malta after a high-speed chase. That's like fifteen miles north of Albany, just below Saratoga Springs."

Sammie pressed her lips together with irritation. Murphy—always lurking in the wings. "Okay," she said. "What's the plan? Roadblocks?"

"No. He crashed. He's on foot."

"What? Jesus."

"It gets worse," Gagne told her. "He's in the one place where it's crazy hard to track him—about a square mile of woods. Used to be a secret rocket-testing site."

"Oh, come *on*," she replied, going into the living room, sitting beside Willy, and turning on her phone's speaker as he hit the remote's mute button.

"We got two things going for us," Gagne said. "One is that there's a ginormous semiconductor-manufacturing plant where part of the site used to be—basically blocking off one side of it—and the other is that the woods're surrounded by roads where units have already been dispatched. With any luck, we have him contained, at least."

"Right," Willy groused. "That's really gonna work."

"What?" Gagne asked.

"Nothing," Sammie said. "I'm coming over. Where's your command center?"

Gagne didn't argue with her. "Shoot for the Malta town offices, on Route 9. If we're not there, somebody'll give you directions. The Hermes site is a mile away at most."

"The what?"

"That's what they called it, right after the war—the Hermes rocket-testing site."

"Yeah," she said, half to herself. "Why not? This whole damn thing is like science fiction."

There was some background noise on Gagne's end, before he said, "See ya in a few," and unceremoniously hung up.

Willy leaned toward her and kissed her neck. "Have fun at the office, honey. Try not to get your butt blown off."

At least the travel time was fast. Sam played her blue lights through the Vermont leg of her trip and met little traffic in any case, given the time of night and her chosen route, which went for miles between towns so small, they didn't even have gas stations.

She'd heard of Malta, on the outskirts of Saratoga Springs horse country. By and large, it was groomed, well mannered, and fed by the largesse of wealthy second-home owners, not to mention the huge new semiconductor plant's payroll and the appeal of a nearby lake.

She didn't find anyone she recognized at the town offices, as expected. There was a command post there, or at least a group of people manning phones, and Gagne had left notice for her to be given directions to the Hermes site.

The transition from neatly mown neighborhoods to dense trees—officially the Luther Forest—was abrupt, and made clear by the sudden vanishing of streetlamps, traffic, and urban lighting.

As she'd gotten ready to depart Brattleboro earlier, dressing in her outdoor BDUs, or battle dress uniform, and updating Dispatch and Joe personally by phone, she'd asked Willy to read aloud from Wikipedia about her destination, thereby learning more about the semiconductor plant and the old rocket site. Counting the surrounding forestland, it was—as Gagne had implied—the worst possible environment in which to find a single man on the lam.

She found where she was headed on the appropriately named Rocket Drive, where vehicles beyond counting were clustered, most of them still flashing their eye-piercing, pulsing, multicolored LEDs. Almost in protest, she killed her own headlights as she parked near the tightest assemblage of cars, and walked toward a tent filled with variously uniformed people.

Thankfully, Scott Gagne had kept an eye out for her, and emerged from the crowd as she approached.

"You made good time," he said.

"You got everybody here but the National Guard," she commented, looking around.

His voice dropped as he confided, "Yeah, well. We may've gilded the lily a little, there. You said you're pretty sure Gargiulo killed the Robinson girl—so we kinda advertised that we're after a mad-dog psychopath, just to catch everyone's interest. I'd appreciate it if you don't blow our cover by getting wobbly in your convictions, okay?"

"Got it," she reassured him.

"That being said," he went on, "we still don't have enough people to just lock the place down till morning, so we could do this in daylight, and we weren't able to get the state police chopper with infrared."

Gagne led her to the center of the tent, where a map had been laid out on a makeshift table, surrounded by laptops, radios, and cell phones, all of which seemed to be operating at once. He squeezed her up next to the table's edge and began explaining, "Things have improved a little since we talked. As fast as we could, we dispatched units to the periphery and worked our way in. We found a ski mask in Gargiulo's wrecked car that stank enough of his scent, even I could smell it, so we're cycling through dog teams as we speak. By now, we're pretty sure our guy's somewhere inside this rectangle—basically a quarter mile by half a mile. Problem is it's hilly, wooded in spots, and riddled with tunnels, bunkers, warehouses, and other weird junk I can't even describe that date back to the rocket program. It's also pitch-black, and I already told you about our manpower."

"Then I can help," she suggested.

"Already got you hooked up. You wearing a vest?"

She opened her Windbreaker. "And I have a shotgun in my car."

Five minutes later, after checking in with the incident commander and fetching her 12 gauge, Sam followed Gagne along a dirt road, away from the lights. The break from the noise and flashing LEDs was a relief, but almost immediately, they saw—a hundred yards ahead—a much smaller, quieter, and more dimly lit group near a couple of parked SUVs.

"That's your date for the evening," Gagne said as they closed in. "You're assigned to Deputy Sheriff Lisa Schamberg. I chose her myself 'cause we date back; she used to work for the PD. Good people, great dog handler, incredibly hard worker—a little on the focused side. You two should get along." He smiled. "Normally, we would have a full tracking crew behind each dog, but the perimeter's too big and we don't have people to spare. So, we're making do."

As they got within a few feet of the group, Gagne called out, "Lisa—yo," and was immediately met by a short, strongly built woman dressed like Sam in boots and combat uniform, who came out to meet them leading a handsome, young, powerful German Shepherd on a leash.

She shook Sam's hand. "You Martens?"

"Thanks for taking me on," Sam answered.

Schamberg indicated Scott Gagne. "Thank him. He's says you're okay, that's good by me. This is Brio."

The dog briefly sniffed Sam's outstretched hand—as if obligated by politesse—but otherwise kept by his handler's side, constantly looking up at her with unmitigated devotion. Lisa—Sam was amused to notice—steadily reciprocated, despite her tough-guy demeanor. She repeatedly made small loving gestures with her hand—tiny caresses of the dog's ears, fingertip strokes along the nape of his neck—which reminded Sam of similar displays between humans. There was no doubting the bond between these two.

A voice behind them inquired, "You ready to go in, Lisa?"

Schamberg said something quickly to her dog and glanced at Sam, saying loudly enough to be heard by all, "Good to go." She then explained more quietly, eyeing Sam intensely, "This is a fresh sector, so any scent should be relatively uncontaminated. It's about the only thing we have going for us. Ready?"

Without waiting for a response, she quickly swapped Brio's leash and collar for a thirty-foot tracking lead and harness before telling Sam, "No offense, but if the shit hits the fan, the dog's my partner and my priority. Just so you know. Bullets start flying, he and I hit the ditch. It's up to you to take out the bad guy. You good with that?"

"Yup," Sam replied, having figured as much.

Schamberg studied Sam's shotgun, noticing the flashlight fixed just under the barrel. "You got a remote switch for that?"

"Yeah."

"Keep it off most of the time, if you can. There's no moon tonight, but there'll be enough vision anyhow, once our eyes adjust."

Schamberg suddenly gave her a broad winning smile, transforming her serious face. "Try not to shoot me and Brio in the ass, and never light us up. Deal? 'Cause you're bringing up the rear."

Sam smiled back. "Deal."

As of that moment, watching Lisa and her dog head off, Sam felt as abruptly alone as if she'd been dropped off the side of an ocean liner, and was floating in a vast and empty darkness.

From Sam's own familiarization training at the police academy, she knew better than to converse further. Dog handlers can be an obsessively concentrated bunch, and this one appeared beyond average. Crouching slightly as she trotted behind her dog, Lisa behaved like a half-human, half-canine avatar herself—as quiet, lithe, and loose-limbed as Brio as he gracefully cut back and forth across their line of approach—"casting," in their lingo—his nose seeking Gargiulo's scent on the ground.

In an ideal world, humans leave behind three different scent trails as they walk. One—arguably the strongest—is a triangular-shaped wake, suffused with a trademark odor, which largely hangs in the air like an invisible cloud. The closer a dog's nose gets to the source, the narrower that pie shape becomes. Unfortunately, that plume can be vulnerable to wind and the elements. The second is what we leave behind in our footprints—featuring not just our own smell but also the added flavor, if you will, of the minute disturbances our forging ahead may have caused. The third is even more subtle, involving both the aboveground objects we contact—low-hanging leaves and branches—and the molecular makeup of whatever environment we traverse. Canines trained to pursue these three categories are generally called, respectively: air scent, tracking, or trailing dogs. At the start of his search—once his nose became oriented—Brio began exhibiting the classic traits of a trailing dog.

Sam, however, also remembered being told that whatever the training or technique, problems arise almost inevitably. Topography, weather, temperature, air movement, passage of time, competing odors, and more all regularly conspire to make a dog's job more difficult.

And then there's the dog itself. As sentient creatures, they have moods and feelings, good days and bad, and their handlers need to be sensitive to each. The dogs also know no bounds—their dedication overrides their self-preservation. They will work until they drop, overheat to the point of death, and sacrifice all to protect their human partner or achieve their goal. That creates in the handler a paradoxical dilemma. Like the doting parent of an idiot savant, this person has to manage the actions of a single-minded tracking machine, while preventing her "child" from destroying itself through the excesses of its own nature.

Jogging along behind this intuitively driven team, Sam could only admire them as Lisa escorted Brio through his paces, all while studying his body language for fatigue, assessing for possible threats, and watching for evidence—in near total darkness.

Which is where Sammie fulfilled her role. Widening her eyes for maximum night vision, she swept the nearby possible ambush sites, looking for movement, shadow, and listening for anything amiss. If Lisa was Brio's guardian—watching his back to allow him his full attention—then Sam was Lisa's in turn.

And vigilance was called for. Brio was visibly no longer trailing an elusive scent. After twenty minutes, even Sammie could tell he was onto the real thing—the actual vapor cone of their quarry—which brought his nose up into air scent mode. All three of them picked up their game—more alert, more adrenalized, more mindful of something about to snap.

Lisa and Brio transformed into an offbeat parody of Fred and Ginger in full swing—a taut leash between them—the dog pressing forward, straining against his harness, and his handler fighting to restrain him, increasingly sensitive to a possibly violent encounter looming ahead. Lisa's posture became a sniper's, hunched over to present a smaller target and sighting between the ears of her distant dog, who was aimed like a rifle barrel at his objective.

Sam struggled to not watch them, to keep her eyes on what was ahead and within the surrounding inky blackness. Menacing outlines, arboreal and concrete, natural and man-made, drifted by as they traveled on methodically, each ghostly apparition needing at least a cursory check. Bunkers, pits, steel sheds, and storage buildings arose in turn, the two women knowing the dog's nose would warn them of danger, while aware that the same organ was seriously otherwise occupied, pursuing a single odor and only maybe—or maybe not—aware of anyone else.

After all, who knew if Gargiulo was alone?

The pursuit reached a climax with operatic flourish. The dog coming to a dead stop before the silhouette of a man suddenly separating from the bushes ahead—frighteningly nearby—the flash of a gun, fired at close range and straight at them, its ballooning explosion of blinding light seeming like an onrushing meteor—and followed by the twin yelp of the dog and the scream of his partner.

Lisa, howling with rage and abandoning her promise to drop out of harm's way, filled the night firing at near-automatic speed, shooting into the gloom repeatedly as she threw herself onto Brio's recumbent shape. Sam stabbed the darkness with her light, sighting down the shotgun, waiting for a target.

But the man had disappeared.

Sam ran up alongside Lisa, who'd emptied her magazine and was slapping a second one home while cradling Brio in her arms. Sam saw the dog's bright eyes reflecting back at her, its tongue reaching out to comfort Lisa and lick away the blood coursing from the top of its head, and decided on little evidence that Brio was injured only, and would be okay.

Lisa understood her hesitation without a word being said. "Go, go, go!" she yelled, gesturing with her free arm. "I don't think it did major damage. Go get the son of a bitch. I'll call it in."

Sam pressed on, her hearing replacing Brio's nose as she followed heavy footsteps retreating ahead. This was not proper procedure—exposing herself needlessly to danger, with dozens of armed officers just minutes away. But on the ground, egging her on, she saw regularly spaced drops of fresh blood. Also, from all around, she could hear the shouts of people closing in on her position.

"*Stop*" she shouted as she ran, as if rationalizing her own impulsiveness. "*Police.*"

In fact, in that moment, it was she who suddenly came to a halt, startled by a monolith darker than the night sky beyond it, as tall as a towering building, looming before her as if it had sprung from the earth without a sound. It was one of the abandoned steel gantries, designed to hold rocket engines, six stories high, its walls made of rusting flat metal—silent, still, and as powerful in appearance as a fortress dropped from space.

Around its lower left edge, barely caught by the outermost halo of Sam's flashlight, there was a flicker of a movement as her quarry ducked around the gantry's base for cover.

"I got you now," she muttered, and ran again with renewed purpose.

But she hadn't gotten him. Scrambling down the embankment leading to the tower's foundation, entering the concrete-lined empty pool that had once served to absorb the rocket's fiery blast, she swung around the same corner she'd seen her prey take, and found nothing.

Once more, she stopped dead still, listening.

He was inside, and she could hear the rhythmic pattern of feet climbing a metal ladder.

It defied logic—amid a square mile of forestland, in the dead of night—to climb a tall object with no hope of escape. It spoke of the raccoon heading for a tree, solely in the hope of a little respite before death.

Sam's response was equally impetuous. With backup almost in sight, informed of the situation, and a surround-and-hold scenario available within moments, she nevertheless killed her light and acted like Brio, perhaps influenced by his sacrifice. She ran through the small service entrance she saw in the steel wall, and entered the heart of the empty, cavernous, sixty-foot-tall rocket gantry—abruptly feeling like a mouse at the bottom of an enormous, jet-black, hollowed-out, square-sided silo.

For a fraction of a moment, she almost considered her situation, and how rashly she'd acted.

Until she heard the resumption of heavy shoes pounding on steel rungs, high against the structure's far wall.

Quickly detaching her darkened flashlight from her shotgun barrel, she laid it on the ground, turned it on, and moved far to one side, shouting up and across the darkness, "Drop your gun and come down. *NOW.*"

The flashlight showed little except the rubble-strewn surface of the gantry's battered floor. But that wasn't why she'd placed it there.

Almost on cue, she heard her quarry's footsteps pause on the steel rungs above, just before a volley of gun flashes broke out overhead, and the now distant light's beam became wreathed in splintered stone dust.

Sammie aimed her shotgun at the last muzzle flash and fired two responding rounds of double-aught buckshot. There was a scream of pain, the rattling of a handgun bouncing haphazardly down the ladder, and silence.

Sam commanded, "Come down or the next shot takes you out. *DO IT NOW.*"

Slowly, the sound of his descent drowned out by the arrival of backup troops, Sam first heard and then saw by the glow of a dozen bobbing flashlights, a limping man being escorted toward her. He was bleeding from several wounds to his arms and legs, and had to be supported by both arms.

As they came eye to eye, he snarled, "Bitch."

"Yeah," she replied. "Pisser to be shot by a girl, huh?"

She found Lisa Schamberg and Brio where she'd left them, with Lisa now struggling to control her dog from getting up and running in circles.

"That adrenaline, or is he okay?" Sam asked, drawing near.

"Both," Lisa reported, laughing. "The bullet grazed his skull and disoriented him a little. I'll have him checked out, but he looks like he'll make it."

Sam crouched down beside them as the handler kept running her hands along his body. Lisa buried her face in his fur and gave him a nuzzle. When she looked up, Sam could see that her eyes were damp. "How 'bout you?" Sam asked.

"I'm good."

Sam kept watching her silently. Lisa returned the gaze, blinked a couple of times, and finally added in a broken voice, "I thought I lost him."

Sam slipped a comforting arm across her shoulders.

CHAPTER TWENTY-SEVEN

Willy sat in his car outside his daughter's day-care center, warmed in the morning sun that was slanting through his window. The center was on a residential street, a dead end, which heightened its isolation and sense of security.

His seat was half reclined, his head resting partially against the door post behind him. It was not a good defensive position—atypically for him. He was vulnerable, exposed, and with no sight lines established for any approaching threats. And he was fighting back tears.

His phone lay in his lap, his hand still partially curled around it, from when he'd disconnected just moments ago. He'd been wishing Emma a good day as the call came through.

He was grateful for the timing. The kids were inside for the moment, the street empty of people still doing their morning routines behind closed doors. He was free to be alone with his emotions.

The call had been from a triumphant Sammie, relating that she was fine and unharmed, that they'd grabbed Charlotte Robinson's killer in a showdown and he was spilling his guts from a hospital room under armed guard.

Willy didn't give a damn about any of that. He'd already been told of some of it by Joe, in an earlier call, along with the news that Joe was leaving for Albany to receive a personal briefing on the whole operation—and did Willy want to join him, to congratulate Sammie in person?

Willy had opted out, claiming childcare obligations and a meeting with the Windsor cops in a couple of hours. That hadn't been entirely truthful, of course.

Willy hadn't wept in years—decades, really. And he wasn't quite doing so now. Tears represented an aspect of his emotional makeup he'd pretty much quashed since childhood. He could whip out rage, bitterness, and even humor readily enough. But rarely sadness, and never fear. At the first signs of their looming, he shut them down with the forcefulness of a man fighting for a lifeline.

But after kissing Emma good-bye and hearing Sam's exuberant voice on the phone, he was suddenly overwhelmed. The news of her being okay had startled him with its accompanying relief and gratitude, and—combined with his farewell to Emma just now—had confirmed in him an ingrained sense of insignificance. For all his public self-confidence, Willy was a man who struggled to simply stay alive. He doubted that anyone would feel the same relief for him that he'd just felt upon hearing of Sam's survival. He realized now, for a fact, that he'd be destroyed by the loss of either Sam or Emma—while he had to acknowledge that either of them would survive his being lost to them. They would mourn his passing, and perhaps remember his good traits. But they would go on.

And so the barely withheld tears were also in anger—although not at being marginalized. In a man as complex as he, his slipping from everyone's memory was cynically predictable. Willy's fury was at himself, for thinking selfishly, for appearing narcissistic. He didn't allow himself to weep, to display overt expressions of affection, reliance, or helplessness, less because they were signs of weakness, and more because they might bind him to other human beings—the only species on this earth that had betrayed him as a kid, and was now feeding his reluctant adult heart with love.

He shook his head, frustrated by this disturbance to his long-standing, now threatened, view of reality, righted his seat back, started his car, and headed toward Windsor.

"They here from Springfield yet?" Willy asked Colin as he was buzzed through to the back of the Windsor Police Department and met his old friend in the hallway.

The sergeant pointed over his shoulder at a closed-circuit television mounted onto Dispatch's wall. "If I were a betting man, I'd say that's them right now—sure looks like a car feds would drive."

They walked outside to greet the two men getting out of the tinted-window, gleaming black SUV in the lot.

The driver was of special interest to Willy, who gave the man an affable smile as he made the introductions. "Special Agent Dorman, from Homeland Security; Sergeant Colin Guyette—Windsor PD."

Dorman, not smiling, returned the honors by barely introducing his passenger, whose name Willy didn't catch, before addressing Willy directly. "Before witnesses, I'd like it understood that if whatever you've cooked up here doesn't meet with some high expectations, I'm going to take it out on you by filing criminal charges against you—details and specifics to follow. You and I know what I'm talking about. Is that understood?"

Willy laughed, confident that the man could actually do no such thing, despite his suspicions. "What's understood is that you made the trip, despite your dislike of me, and I appreciate that. I don't think you'll be sorry."

Dorman turned to Guyette. "You good with our being here? This cowboy plays by his own rules. He pulled a fast one on us, and I want to make sure he's not doing the same to you."

Guyette waved his hands. "No, no. It's fine with us. I've been helping him with this—"

"Colin brought it to me, on his own initiative," Willy interrupted. "He deserves an assist if you people do that sort of thing."

Colin was self-deprecating. "Yeah, well, whatever. Anyhow, my boss is on board, too. If you like what you see, we'll be more than happy to see it all go federal."

Dorman pressed his lips together tightly before continuing, "Okay. The bait was you got proof somebody's sabotaging U.S. military equipment. That correct?"

"Basically," Willy said cheerfully as Colin gave him a doubtful sideways glance.

After bringing the two HSI agents up to speed, Willy and Colin drove them to a nearby apartment a short way down Union Street, to where they'd temporarily safeguarded a contented Chris Walker. He'd had no complaints being kept under wraps, with access to TV and all his meals being paid for by the State of Vermont.

"Okay," Willy told him after everyone had settled down inside the small but tidy top-floor apartment, "Chris, it's time for you to earn your keep."

Walker responded with predictable sharpness of mind, "Huh?" prompting Dorman to roll his eyes at his colleague.

"Remember how I told you we'd take care of you if you did the same for us later on?" Willy reminded him.

"I guess."

"This is later on."

Walker had been eating a raw hot dog, without a bun, his teeth and wounded lip having improved at least that much. He paused to swallow before saying, "Okay."

"We need for you to call Robb Haag, tell him you've been in the hospital because of what happened to you—call it an infection of one of your injuries—and that you want to come back to work for him. Tell him you need the money."

"But I don't like working for him."

"I know that, Chris. This is make-believe, okay? We just want Haag to come out and pick you up at the hospital. Tell him they're letting you out in a bit, after a few more tests, and that you'll be waiting for him at the front of the hospital, on the edge of County Road, okay? That last part's important—on the edge of the road, where he can pick you up without having to pull in."

Walker was staring at him intently enough to have been reading his lips, and now nodded solemnly. "Edge of the road. Got it."

"Since we're all so cozy," Alex Dorman said an hour later to Willy as the two of them were clustered together with Colin in the back of an unmarked van in the hospital parking lot, "I hope it's okay if I make it perfectly clear that I know you were the one who fucked us over regarding Sunny Malik—up to and including breaking into his place and torturing him to get information."

As Willy opened his mouth to respond, Dorman held up his hand. "No, no, no. Stop right there. That was a statement of fact. I don't want you to argue, or lie, or do anything about it. You're in deep enough as it is. I just wanted you to know that despite what you woodchucks might think of us, we are not complete idiots. Plus, we got your decoy from the other night and squeezed him hard enough to throw the book at you."

"Okay," Willy said slowly, inviting more.

For all that was coming out of his mouth, Dorman was being perfectly affable, which made Willy almost more nervous than if he'd been screaming at him.

"The bottom line, Kunkle," the fed continued, "is that unlike you, I'm a team player. That's why I'm here right now. But I give you fair warning: You come to my town again, and pull shit like that, I will respond. Does that sound legit?"

Willy was famous for shooting his mouth off, and often using a conciliatory opportunity like this to make matters worse. But this time, perhaps moved by his morning's moment of self-reflection, he merely said, "Yes, it does."

Dorman seemed appeased. "Then tell me why the hell you chose this weird spot for an ambush."

Colin laughed as Willy explained, "You mean risk a shoot-out in front of a hospital? Can't beat the commute if things go wrong."

Dorman stared at him, not bothering to comment.

Willy laid it out. "The hospital's up the hill behind us, pretty safe from any gunfire; the town forest is directly across the street—great for safety and hiding backup; County Road—the hospital notwithstanding—is pretty empty most of the time; and we've got cutoff driveways in front of and behind the pickup spot."

"Not to mention the road's boxed in by a ditch on one side and an embankment on the other," Colin chimed in. "The real point of this thing is that Haag has a half dozen heavy weapons hanging on his wall, and we wanted him away from as many of them as possible."

"You guys are the locals," Dorman conceded, his tone doubtful. "If he's that dangerous, you sure about your setup?"

"Guess we'll find out," Willy said airily. In fact, he was, as usual, taking a calculated gamble. There was a school of thought that believed in applying full force and all resources to every problem, almost regardless of known factors. Such believers were never wrong, in Willy's retelling, even when they failed spectacularly, because they could quote "The Book" as their guiding light, chapter and verse, and therefore blame it by extension, win or lose.

He hated the mindless Book approach—always had. In his experience, if you thought an operation through, and used tactics based on real-world calculations, you always had a better chance of success. Was it foolproof? Never. But if Willy screwed up, he wanted to know how, so that he could improve. The Book rarely supplied that latitude or learning curve.

As for Robb Haag, what were they dealing with? Someone disgruntled, presumptuous, impatient, antisocial, not as smart as his own arrogance would have him believe, and probably undermined by a nagging insecurity. This was the portrait Willy had gleaned from tracking the man's footsteps. Yes, he had guns, and yes, he might use them if the circumstances were right, but within the context that Willy had established with this ambush? He thought not.

He found out soon enough. Despite his other character flaws, it turned out that Haag was punctual. Some five minutes after Chris Walker had been all but pushed outside to wander complaining to the curb—where, to Willy's delight, he immediately sat down on the grass—a typical Vermont rust bucket hove into view from the south end of County Road and noisily rolled to a stop right next to Walker.

Colin raised his binoculars to make sure the driver was indeed the man they were after—and that he was alone—before keying the mic on his radio and urging, "Go, go, go, go."

What happened next was textbook, and even impressive from their remote observation spot. Guyette had trained his people well, and briefed them precisely. Mimicking a training film, vehicles appeared, seemingly from nowhere, and black-clad, ski-masked officers burst from the nearby woods, armed to excess, screaming orders at the top of their lungs.

They surrounded Haag's vehicle, pulled open his doors, dragged him from the car, and laid him flat on the pavement. Others quickly checked the car's interior, including the trunk, before the team leader announced on the radio, glancing in their direction, "Scene's secure."

Willy looked at Dorman. "That work for you?"

The fed smiled back. "Yup."

* * *

Lester chose his moment with care. By now, he had his suspicions about what role Pat Hartnett had played in the death of Ryan Paine, but he had no proof, and Hartnett was a fellow police officer—a double circumstance demanding discretion, tact, and timing.

He had dug into the man's past with Nicole LaBrie's help, and had found, if not a smoking gun, at least the history of two failed marriages, several official reprimands for faulty police work from Bellows Falls and the state's attorney's office, and a generalized portrait of a man who—in a way oddly similar to Ryan Paine and Dylan Collier—had managed to stay employed by just barely scraping alongside his employer's expectations.

Sadly, as the public was becoming increasingly aware, police officers were cut from the same broad cloth of competence as most other professionals, despite recruitment efforts to accept only candidates glowing with integrity, dedication, long fuses, and good people skills.

Lester had decided to approach Hartnett off duty, but far from Dee Rollins, and to do so in an open, nonthreatening environment, which explained his now watching the casually dressed officer—fresh from clocking out at the PD and changing clothes—park his car outside Wilmington's local grocery store.

Les additionally thought it would play better if he headed Hartnett off prior to any shopping, just in case ice cream or other perishable items might be on the man's list.

As a result, having stationed his car near the store's entrance, he got out and waited for Hartnett to draw abreast.

"Pat," he called out in a friendly tone.

Hartnett cocked his head, carefully taking him in without breaking stride. Cops are a wary bunch, especially when caught by surprise. "I know you?"

"Lester Spinney," he said, pushing himself off from leaning against his car to walk forward, his hand extended in greeting.

Hartnett stopped and shook hands in an uninterested way, muttering, "Oh, yeah. VBI, right?"

"Yeah. Good memory," Lester praised him. He indicated the store. "I know you're on your own time. I hope this is okay."

Hartnett gave a shrug, his eyes maintaining the wariness common to people too used to being called on the carpet. "No big deal. Just getting a couple of things on the way home. What's it about?"

Spinney pretended to look around uncomfortably, fortunately assisted by a chatty oncoming elderly couple. He indicated his vehicle. "My car's right here, Mind if we talk there? Little more quiet."

Hartnett's distrust grew in his eyes, but he feigned indifference. "Sure. Why not?"

Lester gave him no time to reconsider, retiring immediately to the car and slipping inside. Hartnett followed suit more slowly, pointedly leaving the passenger door ajar and his right foot flat on the pavement.

"Shoot," he suggested.

So far, so good, Lester thought, unconsciously casting a quick glance at the car's tucked-up sun visor. He'd earlier secreted a recorder there, hoping Hartnett would agree to his invitation to sit in his surrogate office—and thereby deprive himself of any legal expectation of privacy.

Lester chose a roundabout start. "I don't know if it's a slow time for us, or some political favor being paid off, but I've been assigned to clean up a few odds and ends hanging around the Ryan Paine investigation."

Hartnett's reaction was one of carefully worded surprise. "No joke. I thought that was dead and buried, no pun intended." He kept his eyes forward, as if watching the passing pedestrians.

"Yeah, well . . . Didn't we all?" Lester said. "Anyhow, I'm basically talking to everybody I can think of, making sure the t's were crossed, et cetera. You know?"

"Uh-huh," was the vague reply.

Lester was struck that Hartnett hadn't asked why he was featured on that list. Les pursued that anomaly by adding, "So I obviously didn't want to miss you."

Hartnett barely nodded.

Lester went for the punch line. "Since you and Dee were acquainted."

That turned out to be one nudge too far. Hartnett looked at him, his face expressionless, and asked, "Who told you that?"

But Lester played it out, pretending to be startled. "What? Nobody. I was at the memorial service—with a half million other guys, I admit. But I saw you. You and Dylan Collier and a bunch of family and friends. I know you had stuff to do, so it wasn't like you were hanging around, but you were definitely part of the inner circle. I saw you and Dee exchanging looks. Made sense to me at the time—Wilmington's right next to where she lives. I thought maybe you knew Ryan, too."

"No," he said, Lester thought a little quickly.

"Right," Les confirmed, almost apologetically. "Just Dee, then."

Hartnett didn't respond.

Spinney took a file from the dash before him and pretended to leaf through it, looking for something to jog a faulty memory. "And Kyle Kennedy, too," he said, almost as an afterthought, his eyes roaming across the paperwork.

Hartnett twisted the rest of his body around, at the same time pulling in his foot from outside. "What? That's bullshit."

Lester looked bemused, holding up a printout and shaking his head slightly. His reply echoed Hartnett's, "What?" Then he chuckled dismissively, studying the man's face. "Oh, of course. That happens to me all the time. Why're you gonna remember every loser you buckle up? You arrested him—when you worked for BF. DUI. No reason to keep that in your head—even with the weird coincidence of your later hooking up with Dee."

Spinney replaced the sheet of paper and smiled broadly, his gaze innocently back to scanning the file. "I mean, that's what they say—

Vermont's got about fifty people, with half of them arresting the other half all the time. Given Kyle Kennedy's habits, I bet ten cops knew him the way you did."

"Yeah," Hartnett said softly, as if convincing himself.

"It is funny, though," Les went on. "Your not remembering—what with the memorial service and getting involved with Dee. You'd think that would've jogged your memory."

He purposefully put Hartnett between two choices: play along or play dumb. Hartnett, like most people in this position, had more ego than smarts.

"Right," he said slowly, as if distinguishing a distant mirage. "DUI. He was just driving through, wasn't he? And I nabbed him out of pure bad luck." He laughed unconvincingly, adding, "For him, of course."

"That must've been it," Lester said agreeably. "Ruined his night, in any case, 'cause you fed him the whole enchilada, including a night in Springfield to sleep it off. You spent hours with the guy."

"Huh," Hartnett said, as if reminiscing with an old buddy about an ancient escapade. "Becomes a blur after a while, don't it?"

"Even more in a busy town like BF," Lester said supportively. "And you were there a long time."

"Tell me about it."

"Wilmington must be a nice break. You and Dee living together by now?"

"Yeah. I still got a place, but I hardly go there anymore. I'll probably let the lease run out."

"That's a good feeling," Les said, and then asked, as if out of nowhere, "Where were you working when her husband got killed?"

"Wilmington," was the casual reply.

"You ever go back to BF, maybe to shoot the shit?"

He shook his head. "Nah. The place was a hole. I never got along with anybody there, anyhow."

"Nicole LaBrie said to say hi if we talked."

Hartnett grunted. "I always thought she was a stuck-up bitch. Don't know why she's so friendly—used to treat me like crap."

"The reason I asked if you'd gone back is 'cause I found something missing from that DUI case file against Kennedy."

"I don't doubt it," Hartnett said. "They never took care of their files or equipment or the evidence locker or anything else. I even once found part of a ham sandwich under the cruiser seat at the start of a shift, for Christ's sake."

"Actually," Les argued pleasantly, "the file was perfect except for one thing. Kennedy's fingerprint card was missing."

"Yeah? Well, guess it don't matter now."

Lester returned to his paperwork prop. He had been hoping to set a trap of sorts—at least enough of one so Hartnett's body language might betray a flash of nervousness. But the man's last response had verged on bored.

Disappointed, Spinney changed topics. "So when did you and Dee become a couple?"

Hartnett stared at him, blinked a couple of times, and asked, "What the fuck's goin' on?"

"Just building a timeline."

Hartnett's voice lowered, and he unconsciously placed his right hand on the door release, as if preparing to leave. "The fuck you are. For the past ten minutes, you been poking around me and Kennedy and Paine and Dee like a dog figuring out where to pee. What do you want?"

Lester decided he no longer had much to lose. He hardened his own tone as he said, "What I want is for you to explain exactly how you fit into one of the tightest little love nests I've heard about outside of a novel. And given your past with skating on official thin ice—and the fact that this is a homicide investigation—I'd recommend that, A, you get off your high horse, and, B, you make whatever you're about to tell me incredibly convincing, 'cause from where I'm sitting, you can either walk away with my blessing—depending on what you say—or go to jail."

It was a make-or-break moment, and Lester's eye fell to Hartnett's hand on the door, expecting him to complete his earlier gesture. Instead, his mouth fell open. "Go to jail? Why? What the fuck did I do?"

"I don't know yet," Lester told him honestly. "You willing to be straight with me? Right here, right now?"

"I got nothin' to hide."

"All right," Lester reassured him, feeling better about his footing. Interviews like this could be like dancing across a stream on a two-by-four beam. "Then answer the question," he urged. "When did you and Dee hook up?"

Hartnett's face shut down for a moment as he studied the car's floor. "Before Paine was killed," he admitted dolefully. "Before I even stopped working for BF. She used to come see me sometimes when I was on duty there—at night, when nobody was around. The sheriff's office handled dispatch, and sometimes there'd just be one of us on duty, depending on the day of the week. It was perfect."

"What about when you had to patrol, or go out on a call?"

"Depended. I'd put her in the car, like we do for official ride-alongs, or I'd leave her at the station if I had something trickier to handle. If I got tied up, I'd just phone her and she'd split. She didn't mind. She was a cop's wife. She liked cops. Still does."

"She ever talk about Paine?"

"Sure. She said he was well named. Pain-in-the-ass Paine. That's what she called him."

"What about Kyle Kennedy? Were you being straight with me there?"

Hartnett looked irritated with himself. "Not exactly. At first, I had no clue what you were talking about. I pretended to remember nailing him for that DUI. But now that we've talked about it so much, I think I really do. I still couldn't swear to it."

"Okay, since the cards are faceup, give me details about you and Dee," Lester prodded him. "How did you meet up?"

"What you'd expect. There was a social thing—VSP and local agencies pretending to get along around a barbecue pit. Kind of crap management loves. It was north of BF, at Herrick's Cove, on a weekend. She and I met there, hit it off. I didn't have anybody in my life, and she was having problems with Paine." He paused before adding, "Things evolved from there."

In fictional portrayals of police interrogations, they often have the cop studying the suspect's nervous twitches, or his heartbeat as seen at his carotid. One of the favorite presumptions is that everyone looks down and to the left when they lie. Or maybe to the right.

Actual cops make these assessments more generally, more intuitively, and never forget that they may be wrong. A compulsive liar can easily fool a lie detector, be it a machine or a seasoned human being.

Nevertheless, Lester's suspicions about Pat Hartnett were lessening by the minute.

"This may be a little indelicate," he forged ahead, "but were you aware of her seeing anyone else at the same time?"

"Like Collier?" he came back without hesitation.

"For example."

Hartnett considered his response before saying, "I knew they were close. She never said they were intimate and I never asked, 'cause the implication I got was more of a brother-sister thing, but if you're saying it was true, I'm not gonna argue. It's definitely possible. She's a woman with a big appetite."

"How 'bout anyone else?"

"On top of me, Paine, and Collier?" he asked, half laughing. "Jeez Louise. I didn't even know about Collier for sure, and her relations with Paine—as far as she told me—had been polite at best for a while. I thought I was the only one."

"Let's talk about Kennedy, then," Lester suggested. "She ever mention him?"

"Before the shooting? Nope."

"And what about after? How did she refer to him?"

Hartnett gave that some thought. "I'm not sure. . . . I don't remember him coming up. There was a lot about the people running the investigation, and how I better keep a super low profile, so as not to bring the two of us into the spotlight. I guess I do remember her saying one night how she was pissed because some cop had asked if she'd ever known Kennedy. 'Can you believe that?' she said—or something like that. That was about it, I think."

"Part of the post-shoot folderol was about Paine's settlement, wasn't it? Insurance, benefits, partial pay, the rest?"

"Yeah. That's where I got it loud and clear that there'd been no love lost between 'em. She had a couple of shaky moments, and she cried at the service, which you probably know. But she was tough with the bureaucrats when it came to what was due her. She gave 'em hell more than once."

"What was the issue?" Les asked. "Timing?"

"Yeah, and the amount Workman's Comp was going to pay. It's based on dependents and years of service, and she accused them of low-balling. Got pretty fierce before they reached a number."

Lester let a moment pass before asking the most obvious of his questions. "Where were you on the night Paine was shot?"

Given the small roller coaster of emotions he'd been sharing with this man, he wasn't sure what reaction he'd get—including a repeat with the door handle, followed by an abrupt departure, or worse.

But there'd occurred a subtle change between them, and they'd almost imperceptibly slid into being fellow cops discussing a case—detached and objective.

"At the movies," was the answer, but said in an almost doubting voice.

"You don't sound sure about that."

"Oh, I'm sure, all right. Dee and I were supposed to go together, 'cause Paine was on duty. That was the routine. But she wasn't feeling good, so we took a rain check and I went on my own. I remember it because of how the rest of that night turned out. It's like people used to ask, 'Where were you when the planes hit the towers?' you know?"

This time, Lester's antenna did pick up something amiss. "But there's more," he proposed.

"Yeah," Hartnett said slowly. "It's stupid—just something I noticed at the time, and completely forgot till now. After I heard about the shooting—which we all did through the grapevine that same night—I went to see her. That's when she really told me to play invisible—she was royally ticked off for my popping up by surprise."

"Okay . . . ," Lester prompted him as he paused.

"Well, what I'm remembering is that she wasn't sick at all—not like she sounded when she canceled on the phone a couple of hours earlier."

"What do you make of that?" Lester asked.

Hartnett gazed at him and raised an eyebrow. "Honestly? Not a thing. Adrenaline, shock . . . I can only guess what it's like to get news like that. I've delivered it enough times. You probably have, too. When did two people on the receiving end ever act the same? Not really sure why I even mentioned it."

Lester mulled it over himself, and saw what Hartnett meant. He also understood that, for the moment at least, he was done with this interview. It hadn't given him what he'd been hoping for, but certainly additional fodder for the sit-down with Dee Rollins—the increasingly less credible grieving widow.

CHAPTER TWENTY-EIGHT

"You have *got* to be kidding," Sam exploded. "What the hell *is* it with this case?"

"Hey," Scott Gagne countered, smiling, having grown somewhat accustomed to her moods. "Expect the unexpected. You know that."

Sam tamped down her response to this platitude, knowing, however unhappily, how often it spoke the truth. It certainly did in this case, where the Albany entry team, assured of Jared Wylie's being in residence, had instead found his home empty.

"What've we got?" she asked instead.

They were occupying a stuffy command center van, parked on South Swan, loaded with the usual array of computer screens, racks of radios, keyboards, and recording equipment. The imperturbable Gagne tapped a monitor on the wall opposite them, featuring a colorful electronic map of the neighborhood. "He had a secret back door we didn't know about—it didn't feature in the house plans. Probably something he did himself for something like this, or maybe to get people in and out unnoticed. Doesn't matter, though."

"Why not?"

"'Cause we got him here." He pointed to a small blinking spot that was crawling across the map's surface, and now somewhere in the back-yards sandwiched between Lancaster and Chestnut. "We got his laptop's GPS, thanks to your Trojan horse."

Sammie rubbed her forehead in frustration. After a long sleepless night in the hospital getting Nick Gargiulo to roll over on his boss, she, Gagne, and their new state police confederates had rapidly created a plan to grab Wylie before he caught wind of their interest and pulled the vanishing act Gargiulo had warned them he would.

This was apparently falling shy of success.

"What now?" she asked in a calm voice, her head pounding and her eyes sore. She was, after all, still a guest in this town.

Gagne had been working with the third member of their tiny tribe—an all-but-mute techie named Tom, who'd appeared as the van's pri-mary accessory. Both men now indicated another monitor, onto which appeared an overhead image of Albany's cluster of differing government buildings.

"Helicopter feed," Tom explained tersely, returning to his keyboard and knobs.

"State police put up a chopper with the same GPS receiver we got," Gagne filled in. "We should be able to track him, and maybe even zoom in enough to be sure we got the right guy—not that I have any big doubts there."

He did sound confident, which Sammie found helpful. On the other hand, she had noticed something else troubling.

"What's that?" she asked, pointing several blocks away, to a dark mass occupying a tree-filled rectangle formed by the architectual hodgepodge of the State Assembly Building, the capitol, and the oppos-ing slabs of the Legislative Office Building and the New York State Edu-cation Department.

"Protest in West Capitol Park," Gagne said, his tone dropping. "Not what you'd call a rare event around here."

Sam glanced back at the map with the blinking dot. "Wylie's headed straight for it. What if he uses it to disappear? There're a thousand people out there."

Gagne got on the radio and alerted the others to Sam's concern. He also asked the chopper crew if they could get a close-up of Wylie. The difficulty was that the initial plan had not involved surrounding an entire city block. An entry team was just that—small—and now additional manpower, along with the helicopter, had been summoned from afar to help out.

It was finally more than Sammie could endure from the innards of a windowless van. She rose from her seat and asked her partner, "Can you get a feed of that GPS map onto your smartphone?"

He held it up. "It's already running."

"Then let's get out there," she urged. "Tom can call us if things go south, can't he?"

"Sure," the techie said without looking up.

Scott needed no prompting. He rose as well and threw open the van's side door. "Let's go."

South Swan ran the length of the Empire State Plaza's western edge, cutting across the bottom of Lancaster and leading directly into West Capitol Park. That put both cops only five minutes away from where Wylie was trying to vanish—assuming Sammie's reading of his intentions was correct.

"Uh-oh," Scott mumbled as they jogged alongside the plaza's tall, cold, bordering marble wall.

"What?"

He touched the earpiece he'd fit into place moments ago, connecting him to the radio on his belt. "Something must've tipped him off. Wylie ditched the computer—it stopped moving and one of our guys just found it under a parked car, along with a drop phone, on Chestnut."

"His paranoia got the better of him," Sam said.

Gagne pointed skyward. "Probably the chopper got him nervous. I bet he thinks the contents of the laptop are bulletproof, or maybe he wiped it clean, either on the run or through a time bomb device. I have no idea. But we sure as hell lost our signal."

He keyed his radio and asked the pilot above if he'd been able to identify Wylie before the computer was dropped. He listened for a minute before telling Sam, "We're looking for a dark suit, which might actually be helpful in this mob."

The crowd he referred to was by now right before them—a teeming, noisy, placard-waving throng of chanters and yellers—almost all dressed in jeans and T-shirts, or other millennial garb. There wasn't a business suit in sight.

"I told them to try to spot Wylie inside this mess," Scott said, looking around somewhat desperately. People were milling around, looking indistinguishable from one another, additionally hard to see because of the trees covering the park's western half. "It ain't gonna be easy."

Sam saw a couple of mounted police officers, comfortably sitting astride two of the biggest draft horses she'd ever laid eyes on. They were positioned near the steps of the low-slung, modernistic Legislative Office Building bordering Rockefeller Plaza, chatting and looking faintly amused by what was stretched out before them.

"I'm gonna ask them," she told Scott before running off in their direction.

She displayed her badge as she approached, hoping to lessen any concerns they might have, which appeared unlikely, given their laid-back demeanor.

"Hey there," the nearer one said, seeing Gagne approaching from farther off. "What're you guys up to?"

"We're looking for a man in a dark suit," Sam told them, further astonished by the height and breadth of the horses. "You see anyone like that?"

Gagne got close enough to display his credentials as well. "The chopper's with us, too," he added.

The two horsemen exchanged glances. "Got something big going?"

"Big enough," Sam replied. "He's wanted for a homicide."

The nearer cop surprised her by reaching into a pouch near his knee—at the same level as her eyes—and removing a pair of binoculars. He surveyed the crowd through the trees from his comfortable vantage point, working methodically from right to left.

"Okay," he said laconically, handing the glasses over to his partner and pointing. "What d'ya think?"

"Yup," was the answer.

The first one gazed down at Sam and Scott. "Forties, dark hair, long in the back like a lounge lizard?"

Scott reacted excitedly. "That's him."

The police officer chuckled. "Yeah. You want him?"

Sammie almost yelled out in frustration, but Scott understood what was afoot. He placed a calming hand on Sam's forearm and asked the horsemen, "You gonna strut your stuff?"

Both men laughed, spurred their enormous steeds forward, and slowly, unhesitantly, and inexorably plowed into the midst of the teeming crowd.

It was like watching an act of nature. Scott and Sam both scrambled to the top of a nearby retaining wall for a better view, and saw the two riders part the crowd as if by magic, with no shouted commands or violent gestures or rapid movements. To Sam, it was akin to seeing twin locomotives languorously invade a herd of cattle, all of which simply made way for them.

The two cops had their target in sight, however, and moved in a straight line toward it. Scott laughed with excitement and reported, "The chopper pilot just said they're almost on top of him. He either can't move or he's too scared. Supposedly, he's just standing there, looking around like a trapped rabbit."

In the wake created by the horses, Sammie could see clear through the assembly to where, suddenly, a single man in a dark suit emerged from the surrounding humanity, intimidatingly framed by the two colossal beasts. Gently nudged into place by their riders, the horses bookended the man, allowing both cops to simultaneously lean in, hook an arm each under Wylie's shoulders, and lift him clear off the ground between them.

One perfectly executed, parade-ground, wheeled turn later, the mounted cops reversed their journey, leaving the startled and temporarily hushed horde behind, and deposited a nonplussed Jared Wylie onto the sidewalk.

"This who you're after?" the one asked Sam, giving her a well-earned cocky smile.

"Thank you very much, Officer," she told him, and added a small bow.

At approximately the same time, back in southern Vermont, Lester Spinney was parked by the side of Route 9, just outside Wilmington. Initially, he'd stopped here following his interview of Pat Hartnett in order to check his recording, which was fine, and to enter notes of the event while they were still fresh in his mind.

This wasn't a unique situation. Many cops take advantage of an available hour, some good weather, and a quiet parking spot to catch up on paperwork. It's an efficient and nice way to concentrate far from office chatter, ringing phones, and the interruptions of an action-filled world.

However, now that he was almost done, he could admit that homework had been the least of his concerns. In truth, he was worried about how he'd left things with Hartnett. From a starting place of suspicion and wariness, Lester had ended up believing in the man's innocence.

Which therefore prompted the question: What to do now?

More relevantly—and this is what troubled him most—might Lester have exposed Hartnett to some form of danger? And might Hartnett, if innocent, now impulsively act on his own?

What the hell had happened on that deserted midnight road? And who'd been the missing third person?

Lester stared out the windshield, his heartbeat growing rapid with apprehension. Regardless of why he thought he'd stopped here, he was now overwhelmed by a sense of dread. He fumbled to update Dispatch of his destination via radio, started the car, and peeled onto the road, his anxiety increasing by the moment.

Dee Rollins lived off Route 100, south of the major east–west road that linked Brattleboro with Bennington. The word "off," however, invoked a wide selection of road surfaces—from smoothly paved to dirt-strewn and weed-choked—and some significant distances over hilly, forested terrain. In Rollins's case, fortunately for Lester, the gravel road he ended up on was well maintained and only five miles long. This was all the more auspicious, given his sketchy but growing concern—allowing him to challenge the road conditions with a dangerous rate of speed.

When he finally reached it, her house was at the bottom of a hill, on the edge of a small pond with a pasture beyond, tucked under three towering, ancient shade trees that shrouded the structure in shadow.

He paused a moment at the crest, observing and taking stock. There were two vehicles in the dooryard—Hartnett's pickup and a sedan Lester assumed to be Rollins's.

Letting his foot off the brake, hoping that whatever was spooking him was a figment of fancy or overwork, Les kept his eyes on the darkened house as he quietly rolled downhill.

Until he saw the single, unmistakable flash of a gun going off, through one of the windows.

"*Damn*," he swore, racing once more to close the distance, fumbling with the radio to summon backup.

He barely waited for the car to grind to a stop near the porch steps before piling out, simultaneously running for the front door and unholstering his gun.

Banking on the element of surprise over the more cautious choice of waiting for help—twenty minutes away if he was lucky—he violated his training by tiptoeing across the porch, quietly turning the doorknob, and slipping inside.

He got lucky. The entrance led directly into a large post-and-beam living room with picture windows overlooking the pond, which in turn clearly illuminated a woman in her late thirties, crouching over the inert and bloody body of the late Pat Hartnett.

She was trying to fit a semiautomatic pistol into his hand.

"Do not move," Lester ordered her, using the doorframe for stability and keeping her center body mass in his sights. "I'm a police officer."

She froze in place, her body tense, the gun still in a position to be used if she was fast enough.

"Don't think about it," he urged her. "Place the gun on the floor."

She hesitated.

"*Now!*" he yelled at the top of his voice.

She jumped slightly, as if hit by an electrical charge, and finally acted on his command.

"Now walk backwards five feet, lie down, and stretch out on your face—arms and legs out straight."

"I was defending myself," she said, beginning to turn toward him.

"*Do it!*" he screamed.

She bowed her head in submission, and again did as she'd been told.

He moved toward her, his arm outstretched and his finger on the trigger, at the same time removing his handcuffs from his belt. Once he reached her, he placed one knee gently but firmly against her upper back, pinning her in place, before quickly securing his gun and buckling her wrists together.

"That hurts," she said.

He ignored her, quickly ran both hands down her body to make sure she had no other weapons, and shifted over to Hartnett's pale, still body.

The man had a gaping hole in the chest, no pulse, and there was relatively little blood on the wooden floor—an indicator that Hartnett's heart had been stopped almost before he hit the ground.

Lester fought off the guilt threatening to overtake him. He should have figured this out; he should have acted sooner.

"The cuffs are hurting," Dee Rollins complained from behind him.

The entitled whine in her voice brought him back. He swiveled around, now focused solely on a checklist of crucial things to do.

He pulled out his cell phone first, called Dispatch, officially declared Pat Hartnett dead, and followed the standard homicide protocol of requests and needs, from notification of the medical examiner and state's attorney to putting the closest funeral home on standby.

He then pocketed the phone, produced his recorder again, and turned it on. He recited his name, the date and time, and the name of the woman he was with, insisting that she state and spell that name and her date of birth. He then rattled off Miranda and seamlessly received her waiver of rights. Through it all, he was direct, emotionless, clear-spoken, and businesslike.

He was also on a mission he absolutely did not want to fail.

"Why did you kill Kyle Kennedy?"

Still lying on her front, her head twisted toward him on the hard floor, she nevertheless managed to look startled.

"What? What're you talking about? Ryan did that," she stammered.

"But you were there," he insisted. "And you shot Ryan. I want it all from the top, Dee. I witnessed you shooting Officer Hartnett through the window just now. That leaves you with one choice only, which is to be completely truthful with me. What just happened is the last act of something that started three years ago, as Ryan was running out of gas as a state trooper, and you were running out of patience with him."

She lay still, absorbing his words.

"Why was Kyle Kennedy targeted that night, Dee?"

He watched her face, his own sense of purpose sharpening his perception, helping him to read her features, which, to his relief, seemed to be registering an almost calming sense of resignation.

"You were angry," he suggested.

"He dumped me," she said.

Lester remembered Dylan Collier's story—fed to him by this same woman—how Kennedy had been gunning for Paine in order to have Dee for himself. It had been the perfect bit of fiction to make the pieces fall into place, and the exact reverse of what actually occurred.

"Who do you mean by 'he'?" Les demanded. "I need names. Right here, right now. This is what's going to help you from being thrown to the feds and the death penalty. Do you understand?"

She did. After a moment, she said slowly, "Kyle Kennedy dumped me. I hated him for it."

"So you conspired to kill him," he stated.

"Yes."

"Why all the theatrics? Why involve your husband?"

"My husband," she sneered. "What a douchebag. All he was worth was the money I could get out of him. It was like figuring out the combination of a safe—how to line up the right numbers."

Lester was following along. "His death benefits," he suggested.

She smiled. "Yeah."

But he needed the missing pieces.

"What did you tell Ryan to get him to play along?"

She actually chuckled. "He was so stupid. I could always count on that. I told him I'd been bitchy lately because Kyle had raped me one night, when Ryan was on duty. I'd gone to a bar and this man had put the moves on me, and followed me out. You know the routine. Blah, blah, blah. The stupid fucker swallowed it all. It was easy to move him from calling his pals to settling things on our own. I just had to make him think it was his idea."

"What was?" Lester prompted her.

"He would shoot Kyle, we'd both fake Kyle wounding him, and him and me would end up with my so-called rapist dead, and Ryan drowning in awards, a pension, line-of-duty bennies, the works. I even told him there could be a movie deal down the line, if we played it right."

"Who came up with faking Kyle's fingerprints on the gun?"

"Ryan did," she exclaimed, enjoying her orchestrations. "Can you believe it? He read an article as part of a training. I had to help him, of course, even after I stole the print card from Bellows Falls, when I was hanging out with Pat—not that Ryan knew anything about that. Ryan couldn't figure out how to get the prints off the card and onto the gun, of course. It wasn't hard, though—not in a world filled with computers and scanners and printers and YouTube."

"You stole the gun from Kyle," Lester suggested.

"Well, duh," she said scornfully. "He was another penis in search of a brain. Total dumb-ass."

Lester had her on a roll now. Even in her absurd and hopeless position, her ego was triumphant.

"Where were you the night Ryan pulled Kyle over?"

"In another car, nearby. I had to play both of them—get Kyle to be at the right place, right time—on a deserted piece of road—and tell Ryan that I'd heard through the grapevine about Kyle's regular night driving routine. That took some figuring out, 'cause I didn't want to leave any messages on Kyle's phone or his answering machine."

Lester recalled how Collier had been fed the story that Kyle had simply driven back and forth over a series of nights, waiting to be pulled over by Paine. Dee had indeed been hard at work.

"All right," Lester continued. "So Ryan pulls over Kyle at a prearranged spot, and then what? Ryan phones you to join him while he's officially radioing in the stop?"

"Pretty much," she agreed. "Ryan was super mad, which was kind of funny later. At the time, I was worried that he'd screw it up. But he was a well-trained dog and followed the rules and did all that crap you people do when you pull people over. Anyhow," she went on, sounding almost conversational by now. "He finished that part, walked up to Kyle's window, and blew him away. Bam. If I'd halfway liked the loser, I would've been proud."

"But instead?" Lester asked leadingly.

She laughed. "Right. Instead, I leaned in through Kyle's passenger window, like we'd planned, and I shot Ryan. You should've seen the look on his face when he realized what I'd done."

"What were you supposed to do?"

"Hit him in the arm. Like in a Western or something."

Lester thought back to the autopsy photos of Ryan Paine. "You almost messed it up," he couldn't resist saying. "Hitting him in the neck."

"Whatever," she replied dismissively. "He died, didn't he?"

Lester cast a mournful glance at Pat Hartnett before returning to her sullen, angry face. "They all did," he said, "and now you'll pay the price for at least two of them."

CHAPTER TWENTY-NINE

Susan Spinney quietly stepped into her husband's office and stood by the door, watching him. It wasn't really an office, nor the "man cave" he kept calling it. More of a messy, cluttered closet in which he could sit and stare out the window.

As he was doing now.

She loved this man, in many ways precisely for times like this, when despite his maleness and cop-ness and his tendency to make light of everything, he showed a frailty, an empathy, and a sadness reflecting the world he worked in. Day after day, through the decades, she'd witnessed his journey through rapes and murders and domestic violence and more, nurturing his sense of humor and love of family, while watching the toll of his job slowly eating into his soul.

"You okay?" she asked.

He turned from his view of the backyard, in which their guests—Joe, Beverly, and Rachel; Willy, Sam, and Emma—were sitting, chatting, or tending to the barbecue grill, along with Dave and Wendy, and gave her a tender half smile.

"Sure."

"That why you're up here?" she asked, smiling back, crossing over, and kissing the top of his head.

He squeezed her forearm in return. "Yeah—life of the party."

"You know you're not to blame," she reassured him.

"She told us later, at her booking, how Pat came home and flat out asked her about killing Ryan. I put that in his head. It's what made her pull the trigger."

"One way or the other, he was the second man she'd killed that we know about, Les," Sue said. "Do you really think she wouldn't've gotten around to it by herself, the next time he forgot to take out the garbage? Or feed the pets? You didn't wind her up. Hell, you were almost incidental."

He looked up at her and raised an eyebrow. "Now you got me nervous about taking out the garbage."

She gave the back of his head a fake smack, in fact relieved to hear him make a joke. He'd been in a down mood for over two days by now—a record for him.

He tilted his head to one side and asked, "Do I tell you enough how much you mean to me?"

She ran her hand across his close-cropped hair. "Never."

After a moment's pause, she reminded him, "You actually invited these people for a cookout."

"I know," he conceded, getting to his feet. "What was I thinking?"

"Probably that you needed your best friends nearby."

Joe rose from his seat as Sue and Lester appeared from the house, bearing a tray of uncooked hamburgers and hot dogs and a large bowl of salad fixings. "Need any help?" he asked, reaching out.

Sue handed him several bottles of dressing that were slipping from her grip, and they all three began distributing their goods onto the long wooden picnic table.

Spinney started organizing himself at the grill, laying out his utensils and the piles of meat, allowing Joe to sidle up to him privately.

"Tough going?" he asked.

"A little," Lester admitted. "I feel responsible."

"You are," his boss told him. "For solving a murder nobody else knew existed. But not for Pat Hartnett. He made some choices, too. You can't forget that."

Lester tapped the side of his head. "I know that in here. I just don't feel it in my heart."

"Remember Eberhard Dziobek?" Joe asked suddenly.

Lester stopped what he was doing to stare at him. "The shrink? He helped you out a few years ago, didn't he?"

"He's done more than that," Joe said quietly.

Lester was startled. "It's an ongoing thing?"

"Now and then, yeah." Joe smiled. "It's off the books, and sure as hell not known by the Bureau. He's a good guy—been a big help."

"And you think I should see him," Lester suggested.

"I think my saying everything's all right ain't gonna make it all right," Joe said. "He's good with this stuff, and knows where and how to direct it. All I can tell you is it takes its toll."

Lester laid out a few burgers and dogs onto the grill. "Thanks," he finally said. "Maybe I will."

Joe eased away to let him soak in the notion, and wandered over to where Beverly and Rachel were standing together. He slipped an arm around Beverly's waist. "Thanks for coming. I know that fraternizing is one of your usual no-no's."

She smiled at him, relaxed and happy. "For you and Rachel? Both at once?" She put on a theatrical voice before adding, "Exceptions must be made, Joseph. Even in the carved-in-stone Hillstrom code of proper be-havior." She then whispered in his ear, "And you are a sweetheart for inviting Rachel."

"Which reminds me," he said in a voice loud enough to carry across the yard. "Let's not forget that while we're working to eat the Spinneys out of house and home, we're also here to celebrate. While I was away playing doting son to my mother—who by the way sends her love—you all up and smacked down not one, but three major cases, almost as if you knew what you were doing."

He raised a glass and bowed his head toward Willy. "Mr. Kunkle, as usual ignoring the rules and pissing off the feds, the Springfield PD, and God knows who else, you successfully used the potentially unremarkable discovery of three broken teeth to shut down a conspiracy to subvert a major military contract. Randomly but nicely done."

Willy shook his head as Emma, in his right arm, gazed up at him fondly. "The feds got the glory," he said, "and the Windsor PD can't believe they finally got to use their tac team."

To general laughter, Joe then saluted Sammie. "Special Agent Martens—my surrogate field force commander. The death of a young woman, a killer lost into the night, a guaranteed dead end in the making, and you ended up handing a case over to the New York State Police and the Albany PD that they'll be chewing on for years. How many people surfaced in that sleazy guy's hard drive?"

"Dozens," Sam said bashfully.

Joe continued, "Blackmails, extortions, conspiracies, sexual assaults, one homicide that we know of, and several more we suspect. Not a bad piece of work. I couldn't be more proud."

He turned toward Lester. "And our host. Down at the mouth right now for something you did your best to prevent, but only after completely reversing one of the highest profile murders in recent Vermont history, and in the process pulling off some picture-perfect police work. Congratulations, sir."

"Time to eat," Willy suggested in the midst of applause. "We gotta go to work tomorrow, and I don't wanna do that on an empty stomach."

More laughter was followed by Joe putting down his glass and holding up both hands. "In two seconds. I just want to say one more thing, and for that, I'd like to invite three missing guests."

He nodded to Rachel, who dug into the backpack she'd earlier placed under the table. She began setting up a display among the paper plates and plastic glasses.

"We're all here for the same calling," Joe said. "It's supposed to be to protect and to serve, and as all of you have just proven, we do a pretty good job of it."

Rachel had laid out three photographs and three candles, which she now went about lighting.

"But sad to say," Joe continued, "it's never that neat and tidy, and sometimes people pay the penalty. We can't always explain to ourselves or to others why this happens, but it seems to be the price of the battle we've taken on."

Rachel straightened, and he unobtrusively held her hand in thanks. Before them, their faces flickering in the reflected candlelight, were portraits of Kyle Kennedy, Pat Hartnett, and Charlotte Robinson.

"These are who we fight for," Joe said in the stillness. "From all backgrounds and walks of life, and regardless of what they may think of us or our mission. These are the ones we serve, and will continue to do our damnedest to protect."

Sam felt Willy shift slightly beside her, and glanced up just in time to see her daughter wipe a tear from his cheek.